THE
SYNDICATE

TIMEWAVES, BOOK ONE

*Would you risk the future
to save your past?*

SOPHIE DAVIS

The Syndicate
Sophie Davis
Published by Sophie Davis
Copyright © 2016 by Sophie Davis Books

Cover design by Regina Wamba of Mae I Design
Book design by Inkstain Interior Book Designing

BOOKS BY
SOPHIE DAVIS

TIMEWAVES SERIES

The Syndicate
Atlic

TALENTED SAGA

Talented
Caged
Hunted
Captivated, a Talented Novella
Created
Exiled: Kenly's Story
Unforgettable
Inescapable

BLIND BARRIERS TRILOGY

Fragile Façade
Platinum Prey
Vacant Voices

NIGHTMARES TRILOGY

Pawn
Sacrifice
Checkmate

For Hunter—

*I'm so proud of the man you've become,
and can't wait to see where you go.*

Work hard, & dream big.

THE
SYNDICATE

TIMEWAVES, BOOK ONE

PROLOGUE

MAY 1796
FLORENCE

THE POUNDING OF my pursuer's feet on the cobblestones echoed behind me in the narrow alleyway. Ancient architectural masterpieces stretched high on my left and right, blocking the bright afternoon sun. The view was every bit as valuable to the people in my time as the document wedged between my heart and the bodice of my wool dress.

Magnificent as the Duomo was, and as lucrative as a digital image would be, the risks involved with obtaining a snapshot were too great. Oil paintings were still used to memorialize men and women of importance in this time. The most primitive camera was centuries away from being invented. If dropped—a very likely possibility given my current predicament—the slim electronic device in my possession would confound the finder and the loss would royally piss off my boss.

Exercising prudence, I left the camera snug against the inside of my wrist, directly over the scrawling text tattooed on my skin.

Maybe next time, I thought regretfully.

"Obtenir son!" a man shouted in French, his command coming out as a wheezy exhalation of breath.

Get her.

His name was Etienne and he was a guard in the palace. For the past ten minutes, he'd been trying to "get" me with no luck. In his defense, it wasn't really a fair match-up. I was lithe, agile, and well-trained in the art of evasion. He was large, clumsy and accustomed to sitting atop a horse and letting the animal do all the cardio. The fact he'd kept up with me on foot for this long was actually pretty impressive. Then again, he had the advantage of not having to navigate the crowded streets of Florence barefoot, corseted, and wearing something called a false rump.

The clomp-clomp of boots intensified exponentially as Etienne's fellow soldiers joined the chase. They sounded like a herd of elephants ready to trample me to death in their stampede.

Welcome to the party, boys.

With numbers on his side, the Frenchman suddenly had the upper hand. Though I was desperate to find out exactly how outnumbered I was, I didn't dare turn my head to count. They sounded close enough that I imagined their hot, fetid breath was blowing on my neck. The split second it would take to look over my shoulder was time I did not have.

Up ahead, a sliver of sunshine illuminated the filthy cobblestones like a ray of hope. Swatches of color, muted blues and greens and yellows, moved past the opening of the alleyway. Fifteen more feet and I'd be among the crowd, just another woman wandering the piazza.

Pushing myself to increase the pace, my stocking-clad feet slapped the cobblestones with bone-jarring force.

Ten feet.

The shapes in the large town square were close, though still blurry through the sweat stinging my eyes and locks of blonde hair that had long since broken free from the pins used to fasten them in place. The cotton shift beneath my petticoat was tangled around my legs, gathering between my knees in an irksome manner that made me grateful the garments had fallen out of fashion eons before I was born.

Five feet.

The piazza was crowded today, even more so than usual. A small smile crossed my lips. Finally, something on this run was going my way. Crowds were good for me. I was a master at blending—you might even say it was in my job description.

My right foot landed in a puddle. That prematurely triumphant smile vanished. Warm, foul-smelling liquid splashed up over my ankle and halfway up my calf. A wave of revulsion made my stomach turn, and I had to suppress the urge to gag. But there was no break in my stride, no pause for a girlie freak-out.

This isn't the first time you've stepped in urine, I told myself as I skidded the last several feet towards the end of the alleyway. Sadly, it probably wouldn't be the last time, either. I made a quick mental reminder to avoid taking missions in times when people simply dumped their chamber pots in the streets. It was seriously unsanitary.

Behind me, the soldiers shouted curse words as they met the ankle-deep pool of human waste.

This time it was a full-on grin that curved my lips upwards. Sometimes the small victories were what made life worth living.

An instant later, I burst into the piazza. Wide-eyed stares came from those closest to the opening, which I promptly ignored. There was no time to care about the impression I was making. All that mattered was losing my tail, meeting up with my partner, making it to customs, and returning to our time. Preferably in that order. And preferably without taking a detour through the Italian prison system.

Speaking of my partner, where the hell was Gaige, anyway? As the backup on this mission, he was supposed to be there to bail me out of sticky situations. Running for my life from a regiment of Napoleon's soldiers definitely fell into that category.

Feet still in motion, I gathered up the soggy skirt of my dress and began weaving through the crowd. My misstep into the puddle proved fortuitous. Men and women alike parted like the Red Sea when I neared, the heat making the stench of my dress even worse.

"Au voleur!" one of the French soldiers shouted behind me.

Stop, thief!

Awesome. Being labeled a thief, while technically true, was *so* not what I needed at the moment.

Anticipating the hands that were surely about to reach out from the surrounding crowd and grab me, I hugged my arms tight against my body in an attempt to make my five-foot-seven frame as small and compact as possible. Only, no one reached for me. Those in my path continued to move aside to allow me to pass. Their curious expressions narrowed into disdainful gazes directed at my pursuers.

"Se déplacer de côté!" Etienne's voice rose above the murmurs of the crowd.

Move out of the way!

Something that felt like an elbow made contact with the soft spot between the bottom of my ribcage and my left kidney. I pitched forward, stumbled several paces before I caught my footing. Against my better judgment, I spared a glance over my shoulder, positive one of the soldiers would be within arm's reach. But all I saw were well-dressed men and women, now damming the stream they'd made for me to traverse the piazza.

The heel of a woman's shoe crushed my three middle toes. I swore in English at the same time the toe-crusher apologized in Italian. And that was when I realized what was happening. French soldiers were chasing me. French soldiers who were currently occupying Florence. And the piazza was full of Italian—or maybe they were technically Austrian, I wasn't sure—citizens. They didn't give a damn if I was a thief, so long as whatever I stole came from the French interlopers.

To the toe-crusher, I spoke in barely passable Italian, assuring her that no harm was done. At least, I hoped that was what I said. Thanks to the Rosetta—a miniscule translation device—tucked inside my ear, I was able to understand most any language spoken from the heyday of the Roman Empire to the post Epic War economic collapse. Unfortunately, my verbal skills and pronunciation with the same were rudimentary at best.

Not waiting to see whether my sentiments were understood, I resumed my getaway. Once again weaving through the crowd, I carefully navigated the makeshift path caused by my malodorous clothing and scanned the area ahead of me for escape. Thanks to the aid of my new allies, the distance between Napoleon's henchmen and me grew with every pounding heartbeat. If I could just maintain my lead, I might be able to lose my pursuers for good in the crowds and winding streets up ahead.

Of course, this getaway would be a lot easier if my backup was actually doing his job. I was going to give Gaige hell once we were back home in our present. Particularly if I found out he was currently preoccupied with a courtesan.

I quickly darted between two buildings and exited the piazza with much less fanfare than I'd entered with. The passage was barely wide enough for me to fit through, so I doubted Etienne, with his much wider girth, would think to check inside.

Though the sounds of the noisy piazza were dulled by the stone walls stretching high on either side of me, muffled shouts of men demanding to know where the thief had gone floated down the alleyway on the cool breeze. Shadows engulfed me like dark shrouds, providing the perfect cover for me to pause, catch my breath, and revise my getaway strategy.

If the map provided by the historians was accurate, this alley was a cut through to the Ponte Vecchio. Once on the bridge, it would be easy enough to blend into the market crowd—just another consumer haggling with the merchants who were hocking their wares for a premium. From there, I could cross to the opposite side of the Arno

River, go through the Palazzo Vecchio, and retrace my path, with its many twists and turns, to customs. As soon as I reached our waystation, I was jumping home. Gaige or no Gaige. For all I cared, he could stay in 18th century Florence and pray the plague didn't claim him.

Since the goal was to blend once I emerged from my hiding place, I spared a moment to evaluate my appearance. One glance down confirmed that I looked as disheveled as I felt. The golden ringlets that the customs hair specialist had painstakingly curled, arranged, and pinned atop my head were now dangling in limp strands around my shoulders. The powder and rouge that the customs makeup artist had pressed all over my face and neck were surely gone, washed away by a river of sweat. Add in my stained dress and filthy, torn stockings, and I was more likely to be mistaken for a lady of the night trolling for midday clients than a consumer.

Still on high alert, I glanced toward the mouth of the alley to ensure I was alone in the darkness. The only visible movement was in the patch of light at the threshold, as the men and women of Florence went about their daily business. The shouts of Etienne and his lackeys were gone and only faint squeaking noises and the sound of tiny, scurrying claws echoed through the dark space. Breathing a sigh of relief, I began pulling pins out of my hair and twisting the rogue strands up as best I could manage.

We'd been in 1796 for five days now, on what should've been a challenging but doable assignment. Our missions were usually covert, the goal to slip into and out of places, times, and people's lives like ghosts. After spending the first day in Florence familiarizing ourselves with the area, as was our standard procedure, it became clear stealth wasn't going to be an option this go-round. Napoleon was exceedingly paranoid, security in the palace akin to that of Fort Knox in the twentieth century. His private rooms were located in a single wing, guarded closely by French soldiers, and impossible for an outsider to infiltrate. So, I'd used the syndicate's local connections to obtain a position on the household staff of Napoleon's Florentine palace.

Posing as a maid was far less exhilarating than some of my other cover stories, and I'd grown bored quickly. Four days of dusting miniature furniture and fluffing miniature pillows under the eagle eye of Napoleon's security team passed before I caught a break. Thanks to an impromptu, mandatory tactical meeting for everyone on the palace's protective detail, I'd suddenly found myself alone and unwatched.

I knew better than to act on impulse. I knew it was smarter to follow the plan.

Nevertheless, my boredom had bred impatience, causing me to ignore the niggling voice inside my head warning me to bide my time, to wait to act until I had become a background fixture at the palace. Seizing the opportunity, I'd bolted to the forbidden wing with the pint-sized warmonger's private chambers.

The mission target was Napoleon's final letter to his wife, Josephine. I'd found easily in the drawer of his desk—exactly where the historians said it would be. Instinctively, I'd busted out my happy dance, taking an ill-advised moment to celebrate my victory. Just as I was about to slide the letter into the artifact pouch—a stretchy, plastic sleeve from my present, impervious to the elements and all known corrosive chemicals— Etienne had appeared out of thin air and caught me, red-handed.

If I hadn't taken the time to revel in my triumph, maybe he wouldn't have found me with the letter in hand. Maybe it would've already been stashed in my dress. Maybe I could've feigned innocence, babbled about being lost in the sprawling estate.

Unfortunately, I loved a good victory shimmy.

Boots scuffling on stone echoed in the passage, pulling me out of my self-chastising. The reasons for royally screwing up this run, while entirely my own fault, were also entirely irrelevant at that moment. I still had the letter and they still hadn't apprehended me. But both of those facts might prove false if I stayed in the alleyway much longer.

There was one thing I wanted to check before leaving, though. Due to Etienne's sudden appearance, and my equally sudden need to disappear, I'd been careless when placing Napoleon's letter into the pouch and was worried it had sustained damage. After glancing again at both exits, I retrieved the letter from its hiding place, withdrew my camera from the wrist holster, turned it on, and examined the single sheet of velum using the light from the camera's display.

Finding no notable rips, stains, or holes, I breathed a sigh of relief.

One point for me, I thought wryly.

Finally, I re-pinned my hair in a loose bun and smoothed my petticoat and dress back into place. I considered ditching my stockings, but figured bare legs were more offensive than torn undergarments. All the while, I prayed that Etienne and his minions weren't waiting for me at the other end of the passage.

Taking a deep breath and steeling myself for the worst, I crept out of the alleyway as inconspicuously as possible.

The sunlight seemed impossibly bright after the shadow-filled enclosure, and it took several moments for my eyes to adjust. Once they did, I scanned the piazza for both French soldiers and Gaige. Seeing neither, I sighed with both relief and exasperation.

Truth be told, I was beginning to worry about my wayward partner. Gaige was both immature and irresponsible when it came to his personal life, but he took his job very seriously. He didn't know as well as I did how harsh the world outside the syndicate could be, but he would never do anything to jeopardize his position. Or my safety, for that matter.

The customs agent will know where he is, I reassured myself. *No need to panic just yet.*

The crowd was even thicker on this side of the square and the sea of people heading for the large footbridge soon swallowed me whole. I entered the bridge at a leisurely pace to avoid drawing any extra attention. Both sides of the wide walkway were lined with market stalls, selling everything from leather goods to goat feet. Pretending to peruse the merchandise of a silver dealer, I used a serving platter as a mirror to discreetly check behind me for a tail.

"There!" someone shouted in French.

Not good.

Chaos erupted. The soldiers began shoving people aside. I immediately dropped the silver platter and took off into the crowd at break-neck speed.

Luckily, this wasn't my first rodeo. Spurred on by the adrenaline coursing through my veins, I was ducking arms and weaving through groups of people before the guards had even made it past the entrance to the bridge. Back in the spirit of the chase, I felt the bizarre mix of exhilaration and apprehension that only such a frenetically charged situation brought about. With every stride of my relatively long legs, the soldiers' shouts grew fainter and fainter. Soon, the sound of my own blood pumping furiously in my ears eclipsed their voices altogether.

I have this in the bag, I thought, grinning hugely.

Confident that victory was within my reach, I spared a glance over my shoulder to see just how many men were looking to take my head. How many would inevitably fail in their pursuit.

That moment of arrogance cost me.

Head still turned, I ran smack into a brick wall.

Okay, maybe not an actual brick wall. Because why would there have been a brick wall in the middle of a bridge? But the impact was hard enough and the obstruction solid enough that my head actually bounced off of it as though made of rubber.

Ringing filled my ears instantly. The side of my face took the brunt of the collision and my cheekbone felt like it had just made contact with a fist.

That's going to leave an attractive bruise, I thought absently as dizziness overtook me.

The searing pain suddenly took a backseat to the spinning world that was careening dangerously around me. It felt like someone had pressed hyper speed on a carousel. I clenched my eyes closed as tightly as possible, hoping to halt the ride with sheer will alone. When that didn't work, I reached out my arm to steady myself on the low barrier along the side of the bridge. Unfortunately, I underestimated my distance from the wall. The ground rushed up to greet me.

This is going to hurt.

Just as I was about to hit the filthy pavement, strong hands caught me around the waist and pulled me to the very thing that had been my downfall. Rough fabric scratched my palms, proving the wall was not a wall at all but a man's chest.

An impressively firm man's chest, I thought absently.

Somewhere, in an alternate universe, this scene was playing out in a romance novel; I was the swooning leading lady and the hero had just drawn me tightly against him. With that thought swimming in my head, I rested my forehead on the imposing chest in an effort to still the spinning. As I forced myself to draw in slow, deep pulls of oxygen to my addled brain, one of the man's hands rubbed my back soothingly.

This is ridiculous, I thought. One moment I was running for my life, the next I was living a passionate parable. No costume change required.

Despite the sheer absurdity of the situation, I was grateful to the chivalrous man. He could've let me fall flat on my face. He could've shoved me away. And I wouldn't have blamed him, considering my stench. Instead, he was acting the part of the gallant knight, swooping in to save the distraught princess before she knocked out a few teeth on the pavement.

The strong hand on my spine slid down to my hip, moving into my still-downcast line of vision.

Interesting, I thought, still dazed from the collision. Maybe this tale was more scandalous than swoon-worthy, my hero more roguish than knightly. Before I could process that this was definitively reality and not a harlequin novel, the hand continued around to my stomach while the other held me firmly against him. Then, to my utter horror, the hand shot up the front of my dress, caressing every inch of my torso as its owner copped a cheap thrill. Finally, when two long fingers climbed over the deep neckline and down the inside of my bodice, the shock wore off. I snapped into action.

"Get off of me, you perv!" I shouted in English as I shoved against that rock-hard chest, too incensed to translate the words.

Skilled in self-defense, I attempted to create enough space for my knee to lock in on its target: my attacker's groin. The creep was apparently accustomed to groping unwilling women, though, because he angled his lower body away at exactly the right moment. My blow landed on his outer thigh, hard enough to inflict pain but not the doubled-over-in agony degree I'd hoped for.

"Is that your idea of foreplay?" the man chuckled in my ear, his English just as perfect and unaccented as my own. "No wonder you never go on second dates."

My eyes went wide. I tipped my head back to get a good look at the man's face. Dark brown eyes that held just a hint of amber sparkled with amusement. Though a casual observer might have only seen delight, I knew fierce determination was hidden in the shadows beneath. Way beneath, in this case.

"Gaige!" I exclaimed, both incensed and grateful to find my partner had arrived at last.

The grin he wore stretched from ear to ear as his arm slid around me once more, bringing me close again. When his fingers slipped down the front of my dress for a second time, they found their mark. As Gaige's groping digits retreated from my bodice, I caught a fleeting glimpse of the artifact pouch between his thumb and forefinger. Then, just like the queen in three-card Monte, it disappeared to parts unknown.

"What have I told you about personal space?" I snapped, shoving him away from me.

"Is that any way for a lady to treat her rescuer?" Gaige taunted. "I'm not asking for much, Stassi, just a little gratitude."

I opened my mouth to respond that feeling me up was more than enough payment for his eleventh-hour intervention, but never got the chance to utter the words. Without warning, my legs were swept out from underneath me. The action was not performed in an enjoyable, romantic manner. Instead, Gaige tossed me over his shoulder caveman-style.

"Are you freaking kidding me?" I screeched. "Put me down, jackass!"

"Good lord, you stink," Gaige intoned.

"You always stink," I replied lamely, pounding my fists against his back.

"You okay?" he asked quietly. "Still dizzy?"

"Oh yeah, I'm just great," I said, still struggling.

"Still dizzy?" he persisted.

"No, I'm clearheaded and going to kill you," I snapped, straining to loosen his grip enough to flip myself over and away from my partner. "Put me down!"

"In that case, can you pretend you're *actually* trying to get away, Stass? Sell it for the audience."

Startled, I remembered that we weren't alone. When I looked up, dozens of shocked expressions met my gaze. Napoleon's guards had nearly caught up to us, pushing their way towards the outer ring of bystanders who'd stopped to gape at the show.

My heart sank as my annoyance rose. It was *so* not the time for Gaige's pranks. I was going to be completely screwed if the moron didn't let me go in the next moment. Probably even if he did. Still, I kicked my legs as hard as I could in a desperate attempt to flee.

Unfortunately, Gaige's arms were well-muscled from all the rock climbing he did in our downtime and they were locked around me in a steel embrace.

"Just a piece of friendly advice," my partner called over his shoulder. "You might want to take a nice big breath real quick. Oh, and definitely keep your mouth closed."

Alarm bells went off inside my head.

Hold my breath?

Realization dawned. I struggled harder against his hold. Not in the hopes of actually getting free from him, but to indeed give the spectators a show.

"You bastard!" I screamed in mangled French.

"After what you did to my brother, you're lucky it's not the gallows!" Gaige roared back in a monstrous tone, taking two steps to the side. In a lower tone meant only for my ears, he added, "You're welcome, by the way."

Without further ado, Gaige threw me over the side of the bridge.

Despite my partner's advice to keep my mouth shut, I couldn't help the scream that tore loose from my throat.

Every expletive in my vast repertoire flew through my mind in the seconds before I hit the fetid water. The instant the stench wafted into my nostrils, I vowed revenge upon Gaige for this little stunt. Maybe he'd just saved me in the moment, but the impromptu bridge dive probably wouldn't have been necessary had my partner been *actually backing me up*.

The landing was as ungraceful as humanly possible—back-first with my legs futilely bicycle-kicking the air. Lips still parted in an involuntary shriek, murky river water seeped into my mouth before I had the wherewithal to clamp it shut.

Pretend it's one of the hot springs on the island, I chanted over and over again in my head like the refrain of a poorly-written song.

Fortunately for my sanity, a reminder of my mortality quickly derailed that train of thought. Once wet, the heavy wool of my dress felt like newly-poured concrete. I sank like a boulder.

As much as I *really* didn't want another molecule of the Arno River inside of me, I reluctantly opened my eyes to gain my bearings. The foul water stung painfully. I blinked several times before straining to keep them open. All I saw was deep, dark, murky brown. I glanced around frantically, searching for lighter water that would indicate the surface. Once I spotted it, I managed to flip my body around. With powerful kicks of my legs and strokes of my arms, I fought against the weight dragging me down and slowly reversed my course.

Contrary to what he would tell you, my partner didn't have superhero-strength, so I couldn't have been far from the large stone construct. Fortuitous, since I needed to be underneath it for Gaige's gamble to pay off.

Through the cloudy water, a shape emerged up ahead, maybe five feet away. The water was dimmer there, too, as though bathed in shadows instead of sunlight. Swimming towards the pool of darkness, I prayed that I was heading closer to the bridge and not away from it. My lungs were already starting to burn. In the very near future, they would be screaming for air.

Seconds that felt like hours to my oxygen-deprived system passed before my outstretched hands made contact with the slimy stone foundation of the bridge. If I could've breathed a sigh of relief without filling my lungs with pure nastiness, I would have.

My heart began to pound harder, anticipating what was to come.

As soon as my entire body was pressed against the inside of the stone pillar, an unnerving tingling began. The dichotomous sensation started in my toes, cool at first, then growing colder and colder as it crawled up my calves. The crown of my head was instantly warm, becoming uncomfortably hot as the feeling slid down my chest. Though not unpleasant at first, the sensation intensified as it traveled down my torso and up my legs, until the tingling felt more like being continually jabbed with a cheese dagger. It was as though I was the fabric of time itself and thousands of sewing machines were simultaneously stitching me together with white-hot needles.

Within moments, hot and cold collided in a clash-of-the-titans match-up in my abdomen. The pain was unfathomable, indescribable to those who have not felt it. And it was rocketing through me.

A burst of light exploded in my line of vision like a star detonating. Golden white swirls twisted and churned before my eyes, illuminating the murky water with preternatural beauty. At the epicenter, the light was pure gold. It pulled me in as though it was a powerful magnet and I was nothing more than a fleck of metal.

This was a bad idea, I thought, panic overtaking me as surely as the light. Shoving the thought aside, I focused with every ounce of my mental capacity on my destination: The Atlic Gate in my present time.

My body bowed backwards, my spine arching as long fingers of light shot out from the supernova and grabbed hold of my waist. The pain in my midsection peaked right before the golden light engulfed me.

And then I was gone.

ONE

I LANDED OFF-BALANCE and disoriented. My hands shot out instinctively to break the fall. Pain shot through my wrists and up my arms when my palms collided with cold, dry rock. I clawed at the smooth surface, desperate to remain upright. Unfortunately, all I received for my efforts were several broken fingernails. Panting, I sank to my knees.

The skin on the inside of my wrist began to hum, bringing an instant sigh of relief. It was a tune I felt rather than heard, but it touched me down to my marrow all the same. The earth around me answered in kind, singing the same silent song with a power and intensity that had scared me at one time but I now welcomed with open arms. A sense of peace enveloped me, the kind of universal harmony that few in the world could understand, and only then from experience.

"A gate," I muttered to myself with a weary smile. "Good sign."

I knew all too well what came next.

Teeth clenched, forehead pressed against the rock wall, I prepared to ride out the after-effects of the unorthodox jump.

Tremors rocketed through my body with bone-jarring force. My muscles seized, not all at once, but each in turn, over and over. My lungs burned, more from the sudden influx of air than the jump through time.

It'll pass. It'll pass. It. Will. Pass, I chanted to myself, even as the spinning sensation in my head made me feel like the lone sock in a dryer programmed for warp-speed.

Unpleasant as the seconds that followed were, I was in far better shape than I should've been. Not travelling through a gate was a shock to the system, one very difficult for the human body to withstand. It was the reason we were forbidden from free jumping, except in dire emergencies.

As the worst of the effects finally began to wane, I surveyed my surroundings to gauge my whereabouts. Not going through customs was not only unsanctioned and dangerous, it left a lot of room for error— there was no way of knowing where and when I'd end up. Between the river water still obscuring my vision and the vertigo whirling through my head, blurry shapes and vague impressions were all I could see.

As I blinked rapidly to clear my vision, the vortex came into focus around me. Absentmindedly, I rubbed the tattoo on the inside of my right wrist. The letters on my skin glowed bright red for several moments, as they always did after coming in direct contact with other *prima.*

The secret to traversing time lay within the precious mineral. *Prima materia* was more rare than a flawless colored diamond, more valuable than the crown jewels, and more sought-after than a relic from the Ming Dynasty. Throughout history, the existence of *prima* had been doubted more than Excalibur and Atlantis combined. But, as any runner could attest, the mineral was very real. Though it didn't turn substances into gold, as many had hoped it would, it did make time travel possible.

Using the energy my body absorbed from the *prima* to bolster myself, I pushed off the floor and climbed unsteadily to my feet. My head spun from the movement. I leaned against the wall until the dizziness subsided. After a few tentative steps, I plodded slowly around the curve of rock wall towards a patch of hazy light at the end of the tunnel.

A form appeared at the far end of the passage, backlit and shadowed.

"Stassi?" The tall, gangly figure rushed forward, youthful male features came into focus as he closed the distance between us. I recognized him immediately, Rupert Rudolph.

I'm home, I thought with another surge of relief.

"Stassi? What happened?" Rupert asked, taking in my sopping-wet appearance. Concern created a deep crease between his dark brows.

"Gaige happened," I intoned, sparing a weary smile for my favorite gate attendant.

Rupert, a teenager just on the awkward cusp of manhood, was one of several attendants who rotated shifts in my syndicate's waystation. The job wasn't glamorous—entering destinations into the customs ports, logging the comings and goings, and assisting those returning from missions. Still, it was a coveted position among those with aspirations of one day becoming runners, but who weren't yet old enough to begin training.

"Are you okay?" the boy asked, curiosity mingling with worry in his dark eyes.

Together, we exited the passageway and entered the rotunda of the underground gate.

"I've had smoother runs," I replied, holding out my dripping arms to prove my point.

"Shoot, I'm sorry," Rupert apologized. "Let me get you a towel before you freeze to death."

As if on cue, a violent chill ran through me. I hugged my arms to my chest to conserve what little body heat remained.

"Thanks."

He darted towards a metal rack on the opposite side of the cavernous room. Fluffy clean towels were arranged in neat stacks beside bottles of water and energy bars. Rupert grabbed one towel, started back towards me, reassessed the situation, and went back for a second one.

The underground room was a magnificent blend of the old and new worlds. The perimeter of the high, domed ceiling was carved with symbols of the ancient alchemist order—a perfect juxtaposition to the advanced technology used to program mission coordinates. The sloping red walls radiated a cool beauty that hinted at their true nature. At first glance, it was easy to mistake the material for clay, but the faint glimmering where light hit belied the power within.

Another violent shiver wracked my body, pulling me from my admiration. As beautiful as the gate was to look at, the temperature left something to be desired. My fingertips were starting to turn blue. The cool, clean air was also making the horrific stench emanating from me more apparent.

I cursed Gaige.

"Here you go." Rupert held out the towels, which I accepted gratefully. "These should help."

I buried my face in the soft fabric and inhaled the scent of fresh, clean laundry detergent.

"I think they work better if you unfold them," Rupert teased.

My quick burst of laughter sounded muffled beneath the towel.

"Is it Pick on Stassi Day? I didn't get the memo," I replied, slinging one towel over my shoulders and using the other on my hair. Noting the lack of activity in the gate, I added, "Slow day?"

"Yep," he responded, popping the "p" for emphasis. "There aren't any outgoing runs today. Before your unscheduled appearance, we weren't anticipating any arrivals, either. So, yeah, pretty boring 'round these parts."

"Do you know when Molly and Tiger got back?" I asked.

Molly was my best friend, roommate, and fellow runner. She and her partner, Tiger, had left the day before Gaige and me on a run to America. It was supposed to be a quick mission, two or three days max.

"I don't think they're back," Rupert said.

The first hints of dread settled in my gut. I didn't want to seem dramatic, but a run that ran too long over the scheduled time allotment was cause for concern.

"You sure? They should've been back yesterday, maybe even the day before that," I prompted.

"They might've come through when I was off-duty," Rupert replied, scratching his head in the perfect caricature of someone thinking. "I don't remember seeing their arrival in the logs, though. Want me to double-check?"

"Do you mind?" I asked Rupert sheepishly.

"For you? Not at all."

That kid's a real charmer, I thought as Rupert jogged over to his workstation and entered his access code. He scrolled through the arrival log for the past week and shook his head.

"Sorry, Stassi. They're still out." Anticipating my next question, he added, "We haven't received any distress communications from Philadelphia customs, so no need to worry. I'm sure they just got held up. It happens."

"You're right," I agreed, forcing a smile that surely didn't reach my eyes. "How'd you get to be so wise?"

"Age and experience," Rupert answered with a wink.

"Mind getting me another towel, old man? This one's soaked."

With the grace of a young deer still adjusting to its long legs, Rupert loped off to fetch me another dry towel. He returned a moment later with a full-length robe instead.

"Ahh, even better. Thanks, Rupe."

I threw a wet towel at him, hitting him squarely in the face.

"I have to get out of here and change my clothes before hypothermia sets in," I said, tossing the other towel to him.

"You'd better hurry," Rupert advised, walking over to deposit them in the laundry hamper by the shelves.

Pausing mid-hair-wring, I stifled a groan.

"What time is it?" I asked.

"Almost five," Rupert answered, before gesturing to the rows of provisions. "Do you want a protein bar? Or a bottle of water?"

"Morning or afternoon?" I asked anxiously, ignoring his considerate offerings.

I had a sinking feeling I knew the answer.

The runner department held daily mandatory meetings at 5pm. And they meant mandatory. If you were anywhere on the island, attendance was not a question.

"Afternoon. You have just enough time to change clothes, but probably not enough to shower." Rupert wrinkled his nose again. "I feel bad for the person who sits next to you. You really do smell ripe." He grinned cheekily.

I hurried towards the exit, ruffling Rupert's hair as I passed.

"Brat," I said affectionately. "Don't you know that a gentleman never tells a lady she smells bad? I'm sure it's somewhere in one of those books you're always reading."

Rupert laughed and swatted at my hand.

"Eww, don't touch me. Now I need a shower, too."

Though he'd never admit it, I knew Rupert loved the attention all the runners paid him. For many of us, he was the younger sibling we'd never had.

When I reached the foot of the staircase, I paused.

"Gaige should be coming through any minute," I added. "Tell him to head straight to the conference center, no dilly dallying. He has our acquisition."

The slimy plant bits still clinging to my hair like some sort of eco-friendly extensions reminded me that I had a score to even with my partner.

"And feel free to give him a swift kick in the ass to get him going."

Rupert snorted in response.

"That guy doesn't listen to me. He doesn't listen to anyone."

"Just tell him that, thanks to his little stunt, I'm not going to cover for him with Cyrus," I called over my shoulder as I climbed the steps leading out of the gate. "Have a good one, Rupe!"

TWO

LOCATED ON AN island in the Caribbean, the Atlic Syndicate was like a small, independent nation isolated from the rest of the world. Technically it was a U.S. territory, but we didn't adhere to any laws other than our own. Cyrus Atlic, the syndicate's Founder and current head of operations, had paid a hefty sum to keep the island off of the Electric Global Railway System, or EGRS. There were only two ways on and off the island: via boat or through a vortex.

Beautiful as it was secluded, the island was truly paradise. Lush vegetation provided a colorful backdrop that was dotted with waterfalls and wrapped in white-sand beaches. Amaryllises and hibiscuses lined the footpaths. The salty ocean breeze always managed to feel both relaxing and invigorating.

A small smile tugged at one corner of my mouth as I headed down the footpath to the bungalow I shared with Molly.

"If the other camp kids could see me now…," I muttered happily.

The short jog took less than five minutes. Pushing open the front door, I sighed contentedly as I entered my very own slice of the island nirvana.

The feeling didn't last long.

The interior lights were all off, the room only faintly illuminated where the sun shone through the gauzy white fabric covering the windows. The French doors that opened to a small patio overlooking the ocean below remained firmly closed, which was only the case when both my roommate and I were away. The patchwork quilt that normally sat sloppily in one corner of the couch was neatly draped over the back instead, a tribute to my compulsive need to clean and straighten only in the hour before leaving on a run.

My gaze landed on the clock in our kitchen and I swore loudly. With only five minutes to change and sprint to the conference center, I was never going to make it on time.

I scurried to my bedroom and beelined for the en suite bathroom. Ignoring the siren call of a hot shower, I shrugged out of the robe Rupert had given me, peeled off the wet layers of my maid's uniform, and tossed them over the shower doors to dry. The atrociously ruined stockings went directly into the wastebasket.

Back in my bedroom, I quickly dressed in a pair of cotton pants and the heaviest sweater I owned. Though the air outside was warm and humid, I still felt the cold river water deep in my bones. Since my feet were scraped and bleeding from my run through Florence, I opted to carry my most comfortable leather sandals until decorum mandated their necessity.

Retracing my steps through the common area of the bungalow, concern for Molly sparked anew and made my chest tighten. Without thinking, I reached for my proverbial safety blanket: a round gold locket of delicate filigree with a sapphire set in the middle. I brought the locket to my lips before letting it fall back in place between my collarbones.

It was the one link I held to *my* past and I never took it off. As a child growing up in the work camp, it had given me hope that one day I'd find my birth family. As a runner, the same still held true.

Exiting through the back of the bungalow, I crossed our patio to the path leading straight to the conference center. At the footpath's crest, the conference center rose into view. It was the largest building of the island compound and the most outwardly modern. The walls were tinted glass that deflected the heat of the beating sun during the day while absorbing the energy of the rays to power the entire island.

The stones surrounding the massive building were warm on my bare soles, soothing the pain. Unfortunately, I was only able to luxuriate in the respite for a moment. I slid on my shoes, pushed open a tall glass door, and hurried through the lobby.

An unoiled door hinge dashed all hope of slipping in to the meeting unseen. Twenty pairs of eyes turned to stare at me. My own eyes found the formidable man at the head of the table, and I muttered apologies as I scurried to my assigned seat.

Keeping my eyes down, I grabbed the Qube sitting on the table in front of my chair and pulled it to me, preparing to take notes like a dutiful employee. An elbow nudging my ribs drew my attention, and I did a double take when I saw Gaige. Somehow, my pain-in-the-ass partner had managed to beat me to the meeting. He smirked at my stunned expression and mimed pinching my lips shut with his thumb and forefinger. I swatted his hand away before he actually tried to close my mouth for me.

"Stassi? Gaige? Do you care to take over the meeting, or is it okay if I continue?" Cyrus asked in a tone that was firm, but not angry.

"Of course, Cyrus. Sorry I'm late. I had to go change. *Someone* sent me on a little swim in Florence," I replied, with a pointed look at Gaige.

"So sorry that I *saved* you from Napoleon's guards, Stass," Gaige shot back with an irritating grin. "Next time, I'll be sure to leave you to the

Frenchies."

Cyrus stifled a smile at our banter. The amusement softened his tanned, weathered features.

"Are you okay?" our boss asked me. The slight crinkle around his eyes was the only sign that his question was more than a polite inquiry.

"Never been better," I grumbled, running a hand through my damp, disheveled hair. It occurred to me in that moment that I probably should've consulted a mirror before I left the bungalow. Maybe run a brush through my mermaid hair.

Too late now.

"As I was saying," our fearless leader continued, addressing the whole table again. "Judah just returned from Lisbon…."

I leaned back in my chair, content to have everyone's attention directed elsewhere. While Judah's run was recapped, I tuned out the sound of Cyrus's voice, but kept my gaze on him.

Cyrus Atlic was a legend. While physically imposing—tall and exceedingly well-muscled for a man in his late fifties—it was his accomplishments and vision that commanded respect. Our syndicate's Founder had actually worked on the Fourth Dimension project—the team that discovered time travel.

The initial finding was met with mixed reactions from the government and the project's financers. With a vested interest in privatizing time travel, several of the corporate investors pushed to launch a time tourism program soon after the discovery, allowing those with enough money to vacation in any time period of their choosing.

Fortunately for the world, the pilot program never grew beyond infancy. Private citizens proved incapable of responsible travel; they caused more trouble and created more holes than money and influence were capable of fixing or explaining. That was when the government officially stepped in and shut down the venture. The Fourth Dimension project was deemed unfit for further exploration, and became one of the highest-level classified files in the government archives. Very few outside of the scientists, contractors, and financial backers ever even knew of the project's short existence.

Cyrus, who was an exceedingly wealthy businessman and brilliant scientist at the time, had been an integral part of the Fourth Dimension project since its inception, as both an investor and a researcher. And it wasn't within his nature to let such an incredible discovery languish in redacted documents.

Though the logic of the ban on time travel did not escape Cyrus, it also did not deter him. He believed that with the right training and preparation, carefully vetted individuals could visit other eras without disrupting history. With that idea in mind, he quietly purchased Branson Isle from the Americans. Cyrus then established the Atlic Syndicate—a business specializing in locating and acquiring objects from the past.

Historical procurement was a lucrative business. For an obscene price, we would obtain any item from any time that a client requested. *Any* item. And a never-ending parade of the world's most affluent lined up for our services. The profits were more than enough to keep the island in pristine condition and provide lucrative salaries to the syndicate's employees. While most of the world lay in ruins as a result of the Epic War, we lived in untold luxury.

But Cyrus's dream went beyond founding the most elaborate black market the world would ever know. Our boss was a patron of the arts, enraptured with the lost works of creative geniuses throughout time. Artwork, literature, plays, films—every colorful aspect of humanity— they were all lost during the fifth world war. Preserving culture was Cyrus's passion. For him, amassing a fortune was simply a fortuitous byproduct of that.

In order to give life to his great imaginings, Cyrus needed employees. First and foremost, he needed runners—gophers sent back in time to fetch the items his clients requested. After working out the kinks that come with any new business model, he developed a solid training program focused more on the art of assimilation than the physical aspects of jumping from one point and place in time to another. Runners studied people, events, and cultures, learning to blend within past societies without becoming a part of recorded history. And without causing ripples in the timewaves.

Another elbow from Gaige interrupted my musings. When I looked up, all eyes were on me once again.

Realizing I was tuned out, Gaige cleared his throat and answered for me.

"There were a few hiccups, but nothing we couldn't handle."

His chestnut eyes glanced pointedly at me.

"Right, sorry," I said, quickly figuring out that Cyrus had asked about our run. As the lead runner on the mission, I was also the one responsible for recounting it to our boss. "I was able to infiltrate the palace without issue. Napoleon's letters to Josephine were exactly where the historians guessed—the desk in his study. There were some 'hiccups,' as Gaige said, but we made it out okay."

"No major incidents?" Cyrus asked, raising his eyebrows.

"Not at all," I quickly answered, before Gaige could.

Cyrus eyed me carefully. The half-smile on his face was unnerving.

"You didn't bypass customs on the way back?" Cyrus turned the full force of his emerald gaze on me.

Crap. How did he always know everything? The man had a sixth sense. Possibly even seven or eight of them. Glancing over at my partner, I knew he wouldn't have offered up this particular piece of information. Neither Cyrus nor the senior runners in the room would approve of our tactics, however successful they'd been.

Gaige squirmed in his chair but said nothing. Evidently, he was choosing to sit this one out.

Awesome.

"Stassi, you cannot keep doing this," Cyrus continued sternly, all traces of his earlier amusement gone. "We cannot afford to leave behind a trail of mysterious disappearances, nor can we afford for you to be out of commission while you recover from time sickness."

"I'm fine!" I exclaimed. "I'm not sick."

"*This* time," Cyrus shot back. "You didn't get sick *this* time. But you will. Everyone does. Time sickness is inevitable for those who don't follow the rules. Which is precisely why we have rules. Coincidentally, that is also why we have customs: for you to use them. Jumping outside of a vortex is incredibly dangerous, I cannot believe that you don't understand that."

"I know, I know," I replied. "You're right."

Arguing with a man like my boss was pointless, so I took the path of least resistance.

"I'm sorry," I added quietly.

Though I almost promised I wouldn't do it again, I held my tongue. It would have been a lie, and we both knew it.

"What happened?" Cyrus asked, my apology softening his tone.

"One of the guards found me in the study. I tried talking my way out of it. I tried making excuses. I even tried flirting—"

"Wow, can't believe that didn't work," Gaige muttered.

Cyrus shot my partner a warning look, and Gaige's trademark smirk disappeared.

"I tried it all," I continued. "I swear. In the end, I had to make a break for it. My loyal backup," with this I turned to glare at Gaige, "was occupied elsewhere. Guards followed me from the palace, but I managed to lose them. I was heading for customs when the soldiers caught up with me again on a bridge."

"And that's when I intervened with my quick thinking," Gaige chimed in. "I staged a struggle and threw her into the Arno to facilitate a clean exit."

"Clean is *not* the word I'd use," one of the senior runners murmured, eyeing my disheveled appearance.

"Yes, you're quite the helper, Gaige," Cyrus replied sarcastically.

"What?" Gaige asked innocently. "I saved her. If not for me, our fair Stassi here would be waiting for her date with the guillotine."

"Are you really okay?" Cyrus asked, ignoring my partner's witty commentary to focus on me.

"Yeah, I'm fine. There was—"

The door to the conference room slammed open violently, interrupting my reply. A tall, lean girl stood in the entranceway. Red, blistered hands gripped either side of the doorframe to support her weight. Her beautiful pale skin was about four shades lighter than usual. Cerulean blue eyes blazed angrily from beneath ebony strands of singed hair.

Molly.

THREE

"MOLLY!" I SHRIEKED.

Shoving my chair back from the table, I was at my roommate's side in an instant.

Two medics appeared in the doorway behind Molly, both panting and out of breath.

"Are you okay? Molls, what happened?" I asked, terrified.

I went to hug her, but stopped myself when I noticed the smoldering holes in her Puritan-style dress. The patches of skin peeking through the holes were a mess of red welts. My arms fell to my sides. Staring helplessly at my best friend, I was overwhelmed by a mixture of horror over her condition and relief that she was alive.

Molly swayed unsteadily on her feet. Her knees buckled, but she didn't fall. One of the medics reached out to steady her. Despite her bedraggled appearance, she warned the man away with a look so hard it was a wonder he didn't turn to stone.

Even with the appalling circumstances, I couldn't help but smile. Molly's spirit was still intact.

She spared me a small, reassuring nod before focusing on our boss. Cyrus suddenly didn't look quite so fearless under Molly's penetrating gaze.

"I quit!" Molly practically screeched.

"Molly, why don't you—"

"I'm serious, Cyrus!" she interrupted him. "I've had enough! I'm done with this shant."

Her words lacked the bite they might normally have carried, but still had the desired effect. The room was stunned silent for several long moments. Every wide-eyed gaze was fixed on Molly, though no one uttered a sound.

"What is that smell?" Gaige asked.

Naturally he'd be the one to shatter the quiet with an asinine question.

"My hair caught on fire!" Molly shrieked. "Thanks for asking, jackass."

Molly's legs gave out as the pain suddenly became too much. I caught her in my arms as she pitched forward, eliciting a cry when my hands made contact with her burned skin. Wincing, I helped Molly to an empty chair and eased her gently onto the cushion.

"Help her!" Cyrus commanded the medics. They'd frozen in the doorway as Molly yelled at our boss, dumbfounded by the scene. No one yelled at Cyrus. *Ever.*

Spurred into action, both men hurried to kneel down beside my roommate. They had their treatment kits open in record time and were attending to Molly's injuries before anyone spoke again.

Squatting, I gently took Molly's hand. She was trembling and her skin felt cold to the touch, but she weakly returned my squeeze.

"I'm fine," she said soothingly, meeting my terrified stare. "I feel like

34

hell, but I'm fine. At least, I eventually will be."

"She should be at the infirmary," Cyrus said harshly, directing his statement to the medics as though they were to blame for the breach of protocol.

And yet, everyone in the room knew there was nothing the men could have done to stop Molly from storming in to the meeting once she'd made up her mind to do just that.

"Sorry, sir," the younger of the two muttered. He didn't look up, either reluctant to meet Cyrus's stern gaze or unwilling to look away from the task at hand.

"She insisted," the other chimed in weakly. "We couldn't stop her."

Cyrus turned his gaze back to Molly. "And what was so pressing that it could not wait?"

"Quitting, obviously," she snapped, not missing a beat. "Seriously, Cyrus, they tried to set me on fire!"

"Tried?" I heard Gaige mutter. When I whipped my head around to shut him up, I was startled to see an intensely concerned expression on his face.

"I had no choice, I had to jump back here from the stake," Molly continued. "Yes, that's right: The. Stake. Where they *set me on fire*. Like I was a witch!"

Relief flooded me. As bad as the burns looked, they evidently weren't to blame for Molly's deathly pallor. They also weren't responsible for her dilated pupils or the clammy texture of her skin.

All those side effects Cyrus had just been warning me about? The consequences of time sickness? I was staring them right in the face. As crappy as it was for her to endure, at least the illness was curable with time, rest, and some drugs to ease the way. It was a far better prognosis than some deadly 17th century virus.

"You need to lay down," Cyrus told Molly, his tone gentle but definitive. "I'll come see you after the meeting and you can yell at me all you want. Just please let the medics do their jobs."

To everyone's surprise, Molly nodded weakly in reply. The anger and adrenaline had been bolstering her bravado. With both wearing off, she seemed impossibly frail.

"I'll come with you," I said, rising to my feet as the medics gently helped her to stand.

"No, you don't need to," she protested, seeming almost embarrassed by my offer. Her response wasn't unexpected; Molly wasn't the type to ask for help, or admit when she needed it. "I'm just going lay down, probably sleep for a year. I'll see you when you get home."

"Are you sure?" I asked, unsure what I should do. Though I desperately wanted to be there for her, I also didn't want to make her uncomfortable by hovering when she wanted to be alone.

Molly knew me well enough to know exactly what debate was going on inside my head.

"I swear," she said quietly, locking my gaze to show she indeed meant it. "Finish up with the meeting, it will give the medics time to patch me up without an audience."

"I'll be home soon, I promise," I assured Molly, my heart swelling up fiercely. "Send me a message if you want or need me to pick up anything on my way home. Anything at all."

"I could probably use some new skin," Molly answered weakly, a glimmer of humor peeking through. "I'm not sure if the canteen stocks it, but you could ask."

With that, the medics practically carried her out of the room and I reluctantly returned to my seat. The room remained silent for several long moments; the elders processed the event while us rookie runners nervously weighed Molly's condition. She was the first in our class to suffer time sickness, and it was a terrifying sight to behold. The mood of the meeting had become decidedly more somber.

After pausing to collect himself, Cyrus took a deep breath and quietly returning to business. Instantly, my mind was wandering once again.

For several minutes, I focused on making a list of things I could pick up for Molly on the way home. I was contemplating items to distract her when Gaige's voice broke through my thoughts.

"You want this one?" he asked me softly, placing his hand on my forearm and giving it a squeeze.

"Huh?" I asked distractedly.

"Cyrus just said he has an assignment in Paris, year 1925. You want it, right?"

Did arctic explorers want hot showers?

"We'll take it!" I exclaimed.

For the umpteenth time since my arrival, the attention of everyone in the room was on me. I'd been so zoned out before Gaige's question that I didn't realize Cyrus was still explaining the mission. My excited utterance interrupted him mid-sentence. The disapproval in the eyes of the councilmembers around the table—those who'd been with Cyrus since he'd founded the syndicate system—was unmistakable.

"Though the enthusiasm is appreciated, may I finish?" my boss asked wryly, not nearly as irritated as I'd have expected.

"Sorry," I muttered, wanting to melt into my chair.

While I wasn't concerned about the glares from the old guys, I never wanted Cyrus to view me as anything less than professional. Not because I feared that he might send me back to the harsh world outside of Branson—which he absolutely could, with or without a reason—but because I owed him immensely for bringing me to the island from the work camp in the first place. Disrespect was the last thing I wanted to give him in return.

"As I was saying," Cyrus continued pointedly, "our client has requested an unpublished manuscript—*Blue's Canyon* by Andre Rosenthal. The historians located what appears to be the only definitive mention of the work in an interview with the author, published in *Le*

Petit Journal in early March of 1925. When asked about his recent projects, Rosenthal replied that he had just completed his initial round of revisions on *Blue's Canyon*. Because the manuscript was never published and no further mention of it was ever made, the historians believe something may have happened to it not long after the interview. Working off of that assumption, they have pinpointed a window of time in which they believe the chances of recovery are highest.

"The author had a reputation for being quite private about his writing after the alleged plagiarizing of a work-in-progress in 1918. This event also made him quite distrustful of outsiders. Luckily, he was part of the expatriate set that lived and worked in Paris during the 1920s. Since many of those individuals are known for being friendly, becoming ingratiated with them will be the best avenue to Rosenthal. Even still, it is going to take both time and finesse to get close enough to him to find out where he is keeping the book. Rumor has it, he became so paranoid after the plagiarism affair that he never kept what he was working on in a single place. Instead, he would divvy up the sections between several hiding spots throughout the city.

"Considering these factors, we are estimating that this mission will take anywhere from three to six weeks. The range is large because Rosenthal's erratic behavior leaves a lot up to chance. Also, because his most popular work, *Sparrows of Summer*, was not completed until 1928, it will be imperative to not actually steal *Blue's Canyon*. After the previous pilfering of ideas, an outright theft of this book could discourage him from writing anything else. Instead, a reproduction must be swapped with the original pages.

"Any questions? Any interest?" Cyrus concluded in the same way as he always did.

Unsurprisingly, no one else pounced on the intricate mission. Dealing with a paranoid owner was not appealing, not to mention the complexities of finding multiple locations and performing a switcheroo.

But I'd been waiting to visit Paris in that decade since becoming a runner. I might've felt bad about roping Gaige in to something so complicated, except for the fact I still smelled like human waste.

"I guess we could take it," I said meekly, as if I wasn't prepared to throw down for the run.

Cyrus's emerald eyes sparkled with amusement. He wasn't fooled by my nonchalance.

"Six weeks is a long time," he hedged. "Are you sure you want this one? Are you sure you're up for it? You just got back."

Though he hadn't actually said it, I got the impression Cyrus was really asking if I was ready for the level of subterfuge this assignment required.

Whether or not I was capable, I honestly wasn't sure. Nevertheless, the time period and city might hold a clue to the identity of my parents. And that was all I needed to know.

"Positive," I answered, with more confidence than I felt.

"We've got this," Gaige added helpfully, putting his arm around my neck and squeezing me in a crushing side-hug. "I'm even willing to bet that we can get it done in three weeks, tops. Any takers?"

"You've got yourself a bet," Arin, a runner who was a year or two older than us, said. "No way you can steal it, copy it, and replace the duplicate in three weeks. Are you forgetting that there are no photo-replicators in the 1920s?"

She smiled brilliantly at Gaige and gave him a long, lingering look. It seemed as though she'd happily offer herself up as the prize, no matter who won their bet.

My thoughts of Gaige's love life—*gross*—swooped right out the window when the full extent of her words hit me. *Steal it, copy it, and replace the duplicate.* In a time when the technology to perfectly replicate items didn't exist. That meant an alchemist would need time to recreate the manuscript by hand.

Clearing my throat, I threw Gaige's arm off of me and gave Cyrus the most competent expression I could muster.

"I'm not willing to bet on three weeks. But I am positive that we can do it in your time frame," I said. "When do we leave?"

Cyrus's gaze held mine for a heartbeat past comfortable.

"Day after tomorrow" he finally said. "And Stassi? Use customs."

I willed myself not to blush.

"Understood, Cyrus. No problem."

FOUR

"YOU'RE WELCOME," GAIGE prompted, as we stepped outside into the waning sunlight.

Stopping to give him my most menacing glare, I propped my hands on my hips defiantly.

"For what exactly?" I asked, daring him to say it.

"Saving your ass," Gaige declared with a look of glee, not the least bit intimidated by me.

"You mean throwing me in the Arno? Are you freaking kidding me?" I asked, itching to smack the grin off his face. "Maybe once I've showered the sewage off of me, I *might* feel some degree of gratitude. Until then, I'll be plotting my revenge."

My partner laughed at my obviously empty threats.

"Come on, Stass, you have to admit that it was pretty brilliant. In fact, you might even say that my quick thinking saved the day."

"I will most certainly *not* be saying that," I snapped.

Sure, it was a pretty smart exit strategy. But until I no longer felt as though ants were crawling up my legs, I simply couldn't give him the satisfaction.

"I'll take that as a 'thank you'. And also as an apology for doubting I'd come through for you," Gaige said, smiling triumphantly.

As we began walking again, my partner grew uncharacteristically quiet. It wasn't like him to not provide an endless stream of babble, so the silence was unnerving. After a full minute of nothing but the sounds of our footsteps and the chirping of the exotic birds, I couldn't take it anymore.

"You okay?" I asked, throwing him a sidelong glance.

"Of course," he said, offering me a reassuring smile. "I'm just thinking about the run."

"I know it's going to be hard," I said, feeling a twinge of guilt. "I'm sorry, we can back out."

"No way, I live for a challenge," he replied without hesitation. "I just know you've been waiting a while for this, I don't want to let you down."

Startled by his serious tone, I thought carefully about my next words.

"I know that it's a long shot," I hedged. "But I also know that the *only* clue I have is that picture. So if there's even a chance of finding answers in Paris, I want to go. I *have* to go."

The photo I was referring to—a shot of an elegant woman wearing my necklace—was the only solid lead I had to my familial origins. I'd stumbled across the picture while in the time archives stored in the Paris home of the syndicate's Godfather when I was there for training the year before. The caption indicated it had been taken in Paris in the year 1924. That was it. That was all I had to go on. Which was precisely why I needed to go to Paris—to learn her identity. If I could just ascertain her name, I might be able to trace the line of her descendants to one of my parents.

The odds of finding the woman were miniscule, like finding a needle in the largest haystack that ever existed. But I was determined to do just that.

"I know, Stass. I get it."

When I didn't answer, Gaige reached for my hand and gave it a squeeze.

"Well, okay, maybe I don't entirely get how you feel. I can't imagine not knowing who my parents are. But if our roles were reversed, I'd want to do the same thing."

"Thanks," I said quietly.

As much as I wanted to know the identity of my parents, I also wanted the opportunity to ask them why. Why they'd left me to grow up in a work camp. Why they'd left me at all. Why they never came back for me.

I was only four years old when the authorities found me wandering the streets of Knoxville, Tennessee. The local police searched for my family for two weeks without any luck, and I hadn't been able to tell them anything useful to aid their efforts. A kind, young officer assigned to my case repeatedly assured me that someone would come to claim me, that my family would find me. But no one did. My family didn't find me. Not then, and not in the years that followed.

Post-Epic War America was a sad, harsh world. People were out of work, poor, and hungry. Children were frequently abandoned when the government's food rations couldn't stretch far enough to feed everyone at the table. The police were bogged down with cases similar to mine. Spending two weeks on one child was considered a long time.

So, when it became clear that none of my relatives were going to come for me, I was taken to the closest work camp to be raised as a ward of the state. There, I was just one of the many orphans. But that fact didn't make my abandonment any easier to cope with. I would never understand how any parent could send their child away to live in a place like that. Saying that life in the camp was harsh was like saying Robespierre was not a nice man—a gross understatement.

Lost in my thoughts, I was surprised to realize that we'd already reached the fork in the dirt path. When I veered right towards the canteen, Gaige stayed in step beside me. Though the Paris assignment had interrupted my list making during the meeting, I had a good idea of what I wanted to get Molly. Recovering from time sickness mostly required several days of rest and fluids, but there were a few things that could help alleviate some of the symptoms.

My bigger concern was getting my roommate to stay in bed long enough to recuperate. No matter how crappy she felt, she'd be itching for something to do by tomorrow, so providing her with distractions was crucial. Otherwise, she'd be up and gallivanting about the island. Which would just prolong her recovery.

"So, going back to Paris should be awesome," Gaige said enthusiastically, breaking the silence that had fallen between us.

Cocking an eyebrow, I asked, "I know why I'm so excited about this run—what's your reason?"

Gaige's wide-eyed expression told me that he thought the answer was obvious. His next words confirmed as much.

"Seriously? We had a blast when we were there for training; I'm amped to go back. It is a fun-loving place, and the 1920s were an especially fun-loving time. The city might be on your list, but the parties are on mine."

Even though I knew it was his way of distracting me, I played along and gave a dramatic eye roll in reply. Gaige was the brother I'd never had and wasn't sure I wanted at times.

"I hear some of those expats were crazy," Gaige was saying.

We'd just reached the canteen, and Gaige moved ahead to hold the door open. This was typical-Gaige-fashion; despite all of his ridiculousness, hidden beneath the layers of ego and self-absorption, my partner was actually a really good guy.

"That's not exactly a desirable thing," I replied, heading straight for the candy aisle.

The antioxidants in dark chocolate were a natural way to combat time sickness. Luckily, Molly had a sweet tooth and a particular penchant for all things salted caramel.

"Crazy people can be paranoid and unpredictable. That will just make our job that much harder," I continued, purposefully ignoring the intended meaning of his words.

"Whatever," Gaige shrugged off my concerns. "I, for one, welcome the challenge."

"I knew you would," I replied, grabbing three bars of a rare and painfully delicious Swiss chocolate.

"Here, let's get these," Gaige said, choosing a bag of salted caramel jellybeans from the shelf. "Molly will love them."

As we continued around the store, my partner and I selected a random assortment of confections from around the world, a six-pack of grape-flavored sparkling water, two trashy romance novels, a book of crossword puzzles, and a wooden peg game that was meant to test the player's IQ. While I knew the latter would frustrate the hell out of Molly, she would undoubtedly play until she won. Hopefully that would take some time.

"What about first-aid supplies?" Gaige asked as we loaded our goodies onto the conveyor belt at the checkout stand. "Do you think Molly needs like burn cream or something? Oh, maybe some aloe? It works for sunburns, so it should be the same idea, right? Does she like flowers? We could get some here. Or maybe pick some on the way back to your place."

"You've never brought me flowers when I'm not feeling well. When was the last time you bought, or even stole, flowers for a girl?"

"When was the last time you were sick?" Gaige asked.

"True," I conceded with a shrug.

Illnesses were rare for runners. We were vaccinated for most known pathogens and took a handful of supplements and vitamins every day to boost our immune systems. Time sickness was our Achilles' heel.

"45 credits," the cashier told me, after ringing up the mélange of items.

I swiped my forearm in the air over the electronic scanner. The light on the display changed from red to green, indicating that my microchip was approved and the cost of Molly's get-well gifts would be deducted from my account.

Once again proving that chivalry was not dead, Gaige grabbed both of the bags without a word. Together, we set off for my bungalow.

I basked in the dying rays of sunlight on my face as we walked, their warmth chasing away the last remnants of the chill left over from my swim in the Arno. The ocean breeze blew my hair off of my face, the snarling strands drifting behind me like a veil. Though I'd always been a blonde, my hair had become even lighter since moving to the island.

Apparently Gaige had been serious about the flowers, because he stopped in front of my bungalow and plucked brightly colored hibiscuses from their stems.

The moment we entered the bungalow, I beelined for Molly's bedroom. Giving Gaige a warning look and gesturing for him to stay put, I carefully opened her door. He hung back just long enough to fill a vase with water and the flowers he'd picked. Then he slid inside Molly's bedroom behind me.

In the dim light, I could just make out a form in the large bed. The soft rhythm of her breathing told me she was already asleep. Though a thin blanket covered Molly's body from the chest down, white gauze bandages were visible on her arms.

Seeing her like that made my heart hurt, and I felt a terrible sadness for all of the other supposed-witches who'd suffered the same way without any means of escape. How long had it taken for Molly to give up any hope of being rescued and make the jump? How much time had she spent bound to that wooden funeral pyre, suffering the horrific price of ignorance? And where had Tiger been during the ordeal? I'd have to speak to him about that.

Though I understood the need for discretion with so many witnesses, she obviously hadn't been left with a choice. Historic tales of a witch simply vanishing in front of an audience of heartless spectators— doubtlessly assuring her tormentors that she was, indeed, a witch—were a small price to pay for Molly's life.

"Want me to keep an eye on her while you shower?" Gaige asked quietly, drawing me from my painful and angry thoughts.

"Seriously?" I whispered back. "You want to watch her sleep? That's not creepy at all."

"I just—," he started.

"Yeah, yeah," I cut him off, pushing my partner towards the door. "Do I need to warn Molly that you'll be trying to watch her sleep now?"

"When you put it like that, it sounds bad," Gaige replied defensively. "It's not like I was going to accost her while she's in a drugged state. I just meant that I know you're worried about her and I thought you might appreciate it if I—"

"Sat in the dark and stared at her like a weirdo?" I interjected.

"No," he replied, drawing out the word emphatically. "I simply considered that it might be a good idea if I—"

"Hovered two inches from her face and creepy-breathed on her?"

"What? *No*, I just wanted to—"

"Hide in her closet and record the little noises she makes, so you can play them back when you're lonely?"

"*Stassi!*" Gaige said my name with so much exasperation it was amazing smoke didn't come out of his flared nostrils.

"Draw pictures of her to wear around, taped under your clothes?"

"*Stassi!*"

"Fine," I declared. "I'll stop."

"You're an ass, you know that?" Gaige asked, repeating what was probably the question I posed to him most frequently.

"In all seriousness, thank you for the sketchy-but-*maybe*-well-intentioned offer. Just trust me on this—she definitely wouldn't appreciate waking up to find you lurking in the shadows. If the medics didn't make her go to the infirmary and left her here alone, her injuries obviously aren't life-threatening. Go home for now. I'll call you after Molly wakes up and let you know how she's doing."

Despite the jab at his intentions, this seemed to mollify Gaige. He set the bags from the canteen on the kitchen counter alongside the flowers, then left with a promise to return soon.

The door hadn't even clicked shut behind my partner before I was halfway to my bathroom. After turning the hot water tap to full blast, I studied my reflection in the mirror while the shower heated up.

I was the personification of "something the cat dragged in". Something particularly smelly that had been dragged several miles through an oily muck. My hair was limp and filthy from the river water, the ends tangled in knots from the wind. The temporary dye used by the customs hair specialist had come off in the river, and faint pink streaks peeked out from my bottom layers.

The colored strands were a constant source of annoyance for customs agents in just about every time period I'd visited. According to the hair specialists, the pink locks made me too memorable. Wigs and temporary hair dye were easy solutions, so I never felt bad about refusing to get rid of the pink permanently.

It wasn't that I was super attached to the color. My motivation for keeping it was purely sentimental. Molly had given me the home dye job. We'd been friends ever since. Best friends.

I stepped under the rainfall shower and luxuriated in the feel of the hot water on my aching muscles. After several rinse-and-repeats of my hair, I set to scrubbing the filth off with a sea sponge, rubbing so vigorously that my skin quickly began to redden. Finally, after using up most of the hot water on the island, I decided I was both warm enough and clean enough to exit the shower.

I wrapped myself in a lightweight kimono, a gift from Molly that had required bribing a member of the Yurokuri Syndicate to procure—they controlled the Asian timewaves the same way we controlled those of Western Europe and North America. My stomach was cavernously empty, but I lacked the energy to hike up to any of the five dining facilities on the island.

"Delivery it is," I decided.

As I began to scroll through the options on the digital menu station in the kitchen, the front door to the bungalow eased open.

"Hope you're hungry," Gaige's voice called. "I have enough food to feed an army."

The aroma of melted cheesy goodness and garlic bread preceded Gaige through the doorway.

Propping my hands on my hips, I prepared to give him an often-repeated lecture on boundaries. Knocking, for one, was a practice he really needed to start employing. Showing up unannounced, especially after I'd specifically told him that I'd call, was another thing that needed work.

Gaige set down one of the two bags of food he carried and held up a hand to stop me before I launched in to my spiel.

"We have an early meeting with the historians tomorrow," he said in a hushed tone. "I thought you might want to go over the major players beforehand. You need to eat, so I just figured I'd bring dinner and save you the trouble of ordering for yourself."

My irritation waning with every sniff of the delicious aromas wafting from the bags, I cocked an eyebrow.

"Really? You brought lobster mac and cheese and garlic bread for *me*? How sweet of you. I shall eat every last bite."

"That nose of yours is scary accurate." Taking the fact I didn't immediately throw him out as consent, he carried both bags into the kitchen and set them on the counter. "I got one of your favorites, too." Gaige withdrew plastic containers until he found the one he was looking for and opened the lid. "Salmon in conch cream sauce."

My eyes lit up as he waved the plastic container in front of my face. Sure, he was bribing me to hang around, but I wasn't above a good bribe.

Seeing my expression, he shook his head and chuckled.

"I win!" he declared.

My stomach growled again and I reached over, swiping a finger through the cream sauce. As soon as the sherry and butter concoction hit my taste buds, I moaned with pleasure.

"Want me to leave you two alone?" Gaige asked dryly.

With a glare that had zero effect on my partner, I turned to find plates and utensils.

"Actually, leaving me alone with my food isn't a bad idea."

"What do you have on Cook, anyway?" Gaige asked. "Nobody else gets salmon. Are you two having some secret tryst based on your mutual love affair with food?"

"Cook just likes me because I'm nice to him." I glanced at Gaige over my shoulder. "You should try it sometime. What's that saying? You catch more flies with honey than vinegar?"

Gaige finished arranging the food containers on the counter in a buffet-style setup.

"The only flies I like are dead ones, Stass."

"Do I smell lobster mac and cheese?" a sleepy voice asked.

Turning, I saw Molly standing in the doorway to her bedroom. She was leaning heavily on the doorframe and her porcelain skin was devoid of its usual luster.

"What are you doing out of bed?" I demanded.

"I smelled food, *mom*," Molly shot back, big blue eyes sparkling with amusement.

Torn between my anxiety over her wellbeing and a retort, I didn't get a chance to reply. Without warning, Molly swayed and her eyes clamped tightly shut. Gaige and I rushed forward at the same time, but my roommate clung to the doorframe with a white-knuckled grip, remaining upright without our help. She shooed us away once the wave of pain passed.

"Go lay down," I said, my tone allowing no argument.

"But I'm hungry," Molly whined, using the same child-like tone she always did when she thought I was being overprotective.

"Gaige will fix you a plate and the three of us can eat in your room. Fair?"

"Fair," Molly agreed grudgingly.

For a moment, Gaige stood frozen in place, his eyes trained on Molly as if she was the most fascinating creature he'd ever seen. I followed his gaze and realized her robe had loosened, exposing a hint of milky white skin.

Apparently I wasn't the only one who'd noticed Gaige's fixation.

"Like what you see, Fratastic?" Molly taunted.

Her nickname for Gaige had started a couple months back, when Molly and her partner had traveled to the United States in 1979 and infiltrated the Greek system at a big university in search of some trophy. Since then, she'd taken to calling Gaige "Fratastic", in honor of the scores of fraternity guys she'd encountered who reminded her of my partner. I was pretty sure it wasn't a compliment, but he seemed to believe otherwise.

"Huh?" Gaige asked stupidly, snapping out of the trance her flash of skin had caused.

"Come on, Molls, back to bed," I said. Careful not to touch where the gauze covered her skin, I gently took my roommate's arm for support and led her back into the bedroom. Over my shoulder, I called to Gaige, "Fix us plates, will you?"

"On it, boss," he said, giving me a mock salute.

The glowing moonlight outside the windows bathed Molly's room in a soft, silvery glow. The baby blue sheets on her bed were rumpled and the crotched quilt was thrown to one side. Once we were alone, Molly leaned against me for support. I wrapped my arm around her slim waist and guided her towards the bed. She rested her head on my shoulder—not an easy feat since she was several inches taller than me—and limped slowly across the bamboo floor.

"Did I hear right? Did Gaige bring us dinner?" Molly asked as I eased her onto the mattress.

Pulling the covers back so that she could crawl underneath, I waited for her to get situated before tucking the quilt around her thin frame. With her ashen complexion, she looked like a tragic opera heroine. Leave it to her to make deathly ill look dreadfully chic.

"We have an early meeting with the historians," I told her, repeating Gaige's lame excuse for playing delivery boy.

"Sure," she said, drawing out the single syllable, before wincing and emitting a low groan.

"What do you need? You shouldn't have gotten up. Did the medics give you something for the pain?" I asked. "I can call them. Or—"

"Stass, I'm fine," she interjected gently. One of her hands reached out from beneath the covers and clasped mine. Despite her obvious discomfort, she suddenly smirked. "And don't change the subject. Don't think I haven't noticed that Fratastic has been prowling around here more lately."

"He's bored."

"Oh, come on. Spill it. Have you two been getting cozy off island? Have you been enjoying a little international sexy time?"

Unable to help myself, I laughed loudly at the sheer ridiculousness of her question. She was right, though—he'd been lurking around our place a lot in the past few weeks.

"What?" Molly asked innocently, when I refused to dignify her question with an answer. "You wouldn't be the first partners to jump in bed together."

The grossed-out look on my face made Molly erupt into a fit of giggles that quickly turned into hacking coughs. As her trembling fingers reached for the cup of water on her nightstand, I quickly grabbed it. Helping her to sit up, I held the glass as Molly gulped greedily. Once she'd had her fill, Molly's head fell back on the pillow with an exhausted sigh.

Feeling my roommate's forehead with the back of my hand, I found her skin was clammy and cool to the touch. My eyes had adjusted to the dim light and I saw a bottle of pills on her nightstand. I snatched it up and read the instructions: take one every two hours. The Hello Kitty clock Molly had smuggled back on one of her runs read 8:05, meaning she was likely overdue for her next dose. After shaking a pill into my hand, I held it and the water glass out to her.

"Medicine time," I declared.

Eyes closed and face pinched, Molly accepted the pill without protest. She must have been feeling really bad, because she hated taking drugs. After washing the medicine down, my roommate peered up at me from beneath long lashes, her eyes opened just enough for a thin strip of blue iris to show.

"Don't look so horrified, Stass," she mumbled, undeterred from her quest for answers. "Gaige is hot."

"That's the drugs talking," I said with an exaggerated eye roll.

"Seriously," Molly said sleepily. The syndicate's new-age medications worked quickly and she was suddenly fighting to keep her eyes open. She paused. When she spoke again, her speech was slurred slightly. "More importantly, he's a nice guy. I didn't think much of him when we were younger, but now that I've gotten to know him better…." She shrugged one delicate shoulder as she trailed off.

"Molls, nothing is going on between Gaige and me. He's just a friend who doesn't understand personal space."

"I know I give him a hard time, but there's something sweet about him."

A small almost wistful smile crossed her lips and the pain lines on her face smoothed out. Just as Molly's eyelids slid closed, Gaige's heavy footsteps sounded on the bamboo flooring outside her door.

"Dinner is served," Gaige announced.

"Shhh!" I loudly shushed him.

Molly's eyes popped open. "Food?" she asked hopefully, her voice lilting. With a goofy, medication-induced grin that looked out of place on her classical features, she added, "You're a really good guy, you know that?"

That was *definitely* the drugs talking. My roommate rarely said anything to Gaige without a healthy dose of sarcasm.

Evidently he was unsure of how to respond to her unexpected comment, because Gaige placed the tray he was carrying on Molly's vanity without a word. Coming to stand beside me, he looked down at Molly with an adorably worried expression. One of her bandaged hands was resting above the blankets, the white gauze not quite covering the crimson skin riddled with small blisters. As if that wasn't bad enough, when Molly rolled her head to the side to smile up at Gaige, a portion of her neck that had been hidden beneath her hair was exposed. Purplish welts peppered the side of her throat.

One hand flying to my mouth, I gasped. They didn't look like the other areas of her scorched skin, but more like a cross between bruises and some type of communicable rash. I'd never seen such severe burns before.

"Jesus!" Gaige exclaimed. Ever tactful, he added, "What the hell is that? I've seen time sickness and *that* is definitely not a result of it."

"It's Wicca-nitis," Molly replied soberly, sounding less out of it than she had only minutes before.

"I've never even heard of it," Gaige said, looking alarmed.

"Yeah, it's a real witch of a problem," I snickered.

Amusement flickered briefly in Molly's eyes when they met mine, but when she turned back to Gaige her expression was somber again.

"It is," Molly agreed. "The medics said it will be an absolute miracle if I don't succumb to it."

My partner's shocked expression was priceless.

I snorted, unable to hold back the laughter. This was the Molly I knew and loved—mischievous to the core.

"Sorry," Molly said with a sleepy grin. "I couldn't help it, you looked so serious. I needed some levity."

Gaige's relief was palpable.

"Yeah, yeah. Time sickness is a bitch," Gaige said gruffly. The tender expression he'd bestowed upon my roommate when he had thought she might be dying was gone, replaced by his usual cocky smile and look of casual indifference.

"So am I, Fratastic," Molly replied with a wink.

"You said it, not me," he joked.

Molly's eyelids began to droop again. As stubborn as she was, I knew my roommate was going to battle sleep as long as Gaige and I were around to distract her.

"Don't think I'm not aware that your feigned concern is only a ploy," she mumbled. "You just want to tell your buddies you spent tonight in bed with the both of us."

"Meh, it's just an average night for me," Gaige replied. "I don't—"

"We should let you rest," I interrupted.

"Stass, I feel fine," insisted Molly, a light sheen of sweat forming along her forehead. "I'm hungry, I want to eat."

Just the thought of food proved to be too much for Molly. Without warning, she began to swallow repeatedly, as if trying to keep down something that wanted desperately to come up. She sat up with a jerk and I jumped off the bed, unsure what to do. Molly held up a hand and waved me back, the other pressed over her pursed lips.

"I'm okay. I'm okay," she said, voice strained and muffled by her hand.

All three of us waited, holding our collective breaths to see whether Molly would actually get sick. Proving he wasn't as shallow as he would have people believe, Gaige remained next to the bed instead of moving out of the splash zone. I wasn't as keen on being sprayed with vomit, so I ran over to grab the trashcan beside her desk.

After several long moments, Molly lowered her hand from her mouth and leaned back on the pillows again.

"It's all good, no worries. I'm definitely not going to yack."

"Maybe you should pass on dinner for now?" I suggested.

"Probably a good idea," she replied.

"You sure you're okay?" Gaige inquired, worry drawing his brows together.

Molly waved off his concern. "I'm fine, Fratty."

Tucking the quilt up around her shoulders, I said firmly, "We are leaving. You are sleeping. Gaige and I will just be right out in the living room. If you need anything, anything at all, just send me a comm. Or yell."

"So protective," Molly muttered drowsily. "That's why I love you."

After a hurried dinner with Gaige over our mission dossiers, I headed straight for my room and the thrilling prospect of sleeping on my soft, comfortable mattress. Four nights in what they'd called a bed in the eighteenth century had made me stiff and achy, and I couldn't wait to get a proper night's rest.

Crawling under the covers, I took only enough time to set my alarm before allowing my head to fall back on the pile of soft, downy pillows. A low moan escaped my throat—it felt *that* good not to be sleeping on a straw pallet.

As I settled in, thoughts of my locket and what I might find on our trip to Paris whirled through my mind. The digi-board above my desk where I was attempting to track the heritage of my necklace was pathetically empty; only pictures and notes from two possible leads hung there, and both had ultimately been dead-ends.

The Paris lead was far more concrete than either of those, since I had a year, location, and actual photographic evidence. Even still, it would be a nearly impossible feat to find the woman. And yet, for some unknown reason, a part of me was convinced that this time would be different. This time I would uncover a vital clue to my origins.

FIVE

GAIGE STEPPED ATOP the pitcher's mound, replacing a freckled boy named Winks who'd moved to shortstop. I faced him down from home plate, ready for him to send what would surely be a lightning-fast pitch. After winding up, instead of a softball, Gaige lobbed a coconut in my direction. I put every ounce of my being into the swing, a giant tulip clutched in my hands. The flower stem connected with the hairy fruit, and I sprinted to first base. Gaige stood on the mound, waggling his behind and sing-songing at me.

"You're late, you're late, you're late for a very important date."

When I dove for the base, which looked inexplicably like one of the decorative pillows on my bed, a cloud of dirt erupted from the ground and flew up my nose.

"Out of bed!" the umpire cried, slashing his hands through the air in a gesture that meant I was safe.

I woke with a jolt. Four big, brown eyes hovered inches above my face. Blinking rapidly to clear my vision, the twin Gaiges merged into one. With a long, despondent groan, I weakly shoved him away and rolled to the side. Pulling my comforter up to my chin and burrowing in, I clung desperately to the last vestiges of sleep

"I was dreaming about you and your coconuts," I mumbled.

Gaige put both his hands on my shoulders, pushing me so I was again laying flat on my back. He gazed down at me with utter seriousness.

"Stassi. I…. I…."

My partner's humorless tone, coupled with his seeming inability to speak, made me open my eyes and return his penetrating stare. Something was wrong. The enormous, toothy grin was missing from his face.

Is it Molly?

"I can't," he started again, and then held up one finger in a signal for me to wait. He looked down, as if composing himself.

"You're scaring me, Gaige. Just tell me," I gently prodded.

He looked up at me again, his gaze intensifying as he glanced back and forth between my eyes, searching for something. I threw back the covers and sat up.

"Gaige…what is it?" I asked, now fully awake.

"I cannot tell you how long I've waited to hear you say those words. I knew you dreamt about me and my coconuts, I just never thought you'd admit it."

Then something yellow sailed through the air, connecting squarely with my face.

"Ugh, you're the worst!" I groaned and reached for the bright blob he was waving under my nose.

The end tore off in my hand as Gaige leapt backwards off the bed, and I was left holding a stem-less tulip.

Pointing the stem in my direction, he shouted, "Make Stassi a real girl!"

Gaige made a zigzagging motion through the air, like he was a boy wizard brandishing a green wand. He frowned at me for a long moment, and then repeated the theatrics.

"I *said*, make Stassi a real girl!"

I threw the flower at him.

Scowling, Gaige inspected the end of his makeshift wand as if it had betrayed him.

"Damn," he said. "It's broken."

Raising my eyebrows, I waited to see where this was going.

Wagging the stem up and down to punctuate each word, Gaige continued with his rant.

"You know, that wand shop has really gone downhill. I'm going to write them a strongly-worded letter about the dangers of selling inferior products."

Unable to help myself, I burst out laughing.

"You are such a *weirdo*," I told my partner. "Why are you here? Did I oversleep?"

Instead of waiting for his undoubtedly irritating reply, I swung my feet over the side of the bed and padded towards my bathroom. The movement required great effort—I was incredibly sore from my little barefoot jaunt the day before.

"For starters, you didn't oversleep. But you do only have ten minutes to get ready, so…I guess you'll have to wear that face to our meeting."

A grimace accompanied his matter-of-fact statement, implying that I really should've woken up early enough to procure a different face.

Yeah, he was a real charmer.

"And secondly," he called after me, pausing for dramatic effect. When I didn't beg him for answers, Gaige huffed before continuing in a smug tone. "Secondly, I had a breakfast date."

"You mean you gave a bowl of cereal to some willing young thing you ran in to on the way home last night?" I retorted, starting my morning routine.

"Not exactly," he replied gleefully.

I stopped, my toothbrush midway to my mouth, when his words registered.

"Wait, what?" I demanded, poking my head through the bathroom door to glare at him. "You're the reason the term 'manwhore' even exists."

"No," he responded, drawing out the word to seven syllables. "I did *not* find a new pillow pal."

"'New' being the operative word?"

Disgusted with my partner's ever-changing paramours, I stuck the toothbrush in my mouth and went to work cleaning my teeth.

"My date was with Molly!" he declared triumphantly.

Nearly choking on the toothpaste, I swung my head back out into the bedroom.

"Huh?"

"My date was with Molly!" Gaige repeated.

"Does she know that?" I asked. "Or when you say 'date,' do you mean you crawled into her bed and ate while she lay next to you in a medication-induced sleep?"

"You're *so* funny, Stassi," Gaige said, his goofy grin still present. "I don't tell you that often enough, but I genuinely enjoy your wit."

I shot Gaige a pointed look. He was avoiding the question.

"Was she conscious, or were you lurking like a creeper?"

"That's not *exactly* how it happened."

"Do I need to get a restraining order, Gaige? Put an electric fence around our house and a shock collar around your neck? You're not allowed to harass my roommate when she's unconscious."

"Well, it might be *similar* to how it happened," he continued, ignoring my threats. "I mean, she was awake. Sort of. I would say it was closer to a medication-induced haze, not total catalepsy. But we ate, we talked, and I paid, so it qualifies as a date."

I finished rinsing my mouth and then splashed water on my face.

"Where's my breakfast?" I asked.

"Well, I ate it. There's still coffee, though," Gaige said helpfully.

"Good enough," I replied. "Now go wait in the living room while I get dressed."

Gaige dutifully retreated into the hallway.

"Eight minutes, Stass," he called over his shoulder. "Better start trying on other faces."

When I took my hair down from the messy topknot I'd donned after the previous night's shower, I expected it to be a tangled rat's nest. Instead, somehow my blonde hair fell in pretty waves that reached the middle of my back. Even the fading pink streaks looked more vibrant in the light of a new day. I pulled a comb through the tresses to get rid of the tangles, and ran a bit of coconut oil over them to smooth out the frizz. After applying a layer of suncream to my face, I was good to go. I rarely wore makeup while on the island, so this face was my norm. Gaige would just have to deal with looking at it.

Five minutes later, dressed in pink shorts, a navy tee with white writing that advertised some long-defunct clothing brand, and leather flip-flops, I went to join Gaige in the living room. Except, he wasn't there.

Loud laughter and the scent of strong, Ethiopian coffee drifted from Molly's open doorway. I was still groggy from the lack of sleep and unpleasant awakening, but my yearning for caffeine led me to her bedroom, despite being concerned about what I might find there.

Propped up by a bevy of pillows, Molly was sitting in the middle of the bed with her patchwork quilt drawn up over her legs. Gaige perched on the side of the mattress, his body angled so that he was facing her with his back to the door. He was talking animatedly with his hands, making sweeping gestures that looked suspiciously like he was recreating the scene from earlier in my bedroom, when he'd tried to make me a *real* girl.

"Hey, roomie," Molly called when she noticed me, waving her

fingers in greeting.

"How're you feeling?" I asked, pushing away from the doorframe and crossing to stand beside the bed. "You look much better."

She did, too. Her color had improved drastically overnight. The visible burns on her arms appeared far less severe, as well. The *prima* within our tattoos had incredible healing powers, and was more effective than any of the new-age medications developed by the syndicate's med teams.

"I feel a million times better, actually," she said with a tired smile.

"*Prima* power!" Gaige cried, shooting his fist up in the air.

He really needed to stop watching cartoons from the 20th century.

"I was starving when I woke up, though," Molly continued. "Luckily, Gaige was nice enough to bring us breakfast."

"Too bad he ate mine," I said, giving him a pointed look before returning my attention to Molly. "Just take it easy today, okay? Maybe try not to overdo it? It's only been like twelve hours, your body needs time to heal."

She smiled cheekily. "Yeah, yeah, I know."

After saying a quick goodbye to Molly, I scooped up my dossier from the coffee table and practically dragged Gaige out the door.

Our conversation on the walk to the conference center was all business. Gaige and I reviewed the plan we'd made the night before. Despite their reputations for being tough, I felt confident the historians would be impressed by what we'd learned.

Gaige held the door for me when we reached the conference center, then followed me inside. With a wave to the desk attendant, we crossed the large lobby and headed for the library, which made up the entire west wing of the center. The four-story depository held the syndicate's massive book collection, as well as the historical archives. Every time I entered the rotunda, I was awed by the impressive array that lined the shelves.

By the mid-twenty-second century, the depletion of the earth's trees had led to the digitization of books, phasing out the printed word almost entirely. And when the world's technological networks crashed during the Epic War, many of time's greatest works were lost to the ether. Cyrus believed this loss such a great tragedy that he offered a credit bonus to runners who brought back bounds books from their runs. Now the island library had the most impressive collection of titles, both print and digital, on the planet.

Given the vast amount of knowledge located in the Atlic Syndicate's library, it was only fitting that the classrooms for our seminars were located there, as well. Ringing the upper floors of the library's rotunda, each historian had a dedicated space to brief us on everything we needed to know about the times and places we'd be visiting. Most of the history books were located on the upper levels, divided up by the historians' regions near their dedicated classrooms. There was also a loft-type space on each floor that overlooked the rotunda, dotted with overstuffed armchairs and sofas that made for comfortable reading.

As we climbed one of the four spiral staircases, a faint ocean breeze wafted in through the open windows on the uppermost floor. A salty mixture of weathered leather, old parchment, and the organic mint oil used to preserve the books swirled around me. I inhaled deeply, loving every breath of the strange concoction.

"Hey, Stassi. Hey, Gaige," a voice called from above, breaking the quiet.

Tilting my head so far backwards that the ends of my hair grazed my waist, I saw Rupert leaning over the fourth-floor railing and waving excitedly down at us.

"Hey, kid," Gaige said.

"What are you doing in here so early?" I asked. "You should be sleeping in while you still can."

Rupert rolled his eyes and pushed a lock of dark hair out of his face.

"I've got work soon, I'm just looking for something to keep me busy during my shift," Rupert replied with a sheepish grin. He held up a thin book. "I found something awesome."

I squinted, as if that might allow me to read the small print thirty feet above my head.

"It's a biography on Hugh Hefner," Rupert continued. "He was this American guy who ran a club where the waitresses dressed up like bunnies."

"That's just odd," I proclaimed, visions of women in giant furry costumes hopping through my mind. The floor must've been a veritable cocktail of spilled drinks.

Gaige snorted.

"There's a lot more to his story than that," he muttered.

Before I could ask what he meant, the mechanical whirring of a classroom door echoed through the library. A short man with a head of snow-white hair and a black historian's robe came into view on the balcony of the level between Rupert and us.

"Ms. Stassi, Mr. Koppelman, our meeting was to begin promptly at seven o'clock, if I'm not mistaken?" Historian Eisenhower's tone was light and inquisitive, as if he really thought he'd made an error.

Eisenhower wasn't fooling anyone. The scholar was a shrewd old man who never made a mistake. He also never forgot any of ours. Even now, I imagined him placing a black mark beside our names in his mental files.

"No, sir," I replied, lowering my gaze to show I was properly abashed. Gesturing between Gaige and myself, I muttered an apology from both of us.

"No matter," he waved off my words. "You are here now. Come along, come along."

The historian paused to shoot Rupert a meaningful stare.

"Mr. Rudolph, I trust your father has approved your chosen reading material for the day? If not, I suggest you rethink that choice. Mr.

Hefner's biography is not on the list of suggestions that I provided for you. Why not try Theodore Roosevelt or Winston Churchill if you are looking for biographies of twentieth century figures?"

"Y-y-yess, sir," Rupert stuttered, turning a shade of red so dark it verged on purple.

"Very good," Eisenhower replied, before turning his attention back on us delinquents. "Mr. Koppelman? Ms. Stassi? Today, please. We have a lot of ground to cover before the sun sets."

Moments like this one served as a reminder that I was something of an outsider. The historians always addressed runners by their last names, but I didn't have one. Instead of a familial name, I had a numeric signifier given to me by the work camp. I was the eighty-ninth child to arrive in the year 2446, so my full name was technically Stassi 2446-89. Though Cyrus had repeatedly told me that I could choose a last name, I hoped to discover my lineage and claim my rightful surname, as opposed to using a placeholder.

"Sunset? He's joking, right?" Gaige whispered to me as we reached the third floor, drawing me away from my thoughts. "He's not seriously planning to hold us hostage for the next twelve hours?"

I shrugged by way of answer, a sinking feeling in my stomach. Historian Eisenhower was not the joking sort, which meant there was a very real possibility we'd be here the entire day. Since I'd never been on a run that was as long or involved as this one, I had no idea what to expect.

Eisenhower disappeared through the entrance to his sanctuary as we hurried to catch up. Instead of actual doors, some of the bookcases around the perimeter of each floor slid out from the wall to reveal classrooms when the appropriate book was pulled from the shelf. When closed, they appeared like the other countless bookshelves, disguised to preserve the look and feel of the library. It was something Cyrus had once seen in the past, and insisted on replicating in our time.

Eisenhower's room was located behind a shelf of French history books—his specialty.

Stepping through the entranceway was akin to jumping time, without the physical sensations that went along with traveling via vortex. While the library was old-world charm, the classrooms were decked out with modern technology, including floor-to-ceiling digi-boards. The only exception to the contemporary setting was the student desks; they'd been salvaged from a time before computing carrels had been invented. The chairs were made of hard, uncomfortable plastic, and each had a small, connected writing table. When using the beam keyboard with our Qubes—the letters projected onto whatever surface the handheld computer was on—it was absurdly cramped.

Sliding in to one of the desks, I stifled a giggle as Gaige wiggled his way into another. At just over six feet, Gaige's knees bumped the underside of the desk if he tried to sit up straight, so he was forced to sit at an odd angle with his butt resting near the edge of the chair and his long legs stretched out in front of him. Squeezed between the seat back and the writing arm, Gaige looked a like an overgrown child stuffed into a highchair. The spectacle never ceased to amuse me.

"Olivia," Eisenhower called out as he stepped behind the podium at the front of the room where he stood to deliver his lectures. His gold and blue Hyeres FC mug was in the cup holder of the lectern, undoubtedly holding the historian's ever-present jasmine tea.

A soft whirring sound caught my attention and I looked up just in time to see Eisenhower's droid gliding towards us, revived by her wake word. Olivia's presence was as constant as his tea.

Each time we crammed with Eisenhower, Olivia was dressed in clothes that reflected the time period we were studying. Today was no different. Her drop-waist, tunic-style dress was blue with white polka dots. The hem hung just below her pale stocking-clad knees, and several inches of sheer fabric hung down longer than the slip underneath.

Though the dress was downright dowdy for our time, the effect was considered risqué in the twenties, particularly when compared to its fashion predecessors.

Long strands of pearls were looped around Olivia's neck and one perfectly round pearl earring dangled from each of her ears. Her light brown hair was also styled for the period, in the finger waves the 1920s were known for. Brown Mary Janes with a small stacked heel completed her outfit.

"Good morning Miss Stassi. Good morning Mr. Koppelman. May I procure a beverage for you before Historian Eisenhower begins the day's lecture?" Olivia asked. Her voice was cool and detached, touched with a faint French accent. Per usual, she then repeated the question in flawless French.

"Coffee, please," I answered.

"Une café, s'il vous plait," she corrected.

Knowing that she would refuse to continue her task until I did, I dutifully echoed the words. Olivia's painted red lips curved slightly upwards into her version of a smile. Given his specialty, Eisenhower was also the one who conducted the French language courses. Naturally, his bot was programmed to aid our proficiency.

"Your pronunciation is coming along nicely, Stassi 2446-89."

"Merci beaucoup," I replied.

"And for you, Mr. Koppelman?" she asked, turning her entire body to face my partner.

"Ditto," he said.

For a moment, the droid simply stared. I pictured gears turning inside of her head as she tried to puzzle out the translation for "ditto". Of course there weren't actually gears beneath Olivia's synthetic skin, since she was a modern creation and not something from a steampunk novel, but it was a fun visual.

"Mr. Koppelman, the term you speak of has no literal translation. In

American English, 'ditto' is used colloquially to agree with something another individual has just said or to convey that your wishes or feelings are in accordance with those of another individual. Is this to mean that you, too, wish to say: 'Une café, s'il vous plait'?"

Gaige grinned. "Oui."

Historian Eisenhower cleared his throat loudly and tapped the lectern with his laser pointer.

"Mr. Koppelman, I have asked you many times—please do not deliberately confuse her." To the droid, he said, "Carry on, Olivia. Thank you."

The humanoid's electronic parts whirred faintly as she turned and nodded to her boss.

"As you wish, Historian."

She briskly set off for the open door behind Eisenhower to fulfill her task. In the back were a kitchen, the historian's personal study, and a room for a selection of clothing from the wardrobing department.

Not one to waste time, the historian set down his mug and set to business.

"I trust you both have studied the assignment dossier?" he began. Without waiting for a response, Eisenhower continued. "What can you tell me about your primary asset for this run?"

"Andre Rosenthal was a gifted and well-known writer from the twentieth century," Gaige said, quoting verbatim the first line of the author's bio.

"Yes, yes, what else?" Eisenhower made a *hurry-it-along* gesture with his hand.

"His works didn't reach their height of popularity until after Rosenthal's death in 1967," I piped in. "In fact, only four of his novels were published while he was alive. The most critically acclaimed books—those that rendered him one of the era's most influential writers—were actually found after he passed away, and purchased by Dabber and Baehr

Publishing at the estate auction. With the consent of his niece, the house published the novels posthumously."

Gaige scowled at me. "Suck up," he muttered.

"Very good, Stassi." Eisenhower narrowed his muddy brown eyes at my partner. "Now, Mr. Koppelman, maybe you could explain why the target manuscript, *Blue's Canyon*, was never found among his possessions?"

"Yes, sir. *Blue's Canyon* was thought to be his magnum opus, but the manuscript was never found. Some believe that the existence of *Blue's Canyon* was nothing more than a rumor propagated by Rosenthal himself," Gaige began, emphasizing the novel's working title to show he was paying attention.

Our teacher smiled and nodded, sipping his tea. That was high praise coming from Eisenhower.

"Editing notes that were found in Rosenthal's home hinted that he did in fact complete the book," Gaige continued, spurred on by the approval. "But the location has remained a mystery since the writer's death."

As Gaige explained Rosenthal's famous paranoia and his relationships with other notable authors of the day, Olivia whirled back into the room. A serving tray was perched atop one robotic hand, holding two china mugs, a French press, a small pitcher of cream, and a bowl of sugar cubes. She placed one cup and saucer in front of me, poured the coffee, and then offered me the creamer and sugar. As I dumped enough of both condiments into my cup to all but obliterate the bold, rich flavors of the beans, she poured Gaige's coffee.

"Merci," Gaige and I said in unison.

Eisenhower didn't allow our translation chips in his classroom, so when Olivia responded in rapid French, it went in one ear and out the other.

"Thank you, Olivia, that will be all for now," the historian told her in English.

The droid retreated through the open doorway to wait until she was summoned again.

"Stassi," Eisenhower began, his tone a warning of the Socratic method portion of our lecture coming my way. "Why do we believe the complete manuscript may be found in Paris in the year 1925?"

"In a Parisian newspaper's interview of Rosenthal in March of 1925, he was quoted as saying: 'This is a time of extravagance and excess. The art, music, literature and fashion are all exceptional. Here in Paris, society is celebrating. To not document my days spent among those who have shaped and influenced the culture of this age would be a great disservice, not to mention a blatant snub. The manuscript is in its final stages and I am proud of it thus far. In fact, *Blue's Canyon* is my finest work to date.'

"Finally," I concluded, returning my gaze to the historian, "We believe we can find a version of the complete manuscript then because the editing notes found in his home span from 1921 to 1925."

"It is so refreshing to see how seriously you both are taking this assignment," Eisenhower said with a genuine smile.

And on it went.

After we'd talked ourselves hoarse, Eisenhower dimmed the overhead lights and flipped several switches. Behind him, the enormous digital screen came to life. A headshot of Rosenthal that was taken in 1925 emerged, the same one on the first screen of the dossier for this mission. He was twenty-five at the time.

Eisenhower clicked the handheld controller several times, and the daunting cast of characters appeared, arranged in a circle around Rosenthal. Red lines connected his picture with those of the century's most influential minds: Gertrude Stein, F. Scott Fitzgerald, Ezra Pound, James Joyce, Alice Toklas, Sylvia Beach, Adrienne Monnier, Carmen D'Angelo, Ernest Hemingway and his wife Hadley. And those were just the primaries.

With a click of Eisenhower's finger, a second, larger circle of photos ringed the first. Blue dotted lines darted out from it like broken spokes of a wheel. These connected Rosenthal to individuals who orbited the inner sphere of influence, but only played a minor role in his life. Green lines made connections between the entire cast of supporting characters.

Directing his finger beam at each in turn, Eisenhower began the lecture portion of our prep session. While he filled in the gaps that our brief dossier had left behind, Gaige and I furiously tapped notes into our tablets like good little pupils.

A helpful bit of information that was absent from our original mission specifics was the name of an alchemist whose main duty it was to socialize with noteworthy people of the time.

"Ines Callandries." Eisenhower indicated a severe looking woman in the outer ring on the digi-board. "She is known to Rosenthal and will be able to make introductions. However," he held up a finger, warning us not to become too excited by this news, "Ms. Callandries is little more than a background fixture in these individual's lives. Do not expect her to do your job for you. She is available to facilitate your integration into society, nothing more."

By lunchtime, Historian Eisenhower seemed satisfied that we had a solid foundation where the people of the time were concerned. He called Olivia's name and she immediately came to life.

"I believe today's will be a working lunch, Olivia," Eisenhower told her. "Would you please be so kind as to serve the meal you prepared?"

"Oui, monsieur," she replied dutifully and disappeared into the kitchen area.

When she returned, Olivia carried trays with mini ham and Brie baguettes, roasted beet and goat cheese salads served atop endive wedges, and cups of strawberries in heavy whipping cream for dessert. While we dined on the decadent foods common in Paris during our target time, Historian Eisenhower pushed onward.

The screen in the front of the room switched from a collage of faces to a collage of places. Rosenthal's picture was still in the middle, but the surrounding images were of locations, accompanied by addresses: Stein's salon at 27 rue de Fleurus, Shakespeare and Company on rue de l'Odeon, and various cafés in Montparnasse. The latter were the haunts that Rosenthal and his set were known to visit for drinks and lively discussions on everything from their crafts to social issues of the day. The historian cited the significance of each place in turn, highlighting when we'd be most likely to find the asset there.

"Can you tell us where Rosenthal will be on Thursday evening?" Gaige asked. "Do we have a schedule for him that day? I see Friday and other sporadic dates in our spec sheets, but is there anything on the 26th of March? I think we should attempt contact as soon as possible, are you cool with that, Stass?"

He was asking because we normally spent a day acclimating to the period and new location. Since we'd been to Paris before, we didn't need the full twenty-four hour adjustment period.

"That sounds good to me," I replied with a shrug. "We should aim for Thursday night."

Eisenhower closed his eyes, attempting to recall the information from memory. Apparently it wasn't coming to him, because his eyes popped open with a look of annoyance.

"Bob!" he shouted.

A round object zoomed through the air from the doorway at the front of the room.

"How many I be of assistance, sir?" Bob-the-drone asked in a mechanical voice. As he spoke, the lights on one side of his round body came to life and the words appeared in text on his display screen.

"Please fetch me a book that gives us information on Andre Rosenthal's whereabouts on March 26, 1925," Eisenhower commanded.

"Yes, sir. I shall return momentarily."

The drone's internal database held the location of every book in the library, among other things. He was programmed to respond to voice commands such as the one Eisenhower had just given him.

Bob whizzed to the back of the classroom, then hovered in place while the bookshelf door slid open. Three minutes later, Bob returned with the diary of Rosenthal's part-time love interest, Carmen D'Angelo, clutched in his metal graspers. After delivering the book to the lectern, the graspers retracted and Bob hovered to one side while awaiting further instruction.

The historian flipped to the table of contents, slid an index finger down the column of words until he found what he was looking for and turned to the appropriate page. After reading for a minute, Eisenhower snapped the book closed and held it up in the air for the drone to take.

"Bob, return this to the shelf, please," he commanded.

"Yes, sir," the drone replied, disappearing to do the historian's bidding.

"The answer to your question is quite fortuitous," Eisenhower said to us. "*The Great Gatsby* was published in early March 1925. Fitzgerald returned to Paris shortly before you will be arriving to celebrate the release with his friends and colleagues. It just so happens that Gertrude Stein is hosting a party in his honor on March 26th. It is themed and will be held at an American-style speakeasy as a nod to the book's setting. From what I gather, the event is not a private one, so you will not need an invitation."

"I do love a good book release party," Gaige said with a grin.

"I'm so glad," the historian replied drolly. "Hopefully you will enjoy reading the novel between now and then just as much."

"Maybe we should stick with Friday," my partner grumbled.

With a look that silenced Gaige, the historian continued on with the lecture. I made a note on my task list to download *Gatsby*.

After two more hours of tapping away on the beam keyboard, my feet were asleep and my fingertips ached. Thankfully, Eisenhower paused to summon the drone for a second time—I needed the reprieve. Leaning back in my chair, I stretched my legs and watched as he commanded his electronic minions.

"Bob, please fetch Sybil, Charice, Jesma, Claud, Brian, and Jonathon. Olivia, please prepare them for the wardrobing portion of today's session."

The names Eisenhower had listed were other droids. Apparently, the whole gang was coming by for a visit.

"We have one more area to cover," Eisenhower continued, speaking again to Gaige and me. "Then we shall take a brief dinner break before the exam. While we wait, let's go over your plan for integration."

His gaze fell on me, and I took that as my cue.

"Yes, sir. Since we are advancing the timeline, we will make an appearance at Fitzgerald's release party on Thursday night. Hopefully, this will get them all used to our presence in the background. I think we should wait and analyze the situation before we decide whether or not to make the initial contact with Rosenthal that night. Since others in his circle are more open to meeting outsiders, it might be best to become acquainted with those individuals first," I explained, adjusting in my chair to a more comfortable position. "I think we have a better shot at gaining Rosenthal's trust if we don't direct our attention at him, initially."

"From there, we will secure an invite to one of the parties that Stein holds every Saturday," Gaige chimed in. "If it happens organically at the book party, great. If not, we can always have one procured through the customs station. Either way, we will approach Rosenthal directly at Stein's. The goal is to casually befriend him. Depending on which of us he seems more taken with, the other will continue with infiltrating his circle. The more we're seen out and about with these people, the more Rosenthal will let his guard down. If all goes according to plan, we will eventually learn the location information we need from both the writer and his friends over time. Then wham, bam, copy it, ma'am."

Eisenhower took several uncomfortable moments to weigh our proposal. If he vetoed the strategy, we'd be screwed. I honestly couldn't think of another way to broach this run. Time and patience were going to be key.

"Not bad," the historian finally said. "Be prepared, though, Stassi— Gaige is more likely to be accepted by the writing crowd. There's a lot of machismo there, particularly from Hemingway."

With Eisenhower's help, we refined our plan and developed our cover story. We were going to be siblings from Baltimore with too much time and too much money—just another pair of socialites fascinated with the cultural crowd. The artists back then were always looking for benefactors, so it stood to reason a couple of young shipping heirs would be welcomed among them.

"Excusez-moi, s'il vous plait," Olivia said, peeking her head out from the back room. "Nous sommes pets si vous l'etes."

"Gaige, Stassi, is there anything else we need to go over" Eisenhower asked. Gaige and I both shook our heads, and the historian looked back to Olivia. "We are ready, as well."

The lights dimmed even further, and quiet jazz music began playing through unseen speakers. A large spotlight appeared, following Olivia as she glided the length of the room. She'd swapped her polka-dot dress for a pink one with two rows of buttons down the front and a lace collar. A black bell-shaped hat with a white flower covered her finger waves.

"This style is called a cloche," Eisenhower informed us, using his laser finger beam to indicate the hat. While she continued walking, he explained the role milliners played in twentieth century fashion.

Apparently, I'd have an entire wardrobe of headwear.

Olivia turned at the end of the room, sashayed back the way she'd come. Jonathon came next, decked out in a dapper suit. Playing emcee, Eisenhower described the droid's vest, pants, shoes, and tie, pointing out small details that were specific to the 1920s.

Gaige leaned over and whispered in my ear excitedly, "Are we seriously watching a droid fashion show? This is awesome."

While we normally covered the clothes of the time period during these classes, a demonstration like this one had never before been included. The highly amusing spectacle was better than listening to Eisenhower drone on about pictures of clothing, so I wasn't complaining.

Next came Jesma in a blue velvet cape with a poufy collar that Eisenhower told us was typically worn to premiere cultural events, such as the opera. On her return trip down the makeshift catwalk, Jesma swept the cape back behind her shoulders to reveal an asymmetrical dress with one full sleeve and one bare shoulder. The satiny material was gathered above one hip, a large flower holding it in place, and fringe hung from the sleeve and bottom layer of the dress.

Smiling wistfully as the droids continued to showcase the beautiful clothing from centuries past, excitement made me forget my weariness. Normally I wasn't all that interested in clothes and fashion, but something about the elegance of the twenties style appealed to me. To my surprise, I found myself looking forward to wearing the beautiful outfits.

As promised, after the fashion show ended, Olivia returned with more French specialties for dinner. While Gaige and I ate, Eisenhower answered the rest of our concerns and added some final tips.

Once our plates were cleared away, he tapped several keys on the control box and sent exams over to our Qubes. There were a hundred and fifty questions, including some on basic French phrases we should know, even though we'd be posing as Americans. I finished in a little over two hours, scoring a ninety percent. Gaige, being a knowledge sponge, scored a ninety-eight.

"Who's the suck up now?" I joked when he shoved his Qube under my nose and pointed to his grade.

"Too bad we didn't bet on the results," he replied.

"I know better than that."

"At least you know something," he teased.

"You are *both* to be commended," Eisenhower announced. "However, you also both need a lot of work in the language department. You are lucky that all of the expatriates speak English, as do many of the other players. Since you are posing as Americans, your limited French capabilities will be expected.

"Despite this, you should still wear a Rosetta at all times on this run. This will allow you to understand what those around you are saying when not speaking to you directly. It is often helpful to know what people say when they think you cannot comprehend them."

At the height of the nano-neuro craze, similar tech was actually implanted in the brain, but the long-term side effects were, predictably, pretty horrific. Though I didn't quite understand the science involved, the Rosetta's translation outputs were actually heard in the head of the wearer, like creepy little schizophrenic voices; it had definitely taken some getting used to.

After fourteen hours of nonstop cramming, my head felt as though it might explode from all of the information that had been stuffed inside. Dazed, I began gathering my things.

Before we left, as always, Eisenhower ended with the historians' motto: Change not the past, lest we lose our present and destroy the future for all.

SIX

THE STAFF AT the work camp was, in a word, disaffected. They showed little more than apathy towards the orphaned children in their charge, with one exception: the dorm matron. She wasn't physically affectionate—no hugs before bed, no kisses for skinned knees—but she was kind and human enough to comfort a little girl who longed for her family. She used to tell me that my birth parents were among the stars. I took her words literally, and each night before bed I would look out the window and pick one star to be my mother and one to be my father.

Even though I knew better now, old habits died hard.

Standing on the back patio of my bungalow, I gazed up at the sea of diamonds strewn across the blue velvet sky. The bright, twinkling specks were so close to one another, they could've been wrapped in a lover's embrace. I chose two, brought my locket to my lips and made the same whispered promise I had every night for the past fifteen years.

"I'll find you," I told them.

I entered the bungalow through the back and found Molly sitting on the living room sofa. She wore a loose-fitting, long-sleeved gray cotton shirt. A quilt covered her long legs and hid the worst of her burns. Dark brown and bright blue strands of hair were loose around her face and tousled. Dilated pupils shone from eyes shadowed by dark circles, evidence that her medication-induced slumber hadn't been very restful. But the wide grin on her lips was so dazzling it nearly blinded me to her exhaustion.

"You aren't usually this happy to see me," I joked.

Color crept into her ivory cheeks. "Oh, hey, Stass, you're home," she said too loudly. "What's in the bag?"

I'd taken a detour to the canteen on the way home to restock Molly's chocolate supply.

"Goodies," I replied suspiciously. "Why are you yelling at me?"

"Goodies for me?" Molly asked hopefully, her voice much quieter now. "You shouldn't have."

"They're purely medicinal."

"What about me?" a male voice called from another room. "Do I get goodies, too?"

My partner strolled out of Molly's bedroom, a pink cardigan draped over one arm. He held up the sweater for Molly's inspection. "This one okay?"

She nodded. "Perfect. Thanks."

I set the bag of chocolate on the coffee table and concentrated on looking anywhere but at my two friends as Gaige helped Molly into the cardigan. That was when I noticed the digi-screen. Six rectangular film covers all with a different image but the same title sat on virtual shelves.

"Really? You're going to watch the movie instead of reading the book? You are such a cheater," I said to Gaige with mock sternness.

He eased down on the sofa next to Molly.

"I'm a visual learner, Stass. I'll retain more knowledge by watching the movie," Gaige replied.

"In a third of the time," I said dryly. "How convenient."

"You say that like it's a bad thing," Gaige said, feigning confusion.

"Watch with us," Molly said, batting her long lashes. "You can even pick which version."

I was torn. It was late. I was exhausted and the thought of reading an entire book by morning was daunting. Still, I'd been looking forward to a little alone time to mentally psych myself up for the mission ahead.

Molly launched in to a detailed explanation of the different versions of *Gatsby*, listing off pros and cons of each. The oldest was a silent film from 1926, which Gaige vetoed before I could do the same. The most recent was from 2338 and, according to my roommate, was critically acclaimed for its use of a gender-ambiguous cast.

"Might be fun to see if we can guess which characters are played by women and which are played by men," I suggested halfheartedly.

"And, last but not least, we have the 2013 *Gatsby*," Molly continued talking right over me. She went on to describe the beautiful clothes and opulent sets with so much enthusiasm that I didn't have to ask which version she wanted to watch.

"Let's go with that one," I said when she was finished.

"You sure?" Molly asked. "Like I said, it's totally up to you."

I smiled. "I'm sure. Far be it for me to deny an invalid her wish. Here, make yourself useful." I tossed the remote to Gaige.

"It has that one guy from that boat movie you like," Molly added hopefully. "Oh! And the guy who played Bugman."

"You're the one who liked that boat movie," I reminded my roommate. "Remember? I thought it was silly since you knew the whole time how it was going to end."

Rolling his eyes at our banter, Gaige used the universal remote to select the 2013 version of *Gatsby*, dim the living room lights, and, judging by the sweat beads forming on my skin, raise the temperature in the bungalow. I was about to make a snarky comment when Molly shuddered violently. She pulled the cardigan tighter around her thin shoulders.

"Could you turn up the heat another degree or two?" I asked instead, knowing Molly was too proud and too stubborn to make the request.

Gaige did as instructed, and then peeled off his pullover to compensate for the warmer climate.

A haunting melody filled the air as the movie began to play.

The three of us chatted easily about the storyline, clothes, and setting of the film. Molly, who'd apparently seen the other versions, kept up a running commentary on how this adaptation differed from the others.

"I'm so jealous," Molly declared wistfully. On screen, champagne fountains flowed and elegant men and women danced at Jay Gatsby's magnificent home.

"Why?" I asked. "I thought you told Cyrus you were done with this life."

"I know, I know. Getting burned at the stake for being a witch sort of puts a damper on things. It's just that...I love being a runner. You guys get to go live for over a month in that," she replied, gesturing at the screen. "That's going to be so much fun. I know I said I'm done with it, but I really wish I could go with you. I want to experience everything possible, I don't want to be a boring island rat."

"Have you talked to Cyrus again?" Gaige asked carefully.

"He stopped by earlier. He's refusing to accept my resignation until I'm fully recovered," Molly told us.

"I think that's great advice," I said sagely.

Molly shrugged as a chill ran through her, though this time I had a feeling it was a memory that made her shiver.

"Maybe. I don't know. I really don't know what to do. Yesterday I was convinced that running was my past. Now, I don't know. I think maybe I was just upset. And I don't feel like I'm knocking on death's door anymore, so I guess that could be part of it."

"What happened must have been really scary," Gaige said.

The haunted expression still lingered in her big blue eyes. She'd been through a nightmarish ordeal, one that would have landed most any other runner on mental health leave. Suddenly, I felt very selfish for taking the Paris mission, when my roommate so obviously needed moral support.

"I'm sure Cyrus wouldn't mind if we pushed the run back a couple of days," I began.

"No." Molly shook her head decisively. "Totally unnecessary. Come on, Stassi. Who do you think you're talking to? I'll be fine. I *am* fine." With the declaration, she sat up straighter and tucked her gauze wrapped hands beneath the quilt to hide them from view.

Yesterday, when she'd come bursting through the door during the meeting, I'd been terrified. The thought of losing Molly was too much. She meant too much to me. Physically, at least, she was on the mend, I noted. In a couple of days, the burns would start to fade and, thanks to the syndicate's top-notch doctors, she wouldn't have any scars to serve as constant reminders of the ordeal. It was the emotional scarring that worried me. How long would those wounds take to heal?

As I studied her defiant expression, I couldn't help but wonder if Molly was putting on a show so I wouldn't worry about her.

"I'm fine," Molly insisted, when I didn't avert my gaze. "Besides, you have a lead to follow up on. You shouldn't put that off."

"I've waited fifteen years," I replied, brushing off her statement. "Another few days won't hurt."

"No," Molly repeated firmly. "Look, I have my mom and dad if I need anything. And Tiger. He's offered to stay with me while you're gone, just until I'm totally back on my feet."

When the screen faded on the heartbreaking tale of lost love, we called it a night. Gaige offered to help Molly to her bed and, to my surprise, she accepted. I retreated to my own sanctuary for some much needed sleep.

With the doors to the patio open, the screen pulled shut to keep out pesky island critters, a cool breeze swept through my room. Bypassing my usual nightly routine, I collapsed into bed exhausted. For a long moment, I lay snuggled under the light comforter and simply listened to the island's soundtrack. Ocean waves crashed gently on the shore, insects sang chirpy mating songs to one another, wind rustled leaves at a slow leisurely pace.

I closed my eyes and succumbed to fatigue.

SEVEN

THE NEXT MORNING, I was still groggy. Excitement over the impending run and the possibility of hunting down a lead on my locket had replaced my doubts over whether I was truly ready for such a complicated mission. Trudging into the kitchen, I pressed a sequence of buttons on the coffeemaker and waited for my latte to brew.

My roommate shuffled barefoot from her room, her kimono pulled snugly around her.

"You didn't need to get up. You should be sleeping," I said, holding out the latte I'd made for myself to her. "Here, I'll make another."

"You're too good to me," she replied, accepting the mug. "And I wanted to see you off, I can go back to bed later."

I repeated the command sequence on the coffeemaker as Molly sipped foam from her cup. Once my coffee was done brewing, we headed outside to sit on the patio and drink our morning pick-me-ups while watching the island come to life.

"You guys will be careful, right?" Molly asked after we'd been sitting in companionable silence for several minutes.

"Of course, we're always careful," I told her.

"Gaige told me about what happened in Florence. You were almost caught, Stassi. That's not like you."

I'd purposely not told her what had happened, not wanting to worry her while she was dealing with health issues. Gaige had such a big mouth.

"No," I admitted. "It was kind of a mess, but we figured it out. We always do." I smiled at my roommate. "We'll be fine. Gaige has my back and I have his."

Her concern was genuine and not unexpected after her own near miss. Being chased by Napoleon's men had been scary, but was nothing compared to being burned at the stake. Or so I imagined. The thought made me shudder. It was sobering to really think about how dangerous our jobs could be.

"It's not that, exactly. I know you guys take care of each other," Molly replied quietly. "I just have a bad feeling about this one. Like it's...I don't know how to explain it. I just worry about you."

I leaned over and hugged her gently.

"I know you do. I'll check in regularly with customs, though. I'll be sure Cyrus knows that you need to be kept in the loop, okay?"

This seemed to mollify Molly a little, but worry still creased her forehead. My excitement dimmed further at her concern. Molly was the opposite of a worrywart, so this was new territory.

After we finished our coffees, Molly followed me into my room while I changed and packed a few necessities for the run. Untimely possessions were most often confiscated at customs, but a few were allowed, if the agent was a lenient one. Items like my eucalyptus face cream and special mint candies that were made on the island went into my small duffle bag. Once I added my camera, charger, and Qube, I zipped the bag shut. The tech would be necessary for this mission and every syndicate house had numerous safes to keep the items hidden from prying eyes.

I didn't bother with clothes since everything from my underwear to my headwear would be provided by customs, including period appropriate bedclothes in case someone stumbled into my bedroom by mistake. Heaven forbid an intruder find me wearing pink sleep shorts with little green palm trees and run off yelling about some girl in futuristic pajamas.

Molly pulled my rattiest jeans from a drawer, the ones with a huge hole in the left knee from a rock climbing adventure that I'd nearly not come home from. It was my first time climbing with Gaige, Tiger, and Molly, and all three were experts from having grown up on the island. They seemed to forget that the dry, flat farmlands where the work camp was located didn't have hundred foot rock faces over clear blue-green ocean. Nonetheless, after losing my footing numerous times, I'd triumphantly reached the top with bloody knees and blistered hands.

"No, not those," I said when she laid the holey jeans on my unmade bed. "Too many good memories associated with those, it'd be a shame to lose them."

I'd learned to never wear clothes I liked when departing on a run. Ostensibly, customs held the garments we arrived wearing in a locker until it was time for us to return to the island. Yet, when I went back to customs for the return trip, my clothes were not always where I'd left them. It seemed there was as lucrative a black market among the alchemists for items from the future as there was in the future for items from the past. Since our livelihood depended upon them, a few pairs of jeans and some sweaters were a small price to pay. But it was still irritating.

Molly snorted. "Seriously? I thought you were miserable that day."

"No, I had a good time," I said defensively.

Hands on her slim hips, Molly retorted, "You haven't been climbing with us since."

She was right about that fact, but wrong about the reason. The trio didn't need a novice like me holding them back, so I'd found an instructor and paid him to teach me in my spare time: Rupert. Unfortunately I didn't have a surplus of spare time, so I was still nowhere near the level of my friends.

"Whatever. How about the acid-washed ones? They're hideous and don't fit well anyway," I suggested.

Tiger and Molly had made a run to America during the late 80s or early 90s and as a joke Tiger brought back the pleated denim disaster for me.

"Tiger will be so pissed." Molly laughed pulling out the jeans and a ratty t-shirt with a tear. "Is this shirt sentimental, too? Or can you part from this rag?"

"That'll work," I told her.

I changed quickly, and then spared a moment to run a brush through my hair. As I slipped on a pair of dirty sneakers that were well past their prime, Molly grabbed my bag from the bed.

Gaige and Tiger were in the living room when Molly and I emerged from my bedroom.

"What *are* you wearing?" Gaige covered his eyes with his hands like a child afraid of the dark. "I'm blind! I'm blind!" he cried.

Ignoring my partner's theatrics, I turned to greet Tiger. Molly's partner wore straight-legged jeans with a tight yellow tee. A billiard ball appeared to be leaping off of the cotton, and a slogan was scrawled underneath: Yellowbelly Saloon, We Have the Best Balls in Town.

"Nice shirt," I told Tiger.

"Nice pants," he shot back, grinning.

"You're going to watch Molly while I'm gone," I told him in my most no-nonsense tone. "Make sure she doesn't push herself too hard, and that she gets enough sleep. She'll probably need a nap today after getting up so early, make sure you let her rest."

"Did you seriously just declare my naptime?" Molly asked wryly.

At the same time, Tiger saluted me and said, "Aye, aye, Momma Bear, Stassi."

I rolled my eyes and leaned over to give Molly a gentle hug goodbye. "I'll be back soon," I promised her.

"You better," she whispered back, squeezing me hard with her bony arms.

Next I gave Tiger a quick hug, which surprised us both.

Molly must be rubbing off on me, I thought. Normally she and Gaige were only two people I touched.

"Don't worry, Stassi, I'm never letting her out of my sight again," Tiger whispered in my ear and I could hear the regret heavy in his voice. It didn't take a psychoanalyst to know Tiger shouldered the blame for Molly being hurt on their mission. I hugged him a little bit tighter.

After giving my roommate another squeeze, Gaige and I departed the bungalow and headed for the gate. Molly wanted to escort us, but was outvoted. Reluctantly she stayed back with Tiger, who promised to make sure she had a good breakfast, and then returned to bed.

Though it was early, the island was awake and active. Workers tended to the grounds, collectors picked flowers and fruits for both the cooks and scientists, and runners were out and about on their way to meet with historians, eat breakfast in the community dining rooms, or get in some morning exercise on the trails.

We were almost to the gate when Cyrus, face slick with sweat and panting, caught up with us. From his black athletic shorts and gray t-shirt, it was obvious he'd been out for a morning jog.

"Good, I caught you," he said, coming to a stop in front of Gaige and me.

Despite his easygoing smile, the Founder's bright green eyes were troubled. I instantly began to worry something was wrong. "Be careful, you two. Not all things in the past are meant to be uncovered. This manuscript might very well be one of them. If the task proves too difficult or too timely, return home." He winked. "After all, half the payment is due up front and is nonrefundable."

I smiled nervously, reading more meaning into Cyrus's words than I should have. Abandoning a mission was not something the syndicate took lightly. Persistence and ingenuity were the two traits most important to our job.

"Yeah, sure," I said slowly.

"We've got this, old man," Gaige said, clapping Cyrus on the back.

Evidently, our boss didn't take kindly to Gaige's choice of words. He turned one of his infamous glares on my partner. It was a look that could have boiled tap water straight from the faucet. To his credit, Gaige only paled and retreated several steps. I wouldn't have blamed him if he'd simply run away.

"Sir," Gaige corrected. "We've got this, *sir*. I'll take good care of Stassi. No need to worry."

"See that you do, Gaige. And I'll see you both in a few weeks. Check in regularly with customs, and send word immediately if you encounter any trouble."

Both requests were protocol for longer runs, but my partner and I simply nodded our agreement. With a final glare at Gaige, Cyrus continued on his run, and we resumed our path.

When we descended the stone stairs into the gate, we found Rupert and Sara on duty. Like Rupert, Sara held a special place in my heart, but for an entirely different reason. She came from the work camps, too. Sara was one of the only people on the island who understood what it was like to come from nothing to an island with everything.

"Hey, Sara. Hey, Rupert," I called.

"Hi, Stassi," they chorused in unison.

"Kids," Gaige said with a nod.

Rupert waved and Sara gave a shy nod to my partner. Like so many of the females on the island, Gaige dazzled her.

Standing behind the desk, with Sara seated beside him, Rupert tapped away on a beam keyboard.

"Looks like you guys are headed to Paris in 1925, is that right?" he asked, before giving a low whistle. "Six weeks? That's a long time."

The gate attendants weren't given specifics about our missions—only the time period, location, and anticipated length of each assignment. That way, if we didn't return, they could alert Cyrus. Of course our boss studied the logs religiously, so he often knew before the gate attendants if something was amiss. Cyrus was a gruff man, but he cared about everyone on the island and did his best to ensure our safety. I'd seen it in his eyes the moment we met.

"Yeah, try not to miss us too much while we're gone," Gaige joked with the attendants.

"Incoming in vortex five," Sara said suddenly. She glanced at the computer screen. "Should be Duncan and Brie, unless Mateo and Lash are back early."

"Will you check?" Rupert asked her. To Gaige and me, he said, "Sorry, it's a busy day. I have you two set on vortex nine."

As soon as we entered the dark cave, my tattoo began to hum. I rubbed the skin on the inside of my wrist with my thumb. At the turn in the tunnel, Gaige reached for my hand. The blinding white light appeared before us. It began to swirl, gold ribbons weaving through the white background until the two colors were equals. As one, we stepped into the spinning vortex.

Goodbye Branson.

EIGHT

PARIS, I THOUGHT, opening my eyes with a smile on my lips

At least, I assumed we were in Paris. A very cramped Paris, by the feel of it. Gaige's hand no longer held mine, but his body was pressed up against my back, his coffee breath hot on my neck.

"Ugh, personal space," I groaned, trying to put distance between our bodies.

Only, there was nowhere to go. Directly in front of my nose was a stone wall. Dim light shone down on us from a *prima*-powered eternal lamp near the ceiling.

Gaige stepped back, providing me with enough space to turn around. In front of us was a long tunnel lined with the eternal lamps. Slightly unsteady from the jump, Gaige started down the passage. I followed several paces behind, massaging the stiffness from my neck. I lost sight of my partner when he rounded a bend, but could hear him making a racket as he fiddled with something. I rounded the corner and stopped short, nearly running right into his back.

"This damned doorknob won't turn," he remarked, throwing a shoulder against the offending door.

As if he'd said the magic words, it burst open and Gaige tumbled sideways.

"Welcome to Paris, luv," said an amused female voice.

The stout woman bent to offer Gaige a hand, but he waved her off.

"I'm fine. I'm fine. Just a little dizzy," he told her.

The customs agent stepped back, and I patted Gaige on the head like he was an adorable puppy as I passed by. The air was slightly cooler outside of the passageway, but still sweltering compared to the chill of the gate back on the island.

"I'm Isabel, you must be Stassi and Gaige?" the woman said, offering me her hand.

I shook it. "Yes, ma'am."

"You arrived just in time for breakfast. How about something to eat, and then we can get started? Why don't I take your travel bags? I will have them sent up to the townhouse where you will be staying while you're here."

My stomach was queasy from the jump, but I knew the nausea would pass soon.

"Sounds great," I replied, handing her my duffel.

Finally struggling to his feet, Gaige smiled at our hostess. "Just coffee for me, thanks. Watching my figure." He patted his flat stomach, and then shrugged out of the backpack where he'd stowed his personal belongings. "Careful, some of the stuff in there bites," he warned.

Isabel studied Gaige's face, as if trying to decide whether he was joking. After a long moment, she turned without comment.

"Follow me," she called over her shoulder.

I'd jumped to numerous customs ports in my two years as a runner, and all of them were slightly different. This one was a huge, round space set up like the backstage of a fashion runway show. Evenly spaced doors took up the east wall, while the rest of the staging area was fanned out around them. Dressing tables with bright lights were scattered throughout the salon.

Though the Parisian waystation was a busy one, there were still only four doors, which led to the city's four vortexes. Three of the vortexes were exclusively for traveling to and from Branson, since Paris was part of the Atlic Syndicate's territory. The fourth vortex was capable of sending and receiving runners from anywhere in the world.

"The stylists will be down soon," Isabel said, as we crossed through the area designated for hair and makeup.

"You aren't French," Gaige said, his tone almost accusatory.

Isabel pushed open a set of swinging double doors, which led to a sitting area with old velvet couches and a dining table. Having been here before, I knew the second set of doors in this room led to a large kitchen. The smell of pastries wafted out when a server passed through with a coffee decanter.

Isabel chuckled. "No, luv, I'm not. I was born in Baltimore. Lived there until I was sixteen, then came to Paris to live with my aunt and take up the family business."

The sad note in Isabel's voice hinted that her circumstances surrounding the transatlantic move had not been happy ones.

"She's an alchemist?" Gaige prompted.

"Two in a row," Isabel quipped. "My aunt didn't have any children herself, so she sent for me. My parents thought it was to run the hat shop upstairs—that's our cover story here."

Each city had a business front for its gate, from bakeries to pet shops. A southern American port even used a clown college to mask its true nature.

Alchemists manned the customs stations, passing the secrets of our trade down from one generation to the next. The rest of the staff was comprised of family members, along with ex-runners and historians-in-training. Cyrus kept his employee circles closed and tight-knit, allowing the waystations to remain open for centuries without detection.

"Grab something to eat, then we'll get started," Isabel instructed, pointing to the buffet along one side of the room with everything from eggy bread—the French equivalent for what Americans called French toast—to biscuits and fruit.

Once I filled a cup with coffee and piled my plate up with fruit and a buttery croissant, we followed Isabel back into the staging area.

"Pick any stations you like." She waved her arm to encompass the room. "I'll go and fetch the team, they're upstairs working the floor."

Gaige and I plopped down in the nearest swivel chairs. The heat coming off of the bright bulbs caused a line of sweat to form on my forehead. I wound my hair into a bun and fanned my neck. Out of the corner of my eye, I saw Gaige wiping his brow with the back of his hand.

Taking note of our discomfort, Isabel apologized. "Ventilation system is on the fritz. Sorry about that. I'll turn on the fans to get the air circulating."

Good to her word, Isabel flipped a switch on the wall. Warm, stale air began to circulate throughout the room.

"It won't take long to cool off," Isabel promised, disappearing through the doors leading upstairs to the lounge area.

When she reentered the staging area several minutes later, three people were trailing behind her.

"While you eat, let me introduce our staff. This is our resident guise stylist, Felipe. He will handle your overall looks for the mission, including hair and cosmetics." Isabel gestured to the large man standing beside her with shaggy blonde hair and a bulbous nose. He bowed, an overly formal gesture that looked odd coming from such a big guy.

Next, Isabel put her arm around a slim woman with light cocoa skin. "This is our wardrobe stylist, Naomi—a particularly integral part of your team during this time period. She will outfit you in everything from clothing to jewelry and accessories that are appropriate for your cover story."

Naomi smiled shyly and twisted a strand of her long, black hair. Between her flowing locks, bright green eyes, and flawless skin, the wardrober looked as though she should be modeling the latest fashions instead of dressing us in them.

This should be interesting, I thought, giving Naomi a small wave as I wondered how Gaige would handle this unexpected diversion.

When I glanced at my partner, expecting to see unveiled attraction in his big brown eyes. Instead, he was devouring a chocolate-filled pastry like a man who hadn't eaten in years, his attention solely on the confection.

Good boy, I thought wryly, suppressing the urge to pat him on the head as I'd done earlier.

"Finally, this is our resident know-it-all, Ines. She keeps up with all of the latest scandals, trends, and societal haunts. Ines also knows all the most interesting people in our little city."

The severe-looking women stepped forward. I recognized her from one of Historian Eisenhower's pictures.

"Oui," Ines said. "I make it my business to know everyone else's. So, tell me, whose business do you need know?"

I'd just bitten into my croissant, chocolate oozing over my fingers and lips. I hastily swallowed the large bite. She laughed, a tinkling melodic sound that reminded me of wind chimes.

"Do not choke, my dear. We have hours together before we send you out in the world." Ines moved to stand behind my chair, openly appraising me in the mirror. She made a clucking noise with her tongue. "Pink hair? This will not do, I fear. It's too…too…." She tapped her chin with her index finger, searching for the right word. "Futuriste. You will stand out like a virgin in a brothel with that hair."

Gaige snorted.

"Have no worries," Ines continued. "Felipe will have you fixed in no time. Unless you were thinking of wearing a wig?"

I honestly hadn't given it any thought at all. Usually when I arrived at customs, I simply sat down in a chair, then stood up several hours later looking like a different person. No one had ever asked for my opinion before, so I took a moment to consider the pros and cons. Dyeing my hair would mean losing the pink strands that were symbolic of my new life. Wigs were an easy way to alter my appearance. I was accustomed to wearing them, but they tended to make my scalp itch. Six weeks was a long time to have an itchy head.

"No, no wig," I decided, fingering one of the pink strands. Molly would be more than happy to repeat the process when I returned. "Dye it."

"How about a nice auburn, mademoiselle? With your blue eyes and fair skin, it would be lovely," Felipe declared.

"Sure, that works," I said.

"And for you, let's go dark," Felipe said to Gaige. "A little shoe polish and we can make your hair black."

The look of horror on Gaige's face was priceless.

"Shoe polish?" he stuttered.

"I am only joking," Felipe said. "We will use real dye, straight from your time. Do not fret."

Since I had more hair, Felipe started with me. While he set to work, Naomi led Gaige off to select his new wardrobe. Isabel and Ines returned to the milliner's shop above, in case any customers stopped in to browse the hat selection.

Once Felipe had coated my hair in a thick, brownish-red paste, he summoned Gaige and I was sent off with Naomi.

"Dresses in our era are not fitted," she informed me as we walked down a long hallway. Her voice was soft and rich, and seemed to fit her shy nature. "You are fairly tall and slim, so most everything will look good on you. Since you are supposed to be a woman of means with an interest in the arts, only the finest garments will do."

Naomi paused in front of tall oak doors and smiled up at me. "Prepare to be enchanted."

I laughed. Did she think this was my first run?

Naomi pushed the doors open with a two-handed shove.

"Holy shite," I muttered.

Enchanted was an understatement.

The customs closet in Paris was the largest and most extravagant I'd seen, stretching two-stories high and as far back as I could see. Lifelike mannequins were strategically posed around the lower level, displaying beautiful beaded gowns, sequined dresses, fur-collared evening coats, and chic day frocks with flirty details. Some had scarves hanging from the waist or flowing from their shoulders. Some had hats covering their short, wigged hair. Others wore jeweled headpieces that sparkled in the bright lights. And then there was the jewelry: long necklaces of amethysts, pearls, and diamante, gold bangles encrusted with stones in every color of the rainbow, and dangly earrings that added a little something extra.

Behind the mannequins were rows of garments in similar styles. My inner girlie-girl came out, and I longed to run my fingers over the fine fabrics. I found myself wishing that Molly were there; she would've loved this.

"The clothes are all on the first floor, with accessories the second." Naomi gestured to a burgundy chaise in the center of the room. "I hope you do not mind, but I have taken the liberty of selecting a few pieces for you. If you would like to take a seat, I will fetch them."

"Great," I said, still awestruck.

Dutifully, I sat on the lounge and waited while Naomi disappeared behind a winding staircase that led to the second floor. She returned a moment later, pushing a rolling rack. Item by item, she went through the garments she'd selected, explaining what events I was supposed to wear each for and who had designed it. The details went in one ear and out the other—I was too busy gawking at the intricate beadwork and gorgeous embellishments. Usually I found this part of the assignment tedious. Clothes were just clothes, after all. But not this time. This time, I was already scheming on how best to smuggle back my favorite items.

Maybe I could offer to buy the purple silk and velvet loungewear, I thought. *Oh, and that gold evening gown with the rose-patterned jacket thingie. Molly would love them.*

"Time to rinse."

I'd been so caught up in admiring my new wardrobe that I hadn't heard Felipe enter.

"If these items suit you, I will wrap them up and have them delivered to your residence," Naomi said.

"Yes. I mean, oui. They suit me, merci," I said, making use of my minimal French.

Naomi smiled. "Is there anything in particular you would like me to leave out for today?"

I suddenly became quite conscious of the fact I looked like a tragic fashion victim. My acid-washed jeans and ratty t-shirt would be appallingly out of place on the stylish streets of Paris.

"That one," I said, pointing to a red and black day suit with a Peter Pan collar and black bow in the center.

"C'est parfait. I believe there is a matching hat and bag that go with it," Naomi said.

After thanking the wardrober a second time, I returned to the main room with Felipe. A long debate ensued over whether to cut my hair or just pin it up.

"It will take much time to style it appropriately every day if we do not cut it," Felipe warned. "A nice bob will be much simpler to maintain."

"Isn't that why you're here?" I teased.

The guise specialist scowled.

"Please," I begged, sticking out my lower lip in a decent imitation of Gaige's pouty face.

"Fine, fine," Felipe relented. "But I will need at least one hour for daytime and two for evening styles, no discussion, no complaining."

"Deal," I agreed, grinning.

I was surprised to find it was already lunchtime when Ines brought down finger sandwiches and tea. A tall, serious-looking man followed on her heels.

"Stassi, Gaige, may I introduce Pierre?"

The man nodded curtly at us.

"When you are finished here, see me to take the pictures for your passports, s'il vous plait," he said, skipping over the pleasantries.

"Will you also be working with us on copying the manuscript?" I asked, gathering he was the alchemist forger for this era.

"Oui. It would be best to provide me with the photos as you find the document, as I will need time to replicate it," he instructed. "Any other questions?"

When I glanced at Gaige to be sure we were on the same page, he simply shook his head.

"No, not at the moment. Thank you Pierre," I said.

Before I'd finished speaking, the document specialist gave another nod and strode away.

"It was nice meeting you!" Gaige called after him, drawing a giggle from Ines.

Turning back to the lunch provided, I took a small bite of an odd little sandwich with a single slice of cucumber in the middle. Surprisingly, it was delicious. My partner was popping them in his mouth whole, reminding me that I'd need to go over rules for decorum with him. While we ate, Gaige and I asked Ines about Rosenthal and his circle of friends.

"He's a strange little man," Ines said of the author, her French accent becoming more pronounced as she began gossiping. "Secretive and almost paranoid. He speaks to me very little when we bump into one another. In fact, he speaks to very few aside from his writer friends, though he is close to Ernest Hemingway. That might be a good angle; Hemingway's wife loves meeting new people, particularly Americans. She will be there tonight, and is always at Gertrude Stein's house on the weekends."

"Can you handle getting us invited to Stein's salon on Saturday?" Gaige asked.

Ines looked aghast, as if he'd insulted her character by inquiring about her social connections.

"Of course. I can have you invited absolutely anywhere," she insisted with a frown. "But be warned—Stein's wife is an odious woman. She will not like you one bit, Stassi."

"Why is that?" I asked uneasily.

"Does she hate all goofy looking foreigners?" Gaige chimed in helpfully.

"Que'est-ce que c'est, goofy?" Ines asked, looking puzzled. Even though I wasn't wearing a translation device, this was a phrase I knew well. Along with the words for "I don't know", it was the single most-used phrase in my French vocabulary.

"Nothing, ignore him," I answered, reaching over to shove my partner's arm. "I don't know what the translation would be, but it's not important."

"You are much too pretty for her liking," Ines continued with a shrug. "Moi? I'm mannish, no one gives me a second glance."

Hearing her self-assessment, I studied Ines with a critical eye. Her black hair was cut short, just above her ears, with blunt bangs that hung straight across her forehead. She was tall, close to Gaige's height, and angular. Even in a shapeless turquoise dress, it was obvious she was extremely thin. Though she was definitely working the androgynous trend of the twenties, I'd hardly have described her as mannish.

"You're being modest," I said, curious as to whether self-deprecation was a sport among the social elite in this era.

Gaige, oblivious as usual, also gave Ines a once-over. He shook his head decisively.

"I wouldn't say you're mannish. Skinny. Definitely skinny. But that's not a bad thing."

I rolled my eyes. For a guy who spent so much time flirting and talking up women, he didn't have a clue. It was no wonder he struck out more often than not.

"I apologize for my partner," I told Ines. "He lacks couth."

She laughed. "As do so many men. Come now, get changed into your new clothes, and I will show you to your accommodations. You'll be staying in the townhouse next door, a beautiful home. You both must get lots of rest before this evening."

"We must?" I asked, wondering if it was her polite way of telling me I looked haggard.

"But of course," Ines replied. "We all must."

Gaige and I both stared at her, waiting for an explanation.

"This is Parisian society, Stassi my dear," Ines finally said slowly. "The parties start quite late in the evening, and this one will go all night. It is a big event, Fitzgerald and his little book are the toast of the town."

I looked warily at my partner. We were both sleep-deprived, but he didn't seem to be feeling the effects like me. Gaige looked positively giddy.

"Soon, if I do my job properly, the two of you will be, as well," Ines continued. "Paris loves nothing more than a good bit of gossip. News of you will spread like wildfire."

"Best. Run. Ever," Gaige declared.

I didn't share my partner's enthusiasm. A runner's job was to blend in, and for the first time, we were being asked to do the opposite. We were deliberately drawing attention to ourselves, which inevitably led to heightened scrutiny and unwanted questions. I understood why we were taking the path least traveled, but I didn't like it.

That ominous feeling about the run that Molly had expressed? I now felt it, too.

NINE

"WHAT IS YOUR name, dear?" Ines demanded for the third time.

I squared my shoulders and gave her a determined stare.

"Stassi. Like I've said. It's Stassi."

"Stassi," Ines mimicked my American accent. "Stassi is a nickname, not suitable for societal introductions. You are in Paris, not tucked away on Cyrus's island."

That was for sure. We were sitting in the living room of the townhouse next to the milliner's shop, surrounded by opulent furniture, thick Persian rugs, and artwork that would one day be incredibly valuable. The extravagant furnishings went with our cover story as children of a wealthy shipping magnate, but I felt slightly uncomfortable in this environment. Everything in the place looked more suited for a museum. I was almost afraid to touch anything. Gaige didn't have the same problem. He was draped across a brocade armchair, his legs tossed over the side.

For her part, Ines looked just as comfortable. There was an air about her, as if she herself could afford to live in such a place, despite the fact I knew she couldn't. Alchemists were well-compensated for their services, but their salary was paltry compared to a runner's.

I hoped the entitled act was just that—an act. If she were truly as snobby as she came across, the next six weeks would be tedious.

Our Parisian guide gave me a look as though the feeling was mutual and took a long drag from the cigarette she had wedged into a shiny, black cigarette holder. She exhaled a plume of smoke straight into my face, then tapped the end into a crystal ashtray that bore an eerie resemblance to the candy dish Molly had on her desk at home.

"Anastasia," Ines said firmly, blowing a perfect O with the last dregs of smoke. "That is fitting, wouldn't you agree?"

No, I wouldn't agree, I thought stubbornly, *because my name is Stassi.*

Of course, I didn't say that aloud. The elegant French woman was probably correct; Stassi would sound out of place in this time. Truthfully, I just didn't like her very much.

"Fine, I'll go by Anastasia," I relented, reminding myself that I was a professional. "Or Anne or Elizabeth or whatever you say my name should be."

"Don't be silly, Pierre already put Anastasia on your papers," Ines said with a wave of her hand. Irritation at her presumptiveness rose within me, but I tamped it down with several long, deep breaths.

"What about me?" Gaige chimed in. "Did I get a new name?"

"Gaige is a fine name, no need to change it," Ines said, her voice warmer as she spoke to my partner.

If she had a thing for him, we were going to have a problem.

"Of course," he said with a lazy grin. "I'm perfect in every single way."

I had to resist the urge to throw one of the embroidered pillows at his head.

"That is left to be seen," the alchemist replied, raising one perfectly groomed eyebrow.

Ines crossed her legs and drew on her cigarette again as she studied Gaige. The smoke poured from her nostrils in two streams, mixing with the third stream coming from her lips to form one large cloud. Clad in a mauve dress with an intricately arranged hip-line, plunging neckline, and three-foot train, Ines was stylish and sultry. Somehow, the cigarette only added to her sex appeal.

I glanced down at my own emerald dress. It was one of the many creations Naomi selected for me, citing my new auburn locks as a perfect complement to the jewel tone. The silky velvet material was held at the waist with a crystal motif, and a braided train dangled from my hip.

After Felipe had finished styling my hair for the evening and I'd donned the dress, I'd been feeling good about my appearance. But now that the time had come to actually leave, I was second-guessing my choice.

"Are you ready for your introduction to society?" Ines asked, sparing me a glance.

"So ready," Gaige said and stood from his seat.

Putting on the fake smile I always used when nervous, I nodded.

"Totally ready."

"Then let us not waste any more time, my dears. The beautiful people await."

In a haze of Chanel perfume and tobacco smoke, Ines floated towards the door.

Outside, a beautiful white Rolls-Royce idled beside the curb. Ines waited next to the luxury automobile with an entitled air as the driver scurried to exit the vehicle. Gaige waved him off and held the door open himself, turning to roll his eyes at me while Ines climbed inside. Following suit, I settled into the seat of sumptuous beige leather across from the customs agent. Gaige pulled the door shut behind him, plopping down next to me gracelessly.

"Not bad, not bad," he declared, looking around the elegant interior. "I could probably get used to this."

"Good evening," the driver said, turning to greet us through a window in the divider between the front and back of the vehicle.

"Bon nuit," Ines replied absently, waving in our direction. "Stassi, Gaige, this is Jacque. He will be at your disposal while you are here."

"It's nice to meet you," I said warmly, compensating for her dismissive attitude.

Ines relayed our destination and instructions for the evening to Jacque, all in French. With the Rosetta securely inside my ear, I was able to understand every word of their brief conversation.

"This is our private car," Ines said to us once we were underway, as if she'd purchased it herself. "When you have need of Jacque's services, you simply send word to us or telephone the number on the list I gave you."

The old-fashioned phone and number system was new to me, having never visited this time before. The ringer was a separate box mounted on the wall beside the receiver. An operator answered when the handset was lifted, connecting callers based on numbers or sometimes addresses. Before leaving, Ines had handed us each a thick card with the information for contacting the townhouse, the milliner's shop, and our personal driver. It was now tucked securely within my beaded clutch, in case the night took an unexpected turn.

Ines withdrew her silver cigarette case from her purse, then went about lighting her umpteenth cancer stick of the day. I immediately began to turn the crank that opened the windows, filling the car with chilly spring air. After sucking in a deep breath, I nudged Gaige to do the same on his side, much to Ines's annoyance.

"Non, do not do that, my hair will be a mess before the night even begins," she protested.

"Your hair looks absolutely perfect," Gaige insisted with an easy smile. "And the fresh air will liven us all up. It's already giving your cheeks a lovely flush."

Ines fell for the bait, forgetting her objections with my partner's attention.

"How long have you known Rosenthal?" I asked her smoothly, effectively changing the subject. Though we'd discussed the set and players earlier, we hadn't gotten into the specifics of her relationships within the group.

"A year? Maybe two?" Ines said vaguely, shrugging one bony shoulder. "Long enough for your purposes."

"And how well would—"

"This corner, yes, right up here, this is perfect," Ines told the driver loudly in French.

"Are you sure, Miss?" Jacque asked, also in French. "You are still three blocks from your destination. You cannot be too cautious right now."

Ines laughed. "We are not alone. We have an escort, as you can see. He will protect us."

Gaige and I exchanged uneasy glances. Protect us from what? As far as we knew, this part of Montparnasse was considered safe.

"As you say, madam, but the Night Gentleman—"

"Is of no consequence to us, I assure you," Ines interjected.

Still reluctant, Jacque pulled to a stop at the corner Ines indicated.

"Be careful, won't you?" he asked.

"Now where would be the fun in that?" Ines quipped, one hand already pushing the door open.

Gaige and I followed her out of the car and onto the dimly lit pavement. The moment her feet hit the ground, Ines busied herself replacing the cigarette in her holder. When I glanced up and down the street, there wasn't a soul in sight, and only the occasional car.

"The evening is much too nice to ride the whole way, don't you agree?" Ines asked in English, as she joined Gaige and me on the sidewalk.

Jacque had yet to drive away. He was watching our trio, a slight frown on his face.

"Sure," I said, pulling my fur stole tighter around my shoulders to block the cool night air.

"Who is the Night Gentleman?" Gaige asked as we began our short trek.

Ines inhaled deeply.

"You scoundrel, don't you know it's in poor taste to eavesdrop?" she asked with a laugh, as if we hadn't been sitting a foot away. "Speaking of scoundrels, I do hope Ezra is there tonight, he's an absolute gas. One never knows what he will do next."

Gaige caught my eye and a silent message passed between us. She was avoiding the question.

"There was this one time," Ines continued hurriedly, "we drank champagne until dawn out at his country estate and ended up swimming in a lake as the sun rose. He wrote a short story about that night. The character Rosemarie is based upon me."

"Right, that definitely sounds like a gas," I said quickly, cutting her off before the next string of babble burst forth. "So, who is the Night Gentleman? We need to be up on current events."

"What is it you Americans say?" Ines asked. This time her casual laugh sounded forced. "Something about beating a dead horse?"

"I actually don't know if that is an Americanism," Gaige said, scratching his brow as thought he really was considering the origins of the saying.

I rolled my eyes. Ines was definitely evading the question, and not even in a clever way. As Gaige was fond of saying, only sparkly objects distracted me. Our guide's obvious attempts to redirect attention just made me more curious about the subject.

"I'm not a fan of this horse," I said dryly.

"Oh, fine. He's just a man." Ines took another drag from her cigarette and seemed to contemplate what she'd just said. "Or maybe a woman. No one knows for sure."

"And what significance does he have?" I persisted.

"Look, I—," Ines said with a sweep of her arms, cutting off when the end of her cigarette connected with my bare skin. Hot embers flew off to the side, and the sharp sting made me wince.

"Shite, that hurt," I swore through gritted teeth, rubbing my skin.

"Oh, heavens! Stassi, my dear, I am so sorry," Ines gushed.

She yanked the half-smoked cigarette from its holder and threw it onto the sidewalk, stamping the lit end with the toe of her gray heels. She took my hand between both of hers and held my arm up towards the closest street lamp. A red blotch was blossoming where the embers hit my skin.

"I'm fine," I said, snatching my hand back.

"If you are sure, then let us review your cover story one last time," Ines declared, smiling brightly.

A niggling sensation somewhere in the back of my mind told me that she'd burned me on purpose, as if to distract me from the Night Gentleman topic.

Purposeful or not, it worked. As we traversed the final block to the club, Gaige rattled off our cover story.

We were supposedly in Paris on holiday. Our father was both a champion of modern business and heavily invested in the stock market. The latter would've made us dirt poor four years later, but it was a perfect show of wealth in 1925. Prohibition was making our little city too boring, and so we'd departed for a year abroad. Gaige was a supposed arts enthusiast who loved finding hidden gems from undiscovered talents. His hope was that they would one day make him a fortune equal to our father's.

I was fresh out of school and ready to sow my wild oats far, far away from my overprotective parents. My future plan was either to open an art gallery, write a great novel, or make a career spending my father's money on philanthropic causes—I hadn't yet decided. I was to be whimsical and indecisive.

We'd pretty much figured out all the details before our arrival, but Ines helped to fill in some iffy spots to make us more attractive to Rosenthal's crowd.

"And we have arrived, darlings," Ines declared, just as Gaige finished explaining how I was looking to practice my sexual freedom throughout Europe. Obviously he was taking creative liberties.

"Lock it up," I said, pointing at him with a smile.

"You lock it up," he replied, grinning and mimicking my gesture.

It was our standard call to commence acting the part, through and through. Odd phrasing, an offhand mention to history books, or even seemingly-innocuous conversations between the two of us had a way of raising questions and piquing interest in the wrong way. We couldn't have that.

Ines gave us an odd look before crossing to the opposite side of the street. As we followed suit, I glanced around, expecting to see a sign with the name of the nightclub. There wasn't one. In fact, the entire row of storefronts was dark. Many looked abandoned—no mannequins in the windows or fancy writing across the glass declaring the names of the shops.

"Ines, are you sure we're in the right place?" I asked. "It doesn't look like there's a party here."

"Do not be ridiculous, love, of course we are. Do you mistrust me?" She tittered, a sound that was beginning to grate my nerves. "Do not answer that. Close your eyes and listen."

No way was I closing my eyes on that shady Parisian street. But I did listen. At first, I didn't hear it. Then, faint jazz music met my ears. It sounded like it was coming from very far away.

Ines grinned. "You see? We are in the correct place. Come." She strode towards a black door wedged between two store windows and knocked once. A window in the door slid open. Dark eyes peered out at us.

"Ines Callandries," she declared.

The door opened, exposing a broad-shouldered man with what looked like cooking oil coating his dark hair and trim mustache. Gaige snorted, then pretended to cough into his hand to cover it. Blank-faced, the doorman stepped aside to let us enter.

"Gaige! Anastasia! Come along, darlings," Ines called over her shoulder, beckoning us to her like we were dogs.

"I swear on my salary, if she keeps calling me 'Anastasia', I'm going to lose it," I grumbled to my partner as we crossed the threshold.

"Oh, no need to pay me. The spectacle will be compensation enough," Gaige replied with a wink.

I smiled back at him. Thank goodness my partner was a people person. I was good at pretending to like people—emphasis on *pretending*—when the run called for it. Since Ines knew my true identity, and I didn't care one way or the other how she felt about me, there was no reason to pretend with her. Gaige, however, actually did like most people. And most people liked him. I had a feeling that would pay off on this run.

Loud music and thick, sweet smoke engulfed us as we descended a dark staircase with Ines in the lead. I held tightly to the railing with one hand, gathering the scarf trailing from my waist with the other. The last thing I needed was to have the material twist around my legs and send me tumbling down the steps. It would make quite the entrance.

Once we were halfway down the staircase, the wall on my right side ended and I was able to see the underground jazz club through a haze of violet-gray smoke. It was larger than I'd expected, yet small enough to be considered intimate. Only about twenty tables were scattered throughout the middle of the room. Couches ringed the perimeter on a slightly elevated platform, to allow the occupants a better view of the stage.

At the front of the room, musicians played an upbeat tune that featured the saxophone. Couples on the dance floor were doing the

Charleston in a tangling twist of flailing arms and legs. Laughter rang out over the music from those who'd started their night much earlier than we had.

"Over there, you see that group in the corner? Do not stare, darling, it's gauche," Ines said, waving her cigarette holder in the general direction she was indicating with her eyes. "Rosenthal is the one on the far left. The one who looks like he would rather eat his hat than listen to another word from the man beside him."

Despite her chastisement, I continued to stare. No one at the table was paying attention to us, so I didn't see the harm in it. In my ear, Ines was matching faces to names. She included fun facts about each that she'd somehow overlooked during the exhaustive eight hours we'd spent together that day. In her defense, it was her job to know everyone's business. But I was pretty sure she would've been the same scandalmonger even with a different occupation. After she was done with me, Ines leaned over to Gaige and, I assumed, gave him the same speech.

"Oh, splendid, a table just came free," she declared a moment later.

Ines clapped her hands together twice like the head cheerleader at a football game I'd attended on a run to Pittsburgh in the 1970s. I almost expected her next words to be *"Ready? Okay!"*.

They weren't, of course.

"Come, darlings," she trilled.

"Is it just me or is Ines a little…something?" Gaige asked me as Ines beelined for the vacant table.

"She's something, alright," I agreed as we followed our guide through the crowd.

As soon as we settled in to our seats, a waiter appeared with a bottle of champagne chilling in an ice bucket.

"Bonsoir Mademoiselle Callandries, monsieur, mademoiselle," the tuxedoed man said, nodding to each of us in turn. "May I offer you champagne, compliments of Madame Stein?"

Ines readily accepted the bottle on behalf of our group. As he poured the bubbling amber liquid into chipped teacups—they were really going for the prohibition vibe here—the waiter exchanged pleasantries with Ines in a mix of French and English. Thanks to the Rosetta, I understood it all perfectly.

In English, Ines asked, "So, tell me, is there anyone of particular interest here tonight? I promised my American friends a night of fascinating conversation with smart companions."

"But of course, mademoiselle," the waiter replied, subtly tilting his head to indicate each table. "Madame Stein is holding court in the far corner with the gentleman of the evening, Monsieur Fitzgerald, and their closest friends. Lady Beaumont is with the Count at a table close to the dance floor. And Monsieur DuPree and his companions have been here for hours. I believe you can find those gentlemen in their preferred booth—center back, directly across from the stage."

"So kind of you," Ines chirped, discreetly slipping several folded bills into the waiter's palm. She'd essentially just paid him to scan the room for her, but then again it was the syndicate's money, not her own.

"Merci beaucoup, Mademoiselle Callandries, you are too kind," he sang to Ines, then turned to Gaige and I with a bland smile. "We welcome you to our humble establishment. Please, let me know when you are ready for another bottle. Or if Monsieur wishes for a beverage of another sort."

Gaige passed on the stronger stuff, drawing a raised eyebrow from the waiter. Apparently it wasn't manly to drink champagne. Luckily, my partner was exceedingly confident in his manhood.

"A gossip, that one," Ines declared once the waiter was out of earshot. She sipped her champagne, closed her eyes, and sighed contentedly. "But he does know me well. This is my absolute favorite vintage." Her dark eyes popped open. "Try, try. I must know what you think."

I took a small, polite sip from my own china cup. It was good. A bit tangy, but good. Gaige drained his in one, long swallow and smacked his lips.

"Feeling the urge to get drunk already?" I teased.

"Just trying to fit in," he replied, refilling his cup.

Ready to get going, I turned to Ines.

"How do we work this?" I asked her quietly. "Should we go over there and say hello, so you can introduce us?"

The Frenchwoman raised a hand to her chest in mock horror.

"Heavens no, dear. That would be an amateur move." She patted my hand. "You are with me, they will come to us. As the night progresses, they will make their way here. Give it time, you will see."

Much as I hated to admit it, Ines was right. Strolling right over to a tightknit group of assets was a rookie move, but I'd assumed the direct approach would be acceptable since we were with Ines. I wondered, not for the first time, if she'd exaggerated her position within Parisian society. As I watched Stein greet a table of familiar faces, it dawned on me that those at the center of the societal orbit would likely make their way outward as the night progressed and the champagne flowed. Gaige and I being newcomers and unknowns would not warrant immediate attention from the smart set. Or, as we Americans might say, the popular kids. Evidently, Ines didn't either, since the suns of this solar system didn't shine on our table right away.

Heeding her advice, I tamped down my impatience and waited. People did come over, lots of people, but no one from Rosenthal's crowd. We met dukes and counts, fashion designers and wealthy merchants, minor British noblemen and their mistresses, stage actresses and the playwrights who adored them, all gushing about the genius of *Gatsby*. With the women, I lamented the tragic love story and the loss at the end of the book. With the men, I chimed in as Gaige discussed the societal commentary of the novel. All of our thoughts were based on an encyclopedia article I'd downloaded that morning, but no one needed to know that.

At one point, a cattle farmer from the states stopped by to pay compliments to Ines. When he found out Gaige and I were American, he wanted to trade stories about the good ole U.S. of A. Unfortunately, all my knowledge of cattle ranches and Texas was from about fifty years in the future, and even that was spotty. But drunk as our new friend was, he didn't seem to notice my vague answers. Or Gaige's embellished ones. When my partner made reference to me attending the same girls' school as Wallis Simpson, who had yet to rise to infamy as consort to the Prince of Wales, the Texan just grinned.

As Gaige spun a ridiculous tale about a fictitious trip to Texas and the women he'd met there, my mind began to wander. It was already well past midnight. We'd been there for hours and had yet to make contact with any of the targets, even the farthest outliers. If we waited too much longer, anyone we met would surely forget the introductions in their drunken states.

It might be time to make some moves, I decided, trying to catch Gaige's eye.

"Care to dance?"

The question caught me by surprise. I'd been so focused on beaming my thoughts to my partner that I didn't even hear the speaker's approach.

Turning in my chair, I found big brown eyes staring down at me through a mop of blonde curls.

Taken aback by the man's too-handsome-for-his-own-good face, all I could manage was a stuttered, "H-h-hi."

Eloquent, I know.

TEN

"AMERICAN, HOW LOVELY. Ines, you did not tell me you were entertaining guests from across the pond," the man said, straightening to his full height. His English was perfect and only slightly accented, as if maybe he'd attended school at Eaton or Radley.

"Charles, love, I did not know you were here this evening," Ines pouted. "Whatever took you so long to say hello?"

The man leaned over and kissed Ines on both cheeks.

"My apologies," he told her. "I was preoccupied with Dali's talk of big game hunting. You know how he can go on." His gaze traveled back to me. "And then I saw your enchanting friend here."

"Charles DuPree, allow me to introduce Anastasia Prince. Our fathers attended university together."

"And I'm Gaige Prince, Anastasia's brother," Gaige supplied helpfully.

Internally cringing at the name, I did my best to maintain a composed face. Anastasia Prince sounded like Ravenal's secret lover from that long-running space soap in the 2300s.

Charles took my hand and bowed, placing a light kiss just below my wrist. I was startled by the small tingle that ran up my arm. Glancing at my mostly-full teacup, I realized it couldn't be blamed on the alcohol. No, it had just been *that* long since a guy showed interest in me.

Lock it up, Stassi, I coached myself.

"It is a pleasure to meet you, Anastasia Prince," Charles said gallantly. "And you, as well, brother."

"It's Stassi," I told him flatly.

"Pardon?" He arched an eyebrow.

"Stassi," I repeated. "That's what my friends call me, Stassi."

Why was I saying my name so much?

"And you consider me a friend already? I am honored," Charles teased. His tone was light and playful, a half-smile making his expression decidedly flirty.

That tingly sensation from earlier vanished. He was the 1920s version of Gaige—all sugary-sweet one-liners and adorable smiles. Just like with Gaige, I saw through the façade. The guy was the very definition of rakish.

He probably has good abs, too, I thought traitorously.

"So it is that a 'yes' then?" Charles was saying.

"Huh?" I asked, feeling as dense as I sounded.

"If we are friends, then you will dance with me?" His smile practically lit up the room.

He and Gaige are brothers from different mothers, I thought, stifling the urge to poke fun at the debonair stranger.

"My dear Anastasia would *love* to dance," Ines interjected. "Isn't that right, Anastasia?"

No, Anastasia would not like to dance. Nor would she like to be called Anastasia, I thought, wondering when thinking about myself in the third-person became acceptable.

Instead of voicing the babble in my head, all I said was, "Sure."

Accepting Charles's hand, I rose from the table. Gaige's snickers were audible even over the loud music. I longed for a throw pillow. When I glared at him over my shoulder, my partner wiggled his eyebrows and made a ridiculous gesture with his hands that made him look like he was swatting a fly.

"I hate you," I mouthed.

Gaige grinned sweetly, then turned to Ines and began talking in her ear.

I wasn't a great dancer. Not even a good dancer. We'd been instructed in many different types of dance during training, and Gaige had complained the whole time about his poor, trodden-upon feet. The thought made me nervous to step onto the dance floor.

Thankfully, Charles didn't seem to mind my missteps. He took the lead, spinning me in time to the beat. I watched the other women around me and tried to imitate their movements, which served the added purpose of providing my eyes a focal point besides Charles's handsome face. Of course, when he pulled me tight against his chest and swayed for several counts, I couldn't help but notice how toned he was.

"Is this your first visit to Paris?" asked Charles.

Out of the corner of my eye, I saw someone new approach the table where Gaige and Ines were sitting. I recognized her instantly—stout body, matronly face, plaited hair wrapped around her head. She was perhaps the least stylish person in the room, and yet she commanded the most stares: Gertrude Stein.

Distracted by the turn of events, I tried to keep one eye on Stein and answer Charles at the same time.

"Second, actually," I replied absently.

"Oh, really? When was the first?"

Too late, I realized my mistake. I'd arrived in Paris for training almost two years ago in my life's timeline, but I wasn't acquainted with the city that Charles knew.

"Feels like a lifetime ago," I said. "It was when I was young."

Charles chuckled and spun me under his arm once more. I twirled gracelessly, nearly colliding with a well-dressed man crossing the dance floor. The man's deep-set gaze landed on me with keen interest. I smiled apologetically, and the man replied in kind before moving on.

"You are still very young, n'est pas? What did you see while you were here?" Charles was saying.

Magic. Sorcery. The Temple of the Creation, home to an ancient order capable of making something extremely valuable from nothing of consequence.

"I can't recall exactly," I said aloud. "It's been that long."

Stein was sitting in my seat between Ines and Gaige, her hands folded primly on the table. Her expression didn't change, so it was hard to tell how the conversation was going.

"We'll have to change that this time around, won't we?" Charles flirted. "You seem like a fashionable girl, Paris has wonderful boutiques. Or if you prefer the opera, or plays, we have much to offer."

Gaige and Stein were shaking hands. Still, her expression remained annoyingly blank.

"There are many wonderful cafés and restaurants, as well," he persisted.

"I like food," I said, not realizing how trite that sounded until Charles barked with laughter.

"That is excellent to know," he told me.

The song ended. Stein stood, and I noticed then that she was wearing a coat. She was leaving the nightclub.

"Excuse me," I told Charles. "I need to go."

He grabbed my hand as I tried to flee and pulled me back to him, following my gaze.

"Anxious to meet Gertie, I see? So then you are an art enthusiast. Or is it literature? She is the sitting queen of both circles."

"Gertie?" I asked dubiously.

"We are good friends," Charles said of Stein, his tone conspiratorial.

"Does she know that?" I asked.

"I imagine she does or she would not bother inviting me over all the time," he remarked with a grin.

That drew my attention from the departing Stein, who was now joined by Toklas as she climbed the stairs.

"So you attend her salon parties?" I asked Charles, turning up the charm.

"Every Saturday. She has the most interesting friends. All creative types, you know? Creative types are always a good time."

"I'd love to go," I told him, only moments shy of actually batting my eyelashes.

"Beautiful, culturally aware, and independent. What an intriguing woman you are, if I may say so."

It took all my willpower not to blush.

"I've heard about her parties," I explained. "My brother is looking to find a pet painter or writer. We've heard all the best in Paris surround Madame Stein."

"The best in the world," he corrected, studying my face.

The band started playing again, the forlorn call of the trumpet singing above the crowd. The tune was slow and lazy, and several couples left the dance floor. Charles and I remained in the same spot, swaying with his arm around my back and my hand on his shoulder.

"Ines is a frequent guest. I am sure she would be happy to take you both. Or, of course, I would be happy to escort you."

Movement at the corner table drew my attention to where our assets were sitting. Several familiar faces stood to leave, and my hopes for contact dwindled by the moment. Only three people remained on the couch—two men and a woman. Neither of the men was Rosenthal.

I turned my gaze back to Charles. "Maybe I'll see you there. If you'll excuse me, I must get back to Ines and my brother."

Charles's hands clasped mine as I turned to leave. Raising them to his mouth in turn, he pressed a soft kiss on each. His index finger brazenly caressed the inside of my right wrist, his eyes widening when he touched the tattoo. Though I'd covered the ink with makeup, the lines of text were etched into my skin and could still be felt.

I yanked my hands free.

"Excuse me," I said curtly.

The smile Charles gave me didn't reach his eyes. His flirty demeanor was gone, replaced by something akin to suspicion. Evidently, he'd felt the outline of scrawling text.

Way to blend in, Stassi.

He bowed slightly. "Thank you for the dance, Ms. Prince."

I turned and all but ran back to my table, leaving Charles on the dance floor, staring after me.

As soon as I returned to our table, Ines declared that everyone interesting had left and it was time to move on to the next establishment. Since it was nearing four o'clock in the morning by that point, Gaige and I vetoed her plan.

The car ride home was filled with the alchemist's complaints and ever-present smoke, but we were still not swayed by the time we reached the townhome. My partner and I had a job to do, and post-four a.m. was not a productive time.

After removing the beautiful dress and slipping into a pair of silk pajamas, I collapsed into bed, too tired to move. It was startling to think that I'd been home in my bungalow just that morning.

As I lay there, waiting for sleep to carry me away, I toyed with the locket around my neck. It was a reflex to touch the thing that brought me hope of my family. And yet, instead of wondering what answers I might find, I found myself thinking of Charles DuPree.

Not about how his brown eyes were flecked with gold, or how his hair was unruly in an appealing way. Not about how my skin tingled when he touched me, or how good it felt to be held by someone other than Gaige. Not about the fact I knew he was a cad, and therefore too much like my partner to even consider a dalliance.

Instead, I thought about the way he'd looked at me when he touched the tattoo. At the time, I'd thought it was surprise in his expression. But the more I recalled that look, the less I was sure about my initial assessment. There was something else to it, something I couldn't quite put my finger on.

Not important. Focus on the mission.

The night had ended on a high note as far as that was concerned. While I was off dancing, Gaige had managed to charm the stalwart Stein with his praise of her eye for talent. Somehow, he'd even solicited a smile from her frigid wife, Toklas. And when Gertrude learned that we hailed from Charm City, her old stomping grounds—Baltimore was chosen for exactly this reason—she immediately invited him to Saturday's salon, so he could meet her starving artists. Gaige's head was so big on the way back to the townhouse that it took up as much room as a fourth passenger.

"Two weeks, Stass," he'd told me over a nightcap.

"Stein is not our target," I'd reminded him. "She is merely a stepping stone to Rosenthal, we still have a long way to go."

Even my pessimistic attitude did not temper Gaige's ego. He'd gone to bed on cloud nine, confident that we'd be home sooner rather than later. Though I wanted to return to the island as soon as possible, to watch over my recovering roommate, I also needed time in Paris to look into my locket's origins. Since it was the reason I'd insisted on taking this assignment, it would be devastating to leave without discovering anything at all.

As I drifted off to sleep, thoughts of the stars in the sky floated through my mind.

ELEVEN

THE NEXT MORNING, I woke to the smell of coffee and cigarettes. Which could only mean one thing: Ines was already in the townhouse. Lucky me.

Sure enough, she was sitting on the brocade sofa in the living room when I descended the flight of stairs from the second floor. One hand held the offending tobacco, while the other cradled the smallest cup of coffee I'd ever seen.

"Good morning, dear," she chirped. "Did I wake you? I hope not. It looks as though you could use another hour or two of beauty rest."

"I'm good," I told her, choosing to ignore the dig. "Not everyone wakes up looking like they stepped out of a fashion magazine."

She did, too. In crimson silk pajamas with gold beading around the wrist and ankle cuffs, Ines was picture perfect. Her short, blunt bob was sleek and elegant and her makeup was immaculate. I hadn't bothered to look in a mirror.

"Did you actually walk outside in your pajamas?"

"Of course, love. It's perfectly acceptable," she replied, tapping the ash from her cigarette.

"Where's Gaige?" I asked, noting the lack of additional snarky comments about my bedhead and rumpled sleep clothes.

"He went for croissants. Now come sit with me." Ines patted the sofa beside her.

The previous night's champagne had gone to my head, and I was slightly hungover. The smoke filling the townhouse did not help matters.

"I know medical research hasn't made the discovery yet, but I am here to tell you that smoking causes cancer," I told Ines, choosing to sit in the chair farthest from where she was indulging in her bad habit.

Ines's tinkling laughter sent my headache spiking. It was too early for this.

"Oh, I know, dear. I also know that the scientists and medical professionals on Cyrus's island have the ability to cure all types of cancer. Besides," she inhaled deeply, "we all have to die from something."

"Yeah, but I'd rather die quickly, in my own time," I grumbled.

The front door opened, signaling Gaige's return. I sighed gratefully, glad to no longer be alone with Ines. Something about her bothered me. She was nice enough, I supposed. It was just…I didn't know exactly. She just wasn't my type, I decided.

"Hey, Stassi, you're awake," Gaige called.

"Yep." I yawned. "Appears so. Please tell me that bag holds deliciousness, I'm starving."

"As I knew you would be."

My partner joined us in the living room and placed the grease-stained bag on the coffee table in front of me. I dug in immediately, only remembering my manners once I'd taken the first bite of buttery, chocolaty heaven.

Mouth full, I held out the bakery bag to Ines.

"Want one?"

Her nose wrinkled. "Non, merci."

Gaige snatched the bag from my hand.

"It's cool, Ines. You don't need to sugarcoat it—Stassi is a bottomless pit. The girl eats more than I do." Smirking at me, he withdrew a newspaper from under his arm and tossed it on the coffee table. "Here, I got this, too. Thought we could read up on current events, so we don't sound like ignorant tourists."

The thick black font filling the width of the front page immediately caught my eye.

Night Gentleman Strikes Again.

"Oh look, Ines. It's your favorite topic," I said pointedly.

"Utter rubbish," Ines declared, waving at the newspaper as if it had insulted her.

"You don't think this might have been important to tell us?" I asked her, anger rising up. "If it's significant enough to be on the front of the paper, it might be something we need to know about."

"Oh don't be angry, love. I didn't want to spoil the party with talk of it," Ines replied easily, as if it were a perfectly good excuse.

With a disgusted sigh, I pulled the paper towards me and began reading the article. Without context, I quickly found myself confused.

"So who's this guy?" I asked her, pointing to the large picture in the center of the page.

It was a cartoon man in a black mask, top hat, and coattails. The caption underneath asked: A Real-Life Fantômas?

"Who is Fantômas?" I repeated when Ines didn't answer, readying myself to wade through her excuses and diversions.

"No one. No one real anyhow," she replied, refusing to elaborate.

I glared at her until she twitched uncomfortably in her seat.

"Oh, for heaven's sake." Ines removed the cigarette butt from the holder and replaced it with a fresh one. She took three successive drags, barely exhaling one before inhaling the next. "Fantômas is a character from a novel, a villain who spreads terror through the streets of Paris using a series of nasty pranks."

"What kind of pranks?" Gaige asked.

"Just silly things. The works of an overactive imagination."

"Such as?" I persisted.

"I don't read that nonsense," Ines replied. "But I heard that the Night Gentleman used a prank straight from Fantômas last night."

"Acid in place of perfume doesn't sound silly." I pointed to the article as I set down the rest of my croissant. Suddenly, I was no longer hungry.

"He is fictional, dear," Ines stated. Pausing, she sipped her coffee. "Now, on to more pleasant topics. You two should get out and about today, be seen shopping or eating at a café."

"Not so fast," I said incredulously, waving at the paper. "We need to know more about Fantômas and the Night Gentleman."

"There is nothing more to tell," Ines insisted.

"Ines," I warned.

She huffed indelicately. Two long streams of smoke plumed from her nostrils as though she was a dragon.

"Fine, but you're just going to spoil the day," Ines declared. "Last night was not the first time. The Night Gentleman is rumored to be imitating Fantômas's crimes from the novels. So far, he has claimed five victims using poisoned flowers, two with bottles of acid perfume, and one by loosing a manhole cover. The poor dear fell to her death in the catacombs. Last week's attack was particularly sensational because there was a large audience. Supposedly, the depraved little man replaced a snake dancer's harmless python, and it strangled her in the middle of a performance."

"You're joking," Gaige said, his eyes widening in disbelief.

"I mostly certainly am not," Ines professed haughtily.

Gaige turned to me. "You know those old comic books Tiger collects?

The ones from the 2200s, with batboy and his sidekick? The main villain in those is sort of like this."

"Batman," I corrected, without thinking.

Confusion quickly quashed my embarrassment over knowing that fact. Why wasn't this in our dossiers? Why hadn't Historian Eisenhower mentioned the murders? A super villain, or rather serial killer, was sort of an important part of history. Particularly when he was operating at the time and place of our mission.

"You need to tell us everything you know," I demanded with a no-nonsense look at Ines. Something wasn't adding up. "How do they know the same guy is responsible for all of these incidents?"

"Because the self-indulgent man takes credit for each of his acts," Ines replied plainly.

"Like Jack the Ripper?" Gaige asked.

"Jack-the-whom?"

"He murdered prostitutes, then wrote to Scotland Yard and the newspapers about his crimes to take credit for them," I explained.

Ines simply stared.

"Never mind, you would have just been born when he was active. The point is, does Fantômas send notes to the press? Or the authorities?" I demanded.

Sick of having to pry each little speck of information from Ines, I was becoming increasingly frustrated with this conversation. Surprises were not good things on runs. Surprises got runners killed. A serial killer murdering victims like some graphic novel anarchist could get me killed.

Ines shook her head. "No, nothing quite so brazen. Thus far, he has left a poisoned red rose at each scene, with a note signed *The Night Gentleman*."

A poisoned rose and a message? That sounded pretty damned brazen to me.

When I looked over at my partner, the frown lines on Gaige's face matched the anxiety I felt inside. We should have learned about this guy. The historians had a duty to warn us about potential dangers. A freaking serial killer definitely fell into that category.

"How long has this been going on?" Gaige asked, leaning forward to rest his elbows on his knees. There was no trace of his usual good humor, not even a hint of a smirk in sight. This was the guy I trusted my life with.

"A month? Maybe longer? I am not certain, I've only overheard bits and bobs about the subject," Ines replied. "I don't read the newspapers, they are such a killjoy."

Her blasé attitude was transparent. The way she lit one cigarette after another was a clear indication that she was frightened. Our guide's reluctance to discuss Fantômas or the Night Gentleman or whoever he was also spoke volumes.

Eager to learn everything there was to know about our new, unforeseen threat, I started in again. "What have you—"

The look Gaige shot me made the words stick in my throat. I slouched back in my chair, unsure how to interpret his silent signal. My partner turned to Ines, all traces of unease wiped clean.

"Enough of that. What did you have in mind for today? You said something about getting out and being seen? I'm game, but Stassi will need some time to make herself presentable before she faces the world. Like, a *lot* of time. You know what I mean?" Gaige winked conspiratorially at Ines.

Visibly relieved by the topic change, Ines began babbling about Closerie des Lilas, a favorite café of both Hemingway and Rosenthal in Montparnasse. She went on to mention some gardens and a market she thought we should visit, both of which were places Rosenthal enjoyed and would give us something to talk about with him.

I tuned out the alchemist and turned my attention to the article about the Night Gentleman. The mission suddenly seemed decidedly less important than it had when I woke. There was a serial killer prowling the streets, not only creating landmines that we had to avoid, but also posing a potential threat to our safety. I didn't want to be a drama queen, but I wasn't prepared for anything of this caliber.

The newspaper's account was light on detail and heavy on conjecture. The journalist brushed over the facts, focusing instead on drawing comparisons between the Night Gentleman, the comic book villain Fantômas, and also a convicted murderer who'd been executed several years back. The parallels between the three were disconcerting.

The article's author didn't spare a word in his account of how the French police were handling the crimes. He claimed the lead investigator, an Inspector Thoreau, was both inept and willfully ignorant to the facts before him.

The journalist went on to liken the killings to those of Jack the Ripper, positing that, like Jack, it was unlikely the Night Gentleman would be apprehended, even though all the clues he left behind were obvious signs that he wanted to be caught. At the end of the article, the journalist went so far as to invite the Night Gentleman to send his notes directly to the newspaper, so that he may play his game with a worthy foe.

"Sound like a plan, Stass?" Gaige asked.

I glanced up from the paper in my lap. "Hmmm?"

"Get ready, hit up the Luxembourg Gardens, then have a late lunch at Closerie des Lilas?" he recapped the conversation I'd been tuning out.

"Yep, that works for me. Ines, will you be joining us?" I asked, hoping she'd decline the invitation. I wanted some alone time with Gaige to discuss the Night Gentleman, since he evidently didn't want to have the conversation in front of her.

"I am afraid I have another commitment this morning, but I will join you all for lunch," she replied.

"Pity." The word just popped out, and I cringed at my rudeness. Fortunately, Ines spoke almost entirely in rude, offhanded comments without seeming to offend, so she was oblivious to my snarky tone.

"I know, dear," she said, reaching over to pat my hand. "Lucky for us, we still have much time to spend together."

Great, I thought.

Ines scribbled down a crude map of the area and handed it to Gaige.

"Don't forget to call the car around a bit before you are ready to depart, he can be quite sluggish at times. Give this to Jacque," she told him, scrawling an address on another slip of paper.

Finally, after several more instructions, Ines departed in a plume of smoke and perfume. I waited until the door clicked into place before voicing my chief concern.

"Why didn't Eisenhower tell us about a serial killer?" I demanded.

Gaige ran a hand through his newly darkened hair, a weary expression taking over his features. "My question exactly. Do you think it's possible he didn't know about him?"

"Not a chance," I said automatically. "This guy has killed like ten people, there is no way he isn't documented. Eisenhower knows those books inside out. He knows this city, this time."

"Maybe Eisenhower didn't think it was important?" Gaige proposed half-heartedly.

"Seriously? A serial killer operating in the time and place of our run? I don't buy it. He quizzed us on vintners for heaven's sake."

"Right, but that is actually relevant to our mission. These people love their wine," Gaige pointed out.

My partner was right, but still....

"Okay, well maybe the Night Gentleman is arrested today," he suggested. "Or tomorrow. Or maybe he never kills anyone else."

"Are you honestly arguing with me right now? Or are you just playing devil's advocate?" I demanded.

Gaige grinned. "Both."

I rolled my eyes, then sent a brocade pillow sailing through the air to connect with his face.

"Look, Stass, this situation bothers me, too. We should have been told about it, we should have all of the information. You're right about that."

"But?" I asked, correctly guessing his next word.

"*But* it doesn't change anything. We aren't cabaret singers or magicians or snake handlers. We aren't his potential victims. Just follow the golden rule and you'll be safe."

"Golden rule?"

"Stay a virgin. Oh wait, that's not going to work," he teased, holding up the pillow I threw to show me that he was armed against any impending attack. "Just don't take candy from strangers. Or, in this case, perfume and roses."

TWELVE

THE ATMOSPHERE ON rue Mouffetard was more subdued than I'd expected. The crowd was thinner, too. Patrons walked quickly along the market street with their heads down and eyes averted. Shop girls were skittish and storeowners curt. Few wanted to chat, even when Gaige tried to strike up conversations about local tourist attractions and must-see haunts. We were supposed to be mixing and mingling, but there were no willing participants.

Luxembourg Gardens was no different. Only two men sat by the fountain, one reading and the other scribbling furiously in a leatherbound journal. The open circle and meandering paths were otherwise deserted. It should have been crowded and lively, a place for nannies and mothers with prams to stroll with their children; a place for wannabe artists and novelists to come for inspiration; a place for tourists to glimpse true beauty. The entire atmosphere was surreal, like seeing a vacant Times Square in New York City.

"What's the deal?" I muttered to Gaige as we exited the gardens in search of a more populated venue. "I thought Ines said these were good places to see and be seen."

"I couldn't tell you." Gaige shrugged. "The weather is decent. Maybe it's still too early for the fun-loving people? The bright young things aren't exactly known for rolling out of bed before noon."

"I guess. What time is it? Should we head to the café?"

Gaige pulled a pocket watch from his pants pocket, shielding the face with his hand to read the time. "We have an hour before we're supposed to meet Ines, but I guess we could go over now. The writers could all be holed up there, avoiding sunlight while they convey their genius for the masses to consume and praise."

We made our way to Av. de l'Observatoire, stopping in front of Closerie des Lilas to take in the sight. Shrouded in ivy, the landmark café was situated on a corner, its name scrawled across a burgundy awning.

As Gaige and I entered, I couldn't help but think of all of the books written inside of those very walls. As if Ernest Hemingway and Andre Rosenthal weren't enough, the café was home for centuries of beatniks and creative types who would shape so much of culture throughout history.

I took a moment to soak in the atmosphere.

The outdoor patio was informal, with square two-person tables covering the sidewalk space and lush foliage separating the patrons from the outside world. Inside, the floors were hardwood and the tables adorned with glass flower vases atop linen tablecloths. High-backed stools lined a lacquered bar with brass fixtures. A lone man wearing black pants, a white shirt, and a bowtie stood behind the bar, polishing glasses and mugs. He barely glanced up from his task when we entered.

"Can we sit anywhere?" Gaige asked loudly, breaking the serene silence.

"Any empty table is yours for the taking," the barkeep replied, the first acknowledgment of our presence. He made a sweeping gesture meant to encompass the entire café, both inside and outside.

Gaige turned to me. "Lady's choice."

I nodded to an inside table beside a window. It was the perfect vantage point to scope out both the patio and the main bar areas, just in case anyone of interest showed up.

The bartender sauntered over and handed each of us a menu.

"Bonjour, je m'appelle Michel," he said, my Rosetta translating the introduction.

"It's rather quiet in here today," Gaige said conversationally.

The waiter shrugged with indifference. "Typical for this time of day."

"Is that so?" I asked. "My friend promised a lively lunch."

Michel looked around his nearly empty restaurant. One man sat alone at the corner of the bar. He knocked back the last dregs of a scotch and pulled his hat low over his forehead.

"Maybe it is a little slower than usual," Michel conceded. "Would mademoiselle care for a drink? Champagne, perhaps? We have many outstanding vintages. Monsieur?"

Though drinking during the day was par for the course for Parisians, Gaige and I were on the clock. We both ordered coffee and a dessert to split. Between the croissants, sweets, and champagne, my clothes were going to be tight when I returned to the island. Nevertheless, when the waiter returned with the soufflé, I decided the melt-in-your-mouth mixture of chocolate, cream, and fresh strawberries was worth a few extra pounds.

When in Paris..., I thought with a contented sigh.

"We're visiting from the states," Gaige told Michel, even though the man had not asked and did not seemed interested in making small talk.

"You chose a poor time for a holiday in our city," the waiter told us.

Just then, the front door opened, the single bell above the door chiming at the new arrival. A small, disheveled man entered the café with a satchel over one shoulder and a book clutched tightly against his chest. Round spectacles sat atop his squat nose, magnifying beady black eyes that I'd become very familiar with over the past forty-eight hours.

I wasn't the only one who recognized him.

"Is that Andre Rosenthal?" Gaige asked, sounding like a fourteen year-old fangirl who'd just spotted her untouchable movie star crush. "*The* Andre Rosenthal?"

Nice going, Gaige. Way to be totally creepy.

The waiter apparently agreed with me. He narrowed a suspicious gaze on my partner.

"Is this where he writes his books?" Gaige continued to gush, oblivious to how stalker-like he sounded.

In a not-so-subtle attempt to shut him up, I kicked Gaige under the table. He winced and reached down to rub his shin.

"Please forgive my brother," I said. "He's quite a fan of Mr. Rosenthal's work."

This seemed to mollify the waiter some, but he continued to stare at Gaige as though he'd suddenly sprouted a second head.

In my periphery, I saw Rosenthal walk straight to the back corner of the café, to a table shrouded in shadows near a dark hallway with *Toilettes* over the entranceway. Without looking up, the writer readily rearranged the chairs so that they were next to one another. He placed the satchel on one chair, and then sat in the other.

"Have his novels been published overseas? I had not heard," the waiter said.

Crud, I thought, trying to recall the publication facts about Rosenthal's work to bail out my partner.

"*McGrath's Wrath* was released in the U.S. earlier this year, and my father gave me a copy of *Mine Eyes* that he picked up on his last trip to Europe," Gaige said, the lie coming across effortless.

Admittedly, I was impressed. Brain like a sponge, that kid.

Across the room, Rosenthal disappeared down the hallway to bathrooms.

"I'll tell him that he has a fan," the waiter told Gaige. "Be warned, though, Mr. Rosenthal keeps to himself. He comes here to write and not be bothered."

Gaige held up his hands. "Hey, I understand. Wouldn't want to interfere with his genius. One question, though: What's he drink while he writes?"

I wanted to crawl under the table and hide.

The waiter chuckled. "Scotch on the rocks. Would you care for the same?"

"It's five o'clock somewhere," Gaige said by way of answer.

The waiter frowned.

"He means 'oui, merci'," I explained.

As soon as the waiter was back behind the bar, I rounded on Gaige.

"Really?" I demanded.

The fork was halfway to his mouth, loaded with fluffy chocolate. Gaige paused long enough to feign innocence, and then plunged the heaping bite of dessert between his lips. Eyes rolling back in their sockets, he moaned.

I glanced around the café, double-checking that there was no one in the vicinity of our table to overhear our conversation. Or to witness the spectacle my partner was making. In a low voice, I continued scolding Gaige.

"Did you need to advertise that we're here to stalk Rosenthal? Are you trying to send him running for the hills?"

Gaige swallowed, sipped his coffee to wash down any lingering morsels, and smacked his lips noisily.

"I said I'm a huge fan, not that I'm trying to steal from the guy. That's flattering, Stass. Every writer likes hearing his work is appreciated. Are you gonna eat any more of this? Or are you watching your weight these days?"

Stabbing the dessert with my own fork, I scooped up a bite that rivaled the one Gaige had just taken. "You didn't need to be so obvious," I grumbled, right before devouring it.

"You know what?" Gaige asked, the question clearly rhetorical. "You are awfully high-strung today. More so than usual."

"Thanks," I deadpanned.

"No, I just mean you aren't usually this touchy about stuff." He paused, brown eyes studying me intently. "Is the whole Night Gentleman thing really getting to you? We can head back to the island if you want. Cyrus will understand, you know he will."

The waiter returned with two glasses of scotch, setting one in front of me and the other in front of Gaige.

"Compliments of Mr. Rosenthal," he told us. "He says it is not every day he encounters such a voracious fan, particularly an American one."

Gaige beamed up at the waiter, and then turned to look at Rosenthal who had returned to his table in the dark corner.

How does he write without any light? I wondered.

Rosenthal, head bent over his notebook and pen in hand, was scribbling furiously on the pages before him. As if sensing Gaige's stare, his head popped up. His glasses slid forward on his nose and were close to falling over the edge. The writer pushed them back into place with one finger.

Gaige raised his scotch in toast. To be polite, I did the same. With a small half- smile, Rosenthal returned the gesture.

"Let me know when you are ready for a refill," the waiter told us, then returned to the bar.

"Don't say it," I warned, anticipating Gaige's gloating words.

My partner simply grinned and sipped his scotch, leaving his smug expression to do the talking for him.

Much to Gaige's chagrin, Rosenthal did not come over for a meet and greet with his biggest fan. True to his reclusive nature, the writer remained in his corner, ensconced in shadows for the rest of the afternoon. And while Gaige was comfortable openly gushing to the waiter about his love for the author's work, he was not brazen enough to walk over and make a fool of himself. Yet.

"I'll wait until Saturday," my partner replied when I commended him on the achievement.

From our lessons, I knew it was unlikely that Rosenthal was actually working on *Blue's Canyon* that day. At this point, the initial draft was complete and hidden away, awaiting final polishing. Judging by the timeline of his life and career, I guessed he was working on *Sparrows of Summer*.

Unbeknownst to Rosenthal, *Sparrows* would become his highest-grossing work of all-time. The premise sounded interesting—a young American heiress said to be touched in the head falls in love with the Marquis of Mancera, only to learn on the eve of her wedding that he was a notorious conman who assumed the noble title under false pretenses after murdering the real Marquis. *The New York Review of Books* would later describe *Sparrows* as "evocative and spellbinding", "a true work of literary genius", and "just risqué enough to whet the appetite, without being indecent". So, not my usual beach read, but it did sound intriguing.

When our scheduled meeting time with Ines came and went with no sign from the alchemist, I started to worry. Gaige didn't appear the least bit concerned, though he was quickly growing bored with the empty café. With two glasses of scotch under his belt and very little food in his stomach, my partner was somewhat tipsy and entirely ready to leave. I couldn't blame him, watching Rosenthal write for three hours made for a pretty dull stakeout.

Nevertheless, amidst Gaige's protests, I insisted we stay. I wasn't sure how long Rosenthal usually spent writing each day in Lilas, but I was hoping he'd stop by to say hello on his way out. As a conciliation prize for Gaige, I went up to the bar to order another round of drinks for both men.

While Michel busied himself pouring the amber liquid from a bottle on the top shelf, I scanned the titles on a small bookcase behind the bar that appeared to be a lending library of sorts. I'd spent the past two hours flipping through the glossy editions of *Harper's Bazaar*, *Vogue*, and *Vanity Fair* scattered around the restaurant, and my interest in magazines was beginning to wane. Hoping for something more stimulating, or at least more educational, I ran my eyes over the rows of spines.

"Wait, is that a Fantômas novel?" I asked Michel, just as he slid the glasses over the smooth bar.

Following the direction of my stare, the barkeep walked over to the bookshelf and searched for the title in question.

"Second shelf, on the right," I chimed in helpfully.

Michel held up a book with a masked man in a top hat on the front and raised one eyebrow in question. A young American woman interested in graphic novels was apparently quite odd. Or maybe it had more to do with my interest in the character some murderous whackjob was using as a muse.

"Yes, that one," I said, hoping my eagerness wasn't too transparent.

The bartender handed over the book. I opened it to a random page, running my fingers over the pictures of Fantômas. Could it be sheer coincidence that a killer was imitating the comic book character?

"Do you read French, mademoiselle?" the waiter asked as I began flipping through the graphic novel.

I smiled sheepishly.

"Only a little," I admitted. "Would it be okay if I took this over to my table?

"Of course, of course," Michel replied. "That is what the books are here for."

A phone hanging on the back wall rang.

"Pardon me, please," he said.

Novel in hand, I turned and began walking to our table with Gaige's drink. I left Rosenthal's atop the bar for Michel to deliver, since I didn't want to disturb the writer. Though it was an unlikely scenario, if I interrupted Rosenthal at the wrong moment, I might never get to read *Sparrows of Summer* when I got home. Or it might suck.

"Excuse me, Mademoiselle Prince?" Michel's voice called, just as I was about to sit down.

It took me a moment to remember that Prince was the last name Gaige had given us.

"Yes?"

"There is an Ines Callandries calling for you. She apologizes, but she has been detained at her place of work and will be unable to meet with you and your brother."

"Oh, okay. Thank you, Michel," I replied.

"She's obviously a very hardworking and dedicated employee," Gaige grumbled, as I slid his fresh drink across the table.

"Last one, fishy," I warned, watching him take a deep gulp.

"I'm not a fish, I am a man," Gaige declared, just before he belched loudly.

Yeah, the day was off to a great start.

THIRTEEN

"WAIT RIGHT HERE," I said to my partner. "Do not get up out of your chair, understood?"

Gaige's third scotch had somehow brought the idea that he and Rosenthal were old pals, and my partner was resolved to approach the man. I could just picture him pulling up a chair at the author's table and plopping down to offer unsolicited critiques on the man's work.

With a final warning glare to Gaige, I went up to the bar to return the book and settle our check.

"Je voudrais le cheque, s'il vous plait," I said to Michel, drawing an amused smile.

Okay, so I wasn't exactly a linguist. But I also needed to practice, or I never would be.

"Monsieur Rosenthal's, aussi, s'il vous plait?" I added.

"That is very kind of you," Michel replied in English. "I'm sure Monsieur will appreciate the gesture."

"It is the least I can do after my brother's untoward behavior. I hope he has not disturbed Mr. Rosenthal's work for the day."

The bartender looked over at the corner where the writer was still frantically scribbling away.

"I assure you, Monsieur Rosenthal becomes easily lost in his own imagination," Michel said kindly. He scrawled several figures on a slip of paper before turning it upside down and pushing it over to me. "Is there anything else that I may do for you this afternoon?"

I glanced down at the book in my hand, debating whether to ask about buying it from him. The comic was probably in bookstores, and I might even be able to find an English language version. Then again, this copy was in my hands. And if it proved too difficult to understand, I could always read it aloud and hope my pronunciation was good enough for the Rosetta to translate.

"Would you consider allowing me to purchase this?" I asked uncertainly.

"No charge."

"I'd like to buy it," I clarified.

"No charge," the waiter repeated with a wave of his hand. "We have several more copies."

"Thank you."

Adding a generous tip, I paid our check and retrieved Gaige from where he'd remained dutifully in his seat. As we exited, I glanced back at Rosenthal, still working away. I felt a tinge of shame over planning to steal something the quiet man had obviously dedicated a great deal of time to. If *Blue's Canyon* had ever been released, I might have really struggled with the mission, though I never would have admitted it. Only the thought of someone in my time becoming enthralled with the novel assuaged my guilt. Books were meant to be read and enjoyed, not hidden away, lost, and forgotten like a hoarder's treasure.

With the afternoon suddenly free, I suggested we walk for a while to familiarize ourselves with the area. Though European cities weren't completely overhauled on a regular basis like they were in America, we'd never before visited Paris in 1920s. Montparnasse—the neighborhood where the expatriates lived, worked, and played—had been a seedy area with little to offer culturally or socially when we last visited the city. This new mecca for starving artists on the Left Bank was all new to me. Also, Gaige needed to burn off all of the alcohol he'd consumed. Ines had yet to impart our plans for the evening, but it was a safe bet that booze would be included.

We wandered through the streets of Paris, stopping to window shop every so often, when something caught our attention. Gaige kept up a running commentary on Rosenthal's writings the entire time. As he spoke, I realized that my partner was not just pretending to be a fan; he was a genuine devotee of the reclusive author. When Gaige started in on Rosenthal's use of symbolism and how *Sparrows* was actually a metaphor for antiroyalist views, I tuned out of the conversation.

"I mean, I know it sold more copies than any of his other books, but it was *still* undervalued. People just don't properly appreciate—hey, it's that bookstore!"

Gaige stopped in the middle of the sidewalk and pointed up at a sign. A picture of England's most adored bard hung above us, just under the name of the store: Shakespeare and Company. It was a beloved and historically significant establishment, known as much for welcoming and supporting starving artists as it was for selling controversial works like James Joyce's *Ulysses*.

The store would undergo a change of ownership and move locations again in the coming years, so being able to visit the original one was pretty incredible. Stepping back to take in the infamous bookstore's façade—the large windows cluttered with books propped on stands, the front door that always remained open, rain or shine—my attention was immediately diverted.

Several doors down, hung another sign, the same size and shape as the one of Shakespeare. The design was that of an off-kilter five-leaf clover, drawn in a swooping calligraphy style.

No. Fracking. Way.

With my eyes still on the sign, I reached blindly and hit Gaige on the arm several times.

"Ow!" he exclaimed, rubbing his shoulder. "I get it, visiting Shakespeare's is very exciting, but you need to lock it up."

Finally tearing my eyes away from the achingly familiar sight, I smacked Gaige in the arm again and pointed.

"Oh," he said dumbly.

My partner turned back to me, and for a moment we simply stared at each other. A woman walking a toy poodle down the sidewalk, undoubtedly wondering what on earth the two fools in her way were doing, jolted us out of the reverie.

"Let's check it out," Gaige said decisively, already moving away from the bookstore.

I hesitated. We'd come to Paris to find Rosenthal's mysterious manuscript, and Shakespeare and Company owner, Sylvia Beach, was reportedly a good friend of his. It was a contact we needed to make.

Plus…this was something I wanted to do alone. At least, for now.

"Stass? You coming?" Gaige called over his shoulder.

My hand closed around the locket at my throat. I traced the outline of the five-leaf clover carved on the back with my thumb.

"Why don't you go visit Shakespeare and Company? I'll go check it out by myself. We don't even know if this has anything to do with my locket," I said lamely.

My partner scanned the front window of the store beneath the clover. The long strands of gold necklaces and intricately engraved bracelets displayed under bright lights made my response all the more absurd. My partner turned and studied my face.

"Yeah, sure," he replied, running a hand through his dark locks. "No problem. Just, you know, come get me if you need me. For anything."

"I will," I promised.

Taking a deep breath, I reached for the door of the jewelry store. The name was scrawled in white ink across the glass: Bonheur's. I glanced over my shoulder. Gaige was still standing uncertainly on the sidewalk watching me. I gave him what was meant to be a reassuring nod, but I was so tense that the movement was just a jerky twitch.

My partner put a hand over his heart, waited for me to return the gesture, and then walked away.

FOURTEEN

A BELL TINKLED softly as I slipped through the front door of the jewelry shop. Heart already in my throat, the noise nearly caused me to choke on the oh-so-important organ. The utter stillness and absolute silence inside Bonheur's made the accelerated thudding in my chest seem deafening by comparison.

It might be a coincidence, I told myself to calm my nerves.

But it wasn't. The five-leaf clover stamped in the gold of my locket was identical to the five-leaf clover painted on the sign above the storefront. The locket had come from this store or one of its predecessors.

I knew I should have been giddy, over the moon, on cloud nine, or some other silly saying meant to describe a feeling of elation. Finally, *finally,* I was going to learn something that could help me uncover the identity of my birth parents. And yet, now that I was here, standing on a precipice, I was suddenly terrified of the truth.

It was easy to idealize parents you had never met. It was easy to resent parents you didn't know. It was easy to love the people who'd given you life. It was easy to hate the people who'd abandoned you. The truth was never easy. The truth was complicated and messy. Once I knew the truth, my parents would no longer be two stars in the sky watching over me. Was I really ready for that change?

Slowly, like a reluctant bride on her wedding day, I began my march up the center aisle of Bonheur's. My low heels left impressions in the thick jade carpeting with each hesitant step. On my left and right, bright bulbs shone down on glittering jeweled masterpieces in glass display cases. I scanned the rows of gold and gems without really seeing the individual pieces.

"Bonjour, mademoiselle." The man's voice was soft and soothing and came from somewhere near the back of the store.

"Bonjour," I called back, my own voice high and squeaky.

A short man in a tailored navy pinstripe suit stood and emerged from behind a semi-circle glass counter at the rear of the store. His salt and pepper mustache twitched as his lips curved into a polite smile. Red spots of light danced across the ceiling from the stones—rubies most likely— inlaid on his gold wedding band when he made a wide, sweeping gesture around the store.

His next words were spoken in rapid French. Even with the Rosetta, I barely understood his invitation to peruse the merchandise.

"Parlez-vous anglais?" I asked, donning a sheepish expression.

I made sure to mangle the pronunciation to convey just how poor my French speaking skills were. With my anxiety reaching all new heights, I didn't want the added bother of relying on the Rosetta for the impending conversation.

"But of course, mademoiselle," the man said in perfect English.

He joined me in the center of the store, by a hexagonal configuration of display cases with white cushioned stools strategically placed around the perimeter. Ornate hand mirrors were facedown on the glass display cases by each stool, Bonheur's trademark five-leaf clover engraved in the center of the silver ovals.

"Our beautiful city has many visitors, from many cities around the world. I am schooled in a variety of languages," he continued, as if speaking numerous languages fluently was as commonplace as basic arithmetic.

"English is all I know, so that will work for me," I replied, fighting the urge to fiddle with my locket. I wasn't ready to draw his attention to the piece quite yet.

"English it is then. What brings mademoiselle to Paris? On holiday?"

"Yes. My brother and I are touring Europe currently," I answered in a tone meant to be polite, yet also express that I had no interest in idle chitchat.

Clearly an expert in inferences, the man went into sales mode. "How can I be of assistance today? Are you looking for a particular item? A new pair of earrings, perhaps?" He pointed to the gold and crystal dewdrops dangling from my earlobes and nearly brushing my collarbone. "Beautiful pieces, but no doubt heavy. Allow me to show you our selection."

He unlatched a hook beneath one of the cases, and it swung outward on a hinge. He entered the ring of cases, so that we were standing face-to-face over the glass displays.

"Please, sit." He gestured to the closest stool.

I sat, debating how best to segue to my locket.

There was no one else inside the jewelry store, so I didn't have to worry about being overheard. I also didn't have to worry about wasting the man's time, since paying customers were nonexistent.

Best to get to the point. Rip off the bandage, I thought.

"Are you the owner?" I asked aloud.

The man looked up from the cases he'd been examining in search of a new pair of earrings for me.

"I am," he said and held out his hand. "Matthieu Bonheur."

"Stassi Prince," I replied, returning the handshake.

"A pleasure, Mademoiselle Prince. Now allow me to show you our House of Bourbon collection. It is inspired by Louis XIV. You may know him as the Sun King. It is one of my favorite designs."

"Do you design the pieces yourself?" I asked, as Matthieu selected a pair of earrings with a fiery red-orange stone surrounded by delicate spokes of gold that resembled the sun's rays.

From behind the counter, he withdrew a trifold leather book in the same shade of green as the carpet. Matthieu placed the book on the glass and made a great show of unfolding the leaves. He carefully arranged the earrings on the velvet, somehow managing to place them at exactly the right angle for optimal sparkle.

They really are beautiful, I thought with a twinge of guilt, since I had no intention of making a purchase.

"I am the designer, yes. Each piece you see in this store was designed and individually crafted by either myself or another member of my family. It has been this way for generations. My father, my father's father, my father's father's father—they were all artisans," Matthieu Bonheur declared proudly.

"Everything is so lovely," I told him honestly.

"The mademoiselle is too kind." He picked up the oval mirror and pointed to the sun earrings. "Would you care to try them on? Or is there perhaps something else that may be more to your liking?"

I exhaled slowly. "I apologize, Mr. Bonheur, but I am actually here about a specific piece of jewelry."

The jeweler arched a graying eyebrow in question. "Oh?"

"A locket," I hurried on, now desperate to discuss the reason I'd come to the store in the first place.

Bonheur's eyes followed my movements as I unfastened the clasp at the back of my neck. I placed the locket on the white velvet alongside the earrings.

"This locket, to be precise," I added unnecessarily.

Matthieu Bonheur was a man transfixed. His eyes seemed glued to the locket. Only the tiny hairs of his trim mustache moved slightly as he breathed through his nose.

After a long moment that seemed to span eternity, I asked tentatively, "Do you recognize it?"

Bonheur hesitated. Then, as if tearing his gaze from the locket was physically painful, he met my eyes. "I apologize, Mademoiselle Prince, I do not understand. This locket, it belongs to you?"

"It does," I confirmed. Turning the locket over, I pointed to the five-leaf clover. "This is your insignia, right?"

From the pocket of his suit pants, Bonheur produced a jeweler's loop. He picked up the locket, gingerly placing it in the palm of his free hand. "May I?" he asked, indicating the small magnifying tool.

I nodded.

Reading facial expressions, interpreting body language, making inferences based on seemingly inane comments—these were all crucial weapons in a runner's arsenal. And I was very good at all three. I had to be, if I wanted to live to old age. But even a green runner, fresh out of training—hell, a child on the street—would have known Bonheur was putting on a show, stalling for time. Why? That I couldn't answer. Yet there was no doubt in my mind that the jeweler had recognized my locket as one of his own the moment he laid eyes on it.

He muttered to himself in French, so low that the Rosetta couldn't decipher his utterances.

Finally, after eons passed, Bonheur set the locket back on the white velvet. He studied me, the skin around his eyes crinkling like an accordion.

"You are correct, this is one of our pieces."

Hope washed over me like cool rain on a sweltering day.

"So you did make it? Do you remember whom you sold it to? Is there anything you can tell me about her?" The questions came out rapid fire, the end of one word weaving with the start of the next to form one long, mismatched sentence.

Eyes wide, expression vaguely alarmed, Bonheur took several steps backward. I shrunk down on my stool, cheeks burning from embarrassment.

"Mademoiselle's locket is not one of my designs. You see these initials here?" He pointed to two interlocking letters carved into the gold just below the clover. "S.B. for Sebastian Bonheur, my grandfather. May I ask how you came to be in possession of this necklace?"

I averted my gaze. "It belonged to my mother."

Bonheur stiffened. He stared down at the locket with such a tangled web of emotions that I couldn't possibly begin to parse out the individual threads of feeling. His continued silence set off a need to fill the conversational void, and I began to ramble.

"I'm an orphan. I never knew my mother or father. At least, I don't remember knowing them. I was found wandering the streets alone as a child. That," I jabbed a finger towards the locket, "was all I had with me. It's the only thing that connects me to my birth parents. Anything you can tell me about the person who bought it would be helpful," I pleaded.

I would've needed to flip a coin to determine which one of us was more surprised by my outpouring of emotion.

For his part, I couldn't imagine that the jeweler received a lot of young women who sounded on the verge of a nervous breakdown. I was probably the first. The note of raw panic in Bonheur's gaze told me that he prayed I'd be the last.

As for me, I wasn't the sharing, let alone over-sharing, type. I was normally very good at controlling my emotion, as opposed to vomiting them all over strangers.

The thing was, Matthieu Bonheur knew something. Something he didn't want to tell me. It was clear he recognized the locket, yet he'd initially pretended otherwise. His answers to my questions were vague, if he actually answered them at all. More often, he answered a question with a question. They were textbook evasion techniques. I should know; I'd memorized that textbook. That was why I also knew that my previous approach wasn't working. Because I wasn't about to go all Spanish Inquisition on him—I wasn't that desperate yet—appealing to the jeweler on an emotional level was my only option.

"I am afraid I cannot help you, mademoiselle. As I said, the locket was designed by my grandfather, and most likely was purchased during his tenure as owner and head jeweler. I say 'likely', because Sebastian Bonheur officially retired two decades ago, after nearly thirty-five years at the helm. He continued to design specialty items until the day he died, five years ago. It is not possible for me to say when the locket was purchased, and certainly not by whom. I am very sorry," the jeweler finished, refusing to make eye contact.

"Surely you keep records? I know I'm asking for a lot, but maybe you could look for the receipt or purchase order. I'd be happy to pay you."

Bonheur laughed nervously. "I am afraid a search of my records would not produce any results. I do not care to burden myself with paperwork, too tiresome. I am an artist, a craftsman. I create beautiful jewelry for equally beautiful women. It is that simple. I am truly sorry to be unable to aid in your search."

Liar! I wanted to shout. No company stayed in business as long as Bonheur's had without keeping records. Particularly when they did custom design work.

I took a deep breath to calm myself.

"I understand," I said evenly. "But maybe you could at least tell me if this is a custom piece?"

Bonheur hesitated, obviously unsure how much to divulge.

"I cannot be certain," he hedged.

I pushed the velvet-lined leather book across the counter towards him. The jeweler took the hint and examined the locket a second time with his loop. He turned it over in his hand, studying the hinge on one side, and then the seam on the other. Bonheur depressed the catch at the back. The locket sprang open. My heart ached at the sight of the two empty picture frames inside. One day, those frames would hold my parents' faces. Until then, they would remain empty.

Bonheur gently traced one of the empty indentations with his thumb, and then snapped the two halves closed. Cupping my necklace in his hand, he held it out to me.

"The design is unique. I cannot be positive whether a similar one exists, but I can say it does not have an equal. I regret that I cannot be of more assistance to you," Bonheur declared with a note of finality that told me this well of information was tapped.

I still believed Matthieu Bonheur knew more, likely a lot more, than he was telling. I also believed pumping him for that information was useless. What I needed now was a new plan. Well, I needed a plan, period. Storming into Bonheur's and demanding answers had been improvisational. But I wasn't leaving empty-handed, not exactly. Now I knew there were answers behind the glittering walls. I just had to find a different way of unearthing them.

Maybe Gaige would have an idea. He was usually good at thinking outside the box.

Refastening the chain around my neck, I smiled pleasantly. "Thank you, Mr. Bonheur. I understand completely. And you have been more help than you know, honestly."

I offered my hand for a departing shake. Just as I'd anticipated, the jeweler's hand was damp with perspiration. What was that guy hiding? More importantly, *why* was he hiding it?

I was halfway to the door when he called after me.

"Mademoiselle?"

"Yes?" I called over my shoulder.

"I, too, know loss. My own mother died when I was just a few years younger than you are now. She was a beautiful woman, bursting with joie de vivre, as I am sure that your mother was, as well."

Bursting with the joy of living. What a peculiar thing to say.

FIFTEEN

STEPPING THROUGH THE front door of Shakespeare and Company, I did my best to wipe all traces of the odd exchange at Bonheur's from my mind.

Lock it up, Stassi.

Forcing a bright smile, I joined Gaige where he stood in a narrow walkway between two book stacks. My partner was feigning interest in the titles, but dropped the act as soon as he saw me.

"So?" he asked hesitantly.

"We'll talk about it later," I mumbled under my breath. "Let's do this."

"So sorry!" a cheery voice called to us. "I'm afraid I was in the back tending to some jumbled words. Welcome, welcome."

None other than Sylvia Beach herself emerged from the rear of the store. Both her appearance and demeanor were the personification of gentle. Beach was small and prim, something that seemed so out of line with her radical ideas about literature and writers.

Gaige looked at me and raised his eyebrows, then sauntered over to the cash register table where the owner had taken up perch. The hours listed on a small sign posted behind her suggested that our arrival coincided closely with closing time. Nonetheless, the American-born bookseller did not give any indication that our presence was an imposition.

"Now, is there something I can help you with? Perhaps we can find your next adventure," she said warmly.

"My sister could certainly use some adventure," Gaige replied with an easy smile.

"Oh, are you American?" Beach asked delightedly.

"We are," my partner answered. "This is my sister, Anastasia Prince, and my name is Gaige Prince. It is so lovely to meet you. We are in Paris for a spell, visiting from Baltimore, Maryland. Have you been?"

"Sylvia Beach." Beach offered Gaige her hand, and then turned to me and did the same. "Baltimore, you say? What an extraordinary coincidence. I was born and raised there."

Though Gaige feigned surprise at her answer, this fact had been highlighted in Beach's dossier. Still talkative from the scotch, my partner took the opening and ran with it. I hovered nearby, pretending to scan the titles on a shelf. Gaige and Beach swapped names of people and places we supposedly had in common. He easily rattled off details from memory. If I hadn't known better, even I would have bought his story.

"Is this your place?" he asked.

Nice. You sound like you're trying to pick her up, I thought, still lingering close by.

Gaige's comment about my unusually high-strung nature that day came back to me. I was more on edge than normal, he was right about that.

He's a pro. Let him do his thing.

I moved farther away, still close enough to hear them, but deliberately separating myself from the pair. With one ear, I half-listened to Gaige and Sylvia making small talk. Like so many women in so many different eras, Sylvia Beach found my partner charming. She became all the more excited when he told her that he was interested in sponsoring a writer—a common practice where a wealthy benefactor paid for living expenses, so the author could focus on his craft.

For the next forty minutes, the two discussed prospective talent, life in Paris, and great bookstores they'd both visited. Allegedly. Beach appeared oblivious to the fact that Gaige wasn't actually contributing much to the conversation. Instead, my partner was practicing the art of casual evasion—simply agreeing with her, only expounding upon stories when it was a detail we'd studied at length.

"—isn't that right, Stass?" he asked, his voice rising slightly.

"Hmmm?" I'd pulled out a book called *The Weary Blues*, flipped open to a random page, and found myself utterly lost in the lyrical poetry. It was amazing to see how people in this time related to and were influenced by music just the same as we still were in my home time.

"I was just telling Ms. Beach how we met Andre Rosenthal over at that café today. What was it called again?"

"Closerie des Lilas," I supplied automatically.

"Oh, of course. Quaint little place, isn't it?" Beach replied. "Andre enjoys writing there. Here, as well. He stops in one or twice a week and works right over there." She pointed to a wooden table with a matching chair on the other side of the store.

This effectively pulled my mind away from the words of Langston Hughes. I closed the book and joined them at the sales counter.

"So you know him well?" Gaige asked.

"I suppose one could say so," Sylvia said without a trace of pretentiousness.

We knew better than to accept her modesty. The two were great friends, known for contributing to one another's work. In fact, Beach would later publish *Sparrows* on his behalf.

"May I ask you a question about his process?" Gaige asked, only partially feigning the reverence in his voice.

"Of course," she replied.

"We saw him writing in a portfolio with a leather cover. Is that how he writes all of his books?"

"It is."

"Why does he not use a typewriter?" Gaige asked. "It seems a bit dated to be hand writing novels."

"I know, I know," Beach said with a smile. "I am always telling him precisely the same thing. But Andre likes to move about while he works, he says being out among the people inspires the writing. I believe that is one reason he writes in longhand—it is cumbersome to carry a typewriter from place to place."

I didn't need to see Gaige's expression to know we were thinking the same thing: Sylvia Beach had just given us a new clue. *Blue's Canyon* was going to be in a leatherbound notebook.

"What's the other reason?" I asked, genuinely curious.

"I believe it has something to do with Archy," Beach replied with a conspiratorial grin.

"Archy?" Gaige asked.

"Don Marquis? The column he wrote for the *New York Evening Sun*?" she prompted.

"You mean the cockroach who wrote books by jumping around on a typewriter?" I filled in.

"Ah, you've heard of him," the bookseller said with obvious delight. "I do so love that little bug, but I believe Andre finds it insulting to consider that a cockroach might work in the same manner."

"Quite the eccentricity," I said smiling.

"Speaking of eccentricities, I read somewhere that Mr. Rosenthal hides his works-in-progress in various places. Is that true?" Gaige asked, steering the conversation back on track.

Sylvia laughed. "Oh, yes. Andre is a superstitious one. That very well may be the case."

Beach knew it to be true; I could tell.

"I don't suppose he has any hidden around here, does he?" Gaige asked, his tone light and teasing, just right for not incurring suspicion. "It is like a hunt for his great words, what fun."

The alcohol was doing wonders for his game. Maybe I should get him liquored up for work more often.

Sylvia Beach smiled and her bright eyes twinkled. "What kind of friend would I be if I told you that?"

And that's a yes, I thought triumphantly. *Now if only the manuscript he has hidden here is Blue's Canyon.*

"Now I must apologize, I have an evening engagement and need to close up the shop," Beach announced. "I do hope you'll both come visit again soon, I have greatly enjoyed our tête-à-tête."

I held up the copy of *The Weary Blues*. "May I purchase this?"

"Mr. Hughes is a fine poet," Beach declared as she wrote up a sales slip. "The universality of this collection is quite extraordinary."

"That is precisely what I thought," I said, surprised two people from such vastly different worlds could share the same opinion on poetry.

I still had the Fantômas novel tucked under my arm, and set it on the counter as I began counting out francs. Sylvia looked down at it, clucking her tongue.

"Terrible about these murders. What kind of man imitates a literary villain? And one as crass as Fantômas? The whole city is aflutter, people are worried sick."

"Is that why so many businesses are closed today?" I asked her.

"It is. Of this entire block, only Monsieur Bonheur and I opened our doors today."

My ears perked up at the mention of the jeweler. I was torn between asking what she knew about her fellow shop owner and continuing with the Night Gentleman line of questioning. Gaige made the decision for me.

"Word of his presence has not yet reached the States. In fact, we didn't learn about the murders until we arrived. Our friend who lives here said they've been going on for a few weeks. Is that true? I'm concerned for my sister's safety."

I worried that Gaige's first statement was not accurate, that the murders *were* world news by this point. Unfortunately, we were swimming in uncharted waters.

"I would not fret about it," Beach said kindly. "The Night Gentleman seems to seek out women of a particular sort, and your dear sister does not fall into such a category. As to your question about how long he has been active, you are correct. The first killing was about three weeks ago. News does not find significance across an ocean quite so quickly."

Serial killers might not be immediately considered world news, but they usually do make the history books, I thought. Then and there, I made a decision. As soon as I returned to the townhouse, I would send a query through customs to Historian Eisenhower. Gaige and I needed to know what was going on.

"Thank you for your time," I said aloud to Beach, handing her the currency as she gave me the marbled paper bag with my new book.

"I look forward to seeing you both soon," Sylvia replied. She rounded the counter and escorted us to the door. Gaige thanked her as well, and we promised to return soon.

The sun was still shining when we emerged, with nightfall an hour or so away. My partner hailed a passing taxi, and the two of us climbed in while Sylvia watched from the doorway. I waved to her from the open window as Gaige recited our address to the driver.

At least today wasn't a total bust, I thought, striving for optimism. Just twenty-four hours out of customs, we'd already met and mingled with several of Rosenthal's friends, encountered the target himself at one of his regular writing haunts, and managed to weasel a clue out of Sylvia Beach. All in all, we were off to a very decent start. If we could keep up this pace, we'd be back home in no time.

SIXTEEN

WHEN WE ARRIVED back at the townhouse, there was a letter from Ines on our kitchen counter scrawled in her elegant handwriting. Gaige quickly skimmed the contents.

"Ines wants us ready by nine for an 'evening out and about'," he informed me.

"Exactly what does that entail?" I wondered aloud.

Gaige handed me Ines's note. "You can read the details. She says to wear something chic."

"Don't even say it," I warned.

"What? That chic isn't in your repertoire? That you should've started getting ready last night to have even a chance of pulling off chic?" Gaige teased, his eyes wide and innocent.

"Exactly that. Don't say any of that," I replied, scanning the letter and noting that it made no mention of food. Ines must have been too consumed by her comprehensive directives regarding my appearance to think of something as silly as eating. "What time is it?" I asked Gaige.

He checked his pocket watch. "Six."

"Ugh. I guess I am off to see Felipe," I told Gaige. "Want to come?"

He stretched his arms over his head and yawned. "Nah. Naptime. Wake me when you get back."

"Lucky," I grumbled.

"Bring me something delicious!" Gaige called after me.

"Yeah, yeah, yeah," I answered, one foot already out the door.

"Love you!" Gaige sing-songed.

"Love you, too," I said, keeping my back turned so he wasn't able to see the warm smile on my face.

I asked the young girl behind the counter at the hat shop for directions to the transporter's office.

"Through that door there." The salesgirl pointed to a blue door at the back of the store with the word "Privé" above it. "Down one flight of stairs. There you will find a secretary named Ava. She will give you the appropriate form."

"Thank you," I told the salesgirl and set off towards the blue door.

Ava was exactly where I'd been told she would be. After brief introductions, she handed me a communications form and a pen. I gave the message a moment's thought before scribbling down our current dilemma: Serial killer active in Paris. Name = Night Gentleman. Need intel ASAP.

Since we weren't allowed to ask a transporter to jump for any old reason, Ava next had me sign a series of forms. Only requests for immediate assistance, a cleanup crew, or vital information needed to complete the mission warranted dispatching a transporter. Hoping that a murderer fell into the latter category, I signed my name to the last form.

"Your request will be processed immediately," Ava told me.

"Thank you," I called over my shoulder and went to find Felipe.

He was armed and ready when I arrived. As I settled into the swivel chair, my eyes met my reflection in the mirror. I saw a girl who looked harried and anxious, the opposite of a picture-perfect socialite.

Luckily, Felipe was nothing short of a miracle worker. He easily transformed my disheveled mane into sleek, photo-op-worthy locks. After just one hour in the chair, my long, auburn tresses were pinned and arranged in a fashionable bob.

"And now for the fun part," the stylist said with a grin. "No peeking!"

He turned my chair around so I was facing him instead of the mirror, then he wheeled over a cart with dozens of brushes on the top in various sizes and shapes. The trolley had five long drawers, and I knew from experience that they were bursting with eye shadows, foundations, blushes, lipsticks, and eye and lip liners in every color imaginable. Most of the products were time and location specific and would have been purchased at a local department store. Not all, though. Many of the makeup artists favored products from the future, which the syndicate supplied them with.

Another half-hour passed as Felipe dabbed, blended, and brushed his way through the various cosmetics. When he stepped back and clasped his hands together, the guise stylist wore a look of smug satisfaction.

"You, my dear, are a knockout," Felipe proclaimed, spinning my chair to face the mirror with a large flourish. "Voila!"

"Whoa," I said, admiring his handiwork. "I barely recognize myself."

It was true. The auburn hair I still wasn't quite used to was pinned up with elegant finger waves framing my face. My blue eyes were highlighted with dark, smoky shadows, and my lips were traced in a deep red with a pronounced cupid's bow. I looked every bit the part of a fun-loving flapper, ready for mischief and mayhem.

"Do not insult me," Felipe pouted, frowning at me in the mirror. "You are a natural beauty, I simply wish to draw attention to your best features."

I blushed at the compliment.

"Thanks," I muttered. Standing, I smoothed the wrinkles from my dress.

"I am green with envy, love. I hear Ines is taking you to the most fabulous show in all of Montparnasse," Felipe declared. "Even she has yet to pay a visit."

"What sort of show?" I asked. "Ines left a note telling us to be ready by nine, but she was vague about where we're going."

"*Exotique* is all anyone can talk about." Felipe began sweeping the floor around his workstation.

"Is it a cabaret show?" I guessed.

He paused and met my gaze, eyes wide with surprise.

"You have not heard of *Exotique*? It is much more than a simple cabaret show," said Felipe, aghast at my naivety. A look of wonder came over his features. "Yes, there is singing and dancing, but it is so much more than that. It is supposed to be magical, with illusions the world has never seen before."

I stifled a giggle.

"You forget who you are talking to. I have seen quite a bit," I told him.

"Not like this, love. Monsieur Houdini himself is said to have commended the performers after seeing the show in Rome. These men and women can make themselves disappear from the stage, only to reappear next to you in the audience. They pull elephants from hats. The women float on air, and the men walk on water." He wiggled a finger in front of my face. "You doubt, I can see. Just wait, you will understand."

Disappearing and reappearing? A stunt like that during a stage show was merely an illusion. The same could be said for pulling animals from hats, even elephants. Nevertheless, I had neither the time nor the inclination to argue with Felipe. If he still believed that *Exotique* was mesmerizing after watching people materialize in a spinning vortex from the future, then nothing I said was going to persuade Felipe otherwise.

"I'll let you know," I promised the stylist.

To my surprise, Gaige was dressed when I returned to the

townhouse. Sitting on the couch with a cocktail in one hand, my partner was flipping through the Fantômas novel. He was dashing in the tuxedo, complete with coattails and bowtie. Though he'd been a little heavy-handed with the styling product, Gaige's hair gleamed in the light.

"Hey," he called, not bothering to look up.

"You look nice. Catch." I tossed a paper-wrapped tomato and mozzarella sandwich from customs at him.

Hands cupped as if to catch a football, Gaige tore his eyes from the graphic novel just in time.

"Touchdown!" he cried and did a little victory dance in his seat.

"Find anything new about our masked villain?" I asked, climbing the staircase to the bedrooms.

"Not sure. I'm having a hard time translating the words, though the pictures tell quite a tale." He folded back the paper at one end of the sandwich and took a large bite. Around a mouthful of food, Gaige added, "Dude's pretty wicked."

"I'll look at it later," I promised. "Though I doubt I'll understand much more than you do. I'll be ready soon, just need to change. Oh, and just so you know, I sent a message to Eisenhower requesting info about the Night Gentleman."

"Good. I was actually considering doing the same. Let's hope he responds quickly."

"Let's hope," I agreed.

When I finally returned to the living room, I wore a silver and green lamé gown trimmed with pearls, and a matching headscarf. My partner had not moved. The sandwich's paper wrapping was on the coffee table, but otherwise the scene was exactly the same as when I'd left.

A knock on the front door broke the quiet in our Parisian home.

"Oh, no, Gaige, don't trouble yourself," I muttered when he didn't even acknowledge the sound.

"You got it? Thanks, Stass."

The door opened before I reached it. Ines swept in, wearing a daring backless gown of black silk.

"The car is waiting, if you are both ready?" she asked.

I looked to Gaige, since he was the one with his eyes glued to a book.

"Sorry. Are you talking to me?" he said. "Yeah, I'm ready. Oh, wow, Ines, you look great. You too, Stass."

"Thanks for noticing," I said dryly.

A black Rolls-Royce idled on the street in front of our townhouse. Jacque greeted us each formally as he held the back door open.

During the ride, Ines wasn't her usually chatty self. Unsurprisingly, she chained smoked the whole way, managing to suck down two cigarettes on the quick trip. Our guide's obvious anxiety had me glancing over my shoulder as if something or someone might attack me at any moment. Her demeanor improved slightly when the Rolls pulled up in front of a beautiful red and gold theater with *Exotique* spelled out in bright white lights. In contrast to the previous night's club, the sidewalk in front of the theater was teeming with eager men and women.

Starting for the end of the line, I pulled my shawl up to cover my shoulders against the brisk air.

"Stassi, dear, this way!" Ines called after me.

I turned and saw that she and Gaige were heading in the opposite direction. Ines had her arm looped through my partner's. The two made a striking pair. The carefree smile that our guide wore like armor was firmly back in place.

We made our way through the crowd to the front of the line. Ines spoke to the slimmer of the two doormen. When she presented our tickets, the bouncer nodded and unhooked one end of the rope.

"Come along, dear," Ines called, waving me forward with her cigarette hand.

"Enjoy the show, Mademoiselle Prince," the bouncer said as I hurried to catch up with Gaige and Ines.

"Th-thank you," I stuttered in surprise.

What did Ines tell him about me? I wondered.

Somehow, the lobby was even more crowded than the sidewalk. Waiters wove seamlessly through the theater patrons, carrying silver trays with champagne flutes and hors d'oeuvres. Young woman in gold and red quintessentially flapper-style outfits sold cigarettes from trays hanging around their necks.

I took in the festive scene before me, feeling like an extra in the *Gatsby* movie we'd watched with Molly. Smoke curled around the ornate light fixtures, an ominous gray haze hanging over the celebratory night like a storm cloud about to burst. A chill ran up my spine, despite the considerably warmer temperature inside the theater.

"Ah, champagne, merci, merci," Ines cooed, snagging two flutes from a passing tray and handing them to us. "One more, love," she added when the waiter started to move away. He paused long enough for her to claim the remaining glass, and then bowed his apologies. Ines ignored the gesture and turned back to us.

"A toast," Ines declared, raising her glass. "To an exotic night of fabulous entertainment."

Gaige touched his glass to hers. "Here, here," he said.

"Here, here," I echoed, doing the same.

The effervescent bubbles made my nose tingle. Ines was blatantly scoping out the room, doubtlessly cataloguing each of the attendees.

"Not to be rude…," I began.

Gaige snorted. "Which means you're about to be rude," he teased.

I shot him a pointed look. "No, I'm just wondering what we're doing here. This isn't vacation, we're here on business."

"Of course, of course," Ines agreed, taking another sip of champagne as she returned her attention to us. Two red lipstick marks stained the rim of the glass when she was done. "And business, as you say, is why we are here." She waved her cigarette hand lazily, the lit end just missing the coat of an older gentleman passing by.

"Seriously? We saw Rosenthal today, and I didn't really get the pulling-rabbits-from-hats vibe from him," I replied.

"Vibe?" Ines asked, confusion pursing her bright red lips.

"My apologies," I said, remembering my diction. "What I meant to say is that he does not seem the sort to attend an event such as this."

"Ordinarily, I'd agree with you," Ines said. "However, I happen to have it on good authority that your target was sent tickets to tonight's show. A mutual friend of ours owns this theater, and told me that he personally had two tickets messengered over yesterday."

"And you think Rosenthal will actually attend?" Gaige asked doubtfully.

"I was just looking for him," she replied and resumed crowd-scanning.

While she and Gaige perused the faces in the lobby, I leisurely sipped my champagne and let them do the work.

"He is already here," Ines proclaimed triumphantly, pointing. On Rosenthal's arm was a beautiful olive-skinned woman with sleek chocolate waves hanging down to her waist. A short, crimson dress showed off the woman's tanned, toned legs. They were dancer's legs.

Carmen D'Angelo, I thought.

"Andre, dear, over here!" Ines called, waving that damned cigarette wildly about. "And you brought Carmen, how lovely."

The lights in the lobby flickered, and a male voice boomed over unseen speakers.

"The Rochette Theater is pleased to welcome you all. The doors are now open, and we ask that you find your seats so that we may begin tonight's performance. Prepare to be entertained!" the voice thundered in French, the English translation playing in my ear.

Doors at the back of the lobby banged open, though no ushers or theater workers seemed to be standing on either side. Applause rang out from those gathered, as if this was the first illusion of the evening. I clapped politely, though I wasn't nearly as impressed as the rest of the audience. I'd seen true magic. I'd also seen automated doors.

Rosenthal and Carmen made their way over as we joined the line to enter the theater. Ines attempted to make introductions, but the conversations taking place all around us were too loud to hear what she said. I smiled and nodded like I understood anyway, shaking hands with both the author and his date when the time came.

"Fancy running into you here." The voice was deep, sensual, and oddly familiar.

Startled, I spun around.

"Mademoiselle Prince, you look lovely this evening. May I escort you to your seat?" Charles DuPree asked, offering me his arm.

"Sure," I mumbled.

Why could I only manage one-syllable words around this guy?

I cleared my throat and raised my voice. "Excuse me, you startled me, Mr. DuPree. What I meant to say was, yes, that would be fine."

And now I sound like an uptight character from an Austen novel. Way to go, Stassi.

Charles's golden-brown eyes sparkled with amusement. Trying not to blush, I slipped my hand through the crook of his waiting arm. The people in front of us were moving nowhere fast, leaving me scrambling to fill the conversational void.

"I see your brother has found his pet," Charles noted, nodding ahead of us to where Gaige was leaning over and talking into Rosenthal's ear.

I had to suppress a groan. My poor choice of words during our dance the previous night was going to come back and bite me in the ass.

"Gaige is a huge fan of Mr. Rosenthal's work," I said. "We actually saw him earlier today. In fact, he even bought us a round of drinks."

One of Charles's light eyebrows winged upwards. "You must have made quite the impression, Andy is not usually so outgoing."

"Andy? Is that like when you called Gertrude Stein 'Gertie'? Or does Mr. Rosenthal prefer the nickname?" I asked.

"Perhaps you should continue to call him 'Mr. Rosenthal'," Charles replied, grinning down at me.

Suddenly, my throat felt extremely dry. I gulped champagne, swallowing nearly half the glass. Immediately, my head began to spin. I coughed as the liquid scorched my throat. Ever the gentleman, Charles rubbed my back between my shoulder blades with one hand. With the other, he withdrew a scarlet and gray handkerchief from his breast pocket. He brushed the cool, silky fabric over my hand to wipe away the stray droplets. A shiver ran down my spine when our skin made contact.

Lock it up. Lock it up right now, I commanded myself, as if sheer willpower alone could prevent my body from reacting to his touch. Gaige was right—I needed to start dating in our time. Maybe then I wouldn't melt every time a handsome man was near me.

Just then, Rosenthal turned to look over his shoulder, causing his glasses to slip down his nose.

"Charles, there you are," Rosenthal said pleasantly. "We looked for you when we arrived, you must have been hiding."

"No, sir, just late. I had some matters to attend to," Charles explained, his tone deferential and devoid of the playfulness he used in our banter. Turning his attention to Rosenthal's date, Charles took her hand and brought it to his lips. "Mademoiselle D'Angelo, wonderful to see you, as always. What fortune that you have the evening off."

Carmen D'Angelo was more stunning up close than her pictures had let on. Her voice was deep and rich, like dark roast coffee for the ears.

"You as well, Mr. DuPree. It is a rare occasion that I am on this side of the stage. My own show was canceled this evening. Our stage manager says these murders have people scared to leave their homes." Glancing around at the full theater, she added, "Though you would not know from this crowd."

"Carmen is an exceedingly talented dance," Charles explained to me. "Her show, Danza de los Flamingos, is simply the best in Paris. We must go while you are here."

His use of the word "we" was disarming.

"You are too kind," Carmen said demurely, though it was obvious she enjoyed the accolades. I'd learned enough about her to know that complimenting the dancer was easily the quickest way to friendship.

"Apologies, I've forgotten my manners. Carmen D'Angelo this is Anastasia Prince. Mademoiselle Prince is visiting our beloved city from America."

"Charmed," she replied, eyeing me up and down.

"It is lovely to meet you," I said warmly. "I am quite looking forward to seeing your show, I've heard many praises of your talents."

Carmen's false smile immediately turned genuine. Unfortunately, her response was cut off when an usher appeared by my side.

"May I help you find your seats?" he asked brusquely. "The show is about to begin."

Ines produced our tickets from her beaded clutch and showed him our seat numbers.

"Right this way," he replied, his tone noticeably more respectful.

Leaning down so as not to be overheard, Charles whispered in my ear, "It appears you rate highly, Miss Prince." His lips almost brushed my skin when he spoke, sending another pleasant tingle through my body.

The interior of the theater was grandiose, opulent to the extreme. Plush crimson seats were trimmed with gold brocade. Gothic-style light fixtures with electric candles cast an orange-red glow down over the crowd, creating a decidedly creepy ambiance. The brass railings on the balcony level were polished and gleaming to perfection.

Our group, including Charles, followed the usher straight to the area directly in front of the stage. A braided gold rope cordoned off small sitting areas with red velvet couches and matching armchairs. On the table in front of the couch we stopped at was a *Rèservation pour Callandries* sign.

"Your champagne will be delivered straightaway," the usher told us. "All other beverages can be ordered through your waiter. Please enjoy the show."

Ines thanked him as the rest of us filed into our seats. Gaige managed to wiggle his way to Rosenthal's side. Carmen was then relegated to the corner of the couch, a position I was sure she was neither accustomed to nor appreciated.

I sat on Gaige's other side, so that I could eavesdrop on his conversation with Rosenthal. To my surprise, Charles settled in beside me. The couch was large enough to comfortably accommodate all five of us, though having mere inches between Charles and myself was not what I'd expected of the evening.

"I wasn't aware you were joining us," I said plainly. It was a rude statement, but his nearness had caught me off guard.

"I hope you find this a pleasant surprise," Charles replied, cocking one eyebrow.

"I have met so few people in Paris, it is always nice to be in the company of a familiar face," I said, drawing on every ounce of my etiquette training.

"Why Miss Prince, I do believe you would have made an excellent courtesan."

That's an odd choice of words, I thought. *Wait. Did he just call me a prostitute?*

The house lights began to dim, growing fainter until we were shrouded in darkness. Soft, eerie music played, increasing in volume and tempo with each passing heartbeat. Cymbals crashed and a spotlight appeared in the center of the stage. It blinked from white to yellow to orange, before settling finally on red. When the crimson orb appeared, so did a caricature of a man. He was impossibly tall, as if standing on stilts. His black top hat added another six inches to an already impressive height. A handlebar mustache curled across his cheeks and hung down from either side of his face like ribbons on a birthday present. The gold bowtie around his neck stretched from ear to ear. A red dinner jacket with black lapels and striped red, black, and gold pants completed the ensemble.

"Prepare to be entertained!" the emcee boomed into the microphone. "My name is Vladimir, the Viscount of Villainy, the Father of Fear, the Ringleader of Risqué. I will be your host for the evening. We have prepared a special show for tonight. It will shock you. It will amaze you." Vladimir narrowed his eyes and panned the audience. "It will terrify you. Just remember one thing." He held up one finger, paused, and then threw his arms up in the air. "It is all an illusion!" he cried.

The audience's applause was deafening, as if he'd actually done something worth clapping for, instead of merely introducing himself in grandiose fashion. Vlad beamed, drinking in the praise with all the humility of a man accustomed to the spotlight. When the applause died down, the host continued to grin like a fool until it became awkward. I began to squirm in my seat. Finally, the emcee's expression faltered. His smile vanished, and he became alarmingly serious. The man curled into himself, curving his spine to the point he bore a striking resemblance to the hunchback of Notre Dame.

In a stage whisper meant to inspire fear, Vladimir the Vexing—two could play the alliteration game—said, "Or is it?" And the audience went wild.

The show continued in a similar fashion.

Good ole Vlad presented each act with the same vigor he'd used while introducing himself. Every entertainer had a name like Ballantine the Beautiful, Katya the Contortionist, and Niccoli the Neanderthal. Each performance took the trickery to the next level. It started with a run-of-the-mill illusionist named Miguel the Malevolent. His most impressive trick was disappearing from the stage and reappearing overhead on a zipline that ran from one end of the theater to the other.

The last act before intermission was that of Tai Wei Jong, a Chinese dwarf with the skill and grace of an Olympic gymnast. He tumbled across the stage, performing gravity-defying acrobatics as he traversed an obstacle course made up of replicas of the manmade wonders of the Western world: The Eiffel Tower, The Statue of Liberty, Big Ben, and the Colosseum from ancient Rome. The act reminded me of parkour, though the training discipline was over half a century away from becoming popular. Tai Wei's performance was by far the most impressive, despite being the least magical. He received a standing ovation and thunderous applause that shook the very foundation of the theater.

During intermission, my little band of friends discussed the acts we'd seen thus far. Ines and Carmen spoke animatedly about their favorites. Charles proffered guesses as to how the stunts were really done, since the notion of magic was not one he bought into. Naturally, Gaige insisted on playing devil's advocate, poking holes in each of Charles's theories. Then he went a step farther, suggesting ridiculous alternatives. Each one was more outrageous than the one before it.

When Gaige suggested that Tai Wei had been bitten by a radioactive spider and could now shoot webbing from his wrists, which he used to swing from one miniature building to the next, I kicked him in the shin.

"What a delightful idea for a novel!" Ines trilled.

"We could call him Arachnidman," Rosenthal suggested with a chuckle.

"Yes!" Gaige exclaimed. "Just make sure you credit me in the acknowledgments."

Rosenthal raised his champagne flute in toast to my partner. "You have my word, Mr. Prince," he said solemnly.

"Are you serious right now, Gaige? You just put a major would-be comic book franchise out of business," I mumbled under my breath.

Unfazed, my partner simply gave me a wink.

He leaned over and spoke directly into my ear. "Keep them talking, I have to go to the little runner's room." Standing and speaking loud enough for everyone else to hear, Gaige said, "If you will all excuse me."

Charles and I stood to let Gaige pass.

On stage, cabaret dancers were performing to the tune of a jazz band playing from the orchestra pit. Carmen critiqued their moves, declaring the simple dance steps to be "pedestrian" and "amateur".

"Not everyone has your skill, Carmen, dear," Rosenthal said, patting her exposed thigh.

Andre Rosenthal may be a shy recluse, but he likes his women bold, I thought.

"She's bitter because she auditioned for this show and was turned down," Charles whispered in my ear.

I laughed. "Explains a lot," I whispered back.

"In her defense, Carmen is quite talented," Charles continued. "I truly would be honored to escort you to her show. Once it reopens, that is."

"I'm sure the police will catch the Night Gentleman soon," I said absently.

They had to. Otherwise, Historian Eisenhower would have warned us about him, just like Gaige said.

Then it hit me: Charles DuPree had just asked me on a date. The fact pleased me way more than it should have, since improving my social life was not the reason I'd come to Paris. I could hear Gaige now: *Stassi and Charles sitting in a tree, k-i-s-s-i-n-g.*

Thankfully, my partner was still gone and not eavesdropping on my conversation.

"Your brother would be welcome to join us, of course," Charles was saying. "I understand if you would like to have a chaperone. I would not want to besmirch your honor."

He followed up the comment with a sly grin and wink. I had a feeling that, given the opportunity, Charles DuPree would jump at the chance to besmirch my honor.

Heat rushed to my cheeks. Thankfully, at that moment, Ines chose to include me in her conversation.

"Carmen was just saying that her show will be playing on Broadway next year. I told her that she simply had to talk to you, since you have spent time up in New York City."

Yes, 2087 New York City, which is very different from 1926 New York City, I thought.

"I said she needs to visit Hollywood," Rosenthal interjected. "I do believe film will be very popular in the future, and Carmen is made for the pictures."

Thanks to Molly's love of old movies, I actually knew quite a bit about the rise of the film industry and felt a lot more comfortable talking about that than underground clubs and "it" restaurants in prohibition-era New York City. Charles, too, seemed to have an interest in movies. He apparently had a fondness for both Charlie Chaplin and the relatively unknown Greta Garbo.

Charles and I became caught up in conversation with the rest of the group, and I was spared the embarrassment of more alone time with him.

Gaige rushed back to his seat just as the house lights dimmed once more, signaling the start of the second act. When the spotlight reappeared center stage, Vlad was nowhere to be seen. In his place was a woman with fire engine red hair and milky white skin. She wore a bandeau top made of gold coins and baggy, translucent pants held in place by a belt made of the same.

Slow, sensual music started playing. I wondered uncomfortably what turn the night was about to take. *Exotique* was known to be risqué and allegedly pushed the envelope, according to my Parisian companions. Being wedged in between Gaige and a handsome stranger for a salacious show was not ideal. Ignoring the awkwardness, I pasted a pleasant smile on my face and watched candidly.

Sparkly gold eye shadow was painted across the woman's closed lids. Long, dark lashes fanned across her cheeks like spider's legs. Being so close to the stage, I saw them twitch in time to the music as if they had a life of their own. Painted golden flames covered her bare arms and stomach. When she began to move, they appeared to dance across her skin. Wrapping her arms around her midsection, she swayed back and forth, her eyes still closed. Then, from behind her back, she produced two batons, which she twirled and flipped as she floated across the stage. Her movements were fluid, one flowing into the next as easily as water flows over the falls.

The dancer was truly hypnotic to watch. I found myself unable to look away, despite my misgivings about this being a strip show. A man, whose resemblance to the woman was so close they had to be twins, soon joined the redheaded dancer. They were two halves of a whole, moving together as one graceful being to tell a story with their bodies. Behind me, the audience oohed and awed as the couple performed.

My twin theory fizzled when the man dipped the woman low. He brought her back up slowly, his eyes locked with hers, then kissed her deeply. The tempo of the music increased as the couple broke apart, the drumbeat and rhythm giving off a tribal feel.

With one last hungry look at each another, the dancers turned to face the audience, grinning and glowing like twin suns. At some point during the performance, the woman had transferred one of her batons to the man. They each held up the prop in front of them and inhaled dramatically as one, as if to suck in all of the air in the theater. When they blew out their collective breaths, flames erupted from between their lips. The ends of the batons caught fire.

"Shite!" Gaige exclaimed.

"Fascinating," Charles declared, true awe evident in his voice.

This time, when the crowd went wild, I joined them. I had a sneaking suspicion that I knew how the trick was performed—a spark at the end of the baton must have been lit by an accelerant he transferred to her mouth—but that didn't lessen the wow-factor of it all.

Launching into a tap number that was more appropriate with the background music, the couple began dancing with their fiery batons. The audience continued to cheer, clapping in time with the beat.

But, somehow, the performance seemed off. The woman's movements became slower. Her feet barely left the stage. Her arms seemed too heavy, like a windup toy that was losing steam. Someone needed to turn her key. The dancer's cheeks, flushed from the vigorous exercise, went from a pretty pale pink to an alarming shade of purple in the literal blink of an eye.

Immediately, I knew something was wrong.

Twisting an ankle, the dancer fell to her hands and knees with her head bowed down. The fiery baton flew from her hand and skittered across the stage, the flame extinguishing before it came to a stop.

I grabbed Charles's arm. "She's hurt," I cried over the cheers of a crowd who seemed to believe this was all part of the act.

He patted my hand and whispered in my ear, his words confirming my suspicions. "This is part of the show, do not worry," Charles assured me.

Hands clutching her throat, the woman threw her head back violently. The audience gasped. Her eyes, bloodshot and terrified, were bugging out of her face. Veins in her forehead and cheeks protruded from beneath her skin like a grotesque roadmap to hell. Beside her, the man face-planted onto the stage. His baton landed with a thud beside him, continued to burn for several agonizing seconds, and then mercifully went out.

"Don't look," Charles barked in my ear. He placed a hand on my cheek and turned me to face him. His gold-flecked eyes were alight with fear, though his voice was calm and cool. "Do not look," he repeated in a gentler tone.

Staring into his eyes, the sound of men shouting and women crying all seemed far away. I forced myself to hold Charles's gaze, scared to close my eyes for fear I'd see the dancer's disfigured face. His lips moved, but the words never reached my ears. His thumb stroked my cheek soothingly. I clung to his arm with a white-knuckled grip.

Crackles of static were followed by a shrieking reverberation of the microphones. A rhythmic tapping noise came next. The air in the theater stilled, as if time was frozen.

"Hello! Bonjour! Hola! Konnichiwa! Hallo!" a male voice roared. The theater's superior acoustics amplified the words, making them ring in my head over and over again. "I hope tonight's performance was as eye-popping for you as it was for me." The voice cackled manically, like every super-villain from every campy comic book movie that had yet to be filmed. "Let us give our fire dancers a hand, folks. They truly brought the house down."

The Night Gentleman? I wondered. Because there was no way that anyone officially linked with the show could make light of the tragedy on the stage.

After a long pause, when no applause came, the voice called one final line.

"Are you not amused? I know I am."

SEVENTEEN

DURING MY TIME as a runner, I'd encountered numerous difficult situations: Napoleon's henchmen, angry wives, irate husbands, suspicious referees, accusatory townsfolk, and even one sadistic inquisitor who accused me of being a heretic. But never had I matched wits with a homicide investigator. I could say with absolute certainty that I hoped this would be the one and only time.

"We arrived in Paris *yesterday*," I said for the umpteenth time.

Inspector Dog Poo for Brains stared at me across the metal interrogation table.

The French police had arrived not long after the macabre announcement over the loudspeakers and quickly rounded up all of the remaining theatergoers for questioning. Once they'd given witness statements, most attendees were released with the caveat that they be available for further questioning should the need arise.

Unfortunately, we were not included within that group. Something in my statement had apparently sparked suspicion, because the lead inspector requested my presence at the Préfecture de police de Paris for a more thorough interview. And not just me. Gaige was in the adjacent interrogation room, probably answering the same redundant questions.

Though not suspects, Charles and Ines had readily accompanied us to the station. Carmen was so distraught over witnessing the dancers' deaths that Rosenthal had insisted on taking her home. Nevertheless, he promised to wait by his phone if we needed help of the legal variety. Evidently he kept someone on retainer.

"Mademoiselle Prince," the inspector began again, his English heavy with a French accent. "You say that you arrived yesterday—"

"Because I *did*," I insisted.

"But you have no documentation to back up your claims," he finished as if I hadn't spoken. "You must understand how that appears, no?"

"Of course I don't have it *with* me. Who carries their travel papers along to the theater?" I sighed. "I told you—if you let me go to the townhome I'm staying in, I can show you my tickets for both the ship from Baltimore and the train we took from London."

Of course this wasn't exactly true, since Gaige and I had traveled to Paris from the future. But that wasn't going to fly. I'd be carted off to some looney bin before I could say vortex. Thankfully, Pierre could create false documents capable of passing even the toughest scrutiny, given some time.

"Ah, yes," the inspector picked up. "Let us revisit your mode of transportation. You say you sailed to London, then trained over to the continent?"

I was on shaky ground here. The cover story we'd concocted hadn't included travel details, since police interrogation was not something we had anticipated. Gaige and I had been separated immediately upon arriving at the station, and there hadn't been time to get our stories straight. Saying we arrived in Paris by way of London seemed like the best course of action, since it would take the inspector a lot of time to check that fact. Time that Gaige and I could use to leave Paris. If ever there was a reason to abandon an assignment, this was it.

"Yes, that is what I said," I snapped. "Because that is what happened."

Pen poised over a small notepad, the inspector smiled indulgently.

"Mademoiselle Prince, let us try the truth this time, shall we? I care not whether you arrived illegally, only whether you and your brother are involved in the murders."

The truth? The truth was we came to Paris via a vortex, arrived in an underground customs station, and spent the last two days stalking a writer whose manuscript we intended to steal. Yeah, the truth was going to go over *so* well.

"Do I need a lawyer? I believe I want a lawyer," I said instead. "Or better yet, I believe I would like to leave now. You have no evidence of any wrongdoing, because I committed no such act. I am here only as a courtesy, and I have answered your questions to the best of my ability. Now I wish to go home."

The inspector gritted his teeth. He made a notation on his pad, pressing the fountain pen so firmly against the paper that it was wonder the tip didn't crack off.

"Fine, Mademoiselle, you may go. For now. However, I would appreciate it if you remained in Paris while we verify your passage. Perhaps you and I will speak again."

"I look forward to it," I said, smiling triumphantly. "By which, I mean that I look forward to your department's formal apology for this egregious error."

Head held high, I stood and strode to the door without a backward glance at the inspector.

In the lobby, Ines was sitting in an uncomfortable looking chair, smoking and tapping her foot impatiently. Charles stood in the corner at the telephone stand, with his back to the room and the receiver to his ear.

"Stassi, love, there you are!" Ines exclaimed when she saw me. She crushed her cigarette into a nearby ashtray and jumped to her feet, arms spread wide for a hug.

Numb from the long night and still in shock over having had a front row seat to a double homicide, I walked into her arms and let her hold me. Ines patted my back and murmured soothing words into my ear in French. Over her shoulder, I saw Charles slam down the phone receiver and spin to face me. The relief and concern in his eyes was touching. Suddenly, the full impact of the night's events hit me. I felt an overwhelming urge to burst into tears. How had things become so messed up?

Ines stepped back, holding me at arm's length and searching for signs of damage.

"Was it just awful? That horrible little inspector man is such a fool. How anyone could think you had something to do with these tragic deaths is beyond me. Let's get you home. A stiff drink and a hot bath will do wonders."

A glass of wine and a bubble bath sounded pretty amazing, but I doubted either would erase the image of the dancer's bloated, purple face from my mind. Maybe five or six glasses. Of scotch.

"I have called my family lawyer," Charles said, coming to stand beside me. "He does not usually handle criminal proceedings, but is willing to stand in until we find one who does."

"Thank you, Mr. DuPree. That is very kind. Thankfully, I do not believe it will come to that," I said pointedly, my gaze fixed on Ines.

The alchemist's nod was almost imperceptible.

"Of course not. We will show them your travel documents and that will clear up this nightmare," she assured me, for Charles's sake. In a louder voice, one that rang throughout the entire lobby and probably even back to the holding cells, Ines added, "And then we will expect a formal, public apology for your treatment of my dear friends."

"Wait. Where's Gaige?" I asked, realizing for the first time he was nowhere to be seen.

Ines averted her gaze, focusing now on Charles instead of me.

"They're still questioning him. At this point, he is their prime suspect," Charles answered after a long, painful pause.

"Excuse me?" I practically shrieked, sure I'd misheard him. "For what? They have no evidence. This is insanity."

"He left the theater to use the facilities during intermission, and a witness is claiming that he saw your brother near the dressing rooms," Charles explained.

"That means nothing," I said defensively. "He was sitting right beside me when that freak gave his speech. You both saw him. Did you tell the police that you saw him?"

My voice was pleading, begging them to help clear up this unbelievable nightmare. It was the sort of thing that veteran runners warned newbies about. The sort of thing we were cautioned to avoid at all costs. The sort of thing that could irrevocably change history.

Cue more uneasy glances between Charles and Ines.

"What?" I snapped. Having reached my daily limit on social pleasantries, I didn't care that I was being rude.

"It was an audience member," Charles said finally. "What we heard over the speaker was a man from the audience reading from a script—he thought it was part of the show. You know, a side bit where they use audience participation. He told the police that a man approached him during intermission and asked if he'd like to be part of the show."

"So shouldn't that man be able to clear my brother?" I reasoned. "Wouldn't he be able to say it was not Gaige who asked him to do that?"

"I am afraid the man with the script had dark hair, and was wearing a tuxedo and a mask," Ines said slowly. "It could have been anyone."

"So then why all the interest in Gaige?" I demanded.

"Because…," Ines began reluctantly.

"Because the man in the mask had an accent," Charles finished after another awkward silence. "An American accent, to be precise."

"And there were only a handful of men who gave statements at the theater with an American accent. Gaige, of course, being one of those few. Between that and the witness who claims to have seen your brother backstage during intermission…," Ines again trailed off.

My head began to spin. This was bad. Very, very bad. *So* very, very bad. I felt lost and completely alone.

Charles wrapped an arm around my waist and led me to chair.

"That's hardly proof," I said weakly as he lowered me into the seat.

"Ines, would you fetch a glass of water, please?" Charles said.

The customs agent hurried over to a desk worker. "You there, fetch a glass of water," she called loudly, as if she owned the place.

Easing into the seat beside mine, Charles put his arm around my shoulders. The other gently held my hand in the space between us, though I hardly noticed.

"They have arranged for a suspect line-up tomorrow afternoon," Charles explained quietly. "I have spoken on your brother's behalf, so he will be allowed to go home tonight. But only with the promise that we will indeed return tomorrow. We are also to bring your passage receipts. Once you show the inspector your travel documents, this will all be forgotten. Ancient history."

"Ancient history," I parroted.

Which was precisely the problem. Our detainments were now a part of history. It was impossible to know what ripple effects would originate from this incident.

"You vouched for him?" I asked, for lack of something better to say.

If I just kept talking, I wouldn't have to think about the potential fallout from this mix-up.

Charles squirmed uncomfortably. "Well, yes, I did."

"That was very generous of you," I replied absently. "What precisely does that mean?"

He patted my back. "It is nothing more than a formality. I declared that I know him and assured the police of his veracity. Simply put, I swore on my reputation that your brother would return tomorrow. He will be released any minute now, and then we should get you both home."

"Home," I agreed.

I wanted to go home. My *real* home, on the island, not the alchemist townhouse. I wanted to see Cyrus and have him fix everything. Because that's what my boss did. He could dispatch a cleanup crew to fix this mess—it was their area of expertise, after all. They mended history after runners broke it.

When Gaige finally emerged from the interrogation room, I jumped up and squeezed him with all of my might. As long as the two of us were together, we could get the hell out of Paris and return to Branson. Though a glance at Charles brought an immense amount of guilt. Would he get in trouble for vouching for someone who then disappeared? What would his punishment be?

Charles wanted to ride with us back to the townhouse, to be sure we made it home safely. He only backed down when Gaige promised him that Ines and I were in good hands, and we would be returning directly to the townhouse. With a promise to see me the next day, Charles held my gaze as he brushed his lips gently across the back of my hand. Another pang of guilt came with his kiss.

"No more surprises," Gaige declared as soon as we were in the backseat of the Rolls, Jacque behind the wheel. "We send another message through tonight, and leave in the morning if we haven't heard back by then. Ines, we need you to go speak with the forger. Tell him to prepare our papers, just in case."

As though Gaige's declaration had summoned it, one hell of a surprise was waiting in the living room of our Parisian home.

EIGHTEEN

THIS SURPRISE WAS actually a good one. A *really* good one, in my opinion.

Cyrus was sitting on the couch when we walked through the front door. He stood as soon as we entered.

"You came!" I exclaimed, crossing the living room and throwing myself at my boss.

"Stassi, what's wrong?" Cyrus asked, his voice thin and strained.

At first, he simply patted my back awkwardly. When I didn't immediately move away, Cyrus squeezed me tightly against his chest. That was when I realized the error of my ways. Since physical displays of emotion were unusual for me, not to mention the fact that Cyrus was my boss, I'd never shared more than a handshake with him.

"Oh, shite. I'm so sorry, Cyrus." I scrambled backward, feeling mortified. Running a hand over my mussed hair, I scrambled for an eloquent excuse. Nothing came to mind so I simply repeated, "I'm sorry."

Cyrus reached out and took both my hands between his.

"It's okay, it's okay," he assured me, worry creasing his brow. "But you need to tell me what happened, Stassi. What's wrong?"

Refusing to meet his gaze, I mumbled, "Everything."

My boss chuckled softly, easing the tension in the room. "When did you become the drama queen? Hmmm? That's usually Gaige's role."

"Thank you for coming, sir," Gaige said from behind me. His lack of a snarky response to Cyrus's jibe about being a drama queen showed just how serious the situation was.

Apparently, Cyrus agreed. He appeared alarmed by my partner's somber mood.

"Clearly, I am missing something. Stassi is shaking and," he placed one finger under my chin and forced my head upwards, "it appears she's been crying. You," he nodded towards Gaige, "are wearing the same expression as when I told you the canteen would no longer being carrying grape milk. Did something happen?"

"Isn't that why you're here, sir?" Gaige asked, sounding perplexed.

I heard the front door open again. Ines rushed into the room, out of breath.

"I woke Pierre, he is starting on your papers at once. I also had the transport—" Ines abruptly halted when she saw Cyrus. Her authoritative air immediately vanished, replaced with a deferential tone in her voice. "My apologies, sir. I did not know you were here. It is an honor to meet you, my name is Ines Callandries."

"Cyrus Atlic," my boss said, extending his hand to shake hers.

"I-I know, sir," Ines stuttered. "You are the Founder of the syndicates."

Cyrus merely nodded in response to the alchemist as he gently guided me to the sofa and gestured for me to sit. Ines and Gaige joined us. The alchemist was noticeably ill at ease.

Expression weary, Cyrus ran a hand down his face and sighed loudly.

"So, the reason I am here," Cyrus started, picking back up with

Gaige's question before Ines's entrance. "Well, it seems we have a situation…. A missing runner, to be exact."

"Missing runner?" Gaige and I replied in unison.

We exchanged uneasy glances as my chest tightened. Ines lit a cigarette with trembling hands. Our boss studied us each in turn, then reached for a leather portfolio sitting on the coffee table.

"I'm afraid so. Bane Montgomery, head of the Montgomery Syndicate, paid me a visit today. One of his runners took vacation leave about three weeks ago, but never returned." Cyrus flipped open the folder and withdrew a glossy headshot. The man looked to be in his mid-twenties, with black hair and smoky gray eyes. "Do any of you recognize him?" He held the photo up to each of us in turn.

I shook my head. Gaige stared thoughtfully at the photograph, then mimicked my gesture.

"I'm sorry, sir," he finally said. "The guy doesn't look familiar."

We all turned to Ines. Her skin had gone from pale ivory to a shade of green most could only achieve with heavy stage makeup. I felt a fleeting pang of sympathy for the customs agent. All of this had to be nightmare for her, too. A rogue runner wreaking havoc in the city on her watch didn't look so good.

Apparently Ines was still uncomfortable in the presence of such greatness—if I didn't see Cyrus on a regular basis, I'd probably react the same way—because she managed only a jerky headshake as she continued to suck on her cigarette.

Cyrus sighed.

"Ah, well, it was worth a shot." He set the picture on the coffee table before continuing. "His name is Lachlan Shepard, and he's been a runner for the Montgomery Syndicate for five years. Besides a couple of minor infractions, he's never caused any real trouble. Until now, that is."

Lachlan Shepard's personnel file was visible inside the leather folio, but Cyrus never once consulted the printed pages as he spoke.

"When he failed to return from vacation, Bane had a lengthy talk with Shepard's partner about his trip plans. Bane discovered that Shepard is here, now. If his partner is correct, Shepard is in clear violation of Mandate 4.43," Cyrus continued.

Mandate 4.43 was the one about not performing unsanctioned runs.

Along with an awesome salary, beautiful island home, and the chance to touch history, one of the perks of being a runner was the ability to vacation in time periods that interested us. There was some fine print in the mandates about how many time tourism trips a runner could make, and even finer print outlining inter-syndicate travel—trips made outside the territory of the runner's home syndicate. Both the runner's boss and the head of the syndicate whose territory the runner wished to visit needed to approve the request. Judging by Cyrus's angry tone and fierce expression, I was guessing Lachlan did not ask his permission to vacation in the Atlic territory.

"Whoa," Gaige whistled. "What's the penalty on that?"

"Without question, he'll receive an unpaid suspension and a sizeable fine. Shepard will also be on probation for the foreseeable future. Depending on the circumstances and situation, exile is another possibility."

"How did he enter the area?" Ines spoke up. "We would have known if he came through customs."

"We believe he used the catacombs," Cyrus explained, referring to the endless miles of tunnels beneath the streets of Paris. "There are pockets of *prima* down there, so it's not unlike jumping through an actual gate. Many of the passageways are deserted; he could have come through without anyone the wiser. Or, there is always the chance he free jumped. If that's the case, it is even more imperative that I locate Shepard immediately. He may be suffering from extreme time sickness and in need of medical attention."

When none of us responded to this, Cyrus glanced between us again.

"You guys don't know anything about this, do you?" he asked.

"No, sir. This is the first we've heard of another runner being here," I answered.

"So then what has you all worked up?"

Eyebrows raised in question, I looked to Gaige for the answer. My partner wrung his hands in his lap, clearly reluctant to tell our boss about his predicament.

"Have you heard of the Night Gentleman?" I started. "The serial killer who modeled his murders after a comic book character named Fantômas?"

"No," my boss replied uncertainly. "When and where was he active?"

"Now," I said plainly. "Here."

"There are no serial killers operating in this time and location," Cyrus said, his tone definitive.

My stomach dropped. Cyrus's statement confirmed the fear that'd been lingering in the back of my mind. The Night Gentleman wasn't a part of history as we knew it.

"This is not possible. You must be mistaken, Cyrus," Ines said, her high-pitched giggle a mixture of stress and disbelief, as if our boss was playing a joke on us.

"I am certainly *not* mistaken, Ines," Cyrus replied, his tone deadly serious. "We make it our business to know about each and every killer who has ever been active in our territory. Because they are unpredictable, we actively avoid crossing paths with them. There has never been a man named the Night Gentleman killing in Paris."

Silence descended on our group.

"Do you think Lachlan might be the Night Gentleman?" I finally asked, giving voice to the theory we were all probably considering.

"Surely not," Ines declared.

"The timing fits," Gaige suggested. "The killer has been active for two or three weeks now. Lachlan's been MIA for three weeks. The math works out."

"And it would really help us out," I added. "If we know who's *actually* killing people, you're off the hook."

"What do you mean?" Cyrus asked with confusion.

"Um, well...I am the chief person of interest for the murders, sir," Gaige replied uneasily. "That's where we've been all night, at the police station answering questions. Technically, I'm only free right now because a member of society vouched for me."

Cyrus leaned back on the couch and crossed his arms over his chest.

"Start at the beginning," he demanded. "Now."

Between the three of us, we told Cyrus everything we knew about the Night Gentleman and the reasons Inspector Dipstick suspected Gaige was the villain. Recounting it to him only bolstered my belief that the evidence was flimsy and circumstantial. My boss listened with a blank expression, quietly digesting the information.

"This certainly is a snag we hadn't anticipated," Cyrus said calmly when we were finished telling our story. He turned to Ines. "All of this needs to be handled with the utmost efficiency and discretion, do you understand? This situation is strictly need-to-know."

Ines nodded.

"Good. Pierre—that is the document specialist at this customs station, correct?"

Ines nodded again.

"I need him down at customs as soon as possible. If he has an apprentice, it might be good to call him in as well. I need several documents completed by morning."

"I will go wake Pierre immediately," Ines told Cyrus.

"Thank you, Ines. I also need you to contact your connections at local hotels, to see if any of them have a Lachlan Shepard registered. There's a good chance he's using an alias, but we have to start somewhere. Check with your police contacts, too, just in case Shepard was arrested. Or, heaven forbid, found dead. As soon as I finish speaking with Stassi and Gaige, I will be down to meet with Pierre and give him specific instructions."

Ines bid us all farewell and left to go about the tasks Cyrus had assigned her.

"We'll see what, if any, leads the alchemists turn up tonight regarding Shepard," Cyrus told Gaige and me once Ines was gone. "I'm going to have Pierre make a time-period-appropriate replica of that photo." He pointed to the picture still on the coffee table. "That way, I have it to show around, if need be. I'm going to have my passport and travel documents made out in the name 'Cyrus Shepard' so that I can pass myself off as the kid's father. It should help in getting some otherwise reluctant hotel staff to talk."

"Do you really think he might be using his own name?" I asked dubiously.

Cyrus shrugged. "I sure as hell hope so. It'll make tracking him down a lot easier. But that's tomorrow's problem. Right now, you both look like you could use some sleep."

"I sure could," Gaige agreed. My partner stood and stretched. "Night, boss. Night, Stass."

I followed suit, thinking sleep was exactly what I needed. Cyrus remained seated, the portfolio still open in his lap. I hesitated for a moment.

"Is there something else bothering you, Stassi?" Cyrus asked.

"Well, actually, I was just wondering how Molly is doing?"

Cyrus smiled. "She's Molly. I stopped by your place before leaving. In one breath, she told me she would never make another run. In the next, she asked if she could come here with me." He laughed softly. "Said she was worried about you being away from home for so long."

It was my turn to laugh. "Yep, sounds like Molly.

We heard the soft click of Gaige's door closing. Cyrus's expression turned serious.

"Stassi, you wanted this assignment pretty badly. Is there something you aren't telling me?" He didn't sound angry, merely interested.

My hand flew instinctively to my necklace and my fingers closed around the locket.

"No, sir. I loved Paris when I came for training, and I've always wanted to come back. This assignment was the opportunity I've been waiting for."

The lie came easily, since it was rooted in truth.

Cyrus studied me for a long moment. "Well, you'll tell me if there is anything I can help you with? I'm already here, after all."

"Of course," I agreed, forcing a smile. "Goodnight, Cyrus."

"'Night, Stassi."

Just as I reached my room, I heard him call up to me.

"Don't worry about Gaige. We'll get this all straightened out in the morning."

I prayed he was right, yet something told me things would get a whole lot worse before they got better.

NINETEEN

I SLEPT LATE the next morning. Cyrus was gone by the time I finally dragged my exhausted self downstairs. Gaige was sitting at the formal dining table, drinking coffee and reading the paper. An uneaten plate of toast, bacon, and hardboiled eggs was pushed off to one side of him, right next to a bouquet of red roses.

"Coffee's in the kitchen," Gaige called without looking up from his paper.

"I take back every mean thing I've said about you in the last week," I said, stifling a yawn. I pointed to the flowers on my way to the kitchen. "Are those for me? You shouldn't have."

"I didn't," Gaige called after me. "They came by messenger first thing this morning. I have a bottle of 2312 Damiani Merlot that says lover boy sent them."

"I think you mean *I* have a 2312 bottle of Damiani Merlot," I shot back.

"Exactly. And if I'm right, I'll be drinking it with my first meal back on the island."

"That wine was a gift from Molly. So, no, I'm not betting with you—you've probably already read the card and know who sent the flowers. I assume by 'lover boy' you mean Charles DuPree. If so, you should be the one sending him flowers, since he did stake his reputation on you showing up at the station today."

"Dudes don't give other dudes flowers, Stass. I'll send him some scotch—that's a manly gift."

I added sugar and cream to a lukewarm cup of coffee, then joined him in the dining room. Gaige plucked a thick manila envelope from the bouquet and tossed it across the table to me. *Anastasia Prince* was scrawled in bold black strokes across the front. The seal was still intact.

"'I'm sorry' are the words you're looking for," Gaige deadpanned, turning back to his newspaper.

The front page of the paper was facing me. Once again, the prominent front page headline was about the Night Gentleman.

"Whatever," I grumbled, sliding my nail along the flap to break the seal.

Inside was a note written on cardstock the same color and quality as the envelope. Smiling, since I figured the flowers had to be from Charles, I began to read.

Roses are red, violets are blue.
Fire is cleansing, yet deadly, too.
Will you find me, before I find you?
All the best,
Mitchell T. Baylarian.

I threw the note on the table, like a potato too hot to hold. Gaige's head shot up, surprise evident in his dark gaze.

"Was he too forward? Too kinky? Did he say he wants to lick your face?" Gaige teased.

"What? Eww. No. It—it's not from Charles," I stammered.

My partner's expression turned serious. "Who is it from?" he asked, his voice low and a little intimidating.

I couldn't bring myself to touch the vile note again. Mitchell T. Baylarian was not a name I recognized, but I had a strong suspicion the sender often went by a different name: The Night Gentleman.

Gaige snatched the note from the table and read it aloud. All the color had drained from his face by the time he reached the last word.

"Frack me!" my partner exclaimed. "You don't…this can't be…is this from *him*?"

I must have started hyperventilating, because the next thing I knew, Gaige was forcing my head between my knees and urging me to breathe slowly.

That was when Cyrus returned. He might have asked if I was okay. He might have said a bomb just detonated on the street in front of the townhouse. My head was spinning too much to be sure of anything in that moment.

"Baylarian has to be Lachlan Shepard, right?" Gaige was saying when I finally felt well enough to sit up straight.

Cyrus had the note in his hand and a grim expression on his face. "It's possible they are one and the same," he admitted. "I'll have the alchemists look into him. If Baylarian is a real person, they'll find him."

My boss sat in the chair next to me, scooting it closer to mine until our knees were touching. "Are you okay, Stassi?" he asked.

"Yeah. Yeah, I'm fine," I replied, waving off his concern. "I'm sorry, I overreacted. It's just, well, I wasn't expecting *that*." I gestured towards the note in Cyrus's hand.

"You have every right to be upset," Cyrus soothed.

"He's right, Stassi," Gaige chimed in. "This whackjob has singled you out."

Emerald daggers shot from Cyrus's eyes. Gaige flinched.

"We don't know that Baylarian is the Night Gentleman," my boss stated firmly.

I stared at him doubtfully.

Cyrus held up his hands in a placating gesture. "Let's see what the alchemists find on him, okay?"

"Okay," I agreed.

Cyrus stood. "Your travel documents should be ready by now, I'll pick them up while I'm down there. Stassi, why don't you shower and get dressed for the day? The alchemists have located Lachlan Shepard at the Ritz hotel. I want to pay him a visit, perhaps you can join me?"

"Wait. So, Shepard is using his real name? Then who is this Baylarian guy? And which one of them is the Night Gentleman? I'm so confused," Gaige grumbled.

"Lachlan Shepard is registered at the Ritz—that is all I know right now," Cyrus replied calmly. "Hopefully I'll know more after visiting the hotel."

"I'll go with you," I said.

Cyrus smiled down at me fondly. "Good. I'll be back within the hour. Is that enough time for you to get ready?"

"I can make it work."

I remained seated at the dining room table, staring numbly at the flowers, long after Cyrus left. Gaige, loyal as a Labrador, stayed with me.

"I'm gonna get rid of these," he proclaimed, reaching for the flowers.

I held up my hand. "No, not yet. We should probably have them tested for poison and stuff."

My partner snatched his hand back. "Right. Good point." He studied me thoughtfully.

"Stop, please," I begged. "I'm really okay."

But I wasn't. Far from it. That letter had been addressed to me. Like Gaige said, the whackjob had singled me out. Why? Why me?

"If you say so," Gaige hedged, clearly not falling for my ruse.

"I promise, Gaige. It's locked up, swear."

Gaige grinned, though I could tell he was still concerned. "It better be. Because I'm thinking a little late night B&E is in order. After Stein's party, of course. I need my partner on top of her game."

"Shakespeare and Company?" I guessed.

"It's like we share a brain."

"Scary."

By the time I showered and dressed for the day, Cyrus had returned. He and Gaige were talking in the living room when I descended the stairs. And Ines was with them. Goodie.

"There was one slight issue with timing," she was saying. "The *Queen Mary* was the most recent ship to arrive in London from Baltimore, and it pulled into the harbor on Monday, March 2nd. The first murder occurred on March 5th, which would have given Gaige enough time to reach Paris and commit the crime. We created fare receipts for the ship, just with a different arrival date: March 24th. By the time that inspector is able to nullify your story, your run will be complete and you'll be back home." Her smile was tight and strained. "Then you have your boat-train tickets, from London to Paris, arriving on March 26th. Those are legitimate and will standup to scrutiny."

"Cyrus, do you think we should keep going with this run?" Gaige asked. "A lot has gone wrong."

"A lot has gone right, too," I interjected, joining the others in the living room.

All three turned skeptical eyes toward me.

"Since when did you become the love child of Sammy Sunshine and Rita Rainbow?" Gaige deadpanned.

"Funny," I replied, rolling my eyes. "I'm just saying that we've made a lot of progress in a very short time. We've already met the target. We've figured out a place where Rosenthal possibly kept a section of *Blue's Canyon*. We've been invited to one of Gertrude Stein's salon parties. We're making friends. I think we have a good shot of completing this run in a much shorter timeframe than we anticipated."

The Founder wrinkled his tanned forehead as he considered my position.

It was weird. For some reason, I was fighting to continue the run, when I wasn't even sure I wanted to stay. I was conflicted, torn between a desire to return to the safety of the island, where crazies didn't send me ghoulish poems, and the hope that I would find a clue as to who I was if I stayed.

"Stassi's right," Cyrus declared. "You two have made impressive progress. For now, you should continue, as long as it does not cast any additional doubt on Gaige. We'll see how it plays out over the next couple of days with Lachlan Shepard, Mitchell T. Baylarian, the Night Gentleman, and whatever else inevitably goes wrong." He winked. "And if things get worse, it's straight back to the island for you, and I'll bring in a cleanup crew. You two feel okay with that?"

"Yes, sir," Gaige and I said in unison.

Ines cleared her throat loudly to draw the attention her way. "I spoke to Andre this morning, he phoned to see how things went last night. When I told him about Gaige's treatment by the police, Andre was beside himself. It seems you made quite an impression on him last night."

When no one commented on this, Ines continued hesitantly.

"On Saturdays, Andre, Ezra, and Ernest box at this little gym not far from here. Andre wanted me to ask if you would care to join them."

"Awesome," Gaige replied enthusiastically.

"Are you sure that's a good idea? Maybe you should lay low for a little while, until you aren't the chief suspect in a string of murders," I said. "Not to mention that you have to visit the police station, or Charles will be held accountable."

"It is a wonderful idea," Ines argued, as if I'd offended her. "Gaige will visit the station and attend to this line-up business beforehand. Spending time with the menfolk during their masculine pursuits will give him a chance to bond with Andre, and the other two will find him fascinating."

"Fascinating?" I echoed doubtfully.

"Oh yes, dear. The macabre is very compelling."

Cyrus studied Ines, his expression unreadable. If I had to guess, he was weighing her frivolity. I half-expected him to issue some reprimand about her carefree attitude in the midst of several crises, but Cyrus passed over the alchemist in favor of Gaige.

"Gaige, I need you to be honest with me here," our boss said. "Do I need to come down to the stationhouse with you?"

"No, sir," Gaige replied decisively. "The only reasons they have to be suspicious of me will be simple enough to clear up, I can handle this. I will present our new travel receipts to prove I was not here when the killings began. Then the audience member who spoke to the killer will quickly confirm I wasn't the one he spoke to, and that will be that."

Cyrus seemed to appreciate Gaige's confidence. Evidently, a runner being suspected of murder wasn't quite as high of a priority as a runner going rogue.

"Very well, then," Cyrus declared. "Stassi and I should be off to the Ritz. Let's all hope Shepard is there, and at least one mystery will be solved."

With our plan in place, Ines left to contact Jacque to let him know Gaige would need to be driven to the station shortly. Gaige followed her to scour the customs closet, in need of whatever passed for workout clothes in the 1920s.

The alchemists had more than one vehicle and more than one driver, but Cyrus insisted on taking a taxi to the Ritz Hotel. He was the boss for a reason, so I didn't protest.

"The Ritz is an odd choice," I mused, just loud enough for Cyrus and not the driver to hear me. "Isn't it a little upscale for a runner going off-grid?"

Not that I was complaining. In fact, I was genuinely curious to see the lavish hotel where fashion maven Coco Chanel kept a suite.

"It definitely is," Cyrus agreed. "He should have picked something low-key and out of the way. That's what I'd have done if I were him."

The Ritz did not disappoint. As soon as we pulled to a stop in front of the entrance, I knew the hotel was every bit as opulent as I'd imagined. A bellhop wearing an adorable black and gold uniform, complete with top hat, held open the door of our vehicle. His twin did the same with the majestic doors leading inside. My eye was immediately drawn to the crystal chandelier hanging high above the lobby, sparkling brightly in a way no photograph could ever capture. Though I tried not to gape at my surroundings, I felt stuck in a perpetual state of awe.

Unlike me, Cyrus seemed entirely unaffected by the setting. In his defense, he'd probably been there before. Or maybe tracking down a rogue runner simply took precedence over gawking at the elegant surroundings. Whatever the reason, my boss strode purposefully across the marble floors, straight to the hotel's reception desk. He spoke to the female standing behind it in fluent French. The woman seemed to melt a little when he fixed her with his piercing green gaze.

He showed the manipulated photograph of Lachlan Shepard to the receptionist.

"This is my son, Lachlan," Cyrus told her, emphasizing the missing runner's name in an attempt to garner sympathy. "I was told he's staying here. Is it too much to ask for his room number?"

"It is against the hotel's policies to give out personal information about our guests," she told Cyrus regretfully. Leaning over, she rested her ample chest on the marble countertop. "But...I can see how concerned you are for your son."

"Terribly concerned," Cyrus insisted, also leaning in slightly. "My son is delicate, even a little unstable at times. He left home without his medication. His cousin and I have been so worried."

My fictitious family is growing by the day, I thought, realizing this meant I was to be Cyrus's niece for the foreseeable future. The new hereditary ties would prove fortuitous, should Gaige's legal troubles continue. Posing as our uncle would give Cyrus reason to involve himself in any future interrogations or proceedings.

If only I could choose my real parents so easily.

"I understand," the woman said, nodding. "If you will wait one moment, I will check our records, Mr. Shepard."

"Thank you," Cyrus said, reaching across the divide to squeeze her hand.

The attendant walked to the other end of the counter and began flipping through a ledger. Cyrus tucked the picture of Lachlan back inside his leather portfolio.

"Laying it on thick," I teased in a low voice.

Cyrus shrugged. "I may be old, Stassi, but I am not dead. I do know how to flirt, when necessary."

My boss was unarguably good-looking for an older guy, but it was still an awkward exchange. Thankfully, the attendant returned a moment later with a brass key in one hand.

"Your son is indeed a guest here," she told Cyrus, hazel eyes darting back and forth as if worried about being overhead. "He rented a suite and paid in advance for one month. It appears he is scheduled to remain for another week."

One month? Odd. Lachlan's syndicate knew he was missing because he hadn't returned on time for work. Planning to stay after his leave ended didn't make any sense, unless Lachlan never intended to go back.

The receptionist handed Cyrus the key. "Suite 1408. I can show you the way, if you like?"

"That is a kind offer, but I think it best for his cousin and I to check on him alone," Cyrus began, dropping his voice to a conspiratorial whisper. "We cannot be certain what state my son will be in, I would not want to expose you to anything untoward."

Clearly disappointed that she wouldn't be spending the next ten minutes chatting up my boss, the woman forced a smile. "Of course, Mr. Shepard. Just return the key when you are through."

She pointed us towards the elevators. Cyrus and I set off in search of the missing runner.

The door to suite 1408 had a "Do Not Disturb" sign hanging from the handle when we arrived.

"Let me go in first, Stassi," Cyrus said, holding up a hand to force me back. He passed me the portfolio. "Hold on to this for me, will you?"

I clutched the leather dossier to my chest and watched as my boss withdrew a very small, very 25th century revolver from inside his sport coat.

"Is that really necessary?" I whispered loudly and a tad frantically.

"I wasn't kidding when I said Shepard might need medical attention. Bane has been worried about him for while now. He'd thought Lachlan's hectic running schedule might be too much and had hoped the time off would be good for him. Then he learned that this wasn't the guy's first illicit jump. Shepard routinely free jumps, apparently. Too many of those can lead to an illness much worse than time sickness."

"Like a crazy person kind of sickness?" I squeaked.

Cyrus lifted his eyebrows and shrugged. "Just stay out here until I make sure it's safe."

I swallowed hard and took several steps back from the door, nodding my acquiescence.

Cyrus slipped the key into the lock and pushed open the door. Gun barrel first, he entered the room like a trained enforcer.

I chewed my thumbnail, anxiously waiting for my boss to give me the all-clear. The twenty seconds that followed felt more like twenty hours, though every moment without gunfire steadied my nerves just a little bit more.

"He's not here." Cyrus popped his head into the hallway, holstered his gun, and waved me inside the suite.

I exhaled a breath I hadn't realized I was holding.

Molly was right; being a runner is for the birds.

Suite 1408 was made up of one bedroom and a sitting area. A very modern, very out-of-place suitcase and matching duffel bag were sitting by the front door. Perfectly fluffed throw pillows were arranged strategically in the corners of the brocade sofas, and several Paris guidebooks were open on the coffee table. A wet bar in the main room boasted bottles of gin, vodka, and scotch.

The door to the adjoining bedroom was slightly ajar. Through the opening, I could see a queen-sized bed that was immaculately made. Given the "Do Not Disturb" sign on the door, I was guessing that Lachlan hadn't slept in the room the night before. In fact, we had no way of knowing the last time he had.

"Why don't you look through the closet? I'll take the bathroom," Cyrus said.

From an interior pocket of his coat, my boss produced two pairs of latex gloves and several vacu-seal bags similar to the artifact pouches. He handed me one pair of gloves and three of the bags.

Cyrus reached inside his coat again, this time withdrawing a rectangular tin the length of his palm. He removed the lid to reveal a white, waxy substance. I watched with fascination as my boss pressed the hotel room key into the wax.

"Did you just copy that key?" I asked.

"Technically, I made an impression of the key," he replied with a wry smile. "The alchemists can make a duplicate from that. It's a crude method of reproduction, but an extremely effective one. Now we can come back, if need be." He pocketed the tin and the key. "Let's do a thorough search this go-round, that way we can avoid a second trip."

"Of course. But what exactly am I looking for again?" I asked, placing the portfolio on the coffee table so that I could pull on the gloves.

"Anything that might tell us where this guy is now or where he's been."

Following orders, I walked into the bedroom and found the closet.

Period-appropriate men's clothing hung from wooden hangers, the garments divided into shirts and pants, and arranged by color.

"Can you say 'obsessive compulsive'?" I muttered, thumbing through the clothes.

I searched the pockets of everything, hoping for a receipt or ticket stub. The search yielded only a gum wrapper and a 1971 U.S. penny. Just to be safe, I placed both in a plastic pouch to show Cyrus.

Something about the clothing struck me as odd. It looked right for the period, and yet something was bothering me.

They're not reproductions, I realized. So Lachlan hadn't brought the clothes with him. It was slightly surprising, since he wouldn't have been able to borrow from our customs station without drawing unwanted questions. I wasn't sure if this was a real clue or not, but made a mental note to inform Cyrus.

On the floor of the closet, I found a laundry bag with the Ritz logo embroidered on the front. Inside were three pairs of crumpled wool pants, a cream sweater vest, two white undershirts with sweat stains, and several pairs of men's underwear.

"Oh, gross!" I exclaimed, dropping the bag as though it had teeth.

Alarmed, Cyrus rushed into the bedroom. "What? Did you find something?"

"Dirty unmentionables," I groaned, pointing towards the laundry bag.

Cyrus narrowed his gaze, confused. It took him a minute, but realization finally dawned. "Oh, you mean underpants? Anything else?"

I showed him the gum wrapper and penny. "Do these mean anything to you?"

Cyrus shook his head, but he held out his hand for the items anyway.

"Have you checked all the pockets?" he asked.

"The clean ones."

"What about the dirty ones?"

"Do I get hazard pay for this?" I asked.

Cyrus worked unsuccessfully to hide a smile.

"Let me know what you find."

I picked up the first pair of pants and patted the pockets.

"Ah, gotcha," I muttered when my fingers felt the small, hard lump in the right front pocket. Wedging my hand inside, I grasped the slim object and withdrew a camera similar to the one I owned.

Now we're getting somewhere, I thought, slipping the camera into one of the pouches.

I was turning out the pockets in the third pair of trousers when I heard soft, rhythmic knocking from the other side of the bedroom.

I poked my head through an opening in the closet doors and saw my boss rapping his knuckles lightly around the frame of a seemingly random door on the far side of the bed. Cyrus reached for the knob and gave it a tentative twist. The door opened noiselessly.

"What's in there?" I asked.

Cyrus gave a short laugh. "Another door. I assume it leads to the neighboring suite. No knob, though." He repeated the knocking pattern on the second door. "Definitely open space on the other side," he murmured, more to himself than me. Closing the first door, Cyrus gave me his undivided attention. "Find anything?"

"I did—Lachlan's camera." I held up the pouch with the camera inside.

Three long, sharp bangs followed by a muffled, "Housekeeping", from the front door of the suite made us both freeze.

"We'll go through the saved pictures back at the townhouse. Anything else?"

Since we were now running short on time, I turned the pants that I was still holding upside down and shook them. Several coins fell to the carpet in a series of soft thuds. Then, four ticket stubs floated free from their fabric prison. Squatting, I read the information on each one aloud.

My heart pounded harder and harder with every mangled French word that crossed my lips.

I looked up and met Cyrus's intense gaze, knowing even before I voiced my next thought that my boss had already reached the same conclusion.

"These stubs are all for shows where the Night Gentleman struck. Lachlan is the killer."

TWENTY

"DOES THAT HURT? It looks like it hurts," I asked Gaige, squinting up at him from my perch on the sitting room sofa to better appraise the damage to his face. "Who knew a group of erudite men was capable of inflicting so much physical damage?"

This was the first I'd seen of Gaige since we'd parted ways that morning. When he'd sauntered down the stairs to join me in waiting for Ines to arrive, so that we could head over to Gertrude Stein's party, I'd been more than a little shocked. My partner's day of boxing with three of the century's most celebrated authors had left him with one very impressive black eye.

Fingers outstretched, I reached towards his face as if my touch would sooth the shiner. Why? I couldn't say. Maybe it was that mothering nature Molly liked to tease me about.

Gaige swatted my hand away before I made contact. I wasn't sure whether it was because his ego was bruised from getting beat up by a group of intellectuals, or that he was proud of the manly badge and didn't want to feel babied. Either way, he waved off my concern over the dark bruising.

"My eye isn't important right now," Gaige grumbled irritably, though a small, satisfied smile skimmed across his lips when he touched the discolored skin over his cheekbone. He dropped down beside me on the couch.

"How did it go down at the police station?" I asked. "Since you're here, I'm guessing it was okay?"

Gaige grimaced. He held up his hand and wiggled it back and forth to indicate so-so.

"That good, huh?"

"You should have seen that inspector's face just before the line-up, when I handed him the travel documents. Oh, man, Stass. *Priceless*. He turned bright red and his eyes bugged out of his face. It was awesome."

Gaige's colorful description brought to mind the dancer from the night before. The way she'd looked as she knelt dying on stage right in front of us. I felt the blood drain from my face and my stomach started doing backflips. It was still unfathomable that I'd sat fifteen feet away as a woman was murdered.

Though I'd been focusing on the mission all day, distracting myself and keeping busy, every once in a while the scene would pop back into my head like glimpses of a nightmare. My partner's offhand remark brought it all rushing back.

Immediately realizing his mistake, Gaige backpedaled.

"Damn, Stass, I'm *so* sorry. I don't know why I said that. I wasn't thinking, I'm such a donk." He slung an arm around my shoulder and squeezed. All traces of humor were gone when he continued. "Last night was awful." He shook his head, as if to dislodge the memory from his brain. "I still just…I've never seen someone die before."

"Me neither. I'll need therapy when we get home," I tried to joke.

I couldn't think about those poor dancers. Every time I did, it felt like I was the one gasping for breath. I kept hearing the words of the maniac in my head.

"Are you not amused? I know I am."

How could someone be so cruel?

Gaige rewarded my efforts to lighten the mood with a quip of his own. "Me, too. Maybe we can go halfsies on a couple of sessions. You know, like a two-for-one deal. It'll be like couples' counseling…except, not."

And that was why, despite his many flaws, I loved Gaige like the brother I never wanted.

"Now that they have the travel documents, are the police done harassing you?" I asked, needing to change the subject. Any more talk of the previous night's tragedy would make it too difficult to play the part of a whimsical socialite that night.

"Yeah, about that," Gaige started, his quick change in mood making me nervous. "I have good news and bad news."

"Start with the good," I decided.

"The man who was approached by the Night Gentleman did not pick me out of the line-up."

"That's amazing news. Isn't that all that matters?" I asked.

"Unfortunately, no," my partner replied. "He also didn't say it *wasn't* me. Since the Night Gentleman was wearing both a mask and top hat, which is part of why the witness believed he was with the show, the man didn't see enough to say with certainty whether or not it was any of us. So, basically, all his failure to identify me accomplished was preventing the inspector from locking me up today."

"Shant," I swore. "You said you gave the inspector the travel documents, right? Do you think he's going to check on them? We're going to be screwed if he does. Delivering forged papers looks worse than if you hadn't given the police anything at all."

"I know, right? And I don't *think* the inspector is going to check,"

Gaige hedged. "I *know* he is. He told me as much himself."

"What would—"

"Ready, my dears?" Ines's voice suddenly trilled from the foyer, effectively cutting me off. She strode into the living room, the ever-present cloud of smoke trailing her like a shadow. "Jacque is outside."

"Where's Cyrus?" Gaige asked. "Does he not want to join us for this little shindig?"

Ines furrowed her brow, most likely confused by the word "shindig". She must have puzzled out the meaning on her own, though, because she didn't ask for clarification.

"Cyrus has other matters to attend to this evening. I am sure he will explain it all to you in the morning. For now, I can say my people have encountered a small wrinkle. The name on the card you received, Stassi, he does not appear to exist. We have found no mention of a Mitchell T. Baylarian in our records. Cyrus believes your historians will have better luck." She sniffed, as if offended that the syndicate's people, with their advanced technology, would be able to locate a man the alchemists could not. "Now, are you both ready? We are already running behind schedule."

"Whose fault is that?" I mumbled under my breath.

Disregarding my comment, Ines spun and walked purposefully back to the front door, obviously expecting Gaige and me to follow. We both stood and obeyed her silent command.

I opened my mouth, prepared to resume the conversation from before Ines's interruption. Gaige caught my eye and shook his head ever so slightly. His meaning was clear: let's not discuss this in front of Ines. His expression, on the other hand, made it impossible to tell why he didn't want to. Did he not trust the alchemist? Or was he simply not in the mood for the flippant attitude that seemed to accompany anything remotely serious with her?

Personally, I found Ines irritating but harmless.

Either way, there was no more talk of death and psychopaths on the ride over to Gertrude Stein's home. Instead, Gaige gave us a blow-by-blow account of his day in the boxing ring. With his dramatic retelling, it sounded like he'd gone ten rounds with the 2405 Heavyweight Champion, Marcus Maximus, instead of dodging a couple of punches from writers. Or not dodging them, in his case. Nonetheless, I was glad to see him in good spirits. As traumatized as I was over my police interrogation, it was nothing compared to what Gaige had been through.

Judging by the lack of cars and people outside of Stein's house, our trio was among the last to arrive for the night's festivities. Leave it to Ines to feel as though a grand entrance was in order.

Gaige and I followed our guide through the tall front gate and across the courtyard beyond it. The cobblestoned patio had a small fountain in the middle, and paths trailed off into the darkness in either direction. From photographs, I knew that carefully tended gardens lay in the shadows beyond.

Ines paused at the front door to 27 rue de Fleurus and took a deep breath. When she turned to face us, a feigned brightness shone from her expression.

"Lock it up," Gaige said, pointing at me.

"You lock it up," I replied with a smile, mentally preparing myself for the pivotal night ahead.

Ines raised one eyebrow, looking at Gaige and me like we were weirdos. "This little act that the two of you perform, it is very odd," she said.

Gaige shrugged. "Maybe. But it works. Why mess with success?"

"It had better," Ines replied crisply. "Tonight, there is no room for error."

And with those words of encouragement, she pushed the door open and entered without knocking.

TWENTY ONE

ROUGHLY TWO DOZEN people were already milling around Stein's main sitting room, just off the front foyer. They stood chatting in small groups, sipping cocktails and eating delicious-looking hors d'oeuvres from white china plates. I recognized many of the faces from Historian Eisenhower's lecture, though seeing them in person was very different. This was the first time I'd encountered so many notable figures at once. An interaction with any one of them could easily change the course of history. To say I was feeling nervous was like saying the Epic War was a mere skirmish.

Be cool, I thought, slightly worried that my inner fangirl would creep out and embarrass me. *You're a pro, you can do this.*

Even among the group of so many who commanded attention, spotting our hostess was an easy task. Gertrude Stein stood near the fireplace with a group of men that included Rosenthal. They all appeared to be hanging on her every word. At least, until the whispered news of our arrival began to spread throughout the room like a brushfire. Gaige, Ines, and I stood conspicuously in the foyer, every eye in the salon suddenly peering in our direction.

It's like the opening scene of one of my nightmares, I thought frantically. Those horror movie-esque dreams always ended the same way: I'd return to a bloody, unrecognizable present caused by my actions in the past. It was truly one of my greatest fears, right up there with being buried alive. And ostriches—terrifyingly aggressive creatures, something I'd learned the hard way.

Lock it up, Drama Queen, I lectured myself, putting on my practiced, congenial smile.

The volume in the room had gone from an eight to a one. The only sounds were loud whispering and the rustling of clothing. Heads turned and necks craned in an overt attempt to catch a glimpse of the Americans at the center of the latest scandal. For the first time in my life, I understood what it meant to be infamous. I didn't much care for it.

"No need to stare, the Princes will be here all evening," Ines proclaimed loudly.

"No worries, folks, that mess with the police has been cleared up," Gaige added, smiling winningly. "Sorry to disappoint you."

"How positively boring," a short blonde woman declared to her male companion. Her tone that clearly indicated that she'd been hoping my partner was involved in the murders.

"Some people are so strange," Gaige muttered in my ear.

"Mix and mingle, my dears," Ines said. The order leaked through her slightly parted, heavily painted lips, without as much as a twitch of her facial muscles.

Ines ushered us through the entranceway to the salon. Despite Gaige's declaration of innocence, the crowd inched our way in a not-so-subtle manner, making no attempts to hide their curiosity. To me, wanting to meet suspected killers seemed like a blatant disregard for common sense. The partygoers clearly didn't share my beliefs. In this instance, I was grateful since it meant the allegations hadn't ruined our chances of gaining a toehold with Rosenthal's set. In a society where being interesting was the most readily-accepted currency, Gaige and I were currently flush. Evidently, murder suspects bested artists and literati.

Playing the part of hostess, Stein broke away from the group of men and shuffled over to greet us. With her short, practical hair, and round face punctuated by kind brown eyes, the great matriarch of twentieth century literature could only be described as handsome. I found myself drawn to her, fascinated by the intelligence radiating from her like heat from an inferno.

Stein welcomed Gaige and Ines as if they were old friends.

"Tell me that ordeal with the inspector has not turned you off of Paris," she said to Gaige.

"Not at all. These things happen." Gaige waved it off, as though police interrogations where par for the course with him. "Besides, now I have one hell of a story to tell my friends back home."

"Right you are," Stein agreed with an approving nod. "A good story is the spark of inspiration necessary to ignite great novels."

"I couldn't have said it better myself," Gaige replied, drawing me forward into Stein's direct line of sight. "Ms. Stein, allow me to introduce my sister, Anastasia Prince."

I held out my hand, and Stein shook it heartily. "It's such an honor," I gushed, unable to stop myself.

Out of the corner of my eye, I saw Alice Toklas beeline from across the room to stand by her wife's side. Where Stein was rounded edges with soft curves and a keen gaze, Toklas's face was composed of hard lines and mismatched features with a suspicious look in her eye. As subtly as a dog marking its territory, Toklas silently appraised our motley crew.

"An honor?" Stein gave a short bark of laughter. "Did you hear that,

Alice?" She turned to smirk at her wife, who made no reply save a small grunt of acknowledgement. "Are you a writer, Anastasia?"

"Oh, no, ma'am, merely a lover of literature. I love to read," I replied nervously.

"Anastasia is being modest," Gaige interjected. "She has yet to give writing a stab, but she's a great editor. My dear sister here deserves an award for typing up my chicken scratch ramblings. She makes my boring stories worlds more interesting."

"Oh? You're a writer, then?" Stein asked.

"More of a dabbler," Gaige said with faux modesty.

Stein turned her attention back to me. "You and Alice have something in common—she's my typist and editor."

Gaige and I already knew this from our lessons with Historian Eisenhower. And while we hadn't discussed including either Gaige's dabbling or my alleged editing skills, the embellishment to our cover story did make for a nice segue. From there, I was able to turn the conversation to more comfortable ground.

"I'm just glad my brother's hobby has allowed me to put my education to good use," I said.

"You're from Baltimore, right? Where did you attend school?" Stein asked.

"Oldfields, just outside the city. Do you know it?"

"Oh, you must know the DuPont girls. Lovely young women, I hear," Stein inquired.

Thank goodness Historian Eisenhower was so thorough when helping us prep our cover stories. The DuPont girls were among the school's most notable recent alumni.

"We had mutual friends back in school, and even went on a ski trip with a large group one Christmas holiday. Alice is an absolute gas. We haven't kept in touch, though," I replied, the lie coming effortlessly.

"That tends to happen throughout life. You'll encounter those you've lost contact with when you least expect," Stein replied wisely.

"Now, if you'll excuse me for just a moment, Zelda appears to be all lathered up." She nodded towards the blonde who'd termed Gaige's innocence "boring". "The last thing we need tonight is another row with Hemingway. No filter on that one. I'll be right back."

As the hostess made her way across the room to put out the fire brewing in Mrs. F. Scott Fitzgerald—there was no love lost between Zelda and Hemingway—I smiled awkwardly at Toklas.

Gertrude Stein seemed to be a pleasant, albeit-no-nonsense, woman. I couldn't say the same about her other half. Toklas radiated hostility, and her dour expression suggested that she would rather chew glass than spend another second in my company. In the spirit of professionalism, I simply smiled to avoid further offending the woman.

Gaige and Ines were both occupied conversing with other guests, so I was on my own with Toklas. After a moment of tense silence, I scoured my mental database for a neutral topic. Finally, I decided on flattery.

"The food looks delicious," I remarked, knowing Alice had made it all herself. Her culinary expertise was a particular point of pride.

"Oldfields is a fine institution," Toklas said, without acknowledging the compliment. "It's a shame that such a wonderful education is often wasted on young girls with no greater ambition in life than to flit about before becoming a wealthy man's wife."

"Many of my classmates have gone on to attend Barnard, Bryn Mawr, Mount Holyoke, Vassar, and the like," I said, feeling oddly defensive about her judgment of the life that wasn't really mine. "And I did learn typing—that's a useful skill, wouldn't you agree?"

"It can be," Toklas replied with a wave of her hand. "Surely you do not plan to assist your brother with his hobby all of your life. What is it you intend to do with your education, Ms. Prince? After you conclude your holiday in Paris, of course."

First, I'll travel several centuries into the future. Hopefully, I'll have a couple of days off to regroup. Maybe lounge on the beach with Molly, work on my tan. Supposing, of course, that she has recovered from her time sickness and the burns she sustained when witch hunters tried to make her a human torch. Then, it's off to another time period to steal—procure—another artifact for a client with enough gold to be called Midas. Oh, I almost forgot. This plan all hinges on Cyrus finding the rogue runner and putting a stop to his murder spree before time is irreparably altered and the world as we know ceases to exist.

"I'm not certain what the future holds for me, Ms. Toklas," I said instead, speaking warmly in the hopes of thawing her frigid tone. "My father has offered me a position in the philanthropic department of my grandfather's company, though I've always dreamt of owning an art gallery. I was accepted to Pembroke College after graduation from Oldfields, but decided to delay my admission until next year. My brother and I wanted to travel, and our father thought visiting Europe would be a good way to expand our horizons."

Toklas looked at me strangely, as if I'd spoken in a language she didn't quite understand. She'd obviously taken me for a flighty girl with no ambition. It was petty, but I enjoyed watching the smug smile disappear from her face.

For the next twenty minutes, Toklas fired off questions at me as if this were a job interview. I answered in as pleasant a tone as I could muster, making a game of remaining unruffled in the face of her biting remarks. It was good practice, since Gertrude Stein's wife would not be the last hostile asset I'd encounter as a runner.

The conversation with Toklas did nothing to further my knowledge about Rosenthal and where he might be hiding sections of *Blue's Canyon*. But that wasn't my objective in that moment. Alice Toklas was known to be the gatekeeper of the group we were infiltrating—her judgment of a person was the deciding factor in acceptance, superseding even Stein's opinion. I needed her to tolerate me, if not actually like me, so that she would deem me fit to breathe the same air as her wife and their friends.

As Toklas reached into the depth of our cover story, I realized I'd soon to need to change the subject to avoid landmines. I looked to my partner for help. Stein had returned during my odd exchange with her wife. She and Gaige were conversing about Picasso's art—a subject Stein was always eager to discuss. Ines had migrated towards a group of women several feet away. There was no one paying a scrap of attention to Toklas and me, no one to bail me out.

Toklas narrowed her gaze and launched her next attack.

"Our little group here is very close, and yet many have already taken a particular shine to you and your brother. My wife, for instance, seems quite taken with you both. You have managed to integrate yourselves rather quickly, even by our standards. Why do you think that is?" Toklas challenged, studying my face for a reaction as she spoke. Without waiting for an answer, she pressed on. "Perhaps I can make sense of your brother's interest in this crowd, overlooking of course the forceful way he is elbowing in. However, one would think that a young woman such as yourself, with exceedingly limited life experience, might find herself more comfortable with a set that is perhaps less…wise."

I was floored—and, admittedly, a little impressed—by Toklas's ability to cram rudeness into sentences like sardines into cans. It was hard to decide which insult to address first. Toklas was a palpably jealous woman, and I had no desire to spar with her green-eyed monster. Still, I wasn't a doormat.

"I have only just met your wife this evening," I said sweetly. "I do believe it's my brother that Ms. Stein is taken with. As for why I am here, I am a patron of creative minds in all forms—art, literature, theater. To be among the company of so many inspired individuals is an honor I am greatly enjoying. As you say, I have limited life experience, but I am hoping my travels will remedy that."

My self-deprecating admission elicited a satisfied smile from Toklas. Just as I'd expected it would.

"That is not to say I am not well-versed in the works of many here tonight," I continued, causing her smile to falter. "I am quite knowledgeable on a vast number of subjects, if you care for a more intellectual conversation."

I thought I heard Gaige chuckle behind me, but wasn't positive. I just hoped if my partner had overhead my conversation, he would still find it funny when Toklas had me blackballed from future parties.

Yeah, I totally should have heeded the old adage to "quit while you're ahead". If the daggers flying at my head from Toklas's eyes were any indication, my last statement crossed the line from antagonistic and entered the territory of fighting words. Thankfully, Stein loudly announced for her guests to find seats, sparing me Toklas's next attempt at a conversational ace.

Without waiting for me, Gaige strode over to sit beside Rosenthal on a divan situated next to Stein's own throne-like chair. Others filled in around them, all seemingly eager to be as close to Stein as possible. When I moved to join them, Toklas cleared her throat loudly to draw my attention.

"Miss Prince? Would you care to join us in the kitchen?"

It wasn't a question as much as a command.

The segregation of the sexes was expected. Still, I found myself irritated by the exclusion and tried to finagle my way into remaining in the salon. "Thank you, Ms. Toklas, but I think I'll stay with my brother," I told her, matching her frosty smile with one that was sugary sweet and innocent.

"It was not a suggestion," Alice Toklas replied, confirming my earlier suspicions.

Ines appeared at my side.

"Gertrude prefers to discuss writing with the serious novelists and literary connoisseurs," she said cheerily, inserting herself into the conversation. "Alice here is kind enough to keep the rest of us entertained. Their discussions tend to be a bit droll, dear. You will be much happier with us."

Somehow, I doubted that. But before I could formulate an excuse to stay in the salon, Ines placed a hand on my back and steered me away.

Gaige is the primary on this run, I reminded myself as the alchemist herded me away like livestock. Admittedly, he was succeeding quite well in bonding with our target and his friends. Even Gertrude Stein seemed to like Gaige, and she wasn't usually susceptible to a man's charms.

As soon as I stepped into the kitchen, a pretty red-haired woman sidled up next to me. She looked vaguely familiar, though I felt like everyone in attendance did after Eisenhower's exceedingly detailed slideshow.

"Nasty business, what happened last night at the *Exotique* show," she said by way of greeting.

Though I'd been expecting questions about the murders since we arrived, the woman's bluntness surprised me almost as much as Toklas's rudeness. The woman held out her hand.

"Hadley Richardson."

"Stassi Prince," I replied, shaking her hand. A quick flip through my mental archives placed her within the innermost circle—she was Ernest Hemingway's wife.

"Oh, don't be silly dear. Of course I know who you are. You're Gaige Prince's sister."

Evidently, I'd need to get used to this moniker.

"I am," I said warmly. "It is so lovely to meet you. My brother just adored meeting your husband. He had a great time today at the boxing ring. It was very kind of them to include Gaige."

"Ernest had only wonderful things to say about your brother after their boxing lesson. You were with him at the show, I hear." Hadley placed a hand over her heart. "You poor dear, it must have been horrible."

Though Hadley's mouth said "horrible", her bright green eyes shone with interest. Ines was right, I realized. This set evidently found the macabre perversely fascinating.

"It was," I agreed, hoping that my failure to elaborate would serve as a clue to Hadley that I didn't want to discuss the murders.

Lady Luck wasn't smiling down on me.

"You were right there, weren't you? In the front row? You must have been so scared. If I were—"

"Now Hadley, I know you are not bothering my dear Anastasia with morbid questions on such a delightful evening," Ines trilled, swooping in for the save. "It was positively horrid, and I don't wish to talk about it. Neither does Anastasia, I assume."

For the first time since meeting the customs agent, I was actually glad to see her. Ines's timely interruption saved me from further questioning from Hadley.

Unfortunately, it had no effect on everyone else in the kitchen.

Much to the dismay of Alice Toklas, the women at the party were eager for every gory detail I'd witnessed. I got the distinct impression that Toklas wasn't bothered by the subject matter, as much as my being the center of attention. Luckily, the hostess's rancor was no longer reserved strictly for me—she seemed to dislike most of her female guests equally.

"I was at the first performance where the Night Gentleman struck," a woman with a blonde bob and thick British accent said, between bites of a finger cake. She washed down the dessert with a long swallow of champagne. "Bertie and I were near the back, though. He bought the tickets last minute, and all the good seats were sold out."

"I so hate when that happens," another woman added. Though she spoke with the air of the upper classes, the faint hint of a cockney accent made it obvious she wasn't born among them.

"Have you all tried the lemon crèmes?" Toklas asked loudly.

She was obviously trying to reroute the conversation, and I was more than happy to be her copilot.

"I'd love one, Ms. Toklas. Thank you," I said, stepping forward to accept the tiny pastry. I quickly took a bite. "Oh my heavens, this is absolutely divine."

Her scowl deepened when I was the only one who expressed interest. Evidently, sucking up to Toklas wasn't going to make her like me.

"I believe I saw the bloke," the British woman said. She lowered her voice as if worried about being overheard, even though an audience was exactly what she wanted. "He is not nearly so tall as your brother, Ms. Prince. And much slimmer, too. Rubbish what the police are doing to poor Gaige."

"We could not agree more," Ines said. "But Gaige was able to clear up that nonsense today. He took his travel documents to the station and gave them to that awful inspector. We expect a formal letter of apology any day now. I have already spoken with my family's legal counsel, and he believes...."

With everyone's attention focused on Ines, I was able to slide out of the spotlight without too much notice. Not only was the topic making me uneasy, it was also doing nothing to advance the search for Rosenthal's manuscript or ingratiate me to Alice Toklas.

On the plus side, the lemon crème was delicious, and I finished the rest in one bite. I considered moving in next to Toklas to further compliment her baking skills, but decided against it. I could just hear her nasally voice intoning a myriad of thinly veiled insults:

Why thank you, Ms. Prince, it is so nice to hear that from a young woman with rudimentary culinary skills.

That is so kind of you, Ms. Prince. If you like, I will give you the recipe and you can make it for the husband you came to Paris to nab.

As the other women tried to one-up each other with not-quite-close-encounters with the Night Gentleman, I migrated into the hallway just beyond the kitchen. My chances of peeling any of the women away from their gossip circle were slimmer than a runway model in the 1990s, so it was on to plan B: snooping.

Did I actually believe Rosenthal hid his manuscript at Stein's? Nope, not at all.

Nonetheless, she was his mentor and he did frequent these Saturday parties, so it was worth a cursory check of the common areas. Anything further would require a late-night visit, several yards of rope, a lock picking set, and more sensible shoes than the heels currently on my feet.

I was pretending to study a framed Picasso in the hallway, when I sensed someone standing behind me. Careful to keep my expression neutral, I slowly turned and found Hadley Richardson watching me.

"I'm sorry," she began. "It was crass of me to broach that subject. I didn't mean to get them all started and make you feel uncomfortable."

Hadley gestured behind her, to where the other female guests had expanded their boasts from potential glimpses of the Night Gentleman to include sightings of noteworthy individuals around the city. Somehow, comparing a serial killer to a Russian princess in exile just didn't seem right.

"It wasn't my intention to cause such a stir," Hadley continued. "Please forgive me."

"It's okay, truly. He is a curiosity, I understand the interest in what happened," I said politely.

"Yes, but that does not give us the right to be rude. You witnessed something horrible. We are being exceptionally insensitive by asking you to relive it."

This time, she sounded genuinely sorry.

"Thank you for the apology, Miss Richardson, though it really isn't necessary."

"Don't be silly dear, call me Hadley."

She smiled and took a tentative step into the hallway, as if testing the water to determine whether the temperature was to her liking.

"Please, join me," I said, encouraging her along. "I was just admiring this work. There is so much to see within one painting, it is quite remarkable."

"Ah, yes, Pablo is very talented," Hadley said brightly. "And a favorite of Miss Stein's. Her patronage of his work is one of the reasons Gertrude began holding these salon parties—she had to discourage people from constantly stopping by to see them. She said she could never get any of her own work done with the stream of visitors every day."

"It is gracious of her to open her home to so many people each week," I said, finding that I truly meant it. "My brother has been positively giddy since she invited us."

Now that we'd moved past the topic of the Night Gentleman, I was eager to speak with Hadley. According to our intel, her husband was one of Rosenthal's few close friends.

"It was very kind of Ms. Stein to include us," I continued. "You have all been so welcoming, particularly your husband."

"The boys enjoyed his company today. They are accustomed to one another's styles, so a newcomer was probably a nice change for them. Ernest feels simply horrible about your brother's eye, though." Hadley wrinkled her nose in sympathy for Gaige's pain.

I laughed. "Gaige needs a good punch every now and then to keep him in line. Besides, now he can tell people that the great Ernest Hemingway gave him a black eye; he will drink for free on that story for the rest of his life."

Too late, I realized my mistake. Ernest Hemingway wasn't yet the renowned author he would soon be. *A Moveable Feast,* the novel that made him a household name, was still years away from publication.

My first instinct in these situations was to panic. And on my early runs, I did exactly that. Every time I messed up my cover story, accidentally made reference to something that hadn't happened yet, or used a word not yet in Merriam-Webster's dictionary, my heart would start to hammer against my ribs. Experience had taught me to take a beat and wait for a reaction.

Thankfully, Hadley simply laughed it off.

"Your brother must have a lot of faith in my husband's writing, Ms. Prince."

I blushed, feigning the reaction as best I could.

"Gaige will kill me for sharing this, but he has been following your husband since our uncle gave him *Three Stories and Ten Poems*. He believes that Mr. Hemingway is a great talent, and will inevitably be recognized as such."

Hadley waved a hand in the air. "No need for such formalities," she said. "He is Ernest."

"Well, my brother is doing his best to play it cool," I continued, "but he was simply thrilled that Ernest has been so friendly. Mr. Rosenthal, as well."

Behind Hadley, I thought I saw movement in the shadows.

Curious to see where my attention had gone, Hadley turned and followed my line of sight. "Is everything okay, Stassi?"

"Huh? Oh, yes, I apologize. I thought I saw something back there, but I must have been mistaken." I smiled at Hadley to disguise my unease. "I'm just a little jumpy today."

Hadley placed a small hand on my arm and squeezed. "I can imagine you are, after your experience last night. Who wouldn't be?"

And just like that, we were somehow back to the murders.

Though I didn't want the conversation to steer away from topics that were pertinent to the mission, a thought occurred to me. Much as I didn't want to launch back into a useless discussion of the previous night, it was the perfect segue to learn more about Carmen D'Angelo and her relationship with Rosenthal. It was always possible that he'd hidden part of the manuscript at her home.

"Yes, I'm sure the others who were there feel just as ill at ease. Especially those in our section, so close to the stage. Ms. D'Angelo was quite shaken. Mr. Rosenthal took her directly home after the police finished questioning her. I'm curious to know how she's doing today. I don't suppose you're friends with Ms. D'Angelo, are you?" I asked Hadley in my best concerned tone.

Her brows drew together as she mulled over the question, then a flicker of recognition flashed in her eyes.

"You must mean Carmen D'Angelo. Yes, I know her. She is a lovely dancer. I know her socially, but we aren't what you would call friends. You say she was with you at the show? How odd, Andre failed to mention that." Hadley shook her head. "That is very sweet of you to be concerned. I am sure Carmen is fine."

"Are they close? Mr. Rosenthal and Ms. D'Angelo?"

The question was presumptuous, but Hemingway's wife struck me as a gossip—an assumption I hoped was true.

Hadley rolled her eyes.

"On and off. Andre worships at her feet, as if she's a Greek goddess," she replied conspiratorially. "Carmen loves being worshipped, but finds Andre positively boring. They have a pattern of growing close for a time, until Carmen becomes tired of him. Then, they drift apart. But she always comes sniffing around when one of Andre's books is released, or a particularly favorable review comes out. I should've guessed that she'd be interested again—that piece he wrote for the *New Yorker* has been the talk of the town."

"In America, too," I confirmed. "My brother and I both enjoyed it a great deal."

"She must be the reason Andre has been making himself scarce lately," Hadley continued. "I will have to tell Ernest, he's been curious. He is making suggestions on Andre's new manuscript, you know."

My ears perked up. *Jackpot.*

"No, I didn't know that," I said innocently. "Does it have a working title? My brother will be delighted."

"Hadley, darling, have you been keeping our new friend all to yourself?" a voice called.

Hadley and I turned in unison. The British woman was standing in the doorway to the kitchen, hands on her hips, and a mock pout on her thin lips.

"How terribly selfish of you," she continued. "You know well that we all want the chance to learn more about Ms. Prince."

"We were just talking, Maggie," Hadley replied, sounding irritated by the interruption.

That made two of us. I wanted to finish our conversation.

Maggie stepped forward and reached for my hand, as if to drag me back into the kitchen. Since I had no interest in returning to Toklas's domain and being put on a display like a dolphin during feeding time at the aquarium, I firmly pulled my hand free and mustered a polite smile.

"If you will both excuse me, I need to use the powder room. It's down this hallway, correct?"

"Yes, on the left," Hadley answered, pointing in the direction I'd seen the silhouette. Or thought I saw one, at least. As I'd told Hadley, I was jumpier than usual.

"Hurry back," Maggie added.

Because both women were watching my retreat, I did enter the bathroom, even though I didn't actually need to use the facilities. I took the opportunity to touchup my makeup and make sure my auburn locks were all in place. Even though a gold bangle covered my name tattoo, I dabbed another layer of concealer over the letters, just to be on the safe side.

The hallway was quiet when I cracked the bathroom door several inches and peered outside. Neither Hadley nor Maggie was anywhere in sight.

There was little chance I'd get Hadley alone again to finish our conversation. Not with Maggie and the other vultures on the hunt for juicy details about the murders. And Alice Toklas had made it clear that I was not welcome in the salon with the men. So, instead of returning to the party right away, I decided to step outside for some fresh air.

Just for a minute. Just to catch my breath and collect my thoughts.

TWENTY TWO

THE GARDENS THAT wrapped around 27 rue de Fleurus were stunning. The bursting flora was skillfully cut through with winding stone pathways illuminated by the soft glow of electric lamps. Tall shrubs sculpted into artful designs were placed strategically along the walkways, creating intimate pockets of privacy.

From the overall design aesthetic, to each green leafy plant, colorful flower, and carved bench, Toklas had hand-selected it all. Like her wife, Alice clearly knew and appreciated true beauty.

I made a mental note to share my genuine admiration of her hard work. Maybe throwing a couple more gushing compliments her way would crack that seemingly impenetrable shell.

I strolled through the rows of Night-blooming Jasmine, inhaling the intoxicating aroma. As my stress melted away, I wondered again how this mission had gone to hell so quickly. All I needed now was a handbasket, and my journey would be complete

"A woman who prefers solitude to the intellectual conversation of her peers…how very interesting."

I squinted into the darkness, though I was pretty sure I recognized the voice. Sure enough, Charles DuPree stepped out from the shadows.

"How lovely to see you again, Ms. Prince. If I may say so, you look particularly fetching tonight," he said with a small, gallant bow.

Despite my sour mood, I smiled at his formality, as well as the compliment. Too drained to deal with appropriate etiquette, I answered him frankly.

"Do we really need to do this again? Please, just call me Stassi. After all, we have seen the inside of a police station together. I think that qualifies us as more than passing acquaintances."

Charles grinned wickedly. "What if I prefer to call you Anastasia?"

"Trust me when I say, you really don't want to find out," I replied, working hard to sound intimidating. My lips twitched from the urge to smile, though, so I doubted Charles put much stock in my threat.

He laughed good-naturedly. "You are a very interesting woman, Stassi."

"'Interesting'?" I repeated..

"I have decided that I like that about you," Charles continued, as if I hadn't spoken.

"How very magnanimous of you," I replied, sarcasm dripping from each word like grape jelly from an overstuffed PB&J.

He studied my face in the darkness, taking his turn on the carnival ride of uncertainty. Feeling magnanimous myself, I smiled to let him know I was teasing.

"Would you mind some company? Or would you prefer to continue your time of solitude?" he asked politely, shaking off the lingering doubt. "I do not want to disturb you, if you wish to be alone."

"I would love the company," I replied easily. Despite wanting nothing more than to be alone when I'd left Stein's house, I found that

I genuinely meant it.

Obviously pleased, Charles offered me his arm. I hesitated for the space of a heartbeat, and then accepted. Warmth infused my body from the inside out, the night suddenly not as chilly as it had been just a moment before. Trying my best to ignore the spark that had ignited a gentle fire in the pit of my stomach, I let Charles lead me through the gardens.

You can enjoy his attention, and the view he provides. But that's it. Don't go getting any silly romantic ideas, I told myself. *You are here on a run and he is a means to an end, nothing more. You'll be gone soon, and that's that.*

I relaxed and gave myself over to the experience of strolling through beautiful gardens on the arm of a handsome man under the cover of night.

The cool air was refreshing as it blew strands of hair around my face and tickled my neck. The mild bite was a welcome change from the stuffy atmosphere inside Stein's home. Above us, the silvery-white moon played peek-a-boo with an invisible opponent. Ducking behind one cloud after another, it reappeared moments later and shone brilliant white light down on the stone pathway ahead of us.

The scene was amusingly romantic in the most cliché of ways. Because there was no awkward chatter to fill the silence, our physical contact was more apparent, if only to me. If I were a normal girl with a normal job, my thoughts certainly would've turned amorous.

But I was not a normal girl. And I most certainly did not have a normal job.

So, instead worrying about the smudge of lemon crème on my dress or wondering whether Charles was going to kiss me, I focused on the mission. The mission came first. It had to come first. My life, Gaige's life, and countless other lives depended on that simple directive.

Up ahead, the pathway ended in a small cul-de-sac surrounded by hedges, out of view of both the house and the rest of the gardens. There was a stone bench in the middle, and Charles motioned to it with a questioning look in his eyes. I took a seat. He removed the jacket of his suit, draping it around my shoulders before sitting beside me. Though he hadn't asked, I was grateful for the warmth it provided.

"Thank you," I said appreciatively.

"Of course," Charles answered. "Tell me, Stassi, why are you out here alone? With a murderer on the loose, it is perhaps not safe for a young lady to be without accompaniment."

There was subtle chastisement in his tone that normally would have bothered me. After all, I was perfectly capable of watching my own back, probably more so than Charles himself. And yet, my typical irritation didn't come. Maybe it was anti-feminist of me, particularly in such a pivotal era for women's rights, but I found that I appreciated his concern for my wellbeing.

I looked over and met his gaze with a shrug. "I just needed some air. A minute to catch my breath, you know?"

"Ah, yes. To us, you are like the mysterious girl who begins a new school mid-term—everyone is interested in you. Everyone wants to be your friend. Everyone wants to know your story, and perhaps become part of it themselves. It can be rather exhausting, I'd imagine."

"That is an interesting way of putting it, though not inaccurate," I agreed, even though the metaphor wasn't one I could personally relate to. I'd never experienced school in a typical reading, writing, arithmetic fashion. "However, I'm not sure it's me they're interested in. Not *my* story, as much as the story I have to tell. I have already fielded many questions about the show last night, it appears that is where their interest lies."

Charles nodded knowingly.

"This crowd does love a good bit of gossip." He paused, as if debating his next words carefully. "How are you doing?"

"I'm having a wonderful time tonight," I said. "The party is lovely, I've met so many interesting and friendly people."

"That is not what I meant."

I knew what he meant. What I didn't know was how to respond to the question. Was I really okay? I had no idea.

"I've been better," I admitted.

"Yes, well, that is to be expected. Ladies such as yourself are rarely questioned in a murder investigation."

No, but criminals are, I thought with a hint of bitterness that was new for me.

Cyrus and the other syndicate heads could sugarcoat our job description with any flowery language they liked, but it all boiled down to one irrefutable truth: We were criminals. In the past, present, and future, we were criminals. I earned my very lucrative income by stealing. And I was okay with that. Ninety-nine percent of the time.

"I can honestly say that what happened the other night was a first for me," I agreed.

"On a positive note, you can now add the experience to your curriculum vitae. Unless, of course, you only obtained an education to impress future suitors?"

Startled by the insult, I angled my body on the bench and glared over at him, not caring whether he found my reaction as out of line as I found his comment. Only, when Charles's gaze met mine, there was a mischievous twinkle in his golden eyes. And his lips were pursed together, as if trying to suppress a smile.

"Forgive my rudeness. I happened to overhear your earlier conversation with Ms. Toklas," he explained.

His grin was pure mirth, and I found my own lips curving upwards as the weight of the past few days lifted.

"Oh, right, *that*. Is she always so…," I fumbled for an adjective that was both accurate and socially acceptable.

"Yes, I am afraid so," Charles chuckled knowingly. "Her blunt nature still catches many of us off guard. But you handled her with the expertise of a horsewoman accustomed to difficult mounts."

"I've had some experiences with stubborn asses," I replied.

To my surprise, Charles didn't as much as crack a smile. In fact, he seemed to have not heard me at all. The moon had chosen that moment to peek out from between clouds, and his gaze was focused intensely on my throat.

There was very little space between us as we sat facing each other on the stone bench, but Charles leaned in even closer. His handsome features glowed in the iridescent light, his jawline more pronounced, the gold of his hair more brilliant, the flecks of color in his eyes more hypnotic. I swallowed thickly.

Is he going to kiss me?

The question hovered next to my head like a thought bubble from a comic strip that needed to be popped. Kissing a handsome stranger was not going to aid the mission, not even a little bit. Paris was not my home and 1925 was not my time. Nothing could, would, or should come of a romantic entanglement with Charles DuPree. And that wasn't fair to either of us.

Long, strong fingers, like those of a pianist, skimmed my collarbone. I shivered and Molly's philosophy on love, life, and dating came to mind: *All's fair in love, war, and the pursuit of a good time.*

A giggle bubbled up inside my throat, but evaporated when his eyes lingered on my own. Charles cupped my throat. The rough skin of his palm pressed just over my pulse, his thumb sliding underneath the gold chain of my locket. He brought his face impossibly closer, so near that his breath brushed my lips.

And then, voice low and husky, he asked the last question I would've expected.

"When did you get this?"

TWENTY THREE

"STASS? YOU OUT here? Stass?"

Gaige's singsong voice was an instant buzzkill.

Charles and I darted apart like two teenagers caught necking in the backseat of a car at some scenic spot called Lover's Lane or Lookout Point. Charles's fingers were still intertwined with my necklace, linking us together in our embarrassment. He hurriedly yanked his hand free, along with several strands of my hair, and then stood to put even more distance between us. I smoothed my dress into place, before following suit.

Heart still pounding, I called to my partner in a surprisingly even tone. "Back here, Gaige. In the garden."

Footsteps echoing in the still night, as my partner rounded the house. I caught sight of Gaige immediately, the worry lines creasing his brow evident in the soft light from one of the electric lamps. The moment his gaze landed on my companion and me, his concern evaporated.

"Well, well, well, what do we have here?" Gaige's smirk showed enough enamel to see he no longer had his wisdom teeth. My partner crossed his arms over his chest, and stared back and forth between Charles and me.

"It's nice to see you again, Mr. Prince. Beautiful night, isn't it?" Charles replied. He appeared to be the picture of calm, using manners to mask any discomfort he might have been experiencing. Only a slight twitch on the side of his neck belied his tone.

"You're gallivanting around in the dark with my sister, Gaige will do," my partner replied, taking the hand that Charles extended for a gentlemanly shake.

Pebbles crunched beneath the soles of Charles's shoes as he shifted from one foot to the other. Gaige's habit of reveling in awkward situations was clearly not something Charles was accustomed to, and it was making my new friend anxious.

Gaige's gaze lingered on Charles for several beats, purposefully assessing him from head to toe. When my partner turned his attention back to me, his eyebrows had crawled halfway up his forehead, as if to ask, *"This guy? Really?"*

"You were looking for me?" I asked.

"Right. Time to go."

"Go? Is the party over?" I asked, glancing around for a clock as though one of the trees might have a face and hands.

"Yes, dear sister. While you were receiving lessons on the local birds and bees with Mr. DuPree, the earth did continue to rotate. So much so, in fact, that the night's festivities are at a close."

"Then, if you will both excuse me," I said demurely. "I simply must thank our hostesses for such a wonderful evening."

Raucous laughter greeted me in the courtyard at the front of Stein's house. Partygoers had trickled out onto the steps and into the gardens, glasses brimming with champagne and wine in their hands. Several guests had decided to cut out the middleman and were drinking straight from bottles of assorted alcohol.

"Stassi, darling! There you are!" Hadley's voice rang out above the din of boisterous conversations and laughter. She was on the arm of her husband—my first up-close look at Mr. Ernest Hemingway. Though he would go entirely gray later in life, his hair was still inky black in 1925, and ruffled as though he'd been running his hands through it all night.

"Ah, the infamous Miss Prince," Ernest called, his voice a monotone that nevertheless commanded attention. "I had the pleasure of going a few rounds with your brother earlier today, he is quite brave."

"He's something alright," I replied with a smile, walking over to join the couple in the middle of the courtyard.

Stein's other guests flowed past us to the short line of cars waiting on the street. A particularly rowdy bunch made for a gorgeous convertible with the top down at the front of the line that didn't seem nearly large enough for their numbers.

"I'm a fan, Mr. Hemingway, it is such an honor to meet you," I said, refocusing my attention on Hadley and her husband.

And it was true—his was a rare gift. It was as if he possessed a perspective on human nature that few could see, and he conveyed his observations in a precise but illustrative fashion that was timeless. I couldn't fathom having that sort of talent.

"Good, come have a drink with us and you can tell me all about my genius," Ernest declared. Though the remark would've seemed joking from anyone else, his staid expression and my knowledge of his character told me that he was utterly serious.

"Oh yes, you simply must join us!" Hadley cried. "I was such a boar earlier, you must forgive my rudeness. We will be fast friends, you and I. I just know it. Come have a drink with us, say yes."

More than to offer an apology, I got the distinct impression it was a desire for companionship that drove Hadley to extend the invitation.

Still, I couldn't help but laugh at her earnestness.

The lampposts gave off enough light for me to see that Hadley's eyes were a little too bright, her cheeks a little too flushed, and the grip she had on her husband's arm a little too tight. In fact, Ernest was all that was keeping her upright.

Champagne sloshed over the rim of the glass dangling from her free hand. As if the sudden wetness on her skin reminded Hadley that there was still alcohol to drink, she lifted the glass to her lips and drained the contents.

"I wish I could," I replied. Hadley's expression immediately turned to pouty disappointment. "Gaige and I must get home. Our uncle arrived last night, and we promised him a nightcap."

"Oh come now, just one drink?" Hadley pressed. Then, as quickly as her mood had dipped, it swung back up and her expression brightened. "Or you can ring him and he can meet us!"

"Splendid idea," Ernest declared. "We need more menfolk. Your uncle, you say? Is he a military man? I would love to trade war stories with another brave soldier."

"I'm sorry, we really can't tonight," I apologized, legitimately regretful. Not just because the outing would be advantageous for the mission, but also because I genuinely wanted to hang out with these characters. "Perhaps we could get together another day this week?"

"Yes, of course, we will have lunch. Ring me tomorrow and let me know when you're available," Hadley replied, her disappointment forgotten.

"I will," I promised.

A horn honked, followed by a man waving a champagne bottle and calling to Hadley and Ernest from the overstuffed convertible.

"It seems we are being summoned," Hemingway declared.

The three of us said a quick goodbye, and then the couple trotted over to join their friends. All of the seats in the back were already taken, with women teetering on men's laps and clutching anything within reach to keep from falling to the floorboards.

Ernest slid into the front seat beside the driver, while Hadley stumbled over the occupants to perch atop the back of the open-topped car. Someone handed her a bottle of champagne. She attempted to refill her glass, though more alcohol poured down the front of her dress than made it into the cup. A man passing by on the sidewalk nearly became the recipient of a bubbly shower when Hadley raised the bottle in toast to me.

"Au revoir, Stassi!" she called, blowing me a kiss as the driver shifted into gear and the car pulled away.

Hadley's drunken laughter was still audible as I walked inside to say goodbye to Stein and Toklas.

In a weird way, the joie de vivre atmosphere of the 1920s reminded me of a daytrip I'd taken into Nashville with the other work camp girls. Then, just as now, it seemed those who'd lived through the war wanted to celebrate that fact. After so much bloodshed and death, the survivors needed a constant reminder that they were still alive. The parallels made me feel a little less homesick, even though the aftermath of World War Five had never touched Branson.

Inside the foyer, the remaining guests surrounded Stein and Toklas. I stepped to one side to wait discreetly for a break in the conversation. Like bees to honeycomb, a group of women I'd met early in the kitchen swarmed me immediately.

"You positively must join me for dinner," Maggie said, placing one hand lightly on my forearm to draw my attention.

"We should take you to Madame Chanel's boutique," her friend interjected.

"You will be the most fashionable woman in Baltimore, if you return with a trunk full of her designs," a willowy brunette agreed, her voice heavy with a German accent.

The barrage of offers for dinner and shopping dates was so overwhelming, all I could think to do was smile and nod graciously.

Another woman even invited Gaige and me to join a house party on the Riviera in the coming weeks. Thankfully, that was when Ines swept in out of nowhere and expertly handled the situation. She gave noncommittal answers that in no way promised attendance, but were laced with enough flattery for the asker to believe I'd be delighted to join an uncle's eighty-second birthday celebration, or visit the guillotine that had claimed Marie Antoinette's head. In that moment, I was again grateful for our guide and her skillful deflections. Morbid curiosity aside, a blade bathed in more blood than Elizabeth Bathory held little interest for me.

In an unexpected contradiction to our intel about the introverted Andre Rosenthal, the writer stopped at our group on his way out to brush kisses on both my cheeks and hug me goodbye. The embrace was awkward, like one you give an aunt that bathes in mothballs and joint cream, but I still found it touching. The simple gesture brought such guilt that I held on for a few beats longer than socially acceptable. None of my targets in the past were as likeable as Rosenthal, and I felt a shame I'd never before experienced on a run. Using him for profit sat with me about as well as a toddler on a sugar high.

Rosenthal's exit provided the perfect opportunity for me to make my own goodbyes to the group of women inexplicably interested in becoming my new best friends.

I wasn't the only person waiting for an audience with Stein and Toklas, though. I darted in front of several other guests—rudeness be damned, I had places to go and shops to burgle—and reached the hostesses just as a slim man in a well-worn sport coat bid them adieu.

"Americans," I heard someone behind me grumble.

The formidable women were speaking to each other in hushed tones as I approached. I caught Stein rolling her eyes.

"I apologize for interrupting," I began. "I just wanted to thank you again for inviting my brother and me this evening. It was a privilege to be here."

"Sorry about old Dopher, he wasn't too fond of the comments on his novel tonight," Stein replied, gesturing to the departing man. "I hope we did not keep you."

"Not at all," I said with a wave of my hand. "I just didn't want to leave without expressing my gratitude."

"We were happy to have you. Do come back next week," Stein invited. Her wide, welcoming smile was a laughable contrast to Toklas's scowl. "Your brother is going to bring me a short story to look over. I have to admit, I am quite curious."

"Me, too," I replied, stifling a surprised laugh. I couldn't imagine Gaige as a writer, much less one who warranted the opinions of Gertrude Stein. This was going to be interesting.

Ines broke away from the group and joined me in thanking the hostesses.

"Gertrude, Alice, a pleasure as always," she told them. To me, she said, "I do believe Jacque is waiting for us with the car. And poor Gaige is in the courtyard, stuck in an utterly tedious conversation with Vincent. He fancies himself a great artist, and seems to believe your brother is the benefactor he has been waiting for."

We said a final goodbye to Stein and Toklas, and then Ines took my arm and led me outside.

Gaige was indeed in the courtyard, talking excitedly with a group of men who were keenly interested in whatever he was saying. If I had to guess, it looked like an animated, very Gaige-like retelling of his experiences at the Préfecture de police de Paris. Looking as dapper as I'd ever seen him, with one hand tucked into the front pocket of his tailored suit pants and the other waving wildly about, my partner fit right in with the other men of the time.

Gaige waved me over, but I gave him a subtle head shake and smile in response, pointing to where Jacque stood beside our car idling at the curb. After handshakes and lots of back clapping, he caught up with Ines and me just as the driver was opening the backdoor for us.

"That went shockingly well. You were both quite the hits," Ines remarked, once we were settled into the seats and on our way.

"Don't sound so surprised," I said, with a healthy dose of dry sarcasm.

"Ignore her, Ines," Gaige chimed in, poking me in the ribs. "Stassi doesn't always play well with others."

Ines's tinkling laughter filled the car briefly before she eyed me with curiosity.

"Not that it is any of my business, but why did you refuse Hadley's invitation for drinks?" she asked.

Gaige and I exchanged glances. Our late-night plans weren't exactly a secret. Nonetheless, through unspoken agreement, we'd neglected to inform Ines of our plans for a felonious after-party.

The alchemist lit a cigarette and took a long, languid drag.

"Does it have anything to do with the toolkits Cyrus requisitioned from customs earlier?" she asked as she exhaled.

"Nothing gets by you, Ines," I replied.

"Well, whatever your plans, promise to be careful, won't you? I simply cannot abide another visit to that horrid préfecture." Ines paused and stared me dead in the eye. "This city is full of men I would gladly lose sleep to spend the evening with, but that bore of an inspector is not one of them. I am sure you would agree, Stassi. Perhaps Charles DuPree is on your list?"

Yep, nothing got by Ines.

TWENTY FOUR

"WHAT THE FRACKING frack?" Gaige hissed, the curse words leaving his pursed lips on a small, white puff of air. "What's wrong with this damned thing?" Remembering too late that our boss had decided to join us on this excursion, my partner glanced over his shoulder guiltily and muttered a sheepish apology for his use of foul language. "Sorry, Cyrus."

"I'm pretty sure it's user error," I suggested helpfully.

Under different circumstances, the situation might have been funny. But at two o'clock in the morning, with the temperature hovering somewhere just north of freezing, I couldn't find any amusement in Gaige's shortcomings. Even with the state-of-the-art lock picking set from customs, my partner couldn't seem to disengage the relatively archaic deadbolt on Shakespeare and Company's front door.

"I've got this," Gaige declared. "Just give me a minute."

"We don't have a minute," I muttered, trying to keep my agitation to a minimum.

Our position on the sidewalk in front of a closed bookstore left us completely exposed and vulnerable to nosy insomniacs looking for late-night entertainment. Thanks to our night vision contacts, also courtesy of customs, Gaige wasn't using a flashlight, which would've drawn even more attention to our shady business dealings.

In Gaige's defense, having our boss staring over his shoulder had to be intimidating. Cyrus was retired from running, and no longer mentored newbies during the apprenticeship year, so this was the first time either Gaige or me had been on a mission with him.

Declining our boss's offer to assist with the search of Shakespeare and Company had not been an option. Even if it had been, Gaige and I needed all of the help we could get. Locating a single book hidden in an overcrowded bookstore was going to be as difficult as finding a specific grain of sand on the beaches of Branson, so three sets of eyes were definitely better than two. Though if Gaige didn't get that door open soon, three butts were going to be sitting in hard plastic chairs down at the police station instead of two.

"I'm usually so good at this," Gaige groaned, going in for a fifth attempt.

I caught Cyrus's gaze over Gaige's head and rolled my eyes. My boss's lips twitched as he fought a smirk.

"Keep telling yourself that," I shot back, careful to keep my volume low. "Your turn is over sweetie, and you get an A for effort. Now move over, let me try."

With a grumble, Gaige handed me the lock-picking tools. I removed my black leather gloves and blew warm air onto my fingers to restore blood flow, then set to work.

"Wait, wait, wait," Cyrus interrupted, just as I was about to slide the flat metal piece into the lock. He gripped the door handle in one gloved hand and twisted. A soft click sounded, then the door swung inward, emitting a rickety creak.

"Ladies first." Cyrus gestured to the open doorway. I crossed the threshold into the bookstore, followed closely by Gaige.

"How'd you do that?" my partner demanded, annoyed.

"Magic," Cyrus deadpanned. "Now, do either of you have a starting point? Or are you just hoping the manuscript will jump off of the shelves and bite you in the ass?"

"The second one," I replied sheepishly.

"Wonderful, the hope-we-get-lucky method of investigating—my favorite." Cyrus's tone was dry as the Sahara. He ran a gloved hand over his salt-and-pepper hair as he surveyed the overflowing shelves and worn furniture. "Okay, why don't we divide the store into thirds? Stassi, you start with Adventure, Children's Books, and Classics," he instructed, gesturing to the signs hanging above the various bookcases. "Gaige, Horror, Literature, and Mystery. I'll take Romance, Thrillers, and Travel. When you finish with your assigned sections, start in on one of the remaining ones."

"Aye, aye, Captain," answered Gaige, giving our boss a cheeky two-finger salute.

From the pouch at my waist, I withdrew a pair of white, cotton artifact gloves. Sliding them on to my frozen fingers, I set to work. This was the first time I'd used the night vision contacts. They felt very foreign in my eyes and I kept blinking, as if that would help me adjust to the new, odd sensation. Even stranger than the feel of them, was the greenish glow they cast over everything.

The search was tedious, made more so by the fact that we didn't know exactly what we were looking for. Going into this, I'd assumed a handwritten manuscript would be easily identifiable, that it was just a matter of locating Rosenthal's hiding place. Not so much. Every other book I pulled from the shelf was handwritten. Even those that were typed often had handwritten missives in the margins.

"Anyone finding anything?" Gaige called after what felt like forever.

Glancing at the synchronized timepiece on my wrist—yet another goody from the customs toolkit—I saw that it had only been an hour.

"Yes, Gaige, I found it. I figured keeping it a secret would be a laugh," I said dryly, reaching for the next book on the shelf.

"Bite me," came Gaige's eloquent reply from across the room.

"Now, children, play nice," muttered Cyrus, sounding somehow both bored and amused.

Exhausted and annoyed, I snapped closed the edition of *Peter Rabbit* in my hands and replaced it on the shelf. I'd finished with my sections, and was no closer to finding *Blue's Canyon* than I had been when we entered the store.

"This is going to take all night," I proclaimed. "We need a better system."

Cyrus turned from a shelf of travel books, a hardback copy of *Alistair's Guide to London* open in his hands. He arched an eyebrow. "Do you have a suggestion?"

I blew out a breath. "No," I admitted, gesturing helplessly around the store. "But there has to be a better way to do this."

Cyrus replaced the guidebook and gave me his full attention.

"You both spoke with Beach, correct? Something she said made you believe part of the manuscript is here. What was it?"

Gaige was sitting cross-legged on the floor in front of a bookcase of mystery novels. He'd been thumbing through a thick book with a tattered rust-colored cover, but looked up when Cyrus started asking questions.

"I don't remember exactly. She told us that Rosenthal comes in here to write on a regular basis. We asked her about his habit of hiding sections of his manuscripts until he was ready to submit them for publication. Then I flat out asked whether any of his work was hidden here," Gaige replied.

"Subtle," Cyrus remarked.

"Effective," Gaige volleyed. "Beach tried to be coy, but she definitely knows there is a piece of a manuscript in this store. She might even know where."

"Exactly," I said, realization dawning. "She does know where, she has to. Otherwise, she might accidentally sell it to someone."

"Should we go wake her up for a little midnight interrogation?" Gaige asked me doubtfully.

I rolled my eyes. "No, of course not. But think about it—she wouldn't want to risk selling the manuscript—"

"You already said that," Gaige interjected.

"—and she wouldn't want to risk someone walking off with it," I continued, ignoring my partner's snarky comment. "So it's not going to be on one of these shelves."

"Stassi's right," Cyrus chimed in. "Beach would want to keep it in a controlled environment, like—"

"Behind the register," Gaige and I finished in unison.

Since I was closest, I reached the sales counter first. Gaige and Cyrus joined me a moment later. I started with the shelves beneath the register. Beach was organized, with accounting and sales ledgers, handwritten receipts for the past few months, inventory lists, and reminder notes to herself arranged in boxes and folders.

"Nothing," I declared, feeling defeated. I'd been so sure the manuscript would be there. "What about the back of store?"

"No need," Gaige replied, sounding distracted.

He and Cyrus were standing beside me, searching the books Beach kept on a small two-tiered shelving unit behind the sales counter. Gaige was holding a leatherbound book, smaller than the one we'd seen Rosenthal writing in at the café, but similar in style. He held it up to show us. The front cover was blank, save one word embossed in gold calligraphy: Book.

"Well that's specific," I said of the title. "Are you sure?" I stepped closer to my partner as he flipped the cover open to reveal the precise penmanship inside. Sure enough, the handwriting matched the examples Eisenhower had shown us of Rosenthal's works.

Cyrus crowded in on Gaige's other side, staring over his shoulder to read the words along with us. My partner ran his gloved fingers over the words written on the otherwise blank title page: *Blue's Canyon.* Gaige turned the page, and read the first line of text aloud: *Serena was exceptionally lovely when she stood before the window, the golden halo created by the sun's morning rays giving her the appearance of an angel sent from the heavens.*

"Look, there." Cyrus pointed to the bottom right corner, where a "1" was scrawled. The number on the next page was "2". "This must be the first section of the manuscript. Flip to the end," he instructed.

Obediently, my partner followed orders, though the slightly wistful expression he wore told me that he wanted to read the story. I didn't blame him. Rosenthal's writing had a way of capturing readers, sucking them in to tales of love, loss, and heartbreak.

On the last page, the final line of text simply read: *Serena's delicate touch was all Tate needed to…*

"To what?" Gaige demanded urgently.

Cyrus clapped him on the back. "Well, thanks to you, the world will soon know," our boss told him. "Now, start scanning. We've been here way too long already."

"Yeah, okay." Gaige reached into his toolkit and retrieved a handheld image scanner—a long, thin object with buttons on one side and a row of LEDs on the other. He hit the start button and began scanning the pages one by one.

The LEDs normally emitted a soft blue light, but it appeared more greenish-yellow and impossibly bright with the night vision contacts. Nervously, I glanced towards the windows at the front of the store. There were no curtains or blinds to shield us; only the darkness had kept us safe this long. A knot began to form in the pit of my stomach. Something felt off.

"Hurry up," I warned impatiently.

"I'm going as fast as I can," Gaige grumbled.

I caught Cyrus's eye. My boss seemed unusually anxious, as well. He crossed and uncrossed his arms, tapping the toe of his boot on the floor.

Not good, I thought.

Ten silent, agonizing minutes later, Gaige mercifully proclaimed, "Last page. Almost done, guys."

I began to relax. *You're just jittery after last night,* I told myself. *Thirty seconds, tops, and we're in the clear.*

The scanner beeped twice to indicate the imaging was complete. I sighed, relieved. We weren't going to spend another night in an interrogation box.

What's that saying about not counting your chickens before they've hatched? I should really remember it in the future.

A short, sharp siren burst was all the warning we received before a loud voice blared through a bullhorn.

"Come out with your hands up!"

TWENTY FIVE

"IS THIS A bad dream?" I groaned. "Am I going to look down and realize I'm naked, too?"

"That would improve this situation exponentially," quipped Gaige, though his trademark grin was nowhere in sight.

"Backdoor," Cyrus said brusquely. "It leads to an alley. Let's just hope the police don't have people posted there already."

Gaige shoved the leather book back into place. As he and I followed Cyrus to the rear of the store, my partner stowed the scanner in the toolkit attached to his belt. Crouching low to avoid detection, the three of us wound through the many obstacles on the path to our only viable exit.

"We need to lessen the chances of us all being caught. Once we reach the alleyway, split up," Cyrus coached over his shoulder as we made it to the back room, careful to keep his voice just above a whisper. "You both know the drill. Avoid capture at all costs. There is an incendiary device built into the side of your toolkits—it's the small metal disc that looks like an old watch battery. If you are caught, or believe you will be, activate it and toss the whole kit. You'll have approximately ten seconds before the device detonates. Once activated, it can't be deactivated, though. Understand?"

"Yes, sir," Gaige and I answered as one.

From outside, the officer with the bullhorn repeated his command, this time tacking on a warning that we had until the count of ten to comply.

"Un…duex…trois…," he began, pausing between the numbers, as if really expecting we might give ourselves up.

"Synchronize your watches. We'll meet at the car in one hour. If you can't make the rendezvous, head for the townhouse on foot as soon as you are able. If you do get caught, get word to Ines through customs and we'll go from there," Cyrus continued calmly, undeterred by the ticking clock the officers had just set.

Still in the lead, Cyrus reached the backdoor. He hurried through, Gaige close behind, just as the man with the bullhorn shouted, "Dix!"

The front door to Shakespeare and Company flew open with a bang.

Instinctively, I glanced behind me. Wrong move. My shoulder struck the corner of a table, causing a lamp to tumble over the side. I was quick, but not quick enough to catch it. The lamp shattered when it hit the floor.

"Stassi!" Gaige hissed, his voice so distant that I wondered if he'd actually spoken at all.

"Back there!" a man shouted.

"Go! I'll catch up," I whisper-yelled to my partner, unsure whether he heard me over the noise the officers were making.

Flashlight beams crisscrossed the room. While the contacts were adaptable, meaning the sudden brightness did not blind me, the constant switching on-and-off of the night vision was dizzying.

Heart thundering in my chest, I dove through the open doorway into the alleyway beyond. Gaige and Cyrus were nowhere in sight. Behind me, I heard the door to the back room slam open.

Crap.

There was no time to run. I needed to hide.

"I am sure I saw someone go out there," I heard one perplexed officer say in French.

I dropped to my knees and slammed my back against the brick wall behind me.

"Did you hear that?" a man asked.

"I think it came from the alleyway," a second one commented.

I swore silently. If they looked outside, I was done.

Or was I?

A window ledge protruded several inches from the wall, with trashcans sitting underneath. There was just enough space behind the cans for someone thin, someone like me. The noise I'd make getting back there would be a tipoff, but what choice did I have?

One other choice, I thought, grinning as a plan developed in my mind.

I snatched the lid off one of the trashcans, and flung it as hard and fast as I could down the alleyway. It landed with a loud thunk, followed by several more thunks as it skidded across the pavement. Rats scurried from hiding places at the sudden commotion, adding their own soundtrack to the impromptu symphony I'd started.

Perfect.

I eased down to the ground and pressed my body against the brick wall beneath the window ledge, holding my breath.

"We've got one! We've got one!" an overzealous officer yelled excitedly from inside.

I dared a peek over my head. A mustached man was leaning out of the window above me, waving a baton back and forth like it was a butterfly net.

"I do not see anything," the officer in the window declared dejectedly.

"Where did he go? He was just here."

"Move. Move. Let me see."

A second man replaced the first. This one I recognized—Inspector Dumb Dumb. I wasn't sure whether to be relieved or disheartened. The guy was definitely incompetent, but he was also determined. If he caught me in another comprising situation, I wouldn't be able to talk myself out of it.

"Rats, you imbecile. Your imagination is playing tricks on you, unless you want to tell me that our criminal has a long tail and whiskers? No? I did not think so. Finish searching the premises." His voice grew fainter as he spoke.

I counted to thirty, and then eased from my hiding place. Sticking to the shadows, I jogged up the alley.

Shakespeare and Company was not the only establishment on this street with a backdoor. It seemed most of stores had an additional exit, whether for trash or in case of a fire, or just because. And most of them were labeled. That was how I ended up crouched in front of a green door with peeling gold lettering.

Bonheur's: Fine Jewelry since 1435.

I knew I shouldn't. I *knew* I shouldn't.

One close call per evening was more than enough. And yet, when was I ever going to get a chance to search the store at my leisure? Well, maybe tomorrow night. Or the next night, or the one after that. Still, I was already there. And though Gaige was onboard with me running a side mission while in Paris, Cyrus probably was not. With him staying at the townhouse, this might be my only shot at snooping without having to make excuses to my boss.

"Just do it," I muttered.

After checking to make sure the door was in fact locked, I inserted a flat metal object with a small scanner on the end. The display lit up a moment later, depicting the lock schematic. I found the appropriate tools in my kit. Three seconds later, I was sliding through the backdoor to Bonheur's.

Where to start? Records? Invoices? Sales receipts? I didn't know. This was the farthest I'd ever come in the search for my necklace's origins. Until stumbling across Bonheur's the day before, all of my leads had fizzled.

This one might crack the case wide open, whispered the eternal optimist in my head.

I smiled. That cheerful voice wasn't my own; it belonged to the living, breathing, everyday bright spot in my life—Molly. Man, I missed her.

My own pessimistic nature, at least where all things family-related were concerned, began to creep in, overshadowing Molly's influence.

Why am I here? What am I even looking for? Is this a mistake?

These questions were not new. Since joining the syndicate, I'd asked myself the same ones too many times to count. Chasing the past was in my job description. But that was someone else's past, someone else's coveted objects, someone else's link to their ancestors.

Instinctively, my fingers closed around the necklace. The cool metal against my even colder palm felt good, reassuring.

Recent sales information might be kept near the registers, but anything older was more likely kept somewhere in the back. Nearby was a tidy alcove that looked promising.

Meticulously labeled file cabinets sat beside a rectangular desk with a pencil cup in one corner and a calculator in the other. A portrait of a man from a different era—a king, from the look of it—hung above the desk, appearing very out of place.

An hour later, I was dying. Searching electronic files was *so* much easier, and faster, than manually thumbing through paper ones. According to their records, Bonheur's had not sold a necklace matching the description of mine in the last decade, nor had one been commissioned. Like our search of Shakespeare and Company, it occurred to me that my methods were too haphazard. I needed to approach this logically, though the sales records had seemed like a logical place to start at the time.

I stood in the center of the small office and tried to tune out the nagging worry that the information I sought wasn't there. All I knew for sure was that a woman physically present in Paris sometime during 1924 had been wearing my necklace. That didn't mean she bought it in 1924. Maybe it had been a gift. Maybe she'd been borrowing it from a friend. Maybe it wasn't the same necklace at all.

No, I decided. Matthieu Bonheur had recognized the locket. He'd said it had no equal, whatever that meant. To me, his odd choice of words meant that the piece was a custom job. And from Matthieu, I knew for certain that Sebastian Bonheur, who'd been retired for several years, had crafted it. So maybe the real issue was that the records in the filing cabinets didn't go back far enough.

"What do you think?" I asked the portrait above the desk. Dead, black eyes stared back at me, the full pink lips unmoving. "A lot of help you are."

I leaned closer to read the signature on the bottom of the painting, down near the gilded frame. It was illegible. Frustrated by my inability to decipher meaning from anything in that fracking office, I pounded the wall beside the portrait. An almost imperceptible click sounded, and then the painting of some long-dead royal guy swung towards me.

"Whoa," I breathed.

It only took me a second to get over my shock. I pulled the frame until the painting was perpendicular to the wall, revealing a safe. A quick search of the toolkit turned up the necessary instruments. I had the correct three-digit combination entered in under a minute.

The safe was relatively narrow, approximately two feet across, but deep enough that I needed to reach my entire arm up to the shoulder inside to brush the back wall with my fingertips. As expected, the contents were incredibly valuable. High quality round, marquise, and princess cut diamonds were sorted by size and placed inside clear plastic pouches in wooden boxes. Precious stones—rubies, sapphires, emeralds—were divided and stored according to the vibrancy of each colored stone. The semiprecious gems—aquamarines, pearls, amethysts, garnets, opals—were placed in labeled drawers of a miniature bookcase. They were all so beautiful, shining brilliantly out at me like a rainbow after a rainstorm.

Several velvet boxes were stacked in the center of the safe. I opened them one by one, crossing my fingers that just one of the necklaces, earrings, or broaches inside would provide me some insight. Gorgeous as those finished pieces were, none of them bore even a slight resemblance to my locket.

Beneath the stack, I found a black leather portfolio with Bonheur's signature five-leaf clover on the front cover. I traced the clover with my finger, my heart pounding so loudly that I could hear the rush of blood in my ears.

This is it, I thought, though I was unable to say why.

I hesitated, afraid to open the portfolio for fear the documents inside would prove a major letdown. Never in my life was I so happy to be wrong.

Inside there were four sheets of paper. The first was a repair order. From the black and white photograph, it appeared the damaged item was a pair of men's sapphire cufflinks. An up-close inspection of the filigree border around the square perimeters sent my pulse spiking.

It's a match. I'd bet my life on it, I thought excitedly.

I scanned the repair order for a customer name. There, in the bottom left corner, was a name printed in precise block letters: M.L. Worchansky. Next to Worchansky's signature was an address in France. And the pickup date was listed as February 17, 1925.

My heart was so light it could have been made of clouds. Worchansky, whoever he or she was, had those cufflinks in his or her possession at that very moment. This was a solid lead. I could go and actually speak with a living, breathing person with knowledge of…what, exactly? Well, I wasn't sure. Worchansky's cufflinks had to be part of a matching set with my locket. The overall design aesthetic—a large sapphire center stone surrounded by gold filigree—was not unique in and of itself, but the way the gold threads wove together to form a border of interlocking symbols was. It couldn't be a coincidence.

The timepiece on my wrist beeped, reminding me once again that I was overdue for the rendezvous with Cyrus and Gaige. Just as I had earlier, I silenced the watch with a tap to the face. I really did need to hurry, though. Otherwise, it would be light out before I returned to the townhome.

Hurriedly, I flipped through the three remaining pages. These appeared identical to the custom work orders I'd found in the filing cabinet, though much, much older. Age had turned the pages yellow and faded the writing on several of the documents. Rings of water damage obscured the hand-drawn pictures in the center of one, and smudged the notes scrawled in the margins of another.

A cursory scan of each document told me very little. I needed more time, and possibly an ancient documents expert, to study the orders thoroughly. I considered scanning the pages, but the quality was too poor. I worried the images wouldn't come out whole. Once I returned to the island, I could bribe a restoration specialist to recreate the ruined images if I had the originals.

So, despite knowing better, I replaced the papers inside the portfolio and tucked it inside the waistband of my pants, underneath my shirt.

I closed the safe, spun the dial, and repositioned the painting of old King Dour-Face.

Next, how to get home? It wasn't like I could simply call a cab. I considered phoning Jacque, since Ines had said the driver was at my disposal. Given the hour, pulling the alchemist from sleep just felt rude, though. Instead, I decided to ring the townhouse. Cyrus and Gaige were probably waiting by the phone as it was, if they hadn't formed a search party to track me down.

I found a phone behind the sales counter in the main area of the store. When the switchboard operator came on the line, I gave her the address to the townhouse and waited for either my partner or my boss to answer.

Too late, a thought occurred to me—what excuse was I going to give Cyrus for my prolonged absence? Somehow, telling him that I'd been stealing old files from a jewelry store did not seem acceptable or wise.

Should've called Jacque, I thought ruefully.

That, at least, would have bought me time to invent a plausible lie.

TWENTY SIX

"STASSI?" CYRUS SNAPPED into the phone. "Where the hell are you?"

Why couldn't Gaige have answered?

"Yeah, Cyrus, it's me. I—"

"Are you hurt?"

"No," I was quick to assure him. "I just—"

"Please tell me you aren't calling from the police station."

"No, no, I'm fine, I got away."

Over the line, I heard Cyrus let out a relieved sigh.

"Good. That's good. Where are you?" he asked. His tone had lost its hard edge, and he just sounded weary.

I hesitated for the space of a heartbeat before answering, unsure how much truth to insert into my lie. Apparently, it was one breath too long for my boss.

"Stassi, where are you?" he demanded, the sense of urgency back.

"I'm hiding in a shop near the bookstore. The police were on my tail and I needed to wait them out," I said smoothly. "But now I'm sort of stuck out here, and I don't know the way back well enough to walk. Do you think that maybe you could come get me?"

The pause that followed was so long, I worried that the line had gone dead.

"Cyrus?" I asked tentatively. "Are you there?"

"Yeah, I'm here, Stassi. Can you meet us where we parked earlier? We can leave right now."

"I'll be there," I promised.

There was another long pause while Cyrus conveyed the plan to someone in the background. I could hear the replies, even over the old-fashioned telephone. Gaige demanded to know what the hell had happened to me. Ines thanked the heavens that I hadn't become the latest victim of the Night Gentleman. Another male voice, that might have been Felipe, proclaimed that he'd been right all along.

"Fifteen minutes," Cyrus said to me.

It was a command, not a request.

"I'll be there," I repeated.

Fourteen minutes later, the same black alchemist car that we'd borrowed earlier pulled to a stop at the rendezvous point, three blocks from Shakespeare and Company. I stepped out of the shadows, where I'd been waiting, as the backdoor of the car swung open. Ines, looking more disheveled than I'd ever seen her, beckoned me inside.

Cyrus was behind the wheel, with Gaige sitting shotgun. My boss glanced over his shoulder, gave me a once over, and gunned the engine without a word. Picking up his impatience, I slammed the door shut as he pulled away. Gaige's greeting was friendlier, though his tight smile told me something else was amiss.

The telltale flick of Ines's lighter sounded impossibly loud in the silent car. She inhaled deeply, then blew the plume of smoke towards the back of Cyrus's head.

"Ines," he barked, his tone allowing no argument. "Not now."

With shaking hands, she pulled the cigarette from its holder and dropped it out the window.

"You worried us, darling," she declared, peering at me in the darkness as she ran her fingers through her hair. Dark strands stuck out at odd angles from her head, and she was wearing a set of silky pajamas.

"I'm sorry," I said simply, my apology directed towards Cyrus more than the woman sitting next to me.

"Why didn't you call earlier?" asked Gaige, sounding more baffled than accusatory. "I mean, if you were in a store all this time, you could have called sooner to let us know you were okay."

"It didn't occur to me right away," I said lamely.

"Really?" he asked, turning to meet my gaze.

"The phone was behind the counter in the front, and I was hiding in the backroom," I explained, mostly for Cyrus's benefit. "The cops were swarming the street, and I didn't want to risk being seen through the window. I was trying to avoid being hauled down to the police station for the second time in twenty-four hours."

"What store were you in?" my partner asked, suspicion creeping into his eyes.

"Enough," Cyrus suddenly snapped. "It has been a long night, and we have other problems to deal with. Stassi is safe, we found part of the acquisition, and no one was arrested—that's all that matters."

Several minutes passed in tense silence. Cyrus's answer replayed in my head. When I couldn't resist the urge any longer, I risked my boss's wrath.

"What other problems?" I asked tentatively, hoping he wouldn't bite my head off.

Gaige turned again to look at me, the worry in his eyes alarming. He opened his mouth to answer, but never got the chance.

"You'll see," Cyrus said, shutting down further discussion.

When we walked into the townhouse five minutes later, I immediately understood. Another large bouquet of roses sat on the coffee table. The sight left me frozen in the doorway. Cyrus, who'd been holding the door open for us, gave me a nudge from behind so he could enter.

"Is that what I think it is?" I said, approaching the sitting area with slow, tentative steps.

"Unfortunately, yes," Cyrus answered.

Gaige waited until I sank onto the sofa beside him, then handed me the small white envelope that had accompanied the blooms. The front had looping writing in black ink: *For Miss Anastasia Prince.*

"Why is he addressing them to me?" I asked, not really expecting an answer.

"I have no clue," Gaige said.

"But we *will* find out," Cyrus insisted.

"Did you open it?"

"Well yes, we had a feeling that they weren't from your new boyfriend," Gaige replied.

While all three of them watched, I pulled out the card.

Roses are beautiful, violets are nice,
One dose of poison might just work trice.
Drink it down, you'll pay the price,
Will you find me and my grand device?
All my best,
Mitchell T. Baylarian

TWENTY
SEVEN

AFTER ONLY THREE hours of restless sleep, I dragged my tired, achy body from bed. To my surprise, Gaige was not only awake, but already in the living room. His Qube was on the coffee table in front of him, set on projection mode. The pages of Rosenthal's manuscript from Shakespeare and Company appeared before him as a hologram. Looking away for only a moment, my partner gave me a cursory wave as I descended the stairs, then resumed reading without a word.

A French Press was sitting on the coffee table, with a clean china cup beside it.

"Aw, thanks, honey," I said as I sat down in the armchair, hoping to draw him out.

I couldn't tell if he was simply engrossed in Rosenthal's words, or he was in a bad mood. Either way, Gaige didn't take the bait. He seemed oblivious to the world around him.

The rich aroma of strong, jumpstart-your-day coffee tickled my nose as I poured it into the cup, keeping an eye on my partner as I did. The first sip warmed my insides and chased away the hazy remnants of sleep.

"Where's Cyrus?" I asked.

"Out," Gaige said shortly.

I waited for him to elaborate, or at least look at me, but another minute passed in strained silence.

"Gaige? Everything cool?" I was unaccustomed to the attitude he was doling out. Every second that passed without his bubbly, sarcastic banter was making me more nervous.

His dark eyes narrowed on me for a long moment, and then he turned his attention back to the novel without answering.

Um, okay.

Beginning to feel annoyed, I took another sip of my coffee.

"Do we have a problem?" I asked. "Something you want to get off your chest? Or is Rosenthal's book actually *that* good?"

Gaige huffed as though my mere presence was irritating him. Apparently, we were playing the quiet game. I wasn't going to lose; if he had something to say, he needed to just come out with it.

I waited out the silence that ensued.

"Where were you last night, Stassi?" my partner finally asked, his voice barely above a whisper. Had I not been sitting right next to him, the question would have been inaudible.

"You want the truth?" I hedged.

"Obviously," Gaige said impatiently. "That's why I asked. Do you have any idea how worried I was? It isn't like you to miss a meet. And I get that the cops were chasing us, but you could've called sooner."

I opened my mouth to repeat the same lame excuse I'd used the night before.

Gaige held up a hand to stop me. "And don't even think about lying. I'm not buying that whole 'Ohh, I didn't think about a phone' shtick.

You're not an idiot, and neither am I. Where did you go? I swear, if you were shacked up somewhere with that DuPree guy—"

"Don't be ridiculous," I snapped, my irritation rising to match his. "Jeez, Gaige. Do really believe I ditched you guys to go swap pillow-talk with some random guy?"

Exasperated, Gaige threw his hands up in the air. "If the glass slipper fits."

"I was not with Charles!" I yelled, hoping the sheer volume of my words would penetrate my partner's thick skull. "I went to Bonheur's."

The hostility evaporated from Gaige's features, replaced by concern.

"The jewelry store? I should have guessed." He ran a hand through his disheveled hair. "You never told me what happened when you went in there the other day. I mean, I didn't want to bug you about it, or anything. I figured you'd tell me when you were ready."

"I'm sorry, Gaige. I didn't mean to shut you out, there's just been so much going on." My hand reached automatically for the locket, as if drawn by a magnetic force. "I spoke with the current owner, Matthieu Bonheur. I showed him my necklace. It was weird. *He* was weird. He obviously recognized it. Or recognized *something* about it. But he pretended he didn't. At least initially, anyhow. Then, after I basically shoved the locket under his nose and pointed to his company logo, he backpedaled and admitted that his grandfather had crafted the piece."

Excitement danced in Gaige's dark eyes, growing brighter as I rambled.

Though my partner didn't have the same personal stake in the locket that I did, he was just as invested in the search for its origins. The fact he cared so much reminded me how lucky I was to have a friend like Gaige.

"Did the owner know who bought it?" he asked, practically bouncing in his seat.

"Unfortunately, no," I replied, feeling another rush of annoyance towards the storeowner. "He gave me some crap about not keeping records, which was obviously a lie. I mean, seriously—a store that doesn't keep sales records?"

"So that's why you broke in to the store," Gaige deduced. "Why didn't you tell me? I would've gone with you." He had a lost puppy look on his face, the same one he always wore when his feelings were hurt.

"It's not like I was planning the break-in last night, I swear," I said hurriedly. "I've been meaning to talk to you about my discussion with Matthieu, we just haven't been alone for more than a second. Our entire trip here has ranged from crazy hectic to utterly insane, without any breaks. Last night, I just saw the door and seized the opportunity. You'd have done the same thing in my position."

My partner weighed my answer for a moment before shrugging.

"You're right. I'm not upset because you didn't tell me right away. It's just...I want you to know that you're not in this alone. We're a team, Stass. For better or worse, I'm with you. Always."

"'Til death do us part?" I teased. Despite my playful reply, Gaige's sentiment was deeply touching.

Feeling the sudden urge to hug my partner, I got up from the chair and plopped down beside him on the sofa. I leaned in to Gaige, and he wrapped both arms around me.

"You're a pain in my ass, but I'm here for you," he continued, tightening his grip until it felt like a boa constrictor had hold of me.

"I wish you'd been there last night," I replied when he finally let go. "I really could've used your help."

"Of course you needed me. Everyone needs a little Gaige Koppelman in their lives," he declared with a devilish grin, shifting to face me. "So, did you find out who bought your necklace?"

My shoulders slumped. "Not exactly," I admitted.

His expression fell, mirroring my own.

"That's not a 'no'," he hedged. "Does that mean that you found something? You're not usually so cryptic."

I glanced around the living room. "When is Cyrus coming back?" I asked. "And where's Ines?"

"Cyrus is doing another sweep of Lachlan's hotel room. He left just before you came down, so I'm guessing he'll be gone for a while," Gaige replied. "Ines stopped by right after I woke up, and said we'd be on our own until after lunch. Why do you ask?"

"Hang on," I said, jumping up off the couch. "I'll show you."

Taking the steps two-at-a-time, I ran back upstairs and beelined to my bedroom. Like all syndicate hideouts, the townhouse had a wall safe in each bedroom for valuables, techno gadgets, and anything else we brought from the future. After punching in the seven-digit code, I found the leather folder exactly where I'd left it, beneath my Qube.

Gaige's quizzical expression was still in place when I returned to the living room. I launched into an abbreviated explanation of my search of the filing cabinets, finding the portfolio in the safe, and my brief perusal of the documents it contained. Gaige listened with rapt attention, drinking in every scant detail I divulged.

"Now, here's where this gets interesting," I concluded, laying the pages side-by-side on the coffee table.

"You mean, the fact that Bonheur's keeps super-old sales receipts in a hidden wall safe isn't interesting enough?" Gaige quipped.

"No—I mean, well, yes. I'm getting to that. Patience, my friend." I pointed to the most recent order, where 'J. Jacobson' was printed in black ink. "It's harder to read on the other two, but once you know what to look for, it's obvious. All three commission orders have the same customer name on them: J. Jacobson."

"So we have name? Let's go track down this Jacobson person," Gaige proclaimed, bouncing on the sofa cushion like an impatient toddler at snack time.

"'A' for enthusiasm, buddy," I decreed, laughing. "But I'm not sure it's going to be that easy." One by one, I pointed to another box on each order; this one listed the date of commission for each individual piece.

After returning home and learning about the newest bouquet of terror from my apparent stalker, I'd been too exhausted and too consumed with dread to give the papers my full attention. But I had noticed the dates.

Gingerly, Gaige picked up the document closest to him for a better look. He squinted, then moved it so close to his face that it nearly bumped his nose. Next, he held it at arm's length, like an extremely far-sighted man who'd misplaced his reading spectacles. "Does that say June of 1795?" he asked, a note of disbelief coloring his words. "And what are these random characters? Hieroglyphs?"

"Yes to the date. No clue about the characters. I thought maybe I'd run them past one of our cryptologists back on the island."

The syndicate had an expert for everything, and I planned on using as many of them as I needed to solve this mystery.

Gaige whistled and set the commission order back on the coffee table. "No wonder the drawing is so faded. I can't even tell what it's of, can you?"

"No. The coffee cup rings and water stains don't help either." I handed him another of the orders. On this one, too, the drawing was faded, the paper yellow and brittle. Even still, it was significantly less damaged than the first. "Look at the date on there, it's even older."

"1493? Is that right? I can't read the month—one of the 'ember' ones, maybe? You know, September, October, November, December," he recited.

"Yeah, that's my guess, too," I agreed.

"Are those earrings?" he asked, indicating the drawing of two square objects.

"That's what I thought initially. Then, I realized the squares on there look a lot like the squares on here." I found the repair order for M.L. Worchansky's cufflinks, and swapped it for the 1493 commission order still in Gaige's hands. "I'm like 99.9% positive they're the same."

"Holy shant!" he exclaimed, excitedly jabbing at the drawing of the cufflinks with his index finger. "Stass, that frou-frou design stuff around the edges looks just like the frou-frou design stuff on your necklace!"

"I know," I replied, fighting the temptation to laugh. In fairness, I'd been nearly as excited when I first made the connection. I'd just been too tired and too uncertain of the significance to celebrate it. "And that 'frou-frou design stuff', as you call it, is also on this."

I showed him the third and most recent commission order, this one for a broach requisitioned in July of 1918. Being less than a decade old— practically brand new, compared to the other documents—both the drawing and the writing were easy to make out. Unfortunately, aside from being able to verify that the engraving on the metal was identical to that of my locket, the crisp lines of text and legible illustration gave me very little information.

"Wait a second.… You mean to tell me that this J. Jacobson person commissioned three different pieces of jewelry over a span of four centuries? How is that even possible?" Gaige inquired.

I watched as the light bulb inside of Gaige's head switched on, and he was able to answer his own question.

"J. Jacobson is a runner," he declared, reaching the same assumption that I had.

"That's the logical conclusion, right? But to my knowledge, Bonheur's has always been located in France. And France is Atlic territory. So, if J. Jacobson is a runner, he or she is one of Cyrus's."

"Not in my lifetime," Gaige said decisively.

The coil of tension that had formed the instant I'd first thought up the J. Jacobson-is-an-Atlic-runner theory loosened. As much as that would have made my search *so* much easier, I didn't want it to be true. The idea that Cyrus had seen me wearing my locket for the past two years, yet never said a word about knowing its origins, sickened me.

No, my boss didn't know about my quest to find my parents. Or that the locket once belonged to my mother. But he did know I was an orphan. He had to think I was curious about where I'd come from. I just couldn't believe that he'd withheld pertinent information from me on purpose.

"You're sure?" I pressed Gaige.

"Positive. I did grow up on the island, Stass. It's not a big place. We're only the second generation of the syndicate, so I know the names of most everyone who has ever lived on Branson. Jacobson isn't a last name I've ever heard. We should double-check with Molly when we get back, but I'm certain I don't know anyone by that name." His expression turned thoughtful. "Let me see that repair order again, though."

I handed him the repair order for the cufflinks. Gaige nodded, as though a suspicion of his had just been confirmed.

"M.L. Worchansky. Him, I do know."

"Seriously? You have a buddy from the early twentieth century?" I asked doubtfully. "This repair was picked up in February. Unless he's passed in the last two months, Worchansky is alive now."

"No, not a friend. I wish, though. M.L. Worchansky is famous, you haven't heard of him?"

"Famous for what?"

"He was an adventurer, for lack of a better term. And a very rich dude. Like go-for-a-swim-in-his-vault-of-money rich," Gaige explained. "He funded, and went on, a lot of explorations. The guy actually discovered an Amazonian tribe at one point. He also lived with a group of natives in what will one day be Alaska, and learned how to ice fish up there. And, if I'm remembering correctly, he had something to do with finding some pharaoh's tomb. Worchansky is a legend. He's been *everywhere*. Which is quite a feat for someone in this time."

"And he's apparently a hero of yours," I teased.

"Just as I will one day be some young, impressionable boy's hero," my partner replied.

"Scary thought." I patted my partner's arm affectionately. "Anyway, Worchansky lives here in France, according to the address on the repair order. I'd have to look it up to be sure, but I don't think his place is too far from here."

Gaige jumped to his feet. "Let's go talk to him!" he exclaimed.

"We can't right now, Gaige," I told him, my heart sinking. "We have a novel to find, a rogue runner to locate, and a killer to stop. I'd say our dance card is pretty full at the moment."

Even as I said the words, I wished I could take them back.

People in hell want a cold front, I thought wryly.

In the jewelry store, when I'd first realized Worchansky lived nearby, I'd been just as keen to head right over. The second flower delivery and the taunting poem that had accompanied it were game changers for me. I wanted nothing more than to hear anything and everything Worchansky had to say about his cufflinks, their possible connection to my locket, and this J. Jacobson person. So badly, in fact, that remaining seated on that sofa while Gaige was all but begging to go find the guy was physically paining me.

But the run came first. It had to. This run, specifically, was too dangerous to allow distractions to divide my attention.

"Besides," I added quietly, "Cyrus is pissed at me, isn't he?"

Gaige wrinkled his nose and flopped back down on the sofa. "Yeah, sort of. Well, not really pissed, exactly. He's more…I don't know, maybe scared?"

"Cyrus? Scared?" I asked doubtfully.

He shrugged. "I don't know. Last night he was practically pulling his hair out when you didn't show at the car. He freaked when I said we needed to leave because of the cops. We waited at the rendezvous point for almost an hour. He only agreed to leave when I suggested you might be trying to reach us back at the townhouse.

"When we got back and woke up Ines, he bit her head off when she suggested we wait until the morning to worry. After she lit up for the third time, he tore the cigarette out of her mouth and crushed it on the coffee table. Which was, admittedly, pretty entertaining, in hindsight. Regardless, it was scary, Stass, we didn't know what happened to you. And yeah, Cyrus was wicked pissed. Not actually at you, though, more in general."

I was speechless. Cyrus was imposing, maybe even intimidating, but he was always so cool, so together. I'd long suspected he had a temper, though I'd never actually seen him angry. Nonetheless, I was positive I didn't want to be within the fallout zone when he lost it.

"I wasn't gone that long," I said defensively. "And we just got separated, it wasn't *that* big of a deal. Honestly, I don't know where I would've gone if not Bonheur's. The police really were close to catching me."

Gaige held up his hand in a placating gesture. "Don't shoot the transporter. You asked, I'm just telling you what happened. Oh, one other thing." My partner smiled devilishly. "A letter came for you this morning."

My heart skipped a beat. Mitchell Baylarian had sent flowers twice the day before, and the second delivery had been less than twelve hours earlier. What the frack was his obsession with me?

"Oh, no, no," Gaige said, seeing my alarmed expression. "Not from the psycho. It's from lover boy."

"Lover boy?" I asked. "I have no clue who you're talking about." I was trying to play it cool, but my voice came out high-pitched, like a cartoon character.

Still grinning like a moron, Gaige withdrew a creamy white envelope from beneath the electronic tablet he'd been using to read Rosenthal's manuscript. Slowly, he extended his arm towards me. I reached for the letter, only to have Gaige pull it back.

"Stassi and Charles, sitting in a tree. K-i-s-s—oww!"

He rubbed the back of his head where I'd smacked him with a throw pillow. Taking advantage of his distraction, I yanked the letter free, scooped up the leather portfolio from Bonheur's, and headed back upstairs.

"After you're done fantasizing about Mr. Tall, Mysterious, and Frightfully Proper, we need to talk about our lunch plans," Gaige called after me.

I paused at the top of the steps. "Lunch plans?"

"Yep. We are revisiting Closerie des Lilas."

"Why? So you can indulge your mancrush on Rosenthal?" I asked. "Gaige and Andre sitting in a tree…."

I ducked when the same throw pillow came sailing up over the second floor balcony.

"*So* mature, Stass," he intoned. "No, some of us have our minds on *work*. After finding the one at Shakespeare and Company, I'm betting there's another piece of the manuscript hidden at the café. It's at least worth looking in to. There are like four other bars or restaurants in his rotation of writing places, so we need to start checking them off."

"Give me an hour," I replied. "I'll ask Felipe to do something quick with my hair and makeup."

Before I hopped in the bath, I paused to open the envelope I'd absconded with. The letter was, in fact, from Charles. He wanted to know if I would join him for dinner Monday evening, and included his phone number and address for me to send a reply.

It took a moment for it to fully sink in.

Charles DuPree was asking me on a date.

Though he was technically an asset, spending time with Charles wouldn't advance the mission whatsoever. For that reason alone, I should've declined. The fact that I still wanted to go, even when it wouldn't be productive, was even more of a reason to decline.

Call him, Stassi. Tell him no.

Instead of listening to my inner voice of reason and heading straight down to the phone, I tucked the card from Charles in the drawer of my nightstand and went to get ready.

TWENTY
EIGHT

GAIGE AND I strolled into the restaurant an hour later.

"Sit wherever you like," a man behind the bar called.

Thankfully, it wasn't the same bartender who'd helped us the other day. This made it considerably less awkward when we darted straight for Rosenthal's favorite booth in the far back corner. The bartender brought us menus and took our drink orders with polite indifference, for which I was immensely grateful. The less interested he was, and the less conversation we made, the less likely he was to remember us later. We definitely didn't need him and the other bartender comparing notes on the newest Americans in town.

"Where do we start?" I asked, once Gaige and I had minuscule cups of espresso in front of us.

My partner shrugged sheepishly. "I was sort of hoping you'd have an idea. You are the smart one, after all."

"Thanks," I muttered, rolling my eyes.

If I were a secretive, paranoid writer, where would I hide something? Where could you hide something in a public place?

Reaching beneath the tablecloth, I ran my fingers along the sides of the table, looking for some sort of secret compartment that might unlatch. The surfaces were all smooth, without any hint of a concealed opening. I leaned down further and did the same along the bottom of the table, hoping for something similar, or even a hidden ledge. A sticky wad was all I found.

"Gross!" I exclaimed. "Why do people do that?"

"I honestly couldn't say," Gaige replied, not even pretending to hide his amusement.

My partner sat back, sipped his coffee and observed with rapt attention as I continued my search of the table. I tried to check under the seat cushion of the chair beside me, but it was attached. Another strike.

"You're scary good at this," Gaige commented as he watched. "I would've immediately dismissed the table altogether."

Across from me, Gaige plucked the butter knife from his place setting. He spared a furtive glance at the bartender, who wasn't paying a bit of attention to us. Wedging the pointed end of the knife beneath the attached cushion, my partner attempted to pry the seat loose from the base of the extra chair beside him.

"Really?" I asked, torn between disbelief and amusement. "You think no one would have notice a guy dismantling the furniture?"

"Really?" he parroted. "You think it's any less ridiculous than attaching it to the underside of a table where countless people sit every day?"

I glared. "Do you have any better ideas?" I asked sweetly. "Maybe you could go check the men's room. Maybe it's hidden in the back of a toilet tank."

Gaige scrunched up his nose at the thought of searching the public facilities. I didn't envy him a bit, particularly since we were in a time when personal hygiene was just beginning to be a thing of importance.

"The women's room is just as likely," he shot back, managing to keep a straight face despite the absurdity of his comment.

I stared wordlessly at my partner until he let out a dramatic sigh.

"Fine," he said, drawing out the word. "But I want it on the record that you owe me."

"You've got it, Gaige. I will state in my official report that you did your job," I deadpanned. "Just be sure you're extra, *extra* thorough when searching the toilets, or no gold star for you."

With a glare that would've melted rock, Gaige stood. As he passed me on his way to the restrooms, my partner paused and leaned down so his mouth was right next to my ear. "You owe me," he repeated.

"You threw me off of a bridge!" I called pleasantly after him.

The sound of a throat clearing made me jump, and I turned to find the bartender standing just behind me with a confused look on his face.

"Mademoiselle? Is everything okay?"

"Oh, y-yes," I stammered. "My brother knows of my fondness for swimming and was just encouraging me to take a dip, no harm done."

"Very good," he replied, looking at me as if I were utterly deranged. "But you misunderstand…is everything okay with your table?"

"Oh yes, quite lovely," I responded with a pleasant smile.

"It is just…. Well, I saw you looking around," he replied tentatively. "Is there perhaps any way that I may be of assistance?"

Great, even the quintessentially disinterested French guy noticed our search, I thought.

"Everything is lovely," I repeated.

"Very well. Your meals should be ready shortly, I will go and check on them."

"We're in no hurry," I said, again with the pleasant smile that was starting to make my cheeks ache. "My brother is in the restroom, so feel free to take your time."

The waiter raised one eyebrow, but didn't comment.

"He has a delicate stomach," I added unnecessarily. "He might be in there for a bit."

My remark on Gaige's bathroom habits drew a brief look of disgust, but the man nodded and left without another word. Though I always enjoyed messing with my partner, that wasn't exactly why I'd said something. My partner's supposedly-weak stomach would hopefully keep the guy out of there, reducing the likelihood that Gaige would be interrupted while searching the bathrooms.

The bartender returned twenty minutes later to refill my coffee. My dining companion still hadn't returned, prompting the Frenchman to look even more repulsed by us gauche Americans. Truthfully, I was beginning to wonder what was taking Gaige so long. Was he checking the ceiling tiles? Dismantling the plumbing? How many toilets did Closerie des Lilas have?

I breathed a sigh of relief when Gaige's shadowy form finally materialized in the hallway. He strode confidently to the table, his dark eyes alive with giddy excitement.

"Ah, here is my brother," I said to the waiter. "We are ready for our entrées, whenever they are ready for us."

Picking up on my dismissal, the man turned to leave, though not before giving Gaige a long, lingering appraisal.

"Would monsieur care for some ginger ale?" he asked.

"Uh, no thanks. I'm good with coffee," Gaige replied. He waited until the man left to give me a bewildered look. "That was a weird question."

"Uh huh," I said innocently. "So what'd you find?"

"Stassi, you are a fracking genius," he declared.

My eyes widened with surprise, even though searching the bathroom had been my idea. I'd relished the thought of Gaige touching so many unclean surfaces more than I'd actually believed he might find something in there.

"You found it?" I asked.

His expression was triumphant, akin to Alexander conquering Persia. It seemed a little excessive for a man who'd found a handful of pages in a toilet instead of building an empire, but who was I to judge?

Gaige glanced furtively around, ensuring no prying eyes were spying on us. The café had no other patrons, and the bartender was still in the kitchen checking on our meals. Confident we were alone, my partner withdrew one of the syndicate's handheld scanners from the interior pocket of his suit coat.

"The pages are already scanned and ready for the forger," he said gleefully, waving the device around like a wand.

"I'll be damned," I breathed. "Rosenthal and I must share a brain or something."

"Poor guy," Gaige said with a grin.

A bell chimed in the distance, making both of us jump. Gaige quickly stuffed the device back into his jacket pocket as the bartender emerged from the kitchen with our lunch.

Giddy with excitement over our latest find, I was practically bouncing in my seat. The bartender eyed me suspiciously when he placed the croque monsieur—a fancy grilled cheese with ham—on my placemat.

"May I get you anything else?" he asked politely.

"The bill, please," Gaige and I said in unison.

Surprise flitted briefly across the bartender's face, but he recovered quickly. Speaking to Gaige instead of me, he nodded and said, "Very good, sir."

I inhaled my food at an alarming rate, tasting nothing and practically choking on every bite. Across the table, Gaige was keeping up with my manic pace. It was like we were contestants in one of those hotdog-eating competitions, except neither of us resorted to dunking our food in liquid to consume it faster.

Coffee and highbrow cheeses don't really mix well, anyway.

When the bartender returned with our check, a piece of ham flew out of my overstuffed mouth as I attempted to thank him. The meat landed on the table directly in front of the appalled man. It was not one of my finer moments in life.

"Wow," Gaige said when the server left, laughing so hard he nearly choked. "That was almost as embarrassing as the first time you went cliff-diving."

I threw a piece of croissant at Gaige in mock outrage. He wasn't wrong, though I'd always maintained that someone—*anyone*—should've mentioned it would be a bad idea to jump from two-stories high into the water while wearing a bikini. After braving the feat, I'd emerged triumphantly from under the water, fists held high above my head in victory and my bathing suit top nowhere in sight.

It wouldn't have been so bad, had the island children not been off of school that day. Mine were evidently the first boobs the tweens and teens had ever seen, so naturally they'd followed me around for weeks with googly eyes and hopeful grins on the off-chance I might flash them again.

It also had not been one of my finer moments.

When we left Closerie des Lilas ten minutes later, the waiter didn't ask us to visit again soon.

TWENTY NINE

THE PHONE WAS ringing when Gaige unlocked the door to the townhouse. We both went for it, but my hand closed around the receiver first. My partner watched with interest as I lifted the earpiece.

"Hello?" I said in English. Belatedly realizing my mistake, I quickly amended, "Je suis désolée. Bonjour?"

"Anastasia Prince?" the caller asked in English.

I recognized the Midwest-American accent immediately.

"Oh, hi!" I said with enthusiasm.

"This is Hadley Richardson," the caller continued.

In the living room, Gaige had his arms wrapped around himself in a tight embrace and was flicking his tongue through the air. I rolled my eyes and briefly considered throwing the sugar dish at his head.

"Hi, *Hadley*. It's Stassi," I said, loudly emphasizing her name for my partner's benefit.

Gaige's arms dropped to his sides. He shrugged his shoulders, then disappeared up the stairs, no longer interested.

In my ear, Hadley laughed merrily. "So sorry about the formality, Stassi. I figured you might have a housekeeper or butler who answered the phone."

Crap. Were we supposed to have hired help for that?

"No problem," I told her, ignoring the remark. "How are you?"

"Oh, fine, fine. I hope it's okay, but I phoned the milliner's shop and got your number from Ines."

"Of course," I replied easily.

"I was calling to see if you might want to join me for lunch the day after next? Nothing fancy, maybe Closerie des Lilas? Ernest and I just love going there, it's near the apartment he keeps for writing."

I groaned inwardly. After the impression I'd left, I wasn't eager to return to Lilas.

"Gaige and I have been there several times, they have wonderful food," I hinted.

My partner was trooping back down the steps with his Qube in hand, and gave me a quizzical expression at the mention of his name. I shook my head in reply.

Hadley understood the not-so-subtle meaning.

"Oh, then we should try somewhere new for you. I'd hate for you to not experience all the best our city has to offer. I know, let's try the Ritz Hotel. Have you eaten there yet? The bouillabaisse is to die for."

"I actually haven't been there," I said, deciding it wasn't a lie since Cyrus and I hadn't been there for the food. "That sounds lovely."

"How is one o'clock? Will that work for your schedule?"

"One o'clock on Tuesday?" I repeated, loudly enough to catch Gaige's attention. He nodded without looking up, busy attaching the scanner to his Qube.

"One is perfect. I will meet you there," I told Hadley.

We said our goodbyes, then I replaced the receiver in its cradle.

"Do you think she might know where to find another part of the manuscript?" Gaige asked.

"Maybe," I said with a shrug. "It's worth a shot. You should schedule another date with the menfolk, too."

Gaige fingered his bruised eye. "Something other than boxing, I hope."

"Or not," I replied with an innocent grin. "What're you doing over there?"

"Syncing the pages I scanned in the bathroom to my Qube before I take it down to customs. Wanna see?"

As I plopped down beside him, Rosenthal's scrawling handwriting appeared as a hologram over the coffee table. Gaige moved the device so it was between us, and we both settled in to read the immortal words of his new friend.

The will had been very clear. Once Serena Rushforth of Warwickshire, England, now Serena Nolan of Blue's Canyon, North Carolina, she was to inherit all lands, accounts, and businesses formerly held by her husband, Tate Nolan.

Serena smiled wanly, recalling Marta Nolan's outrage upon hearing that her ancestral home was to become the property of an outsider. Even the lawyer had shaken his head whilst making the announcement. A woman, an Englishwoman at that, inheriting Bellerose Manor and the Blue's Falls Hotel and Country Club went against a centuries-long tradition of bequeathing the family properties to the eldest living male of legitimate birth. But that was Tate's way; he had always enjoyed causing a stir.

Standing atop Wind Rock, Serena peered down into the canyon below. A single tear slid from the corner of her eye, followed by another and another, until the scarf around her neck was wet with her painful loss. She wept openly for the first time since his death, as if someone had finally unscrewed the lid on the jar where she kept her emotions hidden from the world. On the Rock she felt safe. It was the site of their first kiss; the place her beloved had gone to his knees and asked for her hand in marriage; where, had fate not so cruelly intervened to cut short their time together, Serena would have told her husband that she was carrying their child.

With Tate by her side, the Canyon had felt like home. Without him, the Canyon felt foreign, just as when she'd first moved there. The majestic beauty she'd once embraced while standing in the same spot with her husband seemed cold and ugly now that she was alone.

"Outsider!" "Interloper!" "Imposter!" the winds seemed to cry in her ear.

Serena wept impossibly harder.

The baby in her womb kicked and she rubbed her belly affectionately. This child, part Tate and part Serena, would prove to be the best of each, of this she had no doubt. The ache in her heart lessened as love for her unborn child helped to mend the fissure left by his father's death.

She breathed deeply. She had not come to the Rock to cry over that which could not be changed. She had come with a purpose.

Fingers stiff with cold, Serena unfastened the sapphire broach nestled in the hollow of her throat and removed the scarf. Once soft and smooth to the touch, the fine silk fabric was roughened by her dried tears. It had been Tate's favorite, the fabric the same azure as his eyes. He had been wearing it the first time they met that fateful day on the train that had changed Serena's life forever.

Oh how Marta Nolan had made a fuss when Serena refused to allow the scarf to be buried with the man that both women loved wholly, unconditionally, and, in Serena's case, with reckless abandon. The act had only caused more tumult in the already rocky relationship with her mother-in-law. That, Serena decided, was a problem she would fix. She owed it to Tate. And to their unborn son who would bear his father's name, another Tate Nolan to watch over Blue's Canyon.

Serena inched forward, until the toes of her shoes hung over the edge of Wind Rock. She secured the broach to one end of the scarf to give it weight. Drawing back her arm, just as Tate had taught her, she hurled the scarf into the fog-filled ravine below.

Her reason for doing so was dismissed by the men in the village as a nonsensical wives' tale. Nonetheless, the women below swore on their firstborn children that the legend was true. Serena was there to prove *once and for all that women were wiser than men.*

For a paralyzing moment, the winds ceased to blow. The air went impossibly still. Serena herself thought she had gone deaf. And then, competing gusts from every direction whipped loose strands of hair from the plait running down her back. Out of the fog, a ribbon of blue appeared. Tears filled Serena's eyes for the second time that day. These, however were tears born of joy. She reached out to pluck it from the wind, the scarf catching around her arm, the broach settling delicately in her upturned palm.

His body may have gone to earth, but Tate's soul was alive in Blue's Canyon. Of this, she was certain.

THE END.

"Wow, that's so sad," I said, wiping a tear as I finished reading the last chapter of *Blue's Canyon*.

Gaige snorted. "Damn women and your sobbing over nothing."

"Heartless misogynist," I shot back.

"Hey now, I love women," Gaige said defensively. "In fact, I love working under a woman. Hell, I prefer having a woman above me."

Just in case I had missed the pervy undertones, Gaige smiled wickedly to drive home his point.

I held up my hand. "Enough. For the future of our partnership, it is best you don't continue that little speech of yours."

"I'm just saying—"

"I know what you're saying, sparky. Save it for someone who cares.

Flip back to the beginning of the section, so we can see what all we have."

In total, the portion Gaige found in the toilet tank contained pages 147-225 of Rosenthal's unpublished manuscript. The excerpt from Shakespeare and Company included pages 1-77.

"So, we're missing the middle third of the book," I announced.

Gaige nodded his agreement. "If all else fails, we could always write those chapters ourselves. I bet our client won't even know the difference."

"You don't think so? Do you think your boss would know?" a wry voice spoke up.

Gaige and I both turned towards the front door. We'd been so engrossed in our task, neither of us had heard Cyrus enter.

"Of course, he'd know. Our boss is a genius, you can't get anything by him. Not that I would try, I have too much respect for him. In fact you might even—" Gaige abruptly halted his babbling mid-sentence, blood rushing to his tanned cheeks.

I was just about to make a wisecrack, when I realized what silenced Gaige—the firm set of Cyrus's jaw. Though he didn't look angry, our boss was clearly in no mood for jokes. His green eyes, normally so vibrant and full of life, were dull and weary. Cyrus gestured to the scanner and tablet in front of us.

"Did you find more of the manuscript?" he asked, with a hint of surprise.

"We did," I replied, pleased that we could offer a bit of good news. "There was another third of it in the bathroom at that restaurant they all frequent."

Cyrus raised one eyebrow at the latter bit of information, but didn't comment on the hiding place.

"Good. That is very good. You are both far exceeding my expectations for this mission. I am really quite impressed."

Gaige and I exchanged a look of disbelief. Given how stressed our boss was, the last thing I'd expected was praise.

Cyrus carried a leather train case into the sitting room, placing it on the coffee table before settling into one of the two plush velvet armchairs.

"Well don't look so shocked," he said with a chuckle. "Am I really that much of a hardass?"

"No, of course not," I replied quickly. "We just know you have a lot on your plate right now, things more important than our mission."

"Which is exactly why I'm so pleased that you guys are staying focused and getting the job done. I honestly thought we have to abandon the run, but you're making remarkable strides towards completion." Cyrus sat back in his chair and gave us a tired smile. "I'm proud of you both."

It was the first time in my life that someone had ever said they were proud of me. I didn't know what to make of it.

"Looks like you found something, too," I said hastily, nodding to the train case to hide my embarrassment. Shifting his focus from Gaige to me, Cyrus's gaze softened. He kept his attention on me for a beat longer than I would've expected—just long enough for Gaige to start fidgeting.

"Sorry, I did," our boss finally answered, shaking his head to clear whatever thought he'd been lost in. "I paid another visit to Lachlan's hotel room. He's been back since we were last there. You remember the door that connected his room to the one next to it?"

I nodded, then quickly explained the room's layout to Gaige.

"We closed the door again, right?" Cyrus continued.

"Definitely," I assured him, recalling the final visual sweep I'd given the bedroom before departing.

"That's what I thought," my boss confirmed. "It was open when I arrived today, so I picked the lock to the adjoining suite."

"Naturally," Gaige said with a chuckle.

Cyrus unlatched the clasps on the train case and the top popped open, as if on a spring. He pulled on a pair of gloves, then plucked several clear plastic bags from inside.

"I didn't find anything new in Lachlan's room, but the one next to it was an absolute mess. I checked on the way out, and both rooms are registered under Shepard. I found these in the second one." Cyrus held up one of the bags. Gaige and I leaned forward in tandem to peer at the contents—a whole mess of empty candy wrappers.

"I'm confused," I admitted. "Unless he's diabetic, I don't understand why eating an excessive amount of candy is significant?"

"He's devolving," Cyrus explained. "As you both know, the combination of sucrose and cocoa will stave off time sickness and lessen the symptoms. Judging by the sheer volume of wrappers I found, I'd guess he's dealing with a bad case of it. Probably from jumping too frequently within a short period of time."

"So he's curing himself?" Gaige asked skeptically.

"Not exactly. Chocolate is neither a vaccine nor a cure, more like a bandage. It treats the symptoms, but not the disease itself. Like using painkillers to treat a broken leg—a cast is still needed for the bone to heal properly." Our boss shook the plastic bag. "I found at least forty of these wrappers on the floor of the second hotel room. It means that Lachlan at least somewhat cognizant of the fact he's suffering from time sickness, which suggests he hasn't devolved completely. Or, at least, he hadn't as of yesterday. The chocolate left on the wrappers has been exposed to air for between twenty-four and thirty-six hours."

I didn't bother asking how Cyrus had reached that conclusion; he'd brought all sorts of things with him from the island that were atypical on an ordinary run.

"Maybe that's why he didn't strike last night?" I proposed.

"That's my guess, as well," Cyrus agreed.

"Do you think he's so far gone that he won't be able to stage another one of his deadly performances?" Gaige asked.

Cyrus shook his head regretfully.

"I have no idea. I wish I did. I showed the photo to the staff on duty today, but no one remembers seeing him in the past twenty-four hours. The maids said the 'Do Not Disturb' sign has been on the door for days, so they haven't been inside either room in some time." He sounded exasperated.

"Maybe he's bribed the staff to say they don't know anything? I mean, he is a runner, after all. He knows the tricks of the trade," Gaige said.

Cyrus eyed him pointedly. "That is precisely why I offered them a substantial amount myself. Lachlan may know the tricks, but I *invented* the game."

For the second time in ten minutes, Gaige turned scarlet.

"What else did you find?" I asked, drawing our boss's attention away from my partner.

"Nothing too helpful, in terms of telling us where he might be now." Our boss reached inside the train case and pulled the remaining evidence bags out, one at a time. Cyrus held them up as he rattled off the contents. "A lock picking set, night vision glasses and contacts, a handheld scanner—all syndicate-issue, from the mission kits that runners can check out from customs." He laid the items in a line on the coffee table.

"Is the Paris station missing a kit?" I asked. "They are extremely organized. Sort of seems like they'd have a record of the theft."

"According to Ines, all of their inventory is accounted for. My guess is Lachlan stole the items from the Montgomery Syndicate before he left. I'll send a message to Bane to confirm they're short." Cyrus withdrew four more plastic bags from the train case. "Stage makeup, also syndicate-issue. Shepard is most likely using it to change his appearance, which might explain why no one at the Ritz can recall seeing him recently." The next bags he pulled from the case were much larger, and contained men's clothing. "The style and fabrics of Shepard's clothes are consistent with this time period. And definitely authentic, not reproductions. Again, he could have stolen the items from customs. Or he could have purchased them once he was here."

"All of this was in the second room?" I asked, leaning closer to inspect the vacuum-sealed evidence bags.

Cyrus nodded.

The bags with the clothing were closest to me and immediately drew my attention. One contained a pair of men's dress pants in navy, while another had a very ordinary white dress shirt. But it was the contents of the third that caused my heart to skip a beat.

Inside was a beautiful silk handkerchief, checkered in shades of scarlet and gray. I'd seen a handkerchief in the exact same pattern peeking out from the pocket of a suit with a coordinating lapel lining.

Charles was wearing it the night we all went to *Exotique*.

I swallowed hard. There was no way. Charles was definitely *not* the Night Gentleman. He'd been sitting right next to me when the killer had made his villainous speech at *Exotique*.

Baylarian didn't make that speech himself, a voice inside my head reminded me.

I shoved the thought aside. It didn't matter. Charles couldn't be the Night Gentleman. Lachlan Shepard, alias Mitchell Baylarian, was the Night Gentleman.

Right?

As I struggled to keep my thoughts from galloping wildly away with the notion that my handsome suitor could be a killer, I remembered an irrefutable fact: the Night Gentleman was a new addition to the time period. His existence wasn't documented anywhere in the history books on the island, nor on the syndicate's vast intranet. Since Charles was a native citizen of this time, if he'd gone on a mad killing spree, it would have already happened. It would have been recorded in the historical archives. It *couldn't* be him.

Right?

"Stassi? Is something wrong?" Cyrus asked.

"Hmm? Wrong? Me? No, I'm good."

Cyrus leveled his patented stare on me. The one he used when communicating to an underling that he knew they were withholding information. The one that said it would be in everybody's best interest if he didn't need to ask again. The one that made the unlucky recipient wish for the power of invisibility.

If I were capable of communicating even a tenth of what my boss could with a single withering look, I would never have to speak again.

"I recognize the handkerchief. I've seen it. Or, rather, I've seen one like it. It couldn't have been this one. Obviously it wasn't this *exact* one. No, definitely not. That's impossible."

My, oh-so-eloquent diatribe came out in a single breath.

Gaige snickered and I shot him a glare. I'd taken the heat off of him, but he couldn't repay the favor?

"Where did you see it?" Cyrus asked calmly.

The lump in my throat proved nearly impossible to swallow around.

"On Charles DuPree," I whispered, feeling impossibly traitorous.

Admittedly, the sudden onset of guilt didn't make a whole lot of sense; I'd only known Charles a few days. I wasn't even sure how I felt about the guy, except that his touch made me all tingly and warm inside. And his fascination with my necklace had kind of weirded me out. Nonetheless, Charles had put his reputation on the line for Gaige. That sort of genuine kindness was rare, and spoke volumes about his character. Dragging him into an inter-century murder investigation was a terrible way to repay a man who had been nothing but a solid friend to both me and my partner.

"And who is Charles DuPree?" Cyrus prodded, forehead wrinkling in confusion.

With Cyrus's attention on me, Gaige began making kissy faces and licking his lips suggestively. The gestures would've earned him several smacks in the face with a pillow, had my boss not been sitting with us.

"Stop that, Gaige," Cyrus warned, without turning. That rumored second set of eyes in the back of his head missed nothing. Gaige jumped in his seat. Without skipping a beat, my boss added, "You look constipated."

"Charles is a man on the periphery of Rosenthal's circle," I explained. "He appears to know all the same people as Rosenthal, and attends the same parties and events. DuPree also has a casual friendship with the author."

"And?" Gaige prompted, drawing out the word for several seconds.

"And he seems to like me." I closed my eyes and sighed. Was this really happening? Was I actually dishing about a cute guy with my boss?

Cyrus cleared his throat loudly. Twice. I opened my eyes to only the smallest of slits and peeked through, like a child afraid to face the scary monster lurking at the foot of her bed. Cyrus opened and closed his mouth several times, as if the words were stuck on the tip of his tongue and he couldn't quite manage to knock them loose.

My eyes popped fully open and I stared at my boss in astonishment. Cyrus rendered speechless was a sight worthy of my undivided attention.

"I know the rules about getting involved with someone on a run," I was quick to add. "You don't have to worry about that."

Cyrus sighed. "The rules regarding fraternization are our least followed. Understandably so. Which is why I don't enforce them, as long as care is given and discretion shown." He shifted position, as if the armchair he'd been comfortably sitting in for the last fifteen minutes had suddenly developed lumps. "How do you know he likes you?"

"He asked her on a date," Gaige chimed in helpfully.

"How did you know that?" I demanded, rounding on him.

My partner shrugged and, with no remorse whatsoever, said, "I read your letter."

The letter had been sealed when he handed it to me. Meaning Gaige had used an infrared optical character recognition scanner to read through the envelope.

Revenge would be mine.

"I thought it might be relevant to the run," Gaige was saying, sounding practical and matter-of-fact. "And Stassi misspoke. Charles DuPree is closer than a casual friend to Andre Rosenthal. In fact, he might even know where the final piece of the manuscript is. I think it's worth checking out."

"That's farfetched, Gaige," I quickly replied, hoping to keep Charles off of our boss's radar. "Hadley Richardson is more likely to know the whereabouts, and I'm having lunch with her on Tuesday."

"Oh, I agree, Hadley is a good bet. But you have an opportunity to meet with Charles before you see her, so why not take it? He might even be the killer," Gaige intoned with a mischievous glint in his eye.

"He is *not* the killer," I shot back, then repeated the words directly to my boss. "Cyrus, he isn't the killer."

"My idea is no more farfetched than yours about the toilet bowl," my partner replied innocently.

"Toilet *tank*," I corrected. "Though it's nice to hear you went playing in the toilet bowl for fun."

Cyrus had been silently watching our exchange with the rapt attention of a line judge at Wimbledon.

"You two bicker like a pair of old ladies," he declared. "And what's this about a toilet?"

I opened my mouth to explain, but Cyrus cut me off before I got out the first syllable.

"Actually, don't answer that. I am confident that I don't want to know. Stassi, accept the date. Ask Mr. DuPree where he shops for his dress clothes. Then we can go to the store with Lachlan's picture and see if they remember him. Perhaps he's even ordered clothes that haven't yet been picked up, or maybe they have a delivery address for him. Though it's a long shot, it could end up being well worth the trouble."

"Yes, Cyrus," I dutifully agreed. "I will."

"So that's it?" Gaige asked, as if he hadn't just thrown me under the bus. "What's our next play?"

"There are a couple other theories I want to explore," our boss hedged. "Left untreated, time sickness can be lethal. From what Bane has told me about Lachlan's running schedule, and the numerous chocolate wrappers in his hotel room, I have no doubt he has the disease. It's very possible he's already succumbed. I am going to check the morgue."

That sent a shiver up my spine.

"For now, let me worry about Lachlan Shepard. You both should focus on finding the final piece of *Blue's Canyon*. Gaige is right." My partner sat up a little straighter at Cyrus's praise. "Cover your bases and ask Charles DuPree about the manuscript."

That night, hand shaking badly enough to smudge the ink, I responded to Charles's invitation, accepting his date.

THIRTY

"YOU LOOK…LIKE a girl."

The next night, my assignment was back to parties, champagne, and a handsome guy instead of death and a psychotic killer.

I spun to find Gaige standing in the doorway to my bedroom, a broad smile on his face.

"She looks beautiful, a true vision," Cyrus added, joining Gaige in the entranceway. His grin matched my partner's, though it lacked the half-stunned, half-amused quality.

I turned again to look in the freestanding oak-framed mirror, feeling very self-conscious. The dress Naomi selected specifically for the evening was stunning. Unlike most women's clothing for the time period, this dress had a natural waist. Layers of black taffeta hung just past my knees, almost like a ballerina's best tutu. Two-inch straps of blue and white crystals started at the small of my back, trailing up over my shoulders and down over the bodice to an oval broach at my waist. With the sparkling embellishments, we'd decided against adding additional bling with jewelry.

My auburn hair—something I still wasn't used to—was pinned up in a sleek bob with a deep side part, so that a portion of my hair was swept across my forehead. Felipe completed the look with minimal makeup, save a deep crimson lip. The overall effect was spot-on for the time period; I'd be just another wealthy woman who had nothing but time to look beautiful.

Honestly, I barely recognized myself.

"Are you sure I look okay?" I asked the two men studying my appearance.

Cyrus pushed past Gaige and walked over to get a better look. He took my hand to spin me back around to face them. In my stacked black heels, I only had to tilt my head slightly to meet his gaze. My boss had a faraway look in his eye, as though his thoughts were somewhere else.

"Your boy is going to have a hard time keeping his hands to himself with you in that dress," Gaige declared as he stepped into my room, snapping Cyrus out of his reverie. He shot my partner a warning look.

"Is that necessary?" Cyrus asked him, releasing my hand and taking several steps backwards. "I would not put it quite so crassly, but yes, Mr. DuPree will undoubtedly be quite taken with you."

Gaige snorted. "He already is."

"Which," Cyrus continued as if Gaige hadn't spoken, "will make it easier for you to get information out of him. If, of course, there is any information to be had."

"Oh, Stassi will be able to get more than information out of him," Gaige interjected with a wicked smile. With Cyrus's attention on me, my partner began thrusting his hips, proving his mental age had yet to catch up with his shoe size. I guessed his expression was supposed to be ecstasy. It missed the mark entirely, landing somewhere closer to pain.

"Gaige," Cyrus snapped, his tone devoid of all traces of amusement.

"Sorry, sir." Gaige straightened and gave our boss a small salute.

Cyrus turned his attention back to me. "Are you ready, Stassi? I believe Mr. DuPree will be here soon, but take as much time as you need."

"Actually...," I started, hesitating. "I will be meeting Mr. DuPree at the restaurant."

As expected, this drew a stern, disapproving look from Cyrus.

"He offered to pick me up," I rushed on. "But I thought it might be best to just meet him there."

My boss appraised me for another long minute. He glanced over at my juvenile partner, who was clearly a bastion of embarrassment.

"I suppose I can understand that," Cyrus said. "Though I strongly disapprove, particularly with a killer on the loose."

"I'll be fine," I promised him. Without thinking, I reached out and gave Cyrus's hand a reassuring squeeze. When I remembered myself—he was my *boss*, not a doting father seeing his daughter off on her first date—I yanked my hand back and began stuffing random items in the matching crystal clutch from Naomi.

Gaige stayed behind when Cyrus went to see if the car Charles was sending had arrived yet.

"You are such a weirdo," he joked, slinging an arm over my shoulder. He turned us both so we were facing our reflections. For a long moment, he looked me over from heels to head, then studied my face.

"What?" I asked uncertainly. I wondered simultaneously if the outfit and styling were too much, or possibly not enough.

"I am damn good looking," Gaige said finally, putting his dimples on full display.

"You're an idiot," I declared, wrapping my arms around his shoulders and giving him a squeeze. "Come on, I'm going to be late."

As it turned out, the car had not yet arrived. Against my better judgment, I waited in the living room with my motley crew. Ines also came over to see me off, compounding the awkwardness. Luckily, she was her usual self, chattering away about random nonsense.

"Hadley is quite taken with you, my dear," she told me between drags of her cigarette. "Have you decided what you will wear for your lunch with her?"

"Hadn't crossed my mind," I replied. "I'm sure Naomi will have something lined up."

"She certainly did an exquisite job tonight," Ines said kindly. "Really, Stassi, you look absolutely stunning."

"Thanks," I muttered, desperate to deflect the attention away from my appearance. "You've spoken to Hadley?"

"Indeed," Ines said with enthusiasm. "She is positively giddy about seeing you tomorrow."

I was positively giddy about our lunch as well, only for a very different reason. I liked Hadley well enough, from the brief interaction we'd had, but I was far more interested in information about Rosenthal and the last piece of the manuscript. If I could get her to tell me about other places he went to work, or other haunts he frequented, we could resume the search and get out of the 1920s. I was ready to go home. This run had been the oddest I'd ever heard of, let alone encountered. Once we had the complete work, we could leave all of the weirdness behind and go back to our own time.

I thought about my other reason for remaining in Paris after the run was complete.

My locket.

Somehow, after almost two years of searching, I had a lead. Maybe not a very good one, but something was better than nothing. I needed to follow it, to find the great adventurer whose cufflinks were somehow linked to my necklace.

Without thinking, I rubbed my throat, where the necklace should have been. Naomi had been so insistent about not ruining the neckline of the dress that I'd relented and taken off my most prized possession.

Without its light weight against my chest, I felt empty inside. The necklace was a part of me. I missed it terribly.

"I mean, even Alice loved—" Ines was saying.

"Excuse me, I forgot something upstairs," I blurted out, jumping to my feet.

Our Parisian guide was visibly affronted by my rude interruption. She huffed out two plumes of smoke. In the kitchen, Cyrus stopped pacing long enough to say, "The car will be here any moment, don't take too long."

"I'll be quick," I promised, running for my room as quickly as the heels would permit.

Once the necklace was securely around my throat, the disjointed feeling melted away. Just as Naomi had predicted, it did not match the dress. It actually looked a little ridiculous between the jeweled straps, but I didn't care. Stupid as the notion was, I felt more confident with my locket on.

I hurried back downstairs to find a short, pudgy man in a chauffeurs' uniform standing in the living room. He bowed slightly when he saw me, his cap clutched between meaty fingers.

"Ah, my dear sister has graced us with her presence," Gaige proclaimed grandly, as if I'd been hiding out upstairs all evening.

I shot him a withering glare.

"I apologize for the delay," I said to the driver. "I am ready whenever you are."

"It is no problem, Ms. Prince, I assure you," the man replied.

There was a round of air-kisses from Ines and a hearty pat on the back from my partner. The affectionate squeeze from Cyrus came with a whispered reminder to pump him for information. They all stood at the door as I descended the steps to the curb, as if they couldn't help but take every opportunity to be embarrassing.

I gave the group one last wave through the window as the car door closed behind me, feeling a simultaneous rush of affection and mortification. We pulled away and, finally, I was off for my date with Charles DuPree.

The restaurant, *La Coupole,* was straight from the history books. From the waiters' white gloves and airs of superiority, to the impeccable coattails worn by the men and latest designer fashions worn by the women, it was classically Parisian. In the middle of the vast dining room, a blue domed ceiling of stained glass overlooked a metal statue of two curved men. The entire space was rife with art deco designs that almost seemed out of place with the old-world elegance, but I sort of loved it.

"Anastasia Prince, here to meet Mr. Charles DuPree," I told the maître d' in French.

Apparently, my grasp of the language was sufficient for his liking—or he found my attempt amusing—because his lips curved into a friendly grin.

"Mr. DuPree has already arrived. If you will follow me this way?" he replied, also in French.

The English translation whispered in my ear as I smiled and nodded deferentially. Butterflies swarmed in my stomach as we wound our way through tables of diners.

Breathe, I told myself. *You have done this before. This is nothing new.*

Okay, so that wasn't *exactly* true. I'd only had occasion twice to truly sidle up to men on a run to gain information, but neither had the charm of Charles DuPree. They hadn't been fascinating, or alluring, or so damned good-looking. This was definitely new.

I saw him before he saw me. I had only a moment to admire the strong line of his jaw and perfect slope of his nose before his head turned and our eyes locked. A slow smile spread across his handsome face, and then he stood.

My breath caught.

What have you gotten yourself into?

THIRTY ONE

"YOU LOOK AMAZING," Charles whispered, placing a light kiss on each of my cheeks.

The slight contact had my heart beating double-time. The steady thumps were so loud in my own ears that I was sure he could hear it.

Releasing me, Charles hurried around the maître d' to pull out my chair. I sat, arranging the bottom layers of my dress over the seat as best I could.

"Please, enjoy your meal," the maître d' told us.

With a bow, he left the table. And I was alone with Charles.

Sure, we'd been alone together before. But this time felt different.

Because this is a date, I thought. *Shite. A date. I am actually on a real flipping date.*

My hand flew to my necklace. With the cool metal beneath my hot fingers, I felt more grounded. I could do this. It was just a meal with an asset. A means to an end.

I wonder if the means is going to kiss me goodnight....

Um, no. You can't just go around kissing assets.

"How are you this evening?" Charles asked, sounding remarkably formal.

Putting an end to my mental debate, I replied just as properly.

"Very well, Mr. DuPree. And you?"

"Very well," he echoed my words. "But, as I've said before, please, call me Charles."

His gaze wandered to my hand, still gripping my necklace like a lifeline. I released it abruptly, tucking it beneath the neckline of my dress. Charles had expressed too much interest in the piece of jewelry last time we'd seen each other, and I didn't want to go down that road again.

Thankfully, Charles made no comment about my locket. I worried for a moment that we had nothing to talk about, or that I'd seem unworldly or uncultured to him when engaged in actual conversation. My worries were unfounded, though. Charles steered the dialogue, bringing up banal topics like our mutual friends and acquaintances. Unbeknownst to him, this was exactly the opening I'd been hoping for.

"My brother is having the time of his life," I told Charles. "He has another boxing date with his boyfriends this week."

Charles eyed me strangely as he poured champagne.

"Is Gaige queer? He does not seem the type."

"Oh, no, no." I laughed, realizing my mistake. "I was referencing his male friends, that is all. I assure you, my brother only has eyes for women."

Charles's reply was interrupted by the waiter coming to take our order. The menus were still closed, set to one side of the table. Without looking at them, Charles rattled off an impressive array of dishes. Taken aback by the fact that he'd ordered for me, I had to remind myself that he was from a different time. This gesture was normal, if not expected. As the

Rosetta tried to keep up with what he was saying, I had to stop myself from giggling at the awkward translations. Hopefully "cock in wine" was more appetizing than it sounded.

"I hope the dishes I selected are to your liking," Charles said, once the waiter was gone. "I should have asked, I just thought it would be easier for me to order, since I speak French."

"I speak a little French," I told him haughtily. Then, remembering my manners, I added in a softer tone, "But the food choices sound wonderful."

"Very good."

When he let out a breath and visibly relaxed, I realized he was nervous, too.

"How is your brother's eye?" he continued. "It must be healing well if he is willing to go another round with the boxing trio?"

I shrugged.

"Gaige believes it is a badge of honor." I sipped my champagne. "You are friends with Rosenthal, no? Do you ever box with him and the others?"

The question sounded innocent enough. Nonetheless, I knew from experience that naming only Rosenthal would, hopefully, lead the conversation to the paranoid writer.

"Me? No." Charles shook his head. "Boxing is not really my sport. We are friends though, yes. Instead of joining him in the ring, I usually attend the theater or a nightclub with Andre. Or parties, like the one for Scott the other night. I float between two sets, Andre's is one of them."

"So you're part of the literary set. Are you a writer? Or a painter?" I asked, though I was confident he was neither.

"No," he chuckled. "Merely an enthusiast, like your brother. Though, perhaps not quite so enthusiastic."

"I think it's the mystique surrounding Rosenthal that he finds so enchanting."

Charles scrunched his brow. "What do you mean?"

"How he hides pieces of his work around town until he is ready to publish," I said. "It's quite…eccentric."

Charles rolled his eyes. Noticing my glass was empty, he paused to pour me more champagne.

Slow down on the booze, Stass, I warned myself. *You don't need alcohol muddling your brain. Your hormones are doing a bang up job already.*

"Oh, that," Charles said with a laugh. "Andre is a paranoid chap. It is quite silly, though none of us have the heart to tell him so. Does he actually believe someone would steal into his home in the night and take his work? Andre is a wonderful writer, and I know he has had trouble with plagiarizing in the past, but this nonsense with dividing his manuscripts and hiding them is extreme."

I chuckled along with Charles, as though the idea of people wanting to steal Rosenthal's manuscripts was funny. As though that wasn't precisely my job.

Even if that wasn't the case, having read two-thirds of *Blue's Canyon*, I didn't find the notion ridiculous in the least. His writing was a work of art. Rosenthal possessed the rare ability to create characters that leapt from the pages and materialized in your mind. They became your friends, you cared about them. When they were going through hard times, you shared their agony. You cried when they cried and you laughed when they were happy. And for someone like me, who'd spent so much of her life being mistrustful of those around her, it was easier to form emotional bonds with Rosenthal's fictitious characters than the living, breathing people I was surrounded by.

"So silly," I echoed hollowly, plastering on a smile as fake as the paste jewels on my dress.

When I brought my champagne flute to my lips—it seemed to be my nervous gesture of the night—I was surprised to find the glass nearly empty again. Charles reached for the bottle to refill my glass for a second time, but I waved him off.

"I'd better wait until the food arrives. My brother will be upset if I'm inebriated when I return home."

Actually, Gaige was more likely to give me a high-five and ask if my clothes came off, but Cyrus would definitely be peeved.

"Where all does he write?" I asked, attempting to keep the conversation on track.

"Andre? Well, let's see. He frequents a bookstore, Shakespeare and Company. Have you heard of it?"

"I have," I said casually, as though I hadn't just robbed the place. "My brother and I paid a visit just the other day."

"He also likes a little café called Closerie des Lilas. Ernest is fan, as well. If you stop in, your brother just might have a chance to see them work."

Charles set his glass down, but continued to run his long fingers around the rim of it. The act was oddly mesmerizing. I found myself staring, transfixed, and wondering what it would be like to feel those long fingers sliding around the nape of my neck.

Wait. No. Inappropriate.

What the hell was this guy doing to me? Cool, calm and collected, Stass. Lock it up.

Charles's laugh was low and throaty, as if he was reading my mind and knew my indecent thoughts. Hell, given the year, my thoughts were probably downright erotic.

"If I did not know better, I would say it's you, not your brother, who is fascinated by Andre," Charles said.

Admittedly, it was a sound conclusion based on my line of questioning.

"Not at all," I said, brushing off the notion as ludicrous. "I only ask because I'd love to take my brother to his favorite writer's favorite places while we are here."

Not a lie. That had been our main objective for the past several days.

"Andre would be tickled to realize he has such a big fan." Charles leaned across the table, fixing me with his honey gaze. "If he really wants to see Andre in action, then he should wander by Carmen's place. As I understand, our boy spends a great deal of time writing in her gardens."

"I've seen Carmen, that is not all Rosenthal does in her gardens."

My face was on fire the moment the Gaige-worthy comment slipped through my lips. Where was my filter? Had the champagne really made me so flippant?

Charles threw his head back and laughed loudly.

"Truer words were never spoken, my Stassi."

The food arrived just then. The waiter drew Charles's attention, so my dinner companion did not see me catch my breath at his offhand comment.

Dinner consisted of the finest foods the City of Light had to offer. Course after course arrived, an impossible amount of food for two people to consume. I ate without really tasting much of anything, though the heavy cream sauces and buttery morsels did smell amazing. We talked more about Rosenthal and his friends, though the topics were more general than those from earlier. I didn't press him further about Rosenthal, yet Charles mentioned two other cafés the writer visited on occasion. Carmen's place seemed like our best bet, which meant another count of breaking and entering would soon be on our rap sheets. Thankfully, we were the only ones keeping score.

After five courses of food that were beyond decadent, a vanilla crème brûlée arrived, the top perfectly golden with burnt sugar. As I cracked the top with my spoon, Charles again complimented me on my dress. Steeling myself for what might come next, I took the opening.

"Oh, that reminds me," I said, reaching for my beaded clutch. I unclasped the top and removed the handkerchief from Lachlan's second hotel room. "Gaige found this the other night at *Exotique*. You must have dropped it during the commotion."

Charles gave me an odd look.

"What a peculiar coincidence. I did have one just like it that night, but the suit was taken to the cleaner's yesterday, including the coordinating kerchief."

"So this is not yours?" I asked hopefully.

His expression turned into one of amusement, though I saw an underlying doubt within his gilded eyes.

"It must belong to another gentleman," Charles replied. "It must be difficult to keep us straight when you have so many courting you."

"Hardly," I assured him. "My brother keeps me quite busy with all of his running around Paris. In fact, Gaige asked that I inquire about the tailor who made the suit this goes with." I held up the silk slip, then put it back in my bag. I felt an overwhelming sense of relief knowing that Charles was not a killer, but I still needed to follow the lead.

"Every Parisian has their favorite tailor, but we don't share that information with just anyone," Charles said with a wink, glancing mockingly from side to side as if someone might overhear him. "Mine is a British gentlemen by the name of Waldorf Hucklesbee, but let's keep that between us."

"Well, Paris is the capital of fashion, right?" I joked. "Everyone is competing to be the best-dressed?"

"That it is, as I see you have noticed. How does a newly-arrived American have so many fine Parisian garments?"

I knew he was teasing me, but the comment hit too close to home. It was one of those small details that I should have prepared an answer for. But I hadn't.

"My father is an extremely influential man," I said quickly. "He had many gowns ordered for me before our departure from Baltimore. Most of my wardrobe was waiting when we arrived here, though I picked this dress up just this morning."

I found that I regretted lying to Charles—another first for me. Lying was a crucial part of being a runner. We lied to nearly everyone we ever met. I lied so often that the truth was a malleable concept. I wished that I could just be myself with Charles, not Anastasia Prince. Unfortunately, it would never happen.

"And you wore it tonight…." He trailed off, leaving the words "for me" unspoken, though I still heard them in my head. "I am honored."

I'd done what Cyrus asked and found out the name of Charles's tailor. If the small square of silk was any indication, my date was not the Night Gentleman, and so my interrogation was done. I vowed to relax and just enjoy the rare evening away from my job, dressed to the nines, and with a handsome guy.

Unfortunately, I was not the only one at our table playing an angle. Complimenting my outfit was a natural segue to my locket. Which he smoothly took. Had I not been well-versed in the arts of interrogation, deception, and manipulation, I may have believed his interest was innocent. Except, of course, he'd asked about the damned thing two nights before. Charles DuPree had a lot to learn about subtle information gathering.

"It is a beautiful piece," Charles continued. "I have not seen many like it."

His hand traveled slowly across the table, towards my throat, as if to touch the necklace. Those golden-brown eyes became unfocused, like he was under a spell.

For the briefest of moments, I wondered if it called to him the same way it did to me. But that was ridiculous. It was *my* necklace. *My* family heirloom.

I drew back out of his reach, inhaling sharply. The action caught him by surprise and he dropped his hand.

"If I didn't know better, I'd say you are more interested in my necklace than in me," I joked, though my tone sounded flat and distinctly not amused.

Then, a horrible realization hit me with the force of an emotional wrecking ball: Charles *was* more interested in my necklace than in me. That was why he'd asked for this date.

I am so stupid.

Why, though? Why would a guy from this time period be interested in something from hundreds of years in the future? I thought about his words, *"I have not seen many like it."* Which implied he'd seen at least one other. Across the table, Charles was rambling excuses to explain away his interest.

"The metal work is just so—"

"Have you seen another like mine?" I cut him off abruptly. I gripped the locket in a tight fist, irrationally wanting it hidden from his view.

"I have," he admitted. "When I was a very young boy. A woman, a friend of my parents, had one very similar."

"Similar?" I pressed, no longer caring about etiquette. "But not the same?"

"No, not the same. At least, I do not believe it was the same. It was so long ago, I cannot really be certain. All of my memories from that time are a bit hazy."

"How long ago are we talking?" I was in full-on future mode, speaking to Charles as if he was one of my island friends. "Ten years? Fifteen? You said you were very young, right? And you're how old now? Twenty? Twenty-two?"

"I am twenty-one. It has been approximately twelve years, if I had to wager." His eyes were rolled up and to the right, as if trying to recall a memory. "Yes, well it would have to be twelve years exactly. It was right before I moved to live with the DuPrees."

"I thought you said the woman was a friend of your parents?" I accused, not liking the holes in his story.

I'd rattled him.

Clearly flustered, Charles replied, "Well, yes, she was. Tessa was a mutual friend of both my natural parents and my adoptive parents."

Tessa? Unsurprisingly, the name meant nothing to me. Even if I had an ancestor by that name, I'd never have known.

I was so focused on the name that the rest of his statement nearly flew over my head.

Nearly.

"You're adopted?"

Was that why I felt so drawn to him? Because we were both displaced as children?

Charles took a deep breath and reached for his champagne.

"I am. It is not something I tell most people. In fact, even my closest friends are not aware of my past. I would appreciate it if you did not share that particular bit of information. I do not care to be the subject of gossip." He sounded impossibly prim and haughty.

"Of course not," I replied, taken aback. "I would never."

Charles relaxed slightly. "I apologize. I did not mean to accuse you of anything. The adoption is a sensitive matter that is all."

"Sensitive? Why is that?"

"It is difficult to explain. The situation was…complicated," he answered, looking as lost as I often felt.

"What happened to your birth parents?" I asked, decorum totally going out the window.

He met my gaze levelly.

"They were murdered." Charles gestured to my locket. "I owe my life to the woman who was wearing a necklace very much like that one."

THIRTY TWO

SO, THAT HAPPENED.

My lips clamped shut, Charles's admission effectively putting an end to the brief interrogation session.

I was at a loss. I'd never known my parents, but Charles had. He'd spent at least part of his life with them. Was that better or worse in the long run? I'd always said I would give anything to spend one day with my mother and father. Now, those words seemed silly, childish even.

In the end, I said the most useless phrase one can utter in these situations.

"I am so sorry, Charles."

Head held high, expression perfectly neutral, Charles replied, "As am I. But things could have been far worse. I could have been with my parents when it happened. I might have even suffered the same fate." His tone was so matter-of-fact that I had to imagine he'd practiced the response for situations such as this one. "The DuPrees are lovely people," Charles continued after a brief pause. "They're wonderfully kind to me, and exceedingly generous. I have been very fortunate."

"I'm glad," I said, truly meaning it. "They should be very proud of the man you've become."

A whisper of a smile crossed his lips at the compliment. His honey-colored gaze became wistful.

Just then, the waiter arrived with the final course, a selection of cheeses and fruits, along with the bill. With six courses already under my belt, I worried that Charles was going to have to roll me out of the restaurant if I so much as nibbled on the newest spread.

It seemed my date did not have the same qualms as I did. He dove in immediately.

The faraway expression was still present in Charles's eyes, and he did not attempt to resume our earlier conversation. In fact, Charles remained quiet through most of the final course, only breaking his silence to insist that I try the Brie topped with fig jam.

To be polite, I sampled the concoction. I was *so* glad that I did. The mixture of salty and sweet was enough to make my eyes roll back in my head, an embarrassing reaction that Charles, thankfully, was too preoccupied to notice.

When it became obvious the few crumbles of cheese and stray grapes still on the wooden cutting board were going to remain there, I decided that enough was enough. I'd given Charles ample time to mourn days long past.

I opened my mouth to apologize for bringing up such a painful topic, when Charles spoke first. "Perhaps you would care to take a walk before returning home?"

Figuring that my inadvertent insensitivity had upset him enough that he'd be glad to see the back of me, I was pleasantly surprised.

"I'd like that."

As Charles pulled a thick stack of Francs in a gold money clip from his pocket, and discreetly counted out the bills, I considered everything I'd learned over the course of a single meal. I wondered how much more information I might be able to glean on our walk. Supposing, of course, that Charles was willing to revisit the topic of Tessa.

His birth parents and their deaths were likely off the table, but Charles brought up Tessa in the first place. He'd hinted, or maybe just hoped, that there was a connection between our necklaces. The reason he'd asked me on this date was the same reason I'd accepted: To get answers.

At the start of the evening, my questions had been business-related. Now it was personal. I wanted to know every scant detail from Charles's spotty memory that involved this Tessa woman.

What did she look like? Did I bear a resemblance to her? Was she still alive? Was Charles looking for her? Did he think that I was capable of helping him locate the woman who'd saved his life? And if Tessa's necklace was identical to mine, were the two lockets actually one and the same?

"Are you ready, Stassi?"

Caught up in my own frantic thoughts, I was startled to find Charles standing beside the table. He extended his hand to help me from my chair.

"Oh, yes. Thank you."

Slipping my fingers through his, I let Charles pull me to my feet. "Tonight was wonderful—the restaurant, the meal, the company." I grinned cheekily, channeling my inner flapper as I dialed up the charm.

My previous approach—the rapid-fire questioning that lacked both finesse and tact—made Charles clam up. This time around, I planned to use a more tried and true method of information gathering. *Flirting.*

Molly always said that lust made fools of even the most brilliant of people. I was going to put her theory to the test.

SOPHIE DAVIS

"Seriously, Charles. Thank you for a lovely evening. After the past couple of days, it was exactly what I needed."

He gave me an adorably embarrassed smile in return.

Once outside, I found that the night had turned cold while we were dining. I shivered as we began walking down the quiet street in front of *La Coupole.*

"Where are my manners?" declared Charles, halting abruptly in the middle of the empty sidewalk and shaking his head.

He shrugged out of his suit coat and draped it over my shoulders.

"Oh, no, I couldn't," I objected.

Charles silenced my feeble protest with a look of mock sternness. "I insist."

"Then who am I to refuse?" I teased.

Charles grinned, and I felt a twinge of shame. For some reason, using him for personal reasons felt more duplicitous than using him to further my mission. I assuaged my guilty conscience by reminding myself that Charles's reasons for inviting me to dinner had not exactly been pure.

I snuggled into his jacket, still warm with his residual body heat, and the scent of freshly laundered clothes left outside to dry in the sun wafted over me.

"Better?" asked Charles, tugging the lapels together in the front to block the wind.

His hands moved to my shoulders under the pretense of smoothing the material into place. Even in my heels, which brought my height to well above average for a woman, Charles towered over me. I tilted my head back to see his face. Those honey-colored eyes churned with an emotion I couldn't quite pinpoint.

"Much better. Thank you," I replied.

The cool breeze ruffled my hair, causing several auburn strands to fall into my eyes. Charles reached down and tucked the wayward locks behind my ear, fingertips skimming lightly over my cheekbone as he did.

His hand lingered on my face for several beats past innocent, before sliding down the side of my neck to rest on my shoulder again.

My stomach performed a series of cartwheels in fast succession. I suddenly felt breathless and acutely aware of just how near our bodies were to one another. Charles's palms slid down my arms to clasp my hands, leaving a warm, tingly trail in their wake. Threading his fingers through mine, he pulled me even closer.

Pulse pounding erratically in my throat, gaze inexplicably drawn to Charles's perfect mouth, one thought drove all others from my mind: *He is going to kiss me.*

Wait…did I *want* Charles to kiss me?

Yes. The answer was a resounding yes. Complications and consequences be damned.

Just when I was positive that Charles was going for the gold, his eyes landed on the locket nestled between my collarbones. The fleeting moment of intimacy passed, leaving me torn between disappointment and relief.

"Stassi…," Charles began tentatively. He inhaled sharply, as though preparing to make a difficult speech. Which was why his next words came as a surprise. "The River Seine is lovely at night, why don't I show you?"

What was he going to say? Why had he changed his mind at the last second?

"Yeah, sure. That sounds great," I said aloud, forcing a smile.

Charles released my hands, but offered me his arm instead. The two of us set off down the sidewalk.

We walked in silence for several blocks. Numerous times, I started to ask about Tessa, but could never seem to find the right words. Charles was distracted, and I had the impression that he was also debating how best to broach a touchy subject. He kept fiddling with something in his pocket, which made me smile. The nervous habit reminded me of the way I toyed with my locket to ease my mind.

Finally, we reached the cobblestone path that ran along the water's edge. By unspoken mutual consent, we paused to admire our surroundings. Twinkling lights off in the distance illuminated the various bridges that stretched from one side of the river to the other. The night sky was velvety black, causing the countless stars to appear brighter than usual as they shone down on the quiet city.

I drank in the beautiful backdrop, committing the intricacies to memory so that I would be able to recall them on a whim. In my present, Paris and many other once-great cities lay in ruins. The Epic War had destroyed sites that'd been standing for centuries.

Beside me, Charles stared out over the Seine, too. It was highly doubtful that his thoughts were as bleak as mine, since he did not know the perils that would befall his city over the next half a millennium.

"It's just as lovely as you promised," I said, when the silence became oppressive.

Charles turned to face me, letting his arm fall away from mine. Light from a nearby lamppost illuminated his handsome features, highlighting the fierce determination glinting in his eyes. I steeled my nerves to hear whatever he'd been working up the courage to say since we'd left the restaurant. Sending up a silent prayer, I hoped it was about Tessa.

"Stassi, I must make a confession." Charles spoke the words quickly as though they'd been fighting to break free for a while. "That first night that we met at Scott's book party? I saw you sitting at the table with Ines and your brother, and I had to meet you."

My cheeks felt like they were on fire.

Now who's flirting to weasel information? I thought wryly.

One look at the regret in Charles's expression, and the flames of embarrassment were quickly doused.

"So, I invited you to dance, anticipating that we would share a few cocktails afterwards and see where the night took us. But we started talking, and I found you so delightfully refreshing compared to my usual dance partners. I thought I would ask you to dinner so that I could get to know you better." He swallowed thickly. "Then, I noticed your necklace."

Almost as though his hand had a mind of its own, Charles reached out and his fingers drifted towards my throat. In my own subconscious gesture, I cupped the locket in my palm. His hand fell to the side, then slid in his pocket to play with the object inside.

Charles cleared his throat loudly. "As I told you over dinner, Tessa always wore a very similar locket. No, not similar. *Identical.* I know that must sound crazy to you. But I am certain of it. The pattern around the sapphire is unique and quite distinctive, and I have never seen another like it. I thought maybe…."

"I might know this Tessa woman?" I guessed, relieved that this was his big secret. I had already surmised as much. "I'm so sorry, Charles," I added, taking his free hand with one of mine. "I would love to help you find her, but I don't know anyone called Tessa. I truly am sorry."

And I *was* sorry. For both of us. Whether Tessa's locket was similar, identical, or the exact same one as mine, I wanted to know her, too.

I squeezed Charles's hand and he squeezed back, smiling sadly.

"May I ask what happened to her? And why you are looking for her?" I inquired, studying his reaction for an indication of how far I would be able to push him on the subject.

"I understand that she saved your life," I was quick to add, when Charles answered my initial questions with a blank stare. "But didn't you say she was a friend of the DuPrees? They must know how to contact her, right?"

Thankfully, Charles was too distracted to pick up on the note of desperation in my voice. I didn't want to tip him off that I wanted to find Tessa just as much, if not more, than he did.

"Tessa passed away some years ago." Charles's voice was gruff with emotion.

"Oh, Charles, that's awful. When did it happen?" I hoped my question came across as innocent curiosity.

"Not long after she arranged my adoption with the DuPrees. It was very sudden, or so I understand. A heart condition, I believe."

I felt as despondent as Charles looked.

"I'm so sorry," I said for the umpteenth time that night.

Charles managed a small smile. "Yes, well, death is a part of a life, is it not?"

"Yeah, I guess so."

Several more minutes of silent reflection passed. I spent the time trying to find a tactful way to ask Charles why he was so interested in my locket if Tessa was dead. It wasn't like I could help him find her, even if the locket around my neck had once hung from hers.

"I did not know Tessa well," Charles said finally, as though there had been no pause in the conversation. "But she was instrumental in relocating me to the DuPrees, and for that I owe her a great debt of gratitude. One I can never repay. She gave me a new life. A second chance. The freedom to become a man of my own making. I would very much like to do something for her in return. Or, as is the case, for her family." The object in his pocket made a jingling noise as he again indulged in his nervous habit. Staring out over the Seine, Charles continued speaking, seemingly embarrassed to have shared such personal information with me. "It was silly of me to think that you and Tessa might have been acquainted at one time."

"It's not silly at all," I told him quietly. "She saved your life. That sort of thing leaves a lasting impression. Wanting to meet and speak with someone who knew her is understandable. When someone disappears from your life, you grasp at every thread of information about that person that you come across, no matter how farfetched it might seem. It's a way of keeping them alive and with you always."

Charles stared deep into my eyes, a small sad smile on his perfect lips.

"You have lost someone close to you." It wasn't a question.

"Yes." I spoke the one word before I'd given any thought to the ramifications of divulging such a sensitive detail about my real life.

"Who?" Charles asked, his gaze holding mine captive.

You have no idea what a loaded question you just asked….

For several long seconds, we simply stared at one another, neither of us blinking. Memories flooded my mind—the countless nights I'd spent with my head tilted back, neck craned, eyes glued to the heavens, while I selected the two perfect stars to call Mom and Dad. Then, I thought about the leads I'd followed to trace my necklace's origins, and how they'd ultimately fizzled. Finally, I thought about Molly and Gaige, and how amazingly supportive they'd both been from the moment they'd heard my tale of woe.

Supportive, however, was the key word. Because neither my partner nor my best friend knew the loss of a parent firsthand. Charles did.

Suddenly, I had an overwhelming desire to tell him the truth. Not that I made my living traveling through time to steal objects for absurdly wealthy clients; I wasn't stupid. But I could tell him *some* version of the truth. One that wouldn't conflict with my cover story.

"My parents," I swallowed around the lump forming in my throat, "disappeared when I was four. James Prince, the man in Baltimore, is not my biological father. I was also adopted." My free hand, the one not linked with Charles's, flew to the locket at my throat. "This necklace belonged to my mother. My *real* mother."

Pain swam across my companion's expression, raw and undisguised. Now that he knew we shared a grief that few others could truly appreciate, it seemed as though Charles no longer felt the need to hide behind stoicism.

Tears pricked the backs of my eyes, and I tried to turn away before he could see.

Charles did not draw me to him, as Gaige or Molly would have done in the same situation. He did not tell me it was okay to cry. He did not spout flowery platitudes meant to comfort, but inevitably sounding hollow. Instead, he squeezed my hand tightly, just once. Just to let me know he was there to listen when I was ready to continue. It was the exact response I needed. His uncanny ability to read me endeared him to me all the more.

I'd planned to let the topic go. I *should* have let the topic go. But fifteen years of repressed bitterness, anger, and heartache were clawing their way to the surface. I couldn't stay silent any longer.

Once my eyes were dry, I faced Charles again. Tone brusque, I picked up the story. "I was found wandering the streets as a child, and taken to an orphanage. This necklace is all I had with me, other than the clothes I was wearing." My brain screamed at me to stop talking. My heart, longing to tell my story to someone who would understand, compelled me to go on. "My earliest memories are from there, the orphanage. I don't remember anything at all about my parents—what they looked like, what they sounded like, what they smelled like. I don't remember my life before the orphanage at all. And I still don't know the circumstances that led to me wandering the streets alone at four years old.

"Mrs. Prince, my adoptive mother, volunteered at the orphanage. I guess something about me appealed to her. Eventually, she brought her husband to meet me, and then they adopted me."

To his credit, Charles didn't immediately begin firing off questions. Instead, he waited patiently, gently rubbing the side of my hand with his thumb in a soothing circles.

"Stassi, I am so sorry," he said finally. "I feel so foolish for prattling on about losing my parents, when you never even knew yours. I can't begin to imagine how awful that would be."

The insensitivity of his statement, though definitely unintentional, made me cringe. Charles blanched. The horrorstruck expression that followed was oddly comical, and I actually giggled.

"I cannot believe—"

"Please, don't apologize," I cut in. "I know what you meant. And please don't feel sorry for me. Like you, I consider myself lucky to have found such an amazing adoptive family. Or, rather, I guess I should say, to have been found by such an amazing adoptive family."

The smile I gave Charles was automatic and genuine. I did have an amazing adoptive family. Gaige, Molly, and, in a roundabout way, Cyrus were my family. I loved Molly and Gaige more than I could imagine loving a blood sibling. And I respected Cyrus, who was always looking out for me, like he was really an uncle.

"I even got a brother as part of the package," I added when Charles didn't say anything.

"So Gaige is not truly related to you?" Charles asked, a hint of something dangerously close to jealousy in his otherwise bland tone.

"No. But I promise you, my affection for him is only sisterly. And he feels the same way about me."

Charles relaxed. "Good to hear."

Chimes from an unseen bell tower began to ring out, signaling the hour.

"Goodness, is it really so late?" Charles asked. "I should get you home before that brother of yours comes after us. Our walk along the Seine will have to wait for another evening, perhaps one where we get an earlier start."

I fought a losing battle to hide the grin his comment elicited.

We resumed strolling back in the general direction of the restaurant as I told him about the friendship between Gaige and me. Though I changed many of the details—swapping out the island for Baltimore, and the future for the present—much of what I told Charles was true.

Then, feeling especially brave, I also told him about Cyrus. Sure, I said his name was James Prince, and that he was a shipping magnate instead of the head of an international crime syndicate. But the underlying truth was there. Feeling bolstered by my ability to deftly swap out incriminating details for those of my cover story, I even told Charles about Molly.

It was oddly liberating, letting someone in without fearing rejection. That was probably why I didn't stop talking once I started.

By the time we were nearing *La Coupole* once more, my date knew more about me than anyone in any time, save my two closest friends.

"My adoptive family has been very supportive of my desire to find my birth parents," I found myself telling Charles. "That's actually a lot of the reason Gaige and I came to Europe. A jeweler here in Paris made my locket."

Immediately, I knew I'd said too much.

THIRTY THREE

I FELT CHARLES stiffen beside me. Out of the corner of my eye, I saw undiluted interest in his expression.

"Your biological mother was French?" he asked, excitement palpable in his voice.

"No, she wasn't. I do know that she was American," I said gently.

Surprisingly, this did not have the dampening effect I assumed it would. I also wasn't sure whether it was true. I figured my parents were American, since I was found in Tennessee, but they could have been born anywhere.

"Did the jeweler tell you that?" Charles asked.

"Oh, no, he was exceptionally unhelpful. He recognized the locket as one of their pieces, but had no record of it being sold or commissioned. Although, he did have sales records for several other pieces of jewelry with sapphires surrounded by this same patterned design." I traced the gold filigree around the stone with my fingernail.

"Who is this jeweler?"

"Matthieu Bonheur, of Bonheur's Jewelry."

Charles abruptly stopped walking. His expression turned to utter disbelief.

"What's wrong?" I asked.

"Do you mean the Bonheur's near Sylvia's bookstore?" Charles asked.

"Yeah, that's the one. It's got the five-leaf clover on the sign, which is the same insignia stamped into the gold on the back of my locket."

"So it is," replied Charles, though I had the distinct impression his mind was a million miles away. After several moments, he snapped back to the present. "You said there were sales records for other items of a similar design?"

I thought carefully about my next words. I couldn't very well tell Charles that the same person had commissioned at least three pieces of jewelry over the course of four hundred years, all of which bore an uncanny resemblance to my locket. Even being a time traveling bandit myself, the idea sounded farfetched.

Ultimately, I decided to gloss over the specifics. Hopefully, Charles was too distracted with his own thoughts to realize I was only giving him a fraction of the big picture.

"And did this jeweler actually show you the receipts for these similar pieces?" Charles was asking.

"Yes," I lied. Then, anticipating his next question, I added, "There wasn't another necklace. I'm sorry, Charles. There was a broach and a pair of cufflinks. There was also a third receipt, but it was badly stained and faded, and I couldn't tell what the item was supposed to be."

"Could it have been a pocket watch?"

The question caught me by surprise.

"I don't know. I guess it could have been. It could have been anything, honestly."

Charles's hand was back in his pocket. This time, when he withdrew his hand, it wasn't empty. One glance at the item cradled in his palm, and the real reason for Charles's obsession with my locket became crystal clear. Suddenly, my stomach felt incredibly hollow.

"I should have mentioned it earlier. It was never my intention to deceive you, I swear. I just, well…," he trailed off, apparently at a loss for words.

He wasn't the only one. My mouth, though hanging open, seemed incapable of forming coherent speech.

The brilliant blue sapphire gleamed up at me enticingly from the gold disk in Charles's hand. I had to suppress the urge to grab the watch and run. Instead, I settled for running my fingertip over the filigree surrounding the stone, tracing each loop and swirl that was so like the design on my necklace.

"Where did you get this?" I asked, my voice barely above a whisper.

"From Tessa." He paused while this nugget of information registered. A million questions floated through my head, though I was unable to focus on any single one. "She gave it to me the day she took me to the DuPrees' home."

"I don't understand."

"Me neither," Charles admitted. "I truly do not know the significance, if any. But this must be one of the other pieces made by Bonheur."

Sure enough, when I flipped it over, I found a perfect five-leaved clover stamped on the back of the watch.

"It could be a coincidence," I hedged, knowing full well that it wasn't. The odds of such a thing were…well, they were as astronomical as me randomly encountering another person with one of the pieces J. Jacobson had commissioned.

"You do not believe that," Charles stated flatly. "Neither do I. Is it not more likely that this pocket watch is the piece on the stained receipt? You did say that it was badly damaged, and that the item could be anything."

"Yes, but all the receipts looked so old, and your watch appears to be nearly brand new."

"As does your necklace," he pointed out.

"True," I conceded.

It was something I'd frequently wondered about with regard to the locket. I wasn't particularly careful with it, and yet the gold never scratched, became dull, or showed any sign of normal wear and tear.

"Perhaps Bonheur treated the gold with some sort of protectant?" suggested Charles.

I had no answer. At least, not one I was prepared to give Charles. If J. Jacobson was a runner, as I strongly suspected, then it was possible he or she had alchemist connections. Which meant it was also possible that the metal wasn't gold, but rather an element unknown outside the ancient and magical order.

I hadn't even considered that until this moment.

How had Tessa come to be in possession of such a precious artifact? And why did she gift it to Charles?

Supposing my many assumptions were true, how my mother came to own the locket was less of a conundrum. Even before I was born, there had been a thriving black market for historical artifacts. She could have purchased my necklace from any number of merchants specializing in illegal goods.

"Did Tessa say anything when she gave you the watch?" I asked, completely ignoring Charles's comment about Bonheur treating the gold.

"No," he said, looking ill at ease. "I have always assumed that it was a family heirloom, since it appears to be quite valuable. But now, I am not so sure. It never occurred to me to ask Tessa where it came from."

"J. Jacobson," I whispered, the name slipping out unintentionally.

"Sorry?"

"J. Jacobson," I repeated. "That was the name on the commission orders Matthieu Bonheur showed me. If this watch really is the item on that damaged receipt, J. Jacobson is the one who had it made."

Charles's gaze was alight with hope.

"We need to find him. We should visit Bonheur's, together this time. Perhaps Matthieu will recognize the watch, and be more forthcoming with information about this J. Jacobson character."

"Not likely," I scoffed, recalling the jeweler's hesitancy to tell me anything about my locket.

I felt Charles's disappointment as keenly as I'd felt his excitement. Which was why, despite the huge warning lights flashing in my head, I told him about Worchansky.

"There is someone who might have information for us," I began tentatively. The current of optimism surging inside of Charles was palpable. "I do have the name and address of the current owner of the cufflinks: M.L. Worchansky." And then, because the light in Charles's eyes was reaching supernova levels of brightness, I quickly backpedaled, "But he might not know anything more than what I've already learned."

"It is just as likely that he does," Charles countered. "We should pay him a visit immediately. Perhaps he even knows Tessa's family. Maybe they are related. As I said, I would really like to do something nice for her relatives to repay the great kindness that she showed me. How is tomorrow? Are you free to call on this Worchansky gentleman?"

His enthusiasm over the prospect of meeting Worchansky eclipsed the enthusiasm he'd shown for me on our sham date.

"I'll have to look at my calendar," I said curtly.

I had no right to be annoyed with Charles for using me. But I was. *You are a big old hypocrite,* I lectured myself.

Charles leaned forward, bending down so our foreheads touched. Because I didn't want to come across like a petulant child, I forced myself not to pull away from him.

"You do know that my interest in you far exceeds my interest in your

347

jewelry, correct?" he asked.

"Do I?" I replied cheekily, not swayed by his sweet talk.

"The moment I saw you sitting at that table, I wanted to know you. Everything that has happened since is simply a fortunate twist of fate. Even if I had never seen your locket, I still would have been desperate to spend more time in your company."

My next breath came out as a shudder. Okay, maybe I was capable of being a *little* swayed by his words.

When Charles's lips found mine, my ability to think rationally took a tumble. Down a very large hill. Without a single boulder, tree, or donkey to slow the descent.

Charles's hands slipped inside the jacket, locking around my waist and drawing my hips closer to his. Next thing I knew, my fingers were running through his silky hair. The kiss was soft but insistent. His mouth tasted like champagne.

Cold hands found their way to the small of my back, just above the waistline of my dress. Slowly, tenderly, he followed the line of the jeweled strap upwards, his touch growing warmer and warmer the longer his skin was in contact with mine. My body responded automatically, moving impossibly closer until nothing but thin fabric separated us.

I couldn't remember the last time I'd been kissed like that. Maybe never. I didn't want it to end. In that instant, I was a normal girl kissing a normal boy at the end of a, relatively, normal date.

When we finally broke apart, we were both breathing heavily. I looked into his eyes. The gold flecks seemed more prominent than before, as if his desire had brought them to the surface. But there was something else there, too—affection. The way Charles was looking at me left little doubt that he'd truly meant what he said about his interest in me surpassing his interest in my locket.

Charles ran a thumb over my bottom lip, his long fingers skimming my cheek with a touch as light as the flutter of butterfly wings. I closed my eyes and concentrated on the feel of his skin on mine. I didn't think about how wrong this was. How pissed Cyrus would be if he found out. How, in several days' time, I would disappear from Charles's life forever.

Cupping my jaw in his hands, he brushed his lips against mine, then lingered for one final kiss.

"I should get you home," Charles said softly.

"That's probably a good idea," I agreed, though the last thing I wanted was to return to the townhouse just then. Without his lips on mine, causing my hormones to muddle my thoughts, I also knew it was best for both of us to let that kiss be the end of our night.

Charles rode in the cab with me back to the townhouse. The driver was only too happy to accept an exponentially larger fare to wait while Charles walked me to the front door. My body and mind were at odds. One hoped for another kiss, while the other urged me to make a clean break before this went any further.

The decision was out of my hands, though. No sooner had my heels hit the sidewalk, than Cyrus appeared in the doorway. No doubt, he'd been watching through the curtains.

"There you are, Anastasia," Cyrus said in greeting, though his focus was solely on Charles. My boss scanned the other man from head to toe appraisingly.

I had a decent command of my facial expressions. If I wanted to convey how I was feeling, I could. If not, my face could appear as a mask. But Cyrus was *the* master. With a single look, he managed to express curiosity verging on disapproval, but absolutely no further insight into the thoughts swirling around in that busy brain of his. It was irritating.

I shot my boss a withering glare for his use of the unnecessarily formal name.

"Hello, Uncle Cyrus."

I was about to make formal introductions, when Charles stepped forward and held out his hand.

"Hello, sir. Charles DuPree. It is a pleasure to meet you."

Cyrus took the other man's hand and shook it firmly, playing up the protective role a little too much for my liking. "The pleasure is all mine," he said in a flat tone, before turning to me. "It is late, Anastasia. Why don't you come inside?"

It wasn't so much a question as a directive.

"Of course, Uncle."

It took all of my willpower not to stress the last word sarcastically.

"Goodnight. Thank you for a lovely evening," I said to Charles. In a lower voice meant only for his ears, I added, "I'll be in touch about our mutual friend."

Charles gave a polite nod to show that he understood.

I started for the door, telling myself to not look back at my date. Not with Cyrus watching.

"Stas—Ms. Prince?"

"Yes?" I replied over my shoulder.

"My jacket?" Charles nodded towards the dinner jacket still hanging from my shoulders. "Unless, of course, you would like to keep it as a souvenir?"

I let out an awkward laugh that reminded me of a schoolgirl's giggle. All I needed were some knee socks and a plaid skirt.

My boss did not find the quip nearly as amusing. As I shrugged out of the jacket, Cyrus took it from my shoulders and handed it to Charles himself.

"Here you go, son. Have a safe night." With those terse departing words, my boss guided me inside and shut the door in Charles's face.

"Was that necessary?" I asked, brushing past Cyrus.

"Of course. It's 1925, Stassi. An overbearing family member is par for the course."

I spared a glance over my shoulder to find my boss grinning.

"We flipped for the honor," Gaige said from the couch. He held up his index finger. "Just one time, I want that coin to come up heads. *Once.* Losing as often as I do is statistically impossible."

"And you're a statistician now?" I asked, plopping down in the chair beside him.

Gaige sat up straighter. "I wear many hats, Stassi."

I rolled my eyes.

"Goodnight, guys," Cyrus called from the stairs. "Don't stay up too late, we have work to do."

More than you know, I thought.

THIRTY FOUR

OVER ESPRESSO AND runny eggs, I briefed Cyrus on my dinner with Charles. Naturally, I forgot to mention our discussion of my necklace. And the kissing.

"A British tailor named Waldorf Hucklesbee shouldn't be hard to track down," Cyrus said when I was finished, taking a sip from his miniscule espresso cup. The sight of such a large man, with such a commanding presence, drinking from a mug that looked like it belonged at a child's tea party was hilarious. Gaige snickered every time our boss raised the tiny cup to his lips.

"Ines may even know him. I'll touch base with customs and follow that lead," Cyrus continued, pointedly ignoring my partner.

"I have lunch plans with Hadley Richardson today. I'll see what she knows about the third part of the manuscript," I added.

"Well aren't you just Miss Social," Gaige teased. "We do all the heavy lifting, while you go on dates and hang out with the cool kids."

"And you go boxing and end up with a black eye," I shot back. "We all have our roles."

"Stassi is learning valuable information," Cyrus said sternly, putting an end to our bickering.

It was odd having my boss on a run with us. Though we normally turned in detailed mission reports and gave oral briefings in the runner meetings, actually having him there to witness the day-to-day was just weird. Not in a bad way, though. And Cyrus was helping us just as much as we were helping him.

"Depending on how things go with Hadley Richardson, we'll have to find a time to search this Carmen's apartment." Cyrus turned to me. "Do you know where she lives?"

"No, sir, but I can find out. Ines might know—they are acquaintances. If not, I can ask Hadley, discreetly of course."

"Good." Cyrus eyed Gaige over the rim of the tiny cup. "What are your plans for the day?"

"Boxing with the menfolk. Ezra, Ernest, and Andre enjoyed my company so much that they asked me to join them again. I guess Ezra has writer's block, and thinks exercise is the way to get past it."

"I think you mean they enjoyed using you as a punching bag," I joked.

"You're not the only one with cool friends," Gaige retorted. "Don't be jealous that you're not allowed to do manly things."

"Is this how the two of you always communicate?" Cyrus asked, his voice devoid of humor.

My partner and I exchanged a look.

"Yes, sir," we replied in unison.

This drew a hearty chuckle from our boss.

JUST AFTER ONE o'clock, I crossed the Place Vendôme and entered the lobby of the Ritz hotel. My stacked heels clicked on the marble floor as I slowly crossed the lobby, taking in the matching marble pillars and staircase. In the center of the lobby was a mahogany table sitting atop a Persian rug, the chandelier overhead making the glossy wood gleam brightly.

As soon as I reached the domed entrance to the public areas of the hotel, I realized my mistake. With two restaurants and three bars currently open, I probably should've asked Hadley specifically where to meet.

I scanned the tables of the main restaurant first, where dozens of people were sipping cocktails and champagne beneath a rounded ceiling painted with a blue sky and puffy white clouds. I was beginning to feel lost in the maze of hallways when a familiar voice called my name.

"Stassi dear, there you are!" Hadley's voice sang out, echoing loudly off the tall ceilings. "So sorry I am late."

"I've only just arrived," I said. "I was just looking around."

"Opulent, isn't it?" she asked, raising both eyebrows with a knowing glance.

"It's something, alright," I replied. Given the modern, utilitarian architecture of my time, I actually thought the stunning hotel was full of character and life. But I could imagine that a woman like Hadley, who didn't exactly surround herself with the finest things, might think it over the top. As I moved to enter the main dining room, Hadley put a soft hand on my arm.

"If you don't mind, would it be okay if we had lunch in the bar? It's quiet, and less crowded."

"Of course," I replied easily, following her down yet another hallway.

There was no maître d' in the bar area, only a bartender wiping down the shiny lacquered surface in front of him.

"Bonjour Frank!" Hadley called out, walking to the back corner of the dark room.

"Good afternoon, Mrs. Hemingway," Frank replied from his post. "Audrienne just ran to fetch me some ice, can I get you started with a drink? The usual?"

"That would be perfect," she replied, then glanced at me. "Fancy a gin fizz, dear?"

"Just a glass of champagne, please. I must admit, I'm a bit of a lightweight," I told the bartender with a conspiratorial smile.

"Nonsense," Hadley protested. "Frank here makes the best gin fizz in all of Paris, you simply must have one."

"In our city, it is never too early for a proper drink," Frank coaxed.

Though it was against my better judgment, given the hour and the fact I was working, I relented.

Frank and Hadley chatted easily while he mixed our drinks and I checked out our lunch venue. Between the dark paneled walls, gold-trimmed mirrors, and dim light fixtures, the bar had a definitively masculine vibe that was in stark contrast to the bright lobby and formal dining room. It was a room designed for men to gather and discuss everything from writing to politics, and would be used for just that over the course of its long, esteemed history.

Ironically, the dark, narrow space would be renamed Hemingway's Bar in the not-so-distant future, due to his frequent patronage and affinity for using the space as a makeshift office. The moniker would remain for centuries, until the hotel closed its doors in 2390. The fact I was seated with Hadley Richardson in the bar made famous by her husband wasn't lost on me—it was one of those surreal moments that demanded I take pause and appreciate the incredible opportunities afforded to me by my job.

Two men with familiar faces sat on tall stools at the bar, scribbling in notebooks and possessing the haggard look of starving artists. Several others were engaged in a lively debate at two round tables that had been pushed together, the tops of both littered with empty glasses and crumpled pieces of paper.

"This is *the* place for struggling writers," Hadley confirmed, catching me staring at the two men I couldn't quite place. "They spend what little money they have on alcohol and smoke their cigarettes, in the hope inspiration will strike. My husband just loves coming here."

"I imagine the people he meets make for interesting characters in his novels," I replied, my heart sinking.

In the following years, Hemingway would meet a woman in this very bar and begin an affair, ultimately leading to a divorce from Hadley. Knowing what was to come for her brought a feeling of sadness that I struggled to shake off. It was a hazard of the job.

Luckily, Hadley chose that moment to tell a joke about two writers who walked into a bar, and my bleak mood was lifted as I laughed at the punchline.

We sipped our drinks and chatted easily until the waitress arrived in a flurry of apologies. Evidently, it wasn't only her husband who frequented the place; Audrienne greeted Hadley by name, just as Frank had done. They exchanged pleasantries, then we chose several small plates from the menu to share.

For the first hour, Hadley gossiped to me about her friends, revealing what she purported to be all of their dirty little secrets. Given the tightknit nature of their group, I had to guess that the tidbits weren't at all secret. If it was similar to the rumor mill that churned on the island, everyone knew everyone else's business.

One gin fizz turned in to two, which ultimately turned in to three. When the food arrived, I compensated by carb-loading like a marathon runner the night before a big race. Hadley didn't feel a similar need to offset the alcohol, which worked well for my purposes.

The more time we spent together, the more I found that I genuinely liked Hadley Richardson. Had we been born in the same time, we probably would have been friends. And so I chose not to rush the conversation. Sitting and talking with her was a welcome respite from all of the somber events of the run, and I was actually having fun. I found myself feeding in to her need to gossip, as if her friends were mine and the stories meant something to me.

"You *must* be joking," I said, eyes wide and fingers covering my mouth to hide my smile. "Her skirt was really tucked into the back of her stockings all night?"

Hadley laughed so hard at the memory that she gasped to catch her breath. "Genevieve was *so* embarrassed. She didn't show her face in town for weeks."

"Why didn't anyone tell her?" I asked, giggling right along with my companion.

Hadley waved her hand dismissively and sipped her drink through the tiny cocktail straw.

"Oh, because Genevieve DuMount thinks she is something special. Her father is some minor duke or lord or something silly like that. She insists that people call her *Lady Genevieve* during formal greetings." Hadley sighed dramatically. "Her time here is supposed to be making her more cultured. Wait until daddy dearest learns she has spent most of her stay on her back. No dowry is large enough to make a man overlook the reputation she's earned."

The waitress arrived with another round of drinks, which we hadn't ordered.

"Compliments of the gentleman sitting by the window." Audrienne gestured to a man sitting alone at the corner of the bar.

Both Hadley and I turned to look at him, only his profile in view from our vantage point.

The generous man wore an expensive suit in charcoal gray. He was attractive in the male model sort of way that would become popular a century later, though his pale complexion was a little too vampire-esque for my taste.

Hadley raised her glass to our benefactor, and I followed her lead. The man reciprocated with his own tumbler of amber liquid. Though I would've expected him to stand and join us, as was customary, he made no indication that he wanted any further interaction.

It was decidedly odd, but I was grateful he didn't expect polite conversation with us in return for the drinks. Since I had yet to broach the topic of the manuscript with Hadley, I didn't need any distractions.

"It seems you have an admirer," Hadley teased.

"How do you know it's me that he's after? Maybe it's you," I countered.

Though Ernest's wife had a very pretty face, she had a matronly air about her that wasn't helped by her masculine style of dress. Between her short, wide-legged gaucho trousers, the blouse buttoned to her neck, and face unadorned by makeup, Hadley Richardson certainly didn't seem concerned with attracting the attention of men.

"Be serious, Stassi." Hadley patted her short, unruly hair. "Of the two of us, you are the more likely candidate. You should go talk to him."

I laughed uneasily. One man in my life was more than enough trouble.

"I am having too much fun with you," I said decisively, raising my glass to clink it against hers.

"Me too," she declared. "Speaking of fun, have you been to Monte Carlo?"

I shook my head.

"Shame you didn't arrive sooner, we could've run away for a few nights down there. There's such excitement, you would just love it."

"I'm sure I would," I agreed.

"Ernest and I leave for Germany at the end of the weekend, otherwise I'd steal you away." The light in Hadley's eyes dimmed slightly, and her smile wasn't quite as wide. The change was so minor that someone less perceptive might have missed it. She drank deeply from her glass. When she set the tumbler back onto the table, the bubbly attitude was firmly back in place. "Everyone simply must experience Monte. Perhaps when I return?"

"Germany? How long will you be gone?" I asked nonchalantly.

My own glass was cupped between my palms, the contents untouched. After the amount of gin I'd consumed already, I resolved to pace myself for the rest of our lunch.

"Three months. Ernest wants to finish his notes on Andre's novel, then get started on his own new one." She took another healthy swig from her glass.

"Is Mr. Rosenthal going with you?" I asked, furrowing my brow.

"Heavens, no. He's not much for traveling. Why do you ask?"

"Oh, I was just curious. I don't know much about the processes of writers, but three months seems like an awfully long time for them to be separated when Ernest is helping him with his novel."

I swapped the cocktail for my water glass, taking several gulps.

"It would be, but the first draft of *Blue's Canyon* is complete," Hadley told me. The next words out of her mouth were music to my ears. "Ernest is taking it along with him, and plans to revise over the coming months." She laughed humorlessly. "It seems I'll be spending a lot of time alone in the German countryside, and I don't speak a lick of the language. But Ernest says the quiet is necessary for his work."

Hadley drained her glass.

"When exactly do you leave?" I asked.

"We are taking an early train on Sunday," she told me, sadness radiating from her eyes.

Just under five days.

"We simply must get together again before you leave, I've had such fun today," I declared. Seeing her so obviously unhappy with her husband's plans, my heart felt heavy.

"Maybe we could do another lunch?" she asked, looking excited.

"Oh! I know—there is a wonderful show we could see. An Italian dance company, the Flying Codonas, puts on an aerial performance. I've heard nothing but rave reviews and have been just dying to go. Say you'll go with me."

Her voice was pleading, her eyes hopeful.

Despite the fact the tasks on my to-do list were reproducing with one another faster than bunnies in springtime, I agreed to attend the show with her.

"Assuming, of course, it remains open," she added. "The Night Gentleman has put a wet blanket over the nightlife."

I smiled thinly, the respite from my problems coming to an end.

Right, that guy. Nombre deux on my list.

"Ring me and we'll make plans," I said. "If not that, we will do something else before you leave."

Hadley grinned, relieved. She had the tumbler to her lips before remembering it was empty.

"Are you going to drink that?" Hadley asked, pointing to the untouched glass on my side of the table.

With a giggle, I pushed it over to her. Hadley resumed her idle chatter as she sipped the cocktail. I downed two cups of very strong coffee. Tiny as she was, it would be a miracle if I didn't need a wheelchair to get her from the bar to the street when we were ready to leave.

"Would you be interested in a walk around the Tuileries Gardens?" she asked when we finally asked Audrienne to fetch the check. "They're right around the corner and absolutely beautiful—a must-see in Paris."

"Definitely," I agreed. "I could use a bit of fresh air."

Once we'd settled the bill, we retraced our steps through the lobby. Hadley looked slightly unsteady on her feet, so I looped my arm companionably through hers.

The sun was still shining brightly as we exited the Ritz, and I slid large black shades over my eyes. I felt a tug on my arm as Hadley swayed.

"Is it remarkably hot?" she asked. "I didn't realize the temperature had grown so warm."

Though it was a beautiful spring afternoon with just the right amount of warmth in the air, I suggested postponing our walk until the weather was more agreeable. As drunk as she was, Hadley was in no shape to be wandering the streets.

There was a single cab idling at the curb, and I insisted that Hadley take it. Despite her protests, I won out in the end.

"I want to walk a bit anyway," I reassured her. "See the sights. That is why I'm here, after all."

A bellhop scurried over from the front of the hotel and held the car door open for Hadley.

"Well, there is a sight right there," she said, pointing conspicuously to a petite woman in black pants and a white blouse that was a feminine version of a man's suit shirt.

I recognized her immediately.

"Coco Chanel," Hadley confirmed my thoughts. "Brilliant designer. She lives here at the Ritz, you know? Has kept a suite for some time. She's going to be somebody one day. Someone big." My new friend waggled her fingers at me. "Toodles. We'll talk soon."

"Toodles," I echoed belatedly, my gaze following the future fashion icon.

Oh, Hadley, you have no idea. Coco Chanel won't just be someone big. She will be a legend.

The coffee had done wonders to counteract the alcohol, and I was once again sober after wandering for an hour in the cool afternoon air. I used the time to consider all the ways we might get our hands on the third part of the manuscript. Learning that Hemingway was in possession of a section was big. It drastically narrowed down the possibilities of the physical location, so the only thing left was to actually find it. Since Ernest wasn't paranoid or neurotic like Rosenthal, the pages would likely be found in his home.

I considered inviting myself over to Hadley's house for cocktails. Once I plied her with a few drinks, I could ask to see the manuscript, and then find a reason for her to leave the room. While she was gone, I could quickly scan the pages.

After considering all of the different angles, I decided that the only potential pitfall in the plan was Ernest. If her husband was home, Hadley was less likely to show me the manuscript. And if Hadley preferred going out to dining in, I would have to make sure we dined at a time when her husband was out writing or beating up my partner. Having Cyrus with us was a huge boon, since it meant there was a third man in the equation. He could search the Hemingway home while Gaige and I distracted the occupants, if necessary.

All in all, it was a sound plan. My lunch with Hadley had proven even more fortuitous than I'd hoped. I gave myself a pat on the back for finding out that Ernest had the target. I couldn't wait to get back to the townhouse and share my news with the guys.

THIRTY FIVE

"HEMINGWAY HAS it," Gaige announced, before I had both feet inside the townhouse.

"Are you kidding me?" I asked incredulously, glaring at my partner.

"Nope, no, Ernest definitely has it," he replied quickly, not picking up on my sarcasm.

I sighed heavily and closed the door behind me.

"That was my line."

With his face sweaty and swollen in spots, my partner was pacing the living room. Gaige's blackened hair stuck out in every direction, as if he'd been running his hand through the strands compulsively. The energy surrounding him was intense, practically crackling with pent-up excitement.

He stopped and stared at me in confusion. "What?"

"Hadley confirmed her husband has the third piece," I said.

Gaige propped his hands on his hips. "Well, did she tell you *why* he has it? Huh? Did you wheedle that detail out of her?"

"Because he is taking it to Germany with him."

Gaige threw his hands in the air, in an overly dramatic gesture of exasperation.

"Okay, she told you, whatever. But do you know what this means?" he demanded, doing a weird little dance that looked like a child in need of a bathroom. Without waiting for me to reply, Gaige answered his own question. "It means we only have five days to finish the run. Unless, of course, you think I'd look hot in lederhosen."

"We're not chasing them to Germany," I replied. "But I have some ideas for getting our hands on the rest of the manuscript."

"Me too!" my partner exclaimed, bouncing on the balls of his feet. "*So* many ideas."

Gaige was so amped over our mutual discovery, he couldn't sit still while we discussed strategies. One minute he was sitting next to me on the couch, the next he was reprising his ridiculous dance around the coffee table.

"I like where your head's at," declared Gaige, after I'd outlined the plan I came up with on the walk, including the contingency with Cyrus.

"I'm not sure I can say the same about you," I decided, peering closely at him. His face was a startling shade of red, with sweat running down in rivulets. "How much caffeine have you had today?"

"None since breakfast." He put up his fists, assuming a fighter's stance. With a quick one-two combination, he took down an invisible opponent. "Boxing is amazing, Stass. I have *so* much energy right now, it's crazy. *Crazy.* I think I'm going to keep at it when we get home."

"Yeah, you do that. Once we're safely back on the island, you can hit all the stuff you like. Right now, though, I need you to focus."

"I am focused. So focused. Like mega-focused. Let's do this. Call Hadley and set up dinner, let's do this tonight!"

"We just had lunch, I can't ask her for tonight," I said, eyeing Gaige suspiciously. "She's probably sleeping off the alcohol right now. I'll call her this evening, see if she can do tomorrow night."

I was definitely excited about this new development. But Gaige was I-just-won-the-Superbowl-and-lottery-in-the-same-day excited. It was sort of freaking me out.

He started doing jumping jacks, and my suspicion turned to concern.

"Are you sure you're okay?" I asked.

"Gravy, Stass. I'm gonna go for a run. Want to come? Never mind, your chicken legs won't be able to keep pace."

I rolled my eyes. Gaige was able to do many things better than me. He was a better rock climber. He was a stronger swimmer. He was the better bullshanter. And, hands down, Gaige was the more annoying of the two of us. But we both knew my chicken legs could run much faster than his hairy man thighs any day of the week.

Abruptly, Gaige dropped to the floor. The coffee table blocked him from view. Alarmed, I jumped to my feet.

"Gaige!" I exclaimed, worried he'd fainted.

My partner grunted as he pushed his body off of the floor, clapped his hands in front of his chest, and let gravity carry him back down.

I let out a relieved sigh. The idiot was doing push-ups.

Gaige continued his manic exercise routine, performing twenty military-style push-ups before rocketing to his feet.

"Time for that run!" he declared, jogging off towards the door.

"Um, no," I decided. "I think you need to chill."

"Chill? I'm crazy chill, like I just came out of the freezer. A run is just the thing to warm me up. Get it? I just owned that metaphor."

"Gaige, seriously, I don't think that's a great idea. I'm going to get you some water, just sit on the couch."

He swayed on his feet. I rushed around the coffee table to help him.

Turning in my direction, Gaige muttered, "Stass, I don't feel so hot...."

My partner's complexion was bone-white, his eyes darting erratically from side to side. It was definitely worth calling the alchemist doctors to have him checked out.

I was just about to march him next door when, without warning, his eyes rolled up in the back of his head and he fell backwards. I was too slow to catch him. Gaige's head hit the door, bounced once, and his eyelids dropped shut.

I screamed as he slowly slid to the floor.

THIRTY
SIX

"HE JUST NEEDS some rest, I am sure of it. Our dear Gaige will be right as rain come morning," Ines declared, waving her cigarette holder over his bed.

She clicked her lighter, producing a small flame.

Like a viper darting out to attack his prey, Cyrus snatched the cigarette holder from her hand. He eyed the startled alchemist levelly. Then, still pinning her with his don't-screw-with-me stare, Cyrus snapped the cigarette holder in two and let the pieces fall to the floor. Mouth agape, Ines began to sputter weak, belated protests.

"Consider this a non-smoking residence," Cyrus told her. He glanced pointedly down at the broken cigarette holder. "Now you won't be tempted."

Dr. Merriweather, the local alchemist physician, cleared his throat awkwardly. "I will run some tests on his blood, but his vitals are stable.

369

His heartrate is still elevated, though it appears to be coming down. I will continue to monitor him throughout the night."

On the bed, Gaige's closed lids twitched rapidly as his eyeballs pinged and ponged underneath.

"Is that normal?" I asked Dr. Merriweather doubtfully. My partner still hadn't regained consciousness, so it certainly didn't seem normal to me.

"It may be," he replied slowly. "Until I run a DOG scan, I cannot be positive."

"Wait, you know what a DOG scan is?" I asked, surprised. This was the first time we'd ever needed a doctor during a run, and I had no idea how it all worked. "How can you possibly do one now? Those giant machines don't even exist yet, let alone the handheld scanners."

The doctor patted me on the shoulder in a grandfatherly gesture.

"I am an alchemist, dear," he said, as if that explained everything.

Dr. Merriweather left to go run his tests without another word. Thankfully, Ines trailed after him, her head down and proverbial tail tucked between her legs like a scolded puppy. Once they were gone, it was just Cyrus and me with the unconscious Gaige.

"You said he was acting manic before the fall?" asked Cyrus, arms crossed over his broad chest.

"Yeah, I think that's the right term. He was bouncing off the walls, doing calisthenics, wanting to go for a run." I shook my head. "At first I thought it was too much caffeine, but Gaige said he didn't drink coffee after breakfast."

"How has he been acting in general? Since you arrived in Paris?"

"Like Gaige," I replied with a shrug. "I haven't noticed anything out of the ordinary, but ordinary is relative with him."

Cyrus cracked a small smile.

"Why?" I asked, confused.

"Your run to Florence and then to Paris were very close together. In fact, your last several runs have been very close together."

"You don't think he has time sickness, do you?" I asked.

My boss gave a little headshake. "The thought crossed my mind. The slow onset form is rare, and gradually builds up. In some cases, the inflicted is able to mask the symptoms, so that those around him don't realize he's sick. Has he been loading up on sugar?"

"No more than usual."

"How have you been feeling?"

"I'm not sick," I said decisively.

Cyrus stared at me long and hard. I squirmed under his gaze. After the moment became awkward and supremely uncomfortable, he spoke.

"You never are, Stassi."

Somehow, those words felt ominous.

Gaige remained unconscious through the night. Not wanting him to wake up alone, I remained by his bedside, taking up residence in a floral print chair that the designer had clearly created to serve only as a decoration. My back was sore, my legs numb, and I had a kink in my neck that only an expert masseuse would be able to remove.

None of that mattered, though. Gaige was hurt and no one knew why.

Dr. Merriweather came in around midnight to check on him and relayed that all of the standard blood tests came back normal. I asked what he meant by "standard" but quickly regretted the question. I kept my eyes on Gaige, tuning out the alchemist's voice when he began listing technical names for drugs and conditions I'd never heard of.

"He does have a mild concussion and a rather large bump on the back of his head," the doctor concluded.

"That's my fault," I said, guilt washing over me. "I couldn't stop him from falling."

"I'm quite certain that I don't need to tell you that it's not your fault," Merriweather said kindly. "Now I'm running the tests for atypical pathogens and the like. The results should be in by morning."

After thanking him for his efforts, I watched the doctor retreat out of the room. Once it was just us again, I wrapped my fingers around Gaige's hand once more and awkwardly curled back up in the uncomfortable chair.

"You're going to be fine," I promised him.

As the rays of dawn were casting a pink glow on the cream curtains behind Gaige's bed, my eyes became too heavy to hold open. I'd been running on espresso and sheer determination until that point, and my body was done.

A hand caressing my hair drew me from a fitful sleep some time later. In that place between the waking and dreaming worlds, my sleep-addled brain conjured images of Charles. The memory of his long fingers whispering over my skin, the kiss that made my toes curl and my head spin, the way he looked into my eyes with so much adoration and longing.

"Mmm," I breathed, snuggling closer to his warmth.

"Stassi." Warm breath fanned over my cheek as he whispered in my ear. "If you wanted to use my abs as a pillow, all you had to do was ask."

I sat up with a jolt.

"You're awake!" I exclaimed.

"So are you," Gaige countered. A mischievous glint appeared in his eyes—that gleam that meant he was about to say something asinine. "What were you dreaming about?" he sing-songed.

"Nothing," I intoned, elated that he was feeling well enough to mock me. I'd probably regret it at some point in the near future, but his teasing was welcome just then. "At least, nothing I remember now. I only recall the pain of trying to sleep in that chair. Why?"

"Those weren't moans of pain," Gaige declared, his devilish grin appearing. "Was Charles rounding third and heading for home? Here, lay back down on me, go back to sleep."

I crossed my arms over my chest and gritted my teeth to hide my relieved smile.

"I take you're feeling better?"

Gaige settled back against his pillows. "I have a wicked headache, though I don't remember any of the guys landing a blow on the back of my head." He shrugged as he rubbed the spot where his head had connected with the door, unconcerned. "Hazard of boxing, I suppose."

"Not exactly," I started, though Gaige didn't seem to hear me.

Yawning lazily, my partner rested his head in one upturned palm. "Dude, Stass, when we get back, I'm totally spending a day at the springs. I need a massage, a spinal adjustment, and a few hours in the healing baths. Manly sports are hell on the body."

I just gawked. How scrambled was his brain?

"What?" he asked. "Why are you giving me the creeper stare? And why are you sleeping in here? I know I'm irresistible and all, but you do have a bed across the hall."

"What's the last thing you remember?" I demanded.

Gaige blanched at my harsh tone.

"Okay, *Cyrus*, chill. And don't look at me like that; it's freaking me out. You have his tell-me-all-your-secrets stare down. I'm not a fan."

"Gaige," I warned.

"There you go again. You sound just like him."

I wanted to smack my partner right in the goose-egg on the back of his skull to jar some sense loose.

"Okay, okay." Gaige held up his palms in a placating gesture. "I was boxing with the guys, then I came home and went to bed." He sat up straighter, light sparking behind his maple syrup irises. "Shit, I almost forgot. Hemingway has the third piece of the book. Sorry, I was wiped when I got back, I can't believe I didn't tell you."

"Don't move," I said with a warning look as I leapt out of the chair.

Taking the stairs two-at-a-time and flying out the front door, I ran to the alchemists' lair to get both Cyrus and Dr. Merriweather.

Our boss began barking questions the instant he laid eyes on my partner. Moments later, the physician appeared with a handheld DOG scanner just like the ones used by doctors on the island. Cyrus and I stood back, while Merriweather performed a scan of Gaige's brain.

"Is he going to be okay?" I asked uncertainly. "How does he not remember anything?"

"We'll figure it out," Cyrus replied with a grim look.

"Are the doctors here enough? Should we get him back to the island?"

"Merriweather has all of the same tech we have at home, and all of the same treatment options. Depending on what he finds, though, Gaige might need to leave." My boss eyed me critically. "Do you think you can get the last bit of the novel without him?"

"Yeah. At least, I'm pretty sure I can. I might need you to run interference with Hemingway."

While Gaige was poked and prodded by the alchemist doctor, I relayed my ideas for getting the rest of *Blue's Canyon* to Cyrus. He nodded approvingly as I spoke.

"Go call Hadley," he said when I was finished. "The fact they're leaving for Germany on Sunday puts us on a tight timetable. Who knows when or where we might get another shot at it."

I glanced at my partner, not wanting to leave him alone. Gaige met my eyes and gave me a weak smile, confusion and fear shining in his expression. Careful to stay out of the doctor's way, I went to my partner's side and took his hand.

"I need to step out for just a second, but I'll be right back," I promised. "Will you be okay? I just need to call Hadley."

"I'm in good hands," Gaige assured me. "Go take care of the mission."

"One quick call," I repeated, heading for the door. "It won't take long."

"Two calls, actually," Cyrus interjected, handing me a folded slip of paper as I passed him.

"What's this?" I asked as I opened it.

"Put him off," my boss said quietly. "Say your brother is sick and you don't want to leave him. Say maybe you can see him next week. There's no additional information to be had from him."

"I know how this works," I replied evenly, then left the room.

First, I called the Hemingway residence. Ernest answered the phone, telling me that his wife had taken ill the day before, and he didn't want to disturb her at the moment. For a brief, horrible moment, I wondered if she and Gaige had somehow caught the same bug. Thankfully, that notion was quashed when Ernest quietly suggested that Hadley had perhaps overindulged a bit the previous day. After apologizing for disturbing him, I asked Hemingway to have Hadley call me when she was feeling better.

The other task wasn't so easy. Apparently, Charles had phoned while I was sitting vigil by Gaige's bedside. I had a feeling I knew why he was calling, and it wasn't for another night of flirting and expensive champagne. M.L. Worchansky, the man with the cufflinks that matched my locket, was a lead that we both wanted to follow. But without telling Cyrus about the necklace and my search, my boss believed the usefulness of the relationship to be over.

Which meant the relationship was also over.

Blowing people off always sucked, even when the person was boring or unattractive or just not someone of interest. You kept promising you'd get together at a later date, citing a headache, prior engagements, or family obligations. In the case of one man, I'd even gone so far as to tell him I'd fallen ill with diphtheria. Eventually the unknowing informant gave up, and we disappeared without a trace. They went on with their lives, and we became nothing more than someone the mark once knew.

Even though I was well aware of our protocols, I waffled over what to do about Charles. The decision had to be made soon. My run would more than likely be over by Sunday. And it was already Wednesday. The window of opportunity to visit M.L. Worchansky was rapidly closing. This side-project of mine had to be completed immediately, if it was to happen at all. Staying to help Cyrus catch Lachlan would not buy me extra time for it. Without the manuscript as an excuse to slip away, I was shant out of luck.

This is why you came to Paris. This is why you dragged Gaige on this run from hell. Answers. M.L. Worchansky may have the golden ticket. He may not. Either way, you'll never know if you don't ask.

Hand hovering over the receiver, fingers itching to make the call, I listened for the sound of feet on steps. Cyrus and Dr. Merriweather were still with Gaige. Ines hadn't returned since Cyrus declared the townhouse non-smoking. I was alone downstairs, and it was as good a time as any.

I snatched up the receiver and punched in the number. The ringing trilled repeatedly in my ear, and my heart sank a little farther with each unanswered jingle. I let my head fall forward until my chin hit my chest, the weight of disappointment too heavy to fight any longer. It was over. Without Worchansky, answers weren't going to be found on this trip.

The receiver was nearly back in the cradle when a breathless male voice answered.

"Bonjour?"

I pressed the phone tightly against my ear. "Charles?" I asked.

"Stassi," he replied, no trace of doubt when he breathed my name.

The smile in his voice made me smile, little butterflies fluttering in my abdomen.

"How are you?" I asked, forcibly calming my voice.

"I am well, thank you. My apologies for the delay, I was in the shower when I heard the phone ringing. I was hoping it would be you. I have been concerned. How is your brother? Your uncle mentioned that he has fallen ill."

"Gaige is doing better," I said, praying it was true.

My partner was awake, which seemed like a good start. The memory loss worried me, though. Nonetheless, until I heard otherwise, I was going to attribute his inability to recall our entire conversation to the huge knot on the back of his head.

"I am glad to hear it," Charles replied sincerely.

There was a long pause, followed by awkward silence.

"I called—" Charles began, just as I started to say, "Are you free this afternoon?"

We both laughed.

"You go ahead," he told me.

I repeated my question, lowering my voice when I heard movement upstairs.

"As it happens, I am free," Charles said, sounding amused. "But is there a reason we are whispering? Did I make such a terrible impression with your uncle?"

"No, not at all," I told him, bringing the mouthpiece closer to my lips. "Gaige is resting in the next room, I don't want to bother him."

"That is very kind of you. Did you have an activity in mind for this afternoon? Or should I plan something? A picnic perhaps?" His tone was still light and joking.

Good. We are on the same page, I thought.

"I think you know exactly what I want to do," I replied, realizing too late how that could be interpreted. How it *would* be interpreted by anyone at all like Gaige. I started to backpedal.

"Wait, no, not *that.* That's not what I meant, I was trying to say…I just meant…Worchansky."

Through the line, I heard Charles chuckling.

"I know what you meant, Stassi. I inquired with a friend who knows Monsieur Worchansky, and got a phone number for him. I took the liberty of calling ahead, I hope you do not mind."

"No, not at all," I replied, impressed with his initiative. "Would he mind if we stopped by this afternoon?"

"He said any day this week is suitable. Though I forgot to ask where precisely he lives. You mentioned you had the address, though, correct?"

"I do. It's in Montrouge. That isn't far, right?"

"Rather close, actually. I have a car. I can drive us if that is okay with your uncle? Or we can hire a driver, if he would prefer."

It most certainly was not okay with my "uncle". But I didn't plan on telling Cyrus about the excursion.

Upstairs, the door to Gaige's bedroom clicked shut, followed by the sound of Cyrus and Dr. Merriweather talking in low voices.

"Pick me up at four?" I asked hurriedly. Before Charles could answer, I added, "I'll be waiting outside. If I'm running late, don't come up. Just wait for me."

Charles chuckled again. "As you wish."

Two sets of footsteps were descending the staircase, the men's voices growing louder as they drew closer.

"See you soon," I whispered, replacing the receiver just as Cyrus came into view.

Engrossed in their conversation, my boss and the alchemist doctor didn't notice me right away, giving my trembling hands time to still. They were discussing the oddity of Gaige's condition. According to the doctor, there was nothing wrong with him aside from the concussion.

"The memory loss is troublesome," the doctor was saying. "He is lucid now, though. And his vitals are all within the normal range. Blackouts are typically a stage five symptom of time sickness, so I don't think that's what we're dealing with. Once a runner reaches that point, he is almost never able to regress. Mr. Koppelman would be confused, delusional even, if this were from his travels. It is generally so severe by then that the runner becomes unable to function independently, and I usually recommend institutionalization. But he appears to be fine now. Mr. Koppelman has no other symptoms of time sickness, either acute or chronic. I don't believe that is the proper diagnosis."

Cyrus and the doctor were standing in the living room, facing each other. Neither man acknowledged my presence, which made eavesdropping entirely too easy.

"What about his behavior before the fall?" Cyrus asked.

Dr. Merriweather's expression turned troubled. "I cannot say just yet." He patted the pocket of his white coat. "With the additional blood I just drew, I will be able to run more tests."

"Is there anything in particular you're looking for? Something you haven't already tested for? Some inkling of an idea?" Cyrus asked, his tan face looking impossibly grim.

Averting his gaze, as if what he had to say next wasn't going to be received well, the doctor continued.

"From Stassi's description…. You know I'd never think the worst of one of your men, Mr. Atlic. You have impeccable instincts. It's just that…well, we might need to consider that Mr. Koppelman was using recreational drugs. There are a number of substances that would cause such behavior."

"Gaige doesn't use drugs!" I exclaimed.

Both men turned to stare at me. Seeing as I'd just outed myself, I slid off the stool by the phone and joined them in the living room.

The doctor shifted from one foot to the other and pointedly avoided eye contact with me. I turned my hard stare on my boss.

"You and I both know Gaige would not do that. I mean, sure, he likes to drink, but that's the extent of it. And, on a run, he is careful to only use alcohol when the situation calls for it."

Cyrus nodded slowly, looking thoughtful. When his perfectly neutral expression wavered for the briefest of moments, I caught sight of something akin to pride.

"Stassi is right. I have known Gaige his entire life. The boy may imbibe. On several notable occasions, he has even gone overboard. But drugs have never been a part of his life."

The doctor held up his hands, conceding the point. "I understand. And I apologize if I have offended either of—"

"You're damned right you've offended me," I snapped.

Cyrus rested a hand on my shoulder. I waited for a reprimand, but none came. Instead, my boss pulled me to his side, a subtle gesture that showed he was on my team. A little of my anger faded away.

Palms pressed together and held in the center of his chest, Dr. Merriweather bowed in my direction. "I am sorry for that." He inhaled deeply. "I do, however, believe we need to consider the possibility—" He held up an index finger to staunch the flow of irate rambling threatening to flow from my lips. "—that he was drugged.

"I have asked Gaige to write down every detail of his day, from the time he woke up to the last thing he remembers. If he tests positive for an unnatural substance, that should give us a timeline with which to work. From there, we will be able to narrow down where and when he was exposed to the toxin."

"Thank you, doctor. That sounds like the best way to proceed." Cyrus turned to me. "Does that sound okay to you, Stassi?"

I nodded in agreement.

Now that no one was accusing my partner of going on a bender, the fight had gone out of me, replaced by exhaustion. In hindsight, my outburst seemed childish and silly. I should have defended Gaige in a more mature, professional manner.

"I'm sorry, Dr. Merriweather," I said. "I didn't mean to be so reactive, I'm just worried about my partner. Thank you so much for taking care of him."

"I understand completely," Merriweather replied with his kindly smile. "We'll get this all sorted out, one way or another."

"Let me walk you out, doctor." Cyrus gestured to the door.

I turned toward the stairs, figuring I had time for a catnap before

Charles was due to pick me up.

"Stassi?" Cyrus called without looking back. "I'd like a word when I return."

Crap. Was that word going to be "probation"?

Yelling at an alchemist doctor was likely frowned upon. There were worse crimes, like Lachlan's, but the price for defiance was much higher in the syndicates than other workplaces. Without strict obedience and absolute fealty, the syndicate system would break down.

Hopefully, my boss would consider stress a mitigating factor in this situation. This run, with all of its twists and turns and serial killers, was stressful. Cyrus understood that, right?

Of course, if he'd overheard me on the phone with Charles…that was direct insubordination. I tried to recall my side of the conversation, so I'd know just what circle of hell I'd damned myself to if Cyrus had been listening.

Forewarned is forearmed and all of that.

With my mind racing at a million miles a moment, I was sitting on the couch and making mincemeat of my thumbnail when Cyrus reentered the townhouse. He took a deep breath, met my anxious gaze, and then said the last words I was expecting.

"How do you feel about sanitariums?"

THIRTY
SEVEN

"YOU'RE GOING TO have me committed?" I asked uncertainly.

Cyrus stared at me with flat green eyes. "That depends."

"On what?" I shot back, apprehension creeping up my spine.

My first question had been a joke. Sort of. The jury was still out on whether Cyrus's answer had been in the same vein.

"On how much information the employees are willing to share with a man claiming to be searching for his missing son."

"I see," I said, drawing out the second word as his meaning sunk in. "Oh, no. No, no, no, no. Cyrus, you aren't seriously sending me undercover in a sanitarium? In the 1920s? They still use electroshock to try to zap the lesbian out of women. And zipper you shut in bathtubs. No fracking way."

"Did you become a lesbian in the last twenty-four hours?" he asked.

"That's not the point."

Much to my relief, Cyrus cracked a wide smile and chuckled.

"No, Stassi, you will not be going undercover," he said, his emerald eyes twinkling. "Gaige may not have time sickness, but I think that Lachlan does. As I told you before, his syndicate's Founder was concerned over Lachlan's mental health prior to his disappearance. Far as we can tell, Lachlan isn't using customs stations to enter and exit territories. We have no idea how many jumps he's made over the last several weeks. The chocolate wrappers suggest he knows he's sick and is trying to counteract the effects. And the police reports from the Night Gentleman crime scenes point to a deranged, very unstable man."

"Aren't all serial killers deranged?" I asked.

"One could make that argument," Cyrus agreed. Rounding the coffee table, he joined me on the couch. "The Night Gentleman has not taken a victim in four days, which is longer than his last cooling-off period. Serial killers typically speed up their timetable, not slow it down."

"Which must mean Lachlan is out of commission," I reasoned, picking up where Cyrus had left off. "You didn't find him in the morgue, so he probably isn't dead. If he's not wandering freely but is likely still alive, that leaves incarceration or institutionalization."

"Very good," Cyrus told me, nodding his approval. "I made an inquiry at La Sante Prison here in Montparnasse, and no one matching his description is currently in holding."

"And then there was one," I proclaimed. "One likely possibility remaining—a sanitarium."

I leaned back against the couch cushions, exhausted beyond belief.

"And then there was one," Cyrus echoed, a small smile tugging at the corners of his mouth. "Salpêtrière."

"The place that rounded up all the prostitutes and treated them for hysteria?" I asked incredulously.

Horrific images began to invade my mind's eye: Glassy-eyed men and women with electrodes at their temples and bits in their mouths strapped to metal gurneys with leather restraints; doctors and nurses taking perverse pleasure in "curing" their charges through sadistic methods; patients muttering nonsensically to their shadows after one too many electroshock sessions.

"That's the one," Cyrus replied. "I'm impressed by your knowledge of its history, but Salpêtrière is now a state-of-the-art psychiatric facility. If Lachlan has been committed, I'd guess that's where they took him."

"Next stop, Salpêtrière," I said, doing my best impression of a train conductor. "Toot, toot! When do we leave?"

Cyrus studied me. If I looked at all the way I felt, I was not a pretty sight. I felt like a girl who'd spent the night cramped in an uncomfortable chair.

"Go lay down for a bit, Stassi. You need to catch up on sleep," Cyrus said, not unkindly. His tone turned stern when he added, "That's an order."

I stood and stretched, the vertebrae in my spine crackling like pop rocks. Stifling a yawn, I mumbled, "Right after I check on Gaige."

"Gaige is fine. He's doing crossword puzzles and eagerly waiting for the all-clear from Dr. Merriweather, so that the two of you can complete the run. You, on the other hand, look about one breath away from an all-gray-matter diet. Bed. Now." He pointed towards the stairs.

"Did you just say I look like the undead? Not cool."

Despite his tactful choice of words, my boss was right. Now that I wasn't fearful for my partner's welfare, all of the adrenaline that'd kept me going was rapidly dissipating. Exhaustion swept over me as I trudged towards the stairs, my feet feeling like they were encased in cement blocks. The sensation intensified as I navigated the steps, using the bannister like a crutch.

No mattress had ever felt so soft, no pillow so perfect, as the ones on my bed in the Paris townhouse.

WHEN I WOKE, I went straight across the hall to check on Gaige. *Blue's Canyon* was being projected as a hologram from the Qube in his lap, a mug of mint tea steaming between his large hands as he read Rosenthal's novel.

"Have it memorized yet?" I asked from the doorway.

"Just about. The story will make a lot more sense once we have that middle piece, though. I've been trying to figure out what happened to Serena's cat for the last hour." Gaige tapped the screen of his Qube and the hologram disappeared. "You look way better, not like a rabid raccoon anymore."

"Nice gratitude, ass. I stay up all night, holding your hand, and that's the thanks I get?" I rolled my eyes. "Next time, I'll let you die alone."

Hand over his heart, Gaige batted his long lashes.

"Aww, Stass, you were worried I'd die? I didn't know you cared."

"Dead runners generate a lot of paperwork," I deadpanned.

"Come sit."

My partner beckoned me forward and gestured to the floral torture chair. My gaze darted between the chair and Gaige's bed.

"Move," I said, indicating that he should make room.

Stretching out beside him, I rested my head on his shoulder. Gaige leaned his cheek on my hair and wound an arm around my shoulders to pull me close. The embrace was affectionate without being romantic, as though we truly were brother and sister.

"Thanks, Stass," Gaige murmured.

He didn't elaborate, but there wasn't any need to.

"We're a team," I replied, patting his arm.

"Teamwork makes the dream work," he intoned, bringing a smile to my face.

In companionable silence, we sat like that, pseudo-cuddling, for several minutes. He didn't need to tell me how scared he was. Between the rigid set to his muscles and the uncharacteristic grinding of his teeth, it was readily apparent to me. His large fingers nimbly picked at the stitching on the brocade blanket.

"You wanna talk about it?" I asked finally.

"Doc says I'm healthy as an ocelot. He came in while you were sleeping to give me the good news." Gaige's voice lacked its normal flippant tone.

"I think you mean 'horse'. The saying is 'healthy as a—'"

"I know how the saying goes, Stass."

"So, if Merriweather gave you good news, what's the problem?" I asked, slanting my gaze to see his expression from the corner of my eye.

"Healthy people don't black out."

Right, there was that.

"Did Dr. Merriweather have an explanation for it?" I asked hesitantly.

"Yeah, he did." Gaige snorted derisively and let his head fall back against the pillow. He groaned and gingerly touched the lump on the back of his skull. "Doc Merriweather and I had a heart-to-heart. Five times, in five different ways, the alchemist had the nerve to ask me about my 'drug habit'." The air quotes made me smile. "Five times, in five different languages, I told him to turn his ivory tower into gold and go frack himself."

"You didn't!" I exclaimed, half in awe of my partner and half concerned about repercussions. Though if yelling at alchemists was exile-worthy, at least we'd be together.

"Pig Latin was my next choice, but Merriweather quit asking before I could tell him to ackfray himself. He did say that my blood sample came back negative for common drugs, so they're going to test for the more obscure ones now. He made it sound like it was possible that someone dosed me with something, but I could tell that he didn't really believe that." Gaige paused, looking grim. When he continued, his voice was quiet and grave. "Cyrus is going to have my balls if I test positive for anything."

"Castration is a little bloody for the big boss man. He strikes me as more of a double-tap-to-the-back-of-the-head kind of guy. Neat and tidy," I said pragmatically. "But you have nothing to worry about, because they won't find any drugs in your system. Besides, Cyrus is on your side. He knows you. He knows you wouldn't jeopardize a run for any reason, let alone something as pointless and reckless as drugs."

Gaige shrugged, feigning indifference. "Whatever."

"Do you want to talk about it?" I asked again.

"No, not at all," Gaige replied. "But thanks."

"Is Cyrus around?"

He shook his head. "He's meeting with that tailor Charles told you about."

Thank heavens. I hadn't yet conjured a believable excuse for leaving the townhouse to see Worchansky, so this was extremely good news. Almost like fate wanted to help me with my search.

Checking the grandfather clock in the corner of Gaige's room, I saw that I needed to get moving if I was to be ready when Charles arrived.

I rolled onto my side, so I was facing my partner with a fixed expression of innocence. "Want to help me out?"

"I know that look." Gaige grinned. "What harebrained scheme have you concocted?"

"Well, since you asked…."

As always, my partner's excitement mirrored my own when I told him about my plans for the afternoon. Hoping to avoid a tirade of teasing and inappropriate comments, I left out the part about Charles accompanying me. Gaige spent several minutes trying to convince me that he could sneak out and go with me, though his efforts proved fruitless.

"But we're *partners*, Stass," he pleaded, sticking out his bottom lip and giving me puppy dog eyes. "We're in this together. I go where you go, that's the deal. How will you make the dream work?"

"I know, sweetie. But the doctor hasn't cleared you to get out of bed yet, and I'm running out of time here. We're going to be gone in a couple of days, this might be my only chance to go see Worchansky."

Gaige let out a long string of expletives in Pig Latin, directed at Dr. Merriweather. When my only response was a withering look, he dropped the whole wounded-animal-meets-belligerent-sailor act.

"I don't feel right about you going by yourself," he said in a serious tone. "We don't know anything about this Worchansky guy's connection to your locket, nor what kind of person he really is. For all we know, he's the Night Gentleman. I know we're short on time, but what about just waiting until tomorrow, so I can do with you?"

"Tomorrow is full. I have the sanitarium in the morning, and then I'm going to see the Flying Codonas in the evening."

With Hadley nursing a hangover, the Italian aerialists were still up in the air…no pun intended. Tickets were a whole other issue, but I was confident that Ines could arrange that side of things. Hopefully, Hadley would be feeling up to the outing. It was the last chance I'd have to see her before the Hemingways left for the land of sauerkraut and schnitzel.

"I'm sorry…did you just say you're going to see flying testicles?"

The expression of utter bewilderment on Gaige's face was priceless. I rolled my eyes.

"Codonas, not cahones. They're Italian aerialists. Maybe you can even come with us, if you're feeling up to it."

From the corner of the room, the grandfather clock chimed a quarter to four.

Climbing out of bed, I said, "That's my cue. You'll cover for me with Cyrus?"

"We're a team," Gaige answered, echoing my earlier comment.

I paused in the doorway, one hand gripping the frame, and looked back at Gaige over my shoulder. My partner's big brown eyes were hopeful, as if I might urge him to say "screw it" and come with me after all. My face split into a devilish grin straight out of his arsenal.

"Don't worry, I'm not going alone."

Gaige's expression was approving as he gave me wink.

"Don't do anything I wouldn't do."

"Which would be what, exactly?"

"Bondage, animals, and anything involving whipped cream."

I raised my eyebrows in question.

"I hate sticky stuff. *So* not sexy."

THIRTY EIGHT

WHEN I EMERGED from our front door twenty minutes later, my clothes changed and hair pinned back, Charles wasn't waiting on the sidewalk as expected. Taking a few hesitant steps down the street, I looked to see if he was waiting in a car nearby. No dice.

I was just about to go back inside and call Charles, when I spotted him through the front window of the hat shop. He was inside, pretending to browse the insanely overpriced collection of headpieces while a flustered Naomi hovered nearby. The customs agent appeared to hang on his every word, though she said few in return. I watched their exchange from the sidewalk, gazing through the storefront like a voyeur.

As though he sensed my presence, Charles shot me amused glances as he selected a gauzy lavender nightmare. Fashion-forward Naomi was trying to convince him that the peacock blue fascinator she held in her hands was a much better option.

Only half-listening to her sale's pitch, Charles discreetly gestured for me to join him inside. I shook my head, tapping my wrist to hurry him along. Taking my cue, he pointedly glanced between the two hats, silently asking my opinion.

I pointed to Naomi's choice, giggling in spite of myself.

Charles squinted his eyes and shook his head in question.

I curled my arm behind my head and waved it around, miming a feather blowing in the wind. A formidable-looking man in a business suit stopped, one hand poised to push open the door to the hat shop, and glanced curiously between the store window and me. Embarrassed beyond belief, my cheeks flushed scarlet as my hand fell to my side.

Laughing at my poor charades skills, Charles selected the blue hat and went to the counter to pay, though his hands were empty when he emerged.

"Sorry, I had to do something while I waited for you. Loitering on the sidewalk in front of your townhouse was drawing funny looks," Charles told me when he joined me outside.

"Where's your pretty new bobble?" I asked cheekily.

"Being wrapped and sent to my mother." Taking my hands in his, Charles leaned in, as if to kiss my cheek. Instead, he whispered in my ear, "You are ravishing." His lips brushed my skin as he spoke, sending a jolt of electricity down to my toes.

Flushing from both his touch and the unexpected compliment, all I could muster was a breathy, "Thank you."

"This way." Charles offered me his arm. "I parked two blocks over, so your uncle would not see my vehicle."

"How very clandestine of you," I declared as we set off, earning me a quiet chuckle.

When we arrived at Charles's vehicle, my eyes grew wide in appreciation.

Generally speaking, I was not a car girl. The private transportation vehicles of my time didn't interest me in the least. Few people even owned a transpo anymore, since the public systems were lightning fast and more convenient. With a single body style that came in only three color options—silver, black, and white—the interior amenities and upholstery materials were all that separated the inexpensive models from the luxury ones.

Of course, this had not always been the case. At one time— particularly *this* time—cars were rare things of beauty that could act as a status symbol to declare wealth and social standing, like plumage on a peacock. And the one Charles led me to was definitely not your standard Tauosaki Electrorail Transpo.

Judging by his mode of transportation, Charles DuPree was a man of means and a member of the upper class. Not a surprise, really. His clothes, manners, and overall persona suggested as much, though it was hard to be sure since the other planets in Rosenthal's galaxy did not all calculate their worth in a conventional fashion. Many had more cache than cash, and more intellectual value than inherited wealth.

Charles DuPree evidently had it all, including a 1925 Rolls-Royce Silver Ghost Riviera Town Car.

"Do you like it?" he asked as I stared, holding the front passenger door open for me to climb inside. My eyes were still as wide as the Rolls' white-walled wheels. Charles laughed uncomfortably, as though embarrassed by the opulence.

Reeling in my jaw, I smiled neutrally. My own adoptive father was supposedly a businessman with his fingers in many lucrative pies.

"It is a beautiful machine," I replied easily. "I haven't seen this model yet in Baltimore."

Charles eased the door closed and jogged around to the driver's side. As the engine purred to life, I marveled at the smooth, quiet hum. Even compared to the electric, solar, and hydrogen cars of my own time, it was impressive.

Once I got past fangirling over the car, the thirty-minute trip to

Montrouge flew by with easy conversation.

Locating M.L. Worchansky's street address took equally as long, making me wonder how people survived before navigation systems and smart-driving vehicles. After many slapdash turns and circuitous routes, we finally arrived at a picturesque home in the center of town. With flower boxes in the windows and a terrace overlooking the busy street below, the residence matched my ideal of comfortable French pseudo-suburban living for the time period.

An man in an impeccable butler's uniform answered our knock. His French greeting was heavy with a German accent. As if to set the servant at ease, Charles slipped seamlessly into the man's native tongue.

"Is Mr. Worchansky in?" he asked, my Rosetta translating the hacking and gacking sounds.

"Whom may I say is calling?" the butler replied.

"My name is Charles DuPree and this is my friend, Anastasia Prince." Charles gestured to me as he spoke my name. "I called ahead, Mr. Worchansky is expecting us."

"Very good, sir. This way, please." The butler stepped aside, gesturing us into the foyer.

We followed him down a hallway with vast ceilings and marble floors to a large sitting room near the back of the house. Floor-to-ceiling curtains hung from polished brass rods, the cream-colored fabric tied back with twisted ropes of brown silk to allow the late afternoon sun to light the room. The furniture, though obviously well-made and of recent design, appeared worn, as though used for its intended purpose and not merely as decoration. As I took in the room, ringed with chestnut tables holding various artifacts atop pedestals, I couldn't help but linger on the incredible artwork surrounding me.

There was an impressively large Monet that sprawled across three adjoining canvases, along with several paintings by Picasso, Cézanne, and Dali. One day, many of the pieces would find homes in the most famous galleries in the world. The particularly bizarre gargoyle that was squatting beside the fireplace—a menagerie of animals combined into a single figure with the face of a fox, horns of a goat, talons of an eagle, and the stunted arms of a velociraptor—caught my eye and drew me in. Eventually, it would join its twin outside of Cliffman Brother's World Bank in Manhattan. All in all, we were surrounded by masterpieces and relics that were incomparable throughout history. Worchansky had the most impressive collection of art I'd ever been in the presence of.

"Please wait here," the butler told us, gesturing to the sitting area.

I reluctantly abandoned my circuit of admiration and joined Charles on one of the sofas, as he thanked the butler.

Once we were alone, Charles took my hand and ran his thumb over it in small, soothing circles. Apparently, my anxiousness was painfully evident. Though I was hit all at once with the fact we were mere minutes from possibly finding out about my past, looking around the room quieted my fears. Worchansky was clearly a collector. If he was anything like the collectors I'd encountered in my time, he'd be enthusiastic about telling the stories of his acquisitions.

"Just stick to the story and we will be fine," Charles coached me.

"I can do that," I told him solemnly.

He squeezed my hand reassuringly, and I found his concern adorably endearing.

Charles tucked a lock of auburn hair behind my ear, trailing his thumb across my cheekbone. Golden curls framing his face, pupils dilated, gaze soft, smile small and genuine, he looked like the most beautiful of all angels. His other hand slid around my back, pulling me into him. Through the thin fabric of my day dress, I could feel the warmth of his fingers on my back. Though it was meant to be calming, the lazy trail he was running up and down my spine made my pulse pound. Charles bent until our lips were nearly touching, then his curved into a wicked smile.

Definitely a fallen angel, I thought, right before he kissed me.

A thumping noise sent us springing apart. Another thump, thump was accompanied by a soft chuckle, and I turned to find an elderly man ambling into the room. A cane topped by a two-headed eagle aided his journey, the source of the thumping sound.

I wiped my mouth, though Charles's kiss was not something I wanted to erase.

"My apologies," Charles began in German.

The old man waved a gnarled hand at us like a claw swiping the air.

"I have never been one to stand in the way of young love," he said in English, his accent faint and hard to place. His milky blue eyes twinkled knowingly.

"Oh, no, we're merely friends" I said, hurriedly, sticking to our story.

The man, presumably Mr. Worchansky, laughed harder.

"I had a 'friend' once. That Trudy was a special girl," he said, breathing heavily as he trudged into the room. "Had more spirit than a gelding, and did not mind it when the going was rough. She loved the adventures as much as I, and never complained when we had to stay in an unsavory inn or beg a night in a farmer's barn. Our travels through Africa even led to spending a week with the Makhee tribe, and she pitched right in with the rest."

Even as I listened with rapt interest, I hurried to help him to his seat.

"Oh, thank you, dear," he continued as I placed my arm around his hunched torso and guided him forward. Pointing his cane, he indicated the worn armchair closest to the roaring fire. "Ah, yes, this is perfect, my favorite seat in the house."

There was a handmade quilt hanging over the back of his seat, which I unfolded and tucked around his lap.

"You are too kind." He patted my hand affectionately. "Now, tell me why is it you two youngsters have come to visit. I do so enjoy the company, but I suspect there is something particular that you have come for?"

I looked uncertainly at Charles, wondering if he'd neglected to tell Worchansky what we were interested in, or if the elder man had simply forgotten. With a reassuring wink to me, Charles stood and extended his hand to Worchansky.

"Charles DuPree, sir. And this is—"

"Your friend from America, Anastasia Prince," Worchansky finished for him. "No need for pleasantries, son. And no need for my native tongue. I am aware of who you are, and of course you know who I am, since you came to my door. What I do not know is why. And, please, have a seat." He jabbed his cane again, this time in the direction of the couch. "People hovering over me makes me feel sick and feeble."

Stifling a giggle, I followed orders. Charles, obviously derailed by Mr. Worchansky's lack of decorum, looked to me.

"Mr. Worchansky, we are here about a Bonheur's piece you purchased," I began, watching him closely for some sign of recognition. Much like Cyrus, the man's poker face could've easily doubled his wealth in Monte Carlo. "Do you recall purchasing a set of sapphire cufflinks with gold filigree?"

The old man set his cane across his lap and massaged the eagles' heads.

"My mind is sharp as a dagger, dear—it is only my body that needs a whetstone. I know exactly what you're referring to."

Without conscious thought, my hand went to my locket. Worchansky followed my movement with his keen eyes. Interest flickered in his cataract-affected gaze.

"Oh, I see," he continued, his gaze locked on the necklace. "Were you hoping to purchase them and reunite the set?" Worchansky chuckled good-naturedly. "I'm afraid I have the grave misfortune of informing you that it will not be possible. Those pieces are very valuable to me, and I daresay you cannot afford them."

Baited, Charles's tone turned cool and detached. Evidently, he was not accustomed to being denied. "Name your price, sir."

The testosterone in the air was suffocating. Death by an overdose of male hormones was not the way I wanted to go, so I quickly tried to diffuse the situation. Charles seemed to be forgetting that we were here solely for information.

"No, Mr. Worchansky," I cut in. "We are interested in what you know about them. My necklace was passed down through generations, though I'm not aware of its origins. We were hoping that you might have some history on the cufflinks, which appear to be part of the same set."

Charles remained silent, studying Worchansky carefully.

"It is knowledge that you seek?" the older man asked. "I have spent my life acquiring and learning about each piece that I own. A life's work that you ask for as plainly as a telephone number."

"I apologize," I said quickly. "When it comes to—"

Whipping his cane through the air with impressive speed, Worchansky cut me off and pointed to a statue between two of the windows.

"A Michelangelo. I won it in a card game in my twenties from Viscount Mordimore." The cane made a whizzing sound as Worchansky found his next target. "That Rembrandt painting—the dowry for my third son's wife, Eleanora. Born on the wrong side of the blanket, she was still her father's favorite child." Worchansky scoffed. "And yet, he was more reticent to part with the painting than his daughter." Another crack of the cane. "You see the bauble in that case? It has been called many names: The Heart of Lyons, The Raven's Eye, The Diamond Noose, The Scarlet Death." The old man stopped to catch his breath.

"You forgot the earliest moniker," I said, seizing the opportunity. "The Sorcerer's Prize."

The folds of skin around Worchansky's eyes crinkled, pleased with my knowledge of ancient artifacts.

You have no idea, old man, I thought wryly.

"The lore alone makes its worth unattainable for most any man," I continued.

"Cardinal Wolsey gave it to Anne Boleyn when she gave birth to her daughter," Worchansky added conversationally, the derision wiped from his voice and replaced by intrigue.

I wasn't sure how I knew, but I was positive he was testing me. And the fate of the items we'd come to see depended on my performance.

"The daughter, Queen Elizabeth the first, gave the necklace to Mary Queen of Scots as a goodwill gesture. Before later imprisoning her, of course," I volleyed.

Worchansky's eyebrows shot up his forehead, but he quickly recovered his composure. Feeling smug that I'd managed to surprise him with my trivia, I took a moment too long to realize my mistake. The questionably legitimate daughter of Henry VIII and his ill-fated second wife was still known in this time simply as 'Queen Elizabeth'. The second Queen Elizabeth was not yet born in 1925, and wouldn't be the heir apparent for quite some time.

"—a wedding present to the Archduchess Maria von Habsburg-Lothringen from King Louis XV," Worchansky was saying. Evidently, he'd dismissed my remark as a mistake by an American who was confused as to how monarchs were named.

"History, of course, knows her better as Marie Antoinette," I chimed in automatically, glancing self-assuredly towards Charles. I was acing Worchansky's test, and a part of me wondered if my companion was impressed.

I was startled to find that the color had drained from Charles's face, which was devoid of expression. He'd grown mute during my téte-a-téte with Worchansky. His hands were clutched in fists at his sides, gripped so tightly that his fingernails were likely digging half-moons into his palms.

Had Worchansky's comment about money really insulted him that much? I wondered.

In his defense, the old man had no way of knowing that Charles was exceedingly wealthy. Without the gaudy trappings of the nouveau riche, he looked like any other young man about town.

"Yes, Marie Antoinette, the Austrian who was meant to unite her country with France by marrying the dauphin," Worchansky picked up. "Instead, she suffered the grimmest fate of all."

"A royalist smuggled the necklace out of France after her death, because he thought it was too beautiful, too valuable, and had too much history to be destroyed by Robespierre," I replied without missing a beat, though my attention was divided in too many ways to count.

"His name was Albert Bonneville—" Worchansky started to say.

I held up a finger.

"*Her* name was *Alberta* Bonneville," I corrected with a triumphant grin. "She dressed as a man and helped smuggle French royalists to safety."

Worchansky shook his head wonderingly.

"The stone changed hands many times after that, eventually ending up in mine through a private auction," he finished the tale. "It is one of my most prized acquisitions."

Pride shone brightly in Worchansky's eyes as a deep sadness filled me. The thought that this man, who loved history as much as any historian on Cyrus's payroll, would never experience some of the most turbulent, fascinating times yet to come…it broke my heart. Part of me wanted to tell him the rest of the jewel's history, though I knew it was impossible.

Centuries from now, when your bones are dust and your soul is finally at rest, it will change hands again and again, I thought, mentally reciting it as if he might hear and understand. *Later known as the Black Ruby of Shanghai, it will be a gift from China's Prime Minister to American president Livia LeCroix at a global summit in Cameroon. This gesture will serve as a symbol of the Chinese-American alliance post-World War III.*

Five hundred years from now, it will be one of seven enumerated items banned for retrieval by all five syndicates. It is one of the few sacred pieces that belongs within history.

"Mr. Worchansky, if I may ask, what is your point?" Charles interjected, becoming restless beside me. His words pulled me from my musings. I shot him a pointed look, a silent chastisement for his rudeness.

Worchansky's gaze frosted over as it transferred to my sulky companion.

"My point, young man, is this: all of the objects in this room tell a story. They have history that began long before I was born, and their legacies will continue long after I die. This makes them more valuable than I can say. The cufflinks you have come for also have a story, and I have not heard it yet. Until I do, there is nothing you can offer me in exchange."

Worchansky settled back in his chair and surveyed the room's possessions lovingly. He'd mentioned a son earlier, but the items in that room were his real babies, his legacy.

Inhaling deeply, I made a decision. I made the offer before the logical part of my brain could stop me.

"What if I find out their story?" I asked.

The old man quirked an eyebrow, but didn't speak.

"I will learn where they came from, who owned them, and whatever else you like," I continued, my desperation coming through loud and clear. "All I ask is to see them today, and for you to share any information you do have. In exchange, I promise to return with the answers you seek."

Worchansky drew back. I feared he was going to refuse me.

Charles placed a hand between my shoulder blades, trying to quiet the anxiety inside of me. He threaded the fingers of his free hand with mine and squeezed.

"Mr. Worchansky, sir, I am sure there is some agreement we can reach," Charles said, his tone turning deferential.

Apparently, witnessing the depths of my despair had affected him. When I met Charles's gaze, I saw determination. He would stop at nothing to help me. He wanted answers, too. The adoption story would remain a questionable point in his history without them. Somehow, with just the appearance of a pocket watch, Charles had become as wrapped up in my quest as I was.

Worchansky's focus remained on me.

"I am an old man, Ms. Prince. Eighty-two next month. My heart is bad. My lungs are worse. How do I know you will learn the story before I die?"

I held his gaze. "I give you my word."

After all, even if it took my entire lifetime to learn the story, I could return to him before his death.

Silence hung in the air like the mushroom cloud after a nuclear blast. I half expected all of us, or at least Mr. Worchansky, to keel over before the old man made a decision. Finally, without saying a word, Worchansky raised his cane and brought it down upon the floor three times. The loud thumps echoed through the silent room, followed by the appearance of his butler in the doorway.

"Sir? You called for me?"

The elderly man's face was still so maddeningly expressionless. In that moment, I fully expected him to ask for us to be escorted to the door. The inevitable parting words, "Do not come back," would be repeated in French, German, and English to ensure comprehension. Maybe even Pig Latin.

Was my only lead truly a dead end?

Evidently, Charles shared my concern. He stood resolutely from the couch, reaching for my hand to pull me with him.

"Please bring in Tutankhamun's case," Worchansky said loudly. Though the words were directed to his butler, the formidable man never once broke eye contact with me. I found it more than a little ominous.

Exchanging uncertain glances, Charles and I eased back down onto the couch.

When the butler returned moments later, he carried a reddish-brown clay box in his hands. Hieroglyphs marked the sides and an image of Tutankhamun was carved into the lid. The box alone was worth a fortune in my time. Many of the syndicate's wealthier clients collected Egyptian artifacts.

The butler presented the case to his employer, but Worchansky pointed to me. "For Ms. Prince," he said.

"Wasn't that found recently?" Charles asked, his voice a mix of awe and incredulity. The butler set the box in my lap, and Charles reached over to gently run his finger over the engraving on top.

"Indeed. Howard is a long-time friend of mine. He gave me this as a gift for my eightieth birthday, just after he found King Tut's final resting place," Worchansky replied with a wide smile. "Isn't it just remarkable?"

My heart was in my throat, my hands trembling as I took in the Pharaoh's box. While a small part of me wanted to examine and appreciate it, I was mostly anxious to open it and discover what lay inside.

What if the cufflinks aren't a match? What if all of this was for nothing?

One glance at Worchansky put those fears to rest. His smile reminded me of the one Molly wore whenever she brought me back a present from one of her runs—something she knew I'd love.

Using my thumbs, I slowly lifted the lid and inhaled sharply. The deep blue stones twinkled in the light of the chandelier above, the delicate gold filigree winding an intricate pattern around it. Exactly like the locket I wore around my neck.

Removing the oversized cufflinks from the silk lining of King Tut's box, I turned them over in my hands. The gold gleamed up at me. The large egg-shaped stones were so deep that an entire ocean swam inside. With a deep breath, I ran my finger over the back, feeling for the one thing that would make this all the more real: the five-leaf clover.

There, engraved around the post meant to be threaded through a shirtsleeve, was my proof.

"The craftsmanship is unparalleled," Worchansky said softly. "Though I suppose you were already aware of this."

"Yes…they match my necklace," I breathed.

I placed both small circles in a single palm, then held them out to let the light shine upon them. The cool metal seemed to call to my tattoo, sending a tingle up my arm. If I'd needed confirmation that the cufflinks and locket belonged together, that was it.

Energy coursed through my veins, as a rush of adrenaline made my heart race. Maybe I hadn't found the answers I was looking for, but I was one step closer to my past. I felt it with every cell in my body.

"What do you know about them?" I asked our host. "Where did they come from?"

"It was actually Trudy who selected them. She always had such a keen eye for items of intrigue." Worchansky smiled wistfully, his thoughts clearly in another time with another woman. I gave him that moment with his Trudy, wondering if she and I would ever cross paths.

"We attended an estate auction of my great-grandfather's first cousin," Worchansky finally continued. "I know that he received the cufflinks from his father, but that is as far back as I have found. Though I've searched for their story, it seems to flow only in circles, with looping questions and cul-de-sacs of uncertainty. As you can see, the metal is bright and unblemished, despite being quite old. The compound is not something I've seen elsewhere, so I know there is a tale behind the pieces. It has been an anomaly to me for many years; I do hope you will find answers. Having another piece like it is quite promising.

As Worchansky pointed to my necklace, Charles surprised the hell out of me.

"Two others, actually," he said, taking out the pocket watch.

Worchansky's eyes grew wide.

"A third item?" he said wondrously. "How many more might there be?"

"That's what I hope to find out," I said with a smile. "As you said, there is doubtlessly a legend that accompanies these pieces."

"And you will come back to share it with me?" Worchansky asked, showing the first hints of vulnerability.

"Of course," Charles said, surprising me once again. His eyes had turned soft, a kind smile crinkling the edges. We exchanged a look. I realized that he'd come to see Worchansky as I did—an old man whose adventurous spirit was hindered by an aging body. He was someone who longed for the knowledge of history, and all the intrigue that punctuated the eras of time.

"Thank you for this," I said quietly. "I cannot express how much it means to me."

The old man shook his head, snapping out of the discovery of Charles's watch.

"I feel the same, my dear. I do hope you will succeed where I have failed."

"I promise. As soon as I learn anything, I will come again," I swore.

That promise was one I intended to keep.

I will probably never know what thoughts were swirling in Worchansky's mind when he looked at me just then. But the intensity gave me chills. It was a look that made me feel as if he knew all of my secrets.

With an expression that was a churning mix of wonderment, contentment, and disbelief, Worchansky breathed, "Yes, I do imagine I will be seeing you again soon, Ms. Prince." He smiled blissfully. "Sooner than I expect, if I had to guess."

THIRTY NINE

"YOU MADE QUITE the impression on Mr. Worchansky," Charles said as he drove me back to the townhouse.

"He is a very kind man," I replied absently, my thoughts elsewhere.

The cufflinks were tucked back inside Tutankhamun's box at Worchansky's home, a proper encasement for such exquisite and valuable items. A slip of paper detailing what little the collector knew about his relative was clutched in my hand. Unfortunately, it wasn't a lot. His name was Benjamin Markson, and he'd lived his entire life in France before dying intestate. With no will, and no heirs materializing to claim his many items, an estate auction had been held.

Much to my surprise, the listing of those who'd bid on the cufflinks was short but notable: Bonheur's had volleyed back and forth with Worchansky over the pieces. I couldn't help but wonder why the jewelers would've bid so high on a piece they'd crafted themselves.

"Do you honestly believe you will be able to trace the origins?" Charles asked, bringing me back to the moment.

I shrugged noncommittally. "I made him a promise, and I will do my best to keep it."

He reached over and squeezed my hand. "I know you will."

"You know it's not just for him, right?" I asked, watching Charles as he kept his eyes on the winding road. "And it's not just for me?"

Without looking, he released my hand and gently stroked my cheek.

"I know," Charles replied simply.

When we arrived back in the fourteenth arrondisement, we parked several blocks from the townhome. Charles shut off the engine and turned to face me, settling in to his seat.

"Thank you for taking me to see Mr. Worchansky," I said. "I am so sorry that we didn't find any real answers today that would lead you to Tessa's family."

Charles shrugged. "It will, eventually."

"I hope so."

We sat in companionable silence for a long moment. Charles fidgeted in his seat, seeming oddly uncomfortable for such a confident man.

"I should really—" I started.

"When can I see you again?" he blurted out, then laughed sheepishly. "Sorry. That was not supposed to sound so abrupt. What I meant to say is, I would like to see you again. Maybe we could have dinner and see a show? I could even pick you up properly, so your uncle is not so against our courtship."

Courtship....

His gaze was hopeful, his emotions hovering just barely below the surface. Gone was the man with the devilish twinkle and sultry smirk. Charles reached for my hand and brought it to his lips. "Maybe we could even arrange for a private box at the opera. Just you and I, alone in the dark?"

Okay, so that guy was still there.

I laughed. "How very forward of you, Mr. DuPree," I joked.

Charles unfolded my fingers and set his palm against mine, then threaded his fingers through the small gaps. Using our intertwined hands, he pulled me across the bench-style seat. The sun had set while we were inside Worchansky's. Few people were still wandering the streets near my townhouse. Still, cuddling with Charles in a car, in full view of passersby, seemed like a *really* bad idea.

But this was also my last chance to make really bad decisions where Charles was concerned.

His free hand began playing with a lock of my hair.

Seeing those strands of red slip through his fingers made me realize how fake our *courtship* truly was. From my hair to my name to my backstory, everything Charles thought he knew about me was a lie.

Staring into those honey eyes, I wanted to tell him the truth. I wanted him to know my story.

I wanted him to know *me*.

"I like you, Stassi," Charles whispered.

"You don't know me," I told him quietly, mirroring my thoughts.

Charles smiled. "But I want to."

Maybe it was the fact that he called me Stassi. Maybe I was just tired of being boring. Maybe my hormones overpowered my common sense. Maybe I liked him enough that nothing else mattered in that moment.

I pressed my lips to his. This kiss was different than the ones before it. This kiss was hungry, desperate, and filled with everything I couldn't say.

Charles pulled me closer. His hands began to wander, lightly skimming the fabric of my dress. Though his touch wasn't wanton or excessive, it was so electric that my skin tingled beneath his fingers. I ran my own hands over his chest, and the hard muscles tightened in response.

Our lips parted. And then his mouth was on my neck, trailing hot kissing down my throat. His hands were in my hair, pulling my head back to give him better access.

Unfortunately, a car, not matter how opulent, is not an ideal sexy time venue.

The steering wheel dug into my back when he pulled me into his lap. That might have been okay, had I not somehow managed to knock the gearshift into neutral.

The Rolls-Royce began to inch forward.

Caught up in each other, neither of us noticed the movement.

I arched my spine as Charles's gentle fingers found the hollow of my throat. Leaning back for balance, I connected directly with the center of the wheel.

The horn blared a long, loud note, waking both of us from our hormone-crazed haze.

I glanced out the window, looking for pedestrians who might have stopped to watch the show. What I saw sent me into a panic. Streetlamps, storefronts, and a fire hydrant ambled past.

"The car is moving!" I exclaimed. "Charles! The car is moving."

I scrambled off of his lap. Lids still heavy with longing, he tried to hold onto me. I batted his hands away and jabbed the air, trying to draw his attention to the world around us and the fact it was moving past at an increasing pace. Only the empty street had saved us thus far from a collision, and our luck was running out.

Charles swore loudly, using a most ungentlemanly curse word, and reached for the emergency brake. The car came to an abrupt halt, inches away from the bumper of another car parked not far from the hat shop. Given my perilous perch on the seat, my side slammed into the dashboard when we stopped, my head coming worryingly close to bouncing off of the windshield. I groaned.

Charles's breath was coming out in short gasps.

"Are you okay? Stassi? Say something."

I moaned, rubbing my bruised shoulder.

"Stassi? Please, I am so sorry."

"This is why man invented mattress," I intoned.

Needless to say, that was the end of that.

FORTY

AFTER A RELATIVELY chaste goodbye to Charles, I walked into the townhouse alone.

The living room was a beehive of activity. Cyrus was pacing. Ines was crunching hard candies, since my boss had put the kibosh on her nicotine habit. Dr. Merriweather was sitting on the couch looking befuddled. And Naomi and Felipe were staring at one another, as though confused over why they were there. Gaige was noticeably absent from the party.

"Stassi! There you are," Ines announced. Her hands were trembling as she unwrapped another candy.

Cyrus came to an abrupt halt. His laser-like gaze landed on me and, for once, his expression was easily readable. Worry warred with anger, underscored by despondency. I'd never seen my boss so troubled.

"Stassi," he sighed heavily, "we've been waiting for you."

Words I didn't like to hear. Alarm bells began blaring inside my head.

"What's wrong? Where's Gaige?"

Everyone looked at me, but no one answered. My unease ratcheted up another notch.

"Where is Gaige?" I demanded. "Is he okay?"

Green eyes full of sympathy and resignation, Cyrus stared at me for a long moment before answering.

"He's been arrested. The police discovered that his travel documents are fake. They want you for questioning, as well."

The world tilted on its axis. Strong arms were around me, supporting my weight as shapes and colors whirled around me.

"You can fix this, right?" I asked Cyrus. "I mean, you can get him out? Like on bail? He just needs to get out of there, then he can jump home."

Cyrus led me to the couch and guided me down onto the cushions.

"We're working on it," he promised.

Someone handed me a glass of water. I drank deeply from the cup, only to discover it wasn't water. I spit the mouthful of vodka back into the glass and handed it to Ines with a withering glare.

"Thanks for the warning."

"It will help calm your nerves, dear," she told me.

"Like you?" I asked dryly, nodding to her trembling hands.

She bit down hard on the candy in her mouth and pointedly ignored my question.

I glanced around the room, my gaze falling on the doctor.

"What about his condition? Can't you say he's sick?" I pleaded.

Cyrus patted my hand. "We did make that argument. Inspector Thoreau promised to have the prison doctors watch out for him."

"Prison doctors?" I exclaimed. "That is not reassuring, Cyrus. Do we even know what's wrong with him yet?"

Dr. Merriweather's gaze dropped to the ground. "I am doing my very best."

The initial sip of vodka had worked its way into my system. Though

I wouldn't admit it to Ines, I was starting to feel calmer. I sighed and focused on finding a solution to the mess we were facing. Resigned, I snatched up the glass and took another burning gulp.

"Okay, so what's the next move?" I faced Cyrus and fired questions at him in quick succession. "Are you going to pose as his lawyer? Or do the alchemists have a lawyer? Someone who knows what they're doing? You guys have those, right?"

"Slow down, Stassi," Cyrus said soothingly. "There is an alchemist lawyer on his way down to the prison now. He is going to see about bail." His expression turned somber. "Truthfully, I am not sure it will be granted. Gaige stands accused of murdering multiple people in horrific ways. Dr. Merriweather is going to argue his health at the hearing. But I want you to be prepared for the worst-case scenario. The prison doctors will not find anything wrong with Gaige. Whatever caused him to black out is either an uncommon substance, or time sickness, or simply a fluke. In any case, the tests they run *will* come back negative. They will deem him healthy and fit to stand trial."

I closed my eyes.

This can't be happening, I thought, rubbing my temples with both of my hands.

"What's the next move?" I repeated calmly.

Cyrus took so long to answer that I opened my eyes, momentarily worried I'd somehow blacked out and missed his response.

"You and I will go to the sanitarium in the morning, as planned. I will then help you retrieve the last piece of *Blue's Canyon*. In the meantime, the alchemists will work on having Gaige released."

"That's it?" I asked. "That's your answer? To stay the course?"

Cyrus's emerald eyes met mine and held them intently.

"We stay the course," he said evenly.

His confidence raised my own ever so slightly. My boss knew what he was doing. As the Founder of not just the Atlic Syndicate, but the entire system of syndicates, Cyrus was the most capable person I knew. I had to trust him. Squaring my shoulders, I gave him a reluctant nod.

"Okay."

"How is Hadley Richardson?" Cyrus asked, all business once again. "Do you think she will be feeling well enough to go out with you tomorrow?"

"It's just a hangover, I'm sure she'll be fine," I replied. Though I knew my boss deserved my faith, I had to tamp down the urge to defy him and bolt for the police station.

Gaige was my partner and I should be with him. I should be there, arguing for his release.

"Good," Cyrus continued. "Did you get a feel for their apartment? Is the study easy to access? I will start my search there, since that is the most likely place."

I stared at Cyrus, momentarily confused by his questions. How would I know the setup of the Hemingway's apartment? Unless—

"Hadley and I visited on the terrace," I answered quickly. Gaige must have told him I was over at the Hemingways' when I was with Charles and Worchansky. "I didn't really get a chance to look around. She wasn't feeling well, and Ernest was working inside."

Just as so many lies before, this one flowed from my lips like water from a faucet. But there was a big difference: I'd never before outright lied to my boss. Taking a steadying breath, I told myself that it was a minor non-truth, and would not affect the mission.

Lock it up, Stassi.

"Shame. Well, the place is small, I should be fine." Cyrus turned to face the alchemists huddled together on the other side of the coffee table. "It's late. I think it would be best for everyone to turn in and get some sleep. Tomorrow is a full day."

Merriweather, Naomi and the others all nodded and began to gather their things. The doctor closed up his medical case, then came over and squeezed my shoulder.

"Our people are trained for these situations, Stassi. We will have him out as soon as we can," he reassured.

"Really? You guys have freed a runner accused of mass murder?" As soon as the words left my mouth, I instantly felt bad. Even if the man had accused Gaige of using drugs. "I'm sorry, Dr. Merriweather," I quickly added.

"No need to apologize, dear. This is a very stressful time, and we are all on edge." He turned to address Cyrus. "I will inform you as soon as we know more."

While the group of alchemists headed for the door, Naomi hung back and caught my eye. She smiled tentatively. When she opened her mouth to speak, panic made me stiffen.

Was she going to say something about Charles? About seeing me with him when I was supposedly with Hadley?

I needed to preempt the problem.

"Thank you for coming, Naomi," I told her in a rush. "I wish we were seeing each other over beautiful clothes, instead of these circumstances."

The stylist pursed her lips. When she finally spoke, her voice was soft and musical. "I am so sorry about your partner, he seems like a nice man."

I smiled with genuine warmth. "He is."

Naomi held my gaze for a moment longer before following the others out of the house.

Once we were alone, Cyrus headed straight for the liquor cabinet. Pulling two crystal tumblers from the rack, he poured three fingers of scotch into each. He handed one to me and then sank down into one of the armchairs. Leaning back, he closed his eyes and sighed.

"Drink it, Stassi," he ordered. "That woman is right, it will calm you."

Dutifully, I took a small sip of the amber liquid. The slow burn instantly warmed my insides from my throat to my stomach. Cyrus merely held his glass, as if the weight of the tumbler in his hand provided all the comfort he needed.

We didn't speak. My boss seemed content with the silence, so I followed his lead. Though his eyes were closed and his face the picture of serenity, the muscles in his arms and legs were rigid. I wondered what was going on behind those closed lids. Did he really believe we could free Gaige? What did he plan to do if the alchemist lawyer couldn't arrange bail?

Finally, the deafening silence was too much. A question had been marinating in my mind since I'd first learned of Gaige's arrest, one that no one had addressed. I took another sip to steel my nerves—liquid courage, as Gaige would say. I smiled at the thought of my partner, even as tears threatened to fill my eyes. Blinking rapidly, I vowed not to cry. Tears were like lawyers; they only made a bad situation worse.

With another gulp from my tumbler, I found the courage to break the still that'd settled over the living room.

"You said the inspector wanted to question me again? Does that mean he thinks I am involved, too?"

"He hasn't labeled you a suspect. Yet. I believe he wants to speak with you in the hopes of tricking you into either incriminating yourself, or giving him more ammunition against Gaige. I have no intention of letting that happen," Cyrus replied, without opening his eyes.

His tone was so definitive, so matter-of-fact, that I didn't know how to reply.

Cyrus sat up abruptly, drained his glass in one gulp, and stood.

"Try to rest, Stassi." He started for the stairs, pausing at the first step. "Oh, and ask Mr. DuPree to join you tomorrow evening."

"Charles? Why?" I sputtered.

"A double date. I need both Hadley and her husband out of their apartment. Will that be a problem for you? I was under the impression you enjoyed spending time with Mr. DuPree?"

I swallowed thickly, the scotch making the gears in my brain turn slower than normal.

"No, Cyrus, it won't be a problem," I said finally.

My boss stopped at the top of the steps and peered down at me over the bannister.

"It's okay to enjoy yourself from time to time. We sacrifice a lot for the job. I, of all people, understand that." His eyes met mine and held on intently. "Just remember that when the run ends, so does the relationship."

With that single look, I was positive that Cyrus knew I'd spent that afternoon with Charles.

FORTY ONE

SALPÊTRIÈRE WAS ONLY twenty minutes away by car. Cyrus drove, while I watched candidly out the window as the streets of the heart of Paris ambled past. Beautifully dressed pedestrians meandered down the sidewalks, providing the heartbeat of this vibrant city.

It could not have been more different than the area I'd grown up in. The work camps were in the middle of nowhere by design, surrounded by open land. I'd grown up dreaming of making it to the big city, but even my most ambitious hopes never reached Paris. It was moments like these that I couldn't help but appreciate the dramatic shift in the course of my life, one that was due entirely to the man sitting beside me.

Glancing over at Cyrus, the corners of my mouth turned up. I was a lucky girl, indeed.

"Have I ever truly thanked you?" I asked him.

"For what?"

"Everything, Cyrus. My life…I would be…well, I don't know where I'd be if you hadn't come along. So thank you for that." Though it was an awkward display of gratitude, I felt better at least trying.

"You are always welcome," he replied. "I hit the lottery the day I found you."

Not sure how to respond, I watched the Arc de Triomphe sail past in silence.

"Penny for your thoughts?" Cyrus finally asked in a light voice. Without taking his eyes from the road, my boss extended his arm towards me. In the center of his flat palm was a large silver coin.

I laughed. "That's not a penny."

"No, it's much more valuable though."

The coin was tails up. I took his offering and flipped it over, revealing another tail. I pressed the coin back into Cyrus's palm.

"Only to you. Besides, do you really want to part with your two-tailed coin?"

In answer, his fingers snapped shut, like a Venus flytrap swallowing its prey. When he turned his hand over and extended his fingers, nothing fell out. The coin was gone.

"I learned that little trick you just did there before I could tie my shoes," I said with a wry smile.

"Yes, but can you do it while operating an automobile made in 1925?" Cyrus countered.

"I believe the real question there is whether I would want to, or would ever have any need to."

My boss chuckled. "Touché."

I resumed my window-gazing, my mind reverting back to the work camp. Evidently, it was clear to Cyrus where my thoughts had wandered. "We don't have to talk about it if you'd rather not," he began after several moments.

"I'd rather not," I said, tone sharper than I'd intended. Sighing heavily,

I tried to backtrack. "I'm sorry. It's just—"

"No explanation needed, Stassi," he interjected, waving off my attempt at an apology. "I do want to say this though: I am sorry for the time you spent in the camp. You have such strength, such resolve, to have been raised in a manner like that and still turn out to be a kind, thoughtful, and considerate person. Children should not pay for the sins of their parents."

"No, they shouldn't," I agreed. "But you got me out. For that, I will always be in your debt."

"You do not owe me anything," Cyrus said quietly. His gaze was focused on the road in a way that didn't allow me a good look at his expression. Probably by design. But with his hands at ten and two, and his spine ramrod straight, I was guessing his face was as rigid as his posture.

"Well of course not, I've paid back my contract," I joked to lighten the mood.

Cyrus remained silent, staring straight ahead, for the final five minutes of our trip to the sanitarium. Something told me the road was not what he saw.

JUST AS ALL horror-movie-worthy settings tend to be, Salpêtrière was set atop a hill, with a winding drive barred by enormous wrought iron gates. A guard station with one sleepy-looking man in uniform sat on our side of the divide. Overweight, with a cigarette dangling between his generous lips, the guard didn't appear to be capable of running down any potential escapees. His nametag declared him to be Pierre.

Pierre and Cyrus exchanged pleasantries in French through the driver's side window, and then my boss explained the reason for our visit. I listened with my most pleasant smile in place, letting the Rosetta do its job. Apparently Cyrus had phoned ahead, so his name was already on the approval list on Pierre's clipboard. As the guard checked off his name, Cyrus switched to English to introduce me.

"This is my niece, Anastasia Prince, visiting from America," he told the guard. "She will be accompanying me inside."

The man nodded, but said nothing. Turning his back and effectively ending our exchange, Pierre busied himself with unlocking the gates. Once the heavy metal doors parted with a mechanical groan, Cyrus tipped an invisible hat to Pierre and drove through.

A nurse was waiting for us at the end of the drive, wearing the quintessential nurses' attire of the time—a crisp white blouse with matching skirt and cap. Next to her, a male orderly stood dutifully with his hands behind his back. The vacant expression he wore reminded me that it wasn't uncommon for the staff to dip into patients' meds before regulatory agencies were in vogue. While I watched him watching nothing, the nurse's gleaming white heels clicked softly against the gravel as she approached Cyrus's window.

"Bonjour," she said cheerily. "Monsieur Shepard, I presume?"

"Yes. I phoned yesterday, about my son."

"Yes, of course. I am Clara Beaumont, Salpêtrière's head psychiatric nurse." She pointed to herself, and then gestured to the orderly. "This is Renault. We will be assisting you on your tour today. Please, pull to the left."

Cyrus drove around the circular driveway and stopped where she'd indicated, not far from the front doors. There was no parking area in sight, leading me to believe that this part of the hospital didn't receive many visitors.

Whether because she spent her day caring for patients drugged to the point of zombiedom or because she was naturally talkative, Clara began a constant stream of chatter the moment we joined her on the front steps of the hospital.

"Now then, welcome to the Salpêtrière hospital," she began. "We are one of the world's leading psychiatric centers. The hospital was founded by Louis XIV in the seventeenth century as a depository for the city's indigent with psychiatric needs. This main building used to be an old gunpowder factory, which His Majesty hired an architect to convert." She stopped at the top of the chipped stone steps and gestured back to the tall statue in the center of the main drive. "The statue you see there is Phillippe Pinel, who brought humane reforms to our establishment over a hundred years ago."

Though I nodded politely and tried to look interested, I wasn't sure why she was giving us a history lesson. We were looking for my "cousin", not a tour of France's most infamous asylum. For his part, Renault looked like he'd heard this speech a million times.

Clara's voice grew softer as we passed through the front doors.

While the outside of the building resembled an aging manor house whose occupants had either lost their fortune or their will to live, the inside had been completely remodeled and redesigned in clinical-chic. A reception desk was front and center, which we dutifully followed Clara to. After signing in, we were given plastic visitor badges that we were instructed to wear at all times.

You don't have to tell me twice, I thought.

The last thing I wanted was to be mistaken for a patient.

Like a docent leading the creepiest tour in France, Clara continued her spiel as she pulled out a massive key ring and unlocked the door behind the desk.

"Dr. Jean Charcot established his clinic of neurology here in 1882— the first of its kind in Europe. Much of his work is still continued to this day. Sigmund Freud himself studied here under Charcot, and still graces us with his presence on rare occasion for lectures on psychoanalysis. Today, Salpêtrière is home to many of the best minds in psychiatry and neurology from all over the world."

Please say they don't tell the patients that story. Mentally undisturbed people could easily be lulled into a catatonic state by it, I thought.

Suddenly, my heart hurt. I missed Gaige. He would have appreciated that quip.

The nurse's narration continued as we navigated the maze behind the door that separated the sane from the insane. The pale yellow walls of the long hallways were undoubtedly meant to be calming, though the effect was counteracted by the glare of harsh neon lights from above. My stacked heels clicked loudly on the scuffed floors, echoing off-beat with Clara's.

"Ah, here we are. You came at a good time," she said as she stopped to unlock yet another door, this one marked Ward C. "The patients have just finished breakfast and are now enjoying a recreation hour. Five of the unknowns should be in the common room, so we can start with them."

"Unknowns?" I asked.

"Yes, patients whose identities are not known."

"How many unidentified patients do you have?" I asked. Five sounded like a lot.

"Currently eight males and four females." Clara chuckled knowingly at my look of surprise. "That's actually far fewer than we normally have here. Because we are a government facility, many of our patients are sent by the judicial system."

Great. Being locked in with incarcerated insane people was *not* my idea of fun.

"Not to worry," Clara quickly added. My alarm must have been evident, because she patted my shoulder. "That does not necessarily mean they are violent criminals. In fact, most are not. The majority of our patients are men and women with known afflictions who simply stop taking their medication. Like your cousin, for example."

That was the story. Lachlan supposedly suffered from a mental disease that caused memory loss, blackouts, and disorientation. This same fictitious illness, left untreated, caused psychosis, manifesting most frequently in the form of wild delusions. Like being able to travel through time.

I almost felt a little bad for Lachlan. Rather, I would have, had he not been a vicious serial killer.

"Many of our patients arrive in a terrible condition. They are unable to tell us a name, age, or street address where they live," the nurse continued. "Through hypnosis and other treatments, some are able to recall their previous lives."

I didn't want to know the other types of *treatment* the hospital employed in an effort to help patients remember. Despite that statue guy bringing humane treatments to the hospital, it was still a barbaric time for the field of psychiatry.

Clara pushed open the door to Ward C. After a steeling breath, I followed her inside with Cyrus right behind me and the silent Renault bringing up the rear. His presence was a huge comfort in that moment, since I didn't know what we'd find on the other side of that door.

Instead of a dank space filled with raving madmen, like I expected, the door simply lead to another yellow hallway with more doors on either side.

"The recreation center is just down here, past the patient rooms," Clara explained, leading us at a brisk pace.

My earlier relief at the conditions had been decidedly premature. Halfway down the hall, I was hit with a horrific smell—a cross between a men's locker room, a butcher's freezer three days after a power outage, and an outhouse in the middle of the Sahara. My first instinct was to recoil. If flower sachets were still in use during the 1920s, this would've been the moment to reach for mine. The scent was nearly unbearable.

"It takes a moment or two to adjust to the smell," Clara told us matter-of-factly.

I glanced at Cyrus, feeling dubious whether a "moment or two" would suffice. He shrugged and patted my shoulder reassuringly as we reached the ward's common room.

A large group of men wearing hospital gowns were gathered around a standing radio, listening intently to what sounded like a talk show. Other patients were scattered throughout the room on couches and at tables. Some were reading books or playing games. One man, with patches of shoulder length hair the color of freshly fallen snow, played chess against an invisible opponent who seemed to be besting him. Many others simply stared at things only they were able to see.

"That's Winston," Renault said when he caught me staring at the guy playing chess. It was the first time the orderly had spoken, and his voice wasn't what I expected from the strapping young man. It was soft, soothing, and effeminate, and probably helped calm the patients more than any drug in the dispensary. "He is plagued by voices," the orderly continued.

"Is that who he plays chess with?" I asked hesitantly, jumping as Winston slammed his knight defiantly from one square to another.

"No. Diago is his opponent's name," Renault replied with a small smile. "Diago usually wins, but every so often Winston will prevail."

A dishwater blonde with big blue eyes and drool leaking from one corner of his mouth ambled over. He stopped only a foot in front of me and began to rock back and forth. I took a step backwards, but the wall behind me didn't allow for more than that. Just as I mustered a small smile through my unease, he began to chant in a cadence similar to a nursery rhyme.

"Leave it to me. Three times three. A tree is just a tree. Birds, not bees. Leave it to me. Three times three," he sang in accented English, continuing to rock.

"Theo Three," Renault told me quietly. "It's not his real name, of course. But he's an unknown."

"Leave it to me. Three times three. A tree is just a tree," Theo Three repeated.

"Does he ever say anything else?" I asked Renault.

The orderly shook his head sadly. "I am afraid not."

Theo Three lifted an arm and pointed his index finger at me. "Jump, jump, jump, fast as you can. Dance, dance, dance, out of the pan. Sing, sing, sing, for the damned."

Renault laughed uneasily. "You have inspired him, it seems."

"Is everything okay?" Clara asked me in that overly cheerful voice of hers.

While I'd been talking to Renault and rousing verse, Cyrus had given Lachlan's old-fashioned photograph to Clara. She'd paused in her purveyance of the room when she notice Theo standing right in front of me.

"Yes, of course," I said easily, taking a step to the side. Turning to Cyrus, I asked, "Do you see him?"

My boss shook his head.

"Oh, Janna," Clara called to a nurse passing by. "Have you seen this man?"

Janna sauntered over to us, appearing as if to have all the time in the world, and plucked the photo from Clara's hand. The bright red polish on the second nurse's fingernails glinted under the light as she studied the picture of Lachlan.

"It might be him," Janna announced, flipping long brown hair over her shoulder and giving Cyrus a come-hither look. "Who is asking?"

"*Who* might be him?" my boss asked.

"There is a man who arrived about a week ago," she replied shortly, quickly losing interest in our group. "He enjoys the fresh air, you will probably find him on the terrace."

Without another word, Janna returned the photograph and walked away.

Stifling a laugh behind my hand, I followed Clara and the others across the recreation room to a pair of French doors. Two male orderlies stood on either side of them, feet shoulder-width apart and hands clasped behind their backs. Clara greeted them by name. They each nodded in acknowledgement, and then opened the doors for our little group.

A stone veranda that had seen much better days lay before us, with steps leading down to what was once a garden. The overgrown weeds and dry, dead plants served as a vista that was fitting for its cheerless location. Rickety rocking chairs were scattered across the fractured stones of the patio, the wood black in spots from exposure to the elements. All in all, it didn't seem like a suitable place to let mental patients have free rein.

"Not to worry, only patients we consider to be placid are permitted outside," Clara explained, as if she'd read my mind. "The violent ones, and those who might attempt escape, are not." She pointed to a tall fence topped by barbed wire that stood around the perimeter of the lawn area. "Even so, we do take proper precautions for the safety of all our patients."

Tearing my eyes from the fence—a visible reminder that I was locked in with mentally unstable people—I focused on the task at hand and surveyed the patients outside. A few men were enjoying the morning air, along with a couple of women who must've come from an adjoining ward. Though most sat in the rocking chairs, clustered in small groups, one man sat in a wheelchair apart from the rest with his back to us. Oily black hair hung in lank clumps past his ears, almost long enough to brush the moth-eaten cardigan resting over his rounded shoulders.

Cyrus and I exchanged pointed glances.

"Is that the young man the other nurse was referring to?" my boss asked Clara.

"It must be," she agreed. "I recognize all of the other patients out here."

Together, Cyrus and I walked slowly around to the front of the wheelchair. My first look at the man's face caused me to inhale sharply. Dark irises ringed in red stared dead ahead at some unknown fixed point. His lips were dry and cracked, tinged an unnatural shade of indigo. A chipped front tooth compulsively tugged at his bottom lip as the man muttered inaudibly. Ashen skin hung on a too-thin face, as though all of the air had been let out of the balloon that was Lachlan. Only the faintest trace of resemblance to the handsome man in his syndicate profile picture still lingered.

Cyrus squatted in front of the wheelchair, bringing him to eye-level with Lachlan. The man's hands were resting on top of the starch white blanket draped over his lap. Cyrus carefully took them in his own and squeezed gently, rubbing his thumbs over the rogue runner's wrists. To Clara and Renault, the gesture probably seemed nurturing and reassuring. But I knew better.

Just seeing the man was not enough. Cyrus was feeling for the ridges and valleys of a runner tattoo. A quick flit of my boss's eyes in my direction told me that he'd found it. He turned one wrist over, then gently set it back in Lachlan's lap. When Cyrus stood up again, the tightening around his mouth said he was upset. Possibly *really* upset.

A moment later, I understood why.

"Is this your Lachlan?" Clara asked, clueless to the shift in my boss. The nurse was smiling so widely that looking at her made my cheeks hurt.

"What happened to his arm?" Cyrus demanded.

"Pardon?" Clara asked, smile dimming from manic merriment to cheerful concern.

"His arm," Cyrus growled. He yanked back the right sleeve of Lachlan's shirt.

I gasped, covering my mouth to hide my revulsion.

Wrapped around his wrist was a worn, dirty cloth, like a makeshift bandage. The skin peeking out from beneath it was a mess of seeping, swollen scabs. Thin streams of dried blood ran up his forearm to the elbow, with smears that appeared fresher down closer to his palm. Lachlan's fingertips on the opposite hand were also tinged crimson, and his torn and chewed fingernails had more dried blood caked beneath them.

"As a government facility—" Clara began.

"You can't manage basic first aid?" Cyrus snapped.

"I will go fetch fresh bandages," Renault said quietly, then hurried away.

Smart man, I thought. Cyrus was about to blow a gasket.

With a gentleness that belied his rage, Cyrus rested Lachlan's arm across his lap. But his compassion instantly disappeared as he rounded on the nurse, pinning her in place with emerald daggers. I did not envy her in the least.

"How long did you say my son has been here?" Cyrus asked evenly.

Clara relaxed visibly when she heard his calm tone.

Big mistake. Yelling and screaming were one thing. This eerily calm version of Cyrus was far more dangerous.

"Just over a week, Mr. Shepard," the nurse replied automatically.

"And how long have his wounds gone untreated?"

"Sir, the patients are monitored very—"

"There is dried blood and scabbing. Not to mention that his hair has not been washed in quite some time," Cyrus said, disapproval and derision creeping into his scary calm tone. "This tells me that no, you do not monitor your patients. At all."

Renault returned with a small first aid kit. He knelt in front of Lachlan's wheelchair and began cleaning the wounds. I joined him, wanting to stay inconspicuous while Cyrus verbally assaulted the nurse.

"Can I help?" I quietly asked the orderly.

Renault smiled. "Thank you."

He handed me a warm, damp cloth, and I took the runner's right arm while Renault took the left. Thankfully, mine was the side without the grotesque wound. I began gently removing the blood from Lachlan's hand. As Renault carefully rubbed another wet cloth over Lachlan's arm, the runner became agitated. His lips pulled back in a snarl, revealing even more cracked and broken teeth. Saliva, tinged red with blood, flew from his mouth as he hissed angrily.

"Is this how he came in?" I asked incredulously. "With all of these broken teeth? It appears as though he was in a fight."

"Sadly, yes. I was on-duty when he arrived, and he was in bad shape. I didn't even connect this man with the photo you showed us of your cousin—he was unrecognizable. The wounds appeared to be pretty recent at the time. As for his teeth," Renault tapped his own front teeth, "these ones are loose and will likely fall out." The orderly then gestured to Lachlan's jaw, which was swollen on the right side. "Farther in the back, several more are loose, as well."

Instead of answering Renault, I thought about his words as I continued cleaning the blood off the runner's arm, glancing every so often at Lachlan's face to assess the damage there. Who would he have been fighting? Who in this era could possibly hate him enough to inflict such brutal injuries?

I was still lost in my thoughts several minutes later, when I realized that I was running the cloth over skin that was already clean.

Sitting back on my heels, I watched Renault finish wiping up Lachlan's other arm. With the dirty bandage gone and the blood wiped away, bruises in varying stages of the healing process were visible. The ones closer to his elbow appeared to be the oldest, where only faint yellow and sickly green discoloration marred the runner's olive skin. Around his wrist, the skin was tender and red beneath stacked bracelets of purple and blue contusions, as if he'd been struggling against a tight grip.

But, more so than any of the bruises or other injuries, the underside of his right wrist was the most alarming. It was as though something had rubbed or chafed the skin to the point it was missing in some places. Scabs in various sizes and stages of healing ran in a horizontal line nearly half-an-inch thick. In between those were pockets of fresh, open wounds, almost like he'd been compulsively digging for something within the mess.

Renault finished applying ointment all the way around Lachlan's wrist, then traded me the tube of medicine for fresh dressings.

"Merci," he said with a small smile, flushing when our hands brushed.

"You're welcome," I replied, mirroring his expression.

As he carefully wrapped Lachlan's wounded arm in the gauze, the runner began to rock back and forth in his chair. The muttering grew steadily louder. I was just about to lean closer to him, to see if I could make out the words, when Lachlan's voice rose another decibel.

"Not my name. Not my blame," he said clearly. "Not my name. Not my blame."

Lachlan shook his head from side to side in emphatic jerks, causing his greasy strands of black hair to stick to his slick skin. An emotion I couldn't immediately decipher flashed in his dark eyes, then they began flicking back and forth between my face and the wounds Renault was bandaging.

"Not my name. *Not my name.*" His tone was more insistent this time.

"Hang on," I said to Renault. "Can I have a look at his wrist again?"

"If you like." The orderly unwound the dressing.

Off to the side, Cyrus and Clara were still arguing about acceptable care standards for institutions. His full attention was on the nurse, so my attempts to inconspicuously catch his eye failed.

I reached for Lachlan's injured arm. Like trying to avoid startling a horse that had been spooked, I kept my movements slow and deliberate. The other runner flinched when my fingers touched the skin near his wrist, but he didn't pull away. Fighting the urge to look away, I gently pulled his arm closer to examine the scabs on his wrist.

Though it was difficult to see much of the original wound through all of the bruising and infection, not to mention where Lachlan had clearly scratched and picked at the scabs as they healed, the edges looked like they'd initially been precise. Two straight, horizontal lines were still visible among the ravaged flesh.

"Self-inflicted," Renault said softly when he saw me looking. "Your cousin likely tried to take his life."

"Not my name. Not my name. Not my name. Not my name," Lachlan hissed angrily at the orderly.

Is he trying to tell us that he wasn't attempting suicide? I wondered.

Leaning in even farther, I examined the wound more closely. The incisions were shallow. Almost as if—oh shant. No, no, no, no. This was *so* not good.

The incisions were shallow because Lachlan's skin had not merely been cut; it had been excised.

"Not my name. Not my name. Not my name. Not my name."

According to his personnel file, Lachlan was right handed. The skin removal was too exact, the lines too straight to have been made by a non-dominant hand. There was no way that Lachlan could have possibly held the knife in his right hand to make the incisions staring up at me.

Someone else had removed Lachlan's name tattoo.

"Not my name. Not my name. Not my name. Not my name."

"Um, Cyrus...?"

FORTY TWO

LACHLAN'S AGITATION PROMPTED Clara to order a sedative, and he was returned to his room.

Clara then herded Cyrus and me to a cramped administrative office. She disappeared for a short time, returning with a thin medical file in her hand. Soon after, we were joined by Dr. Pierre Marie, the Chair of Diseases of the Nervous System. Introductions were barely finished before Cyrus launched his attack.

"I do hope you understand, but I wish to take my son with me today when I leave," he said resolutely. "Lachlan needs to be with his family during this time."

Dr. Marie raised one eyebrow, but didn't respond. Clara looked hesitantly between the men as a full minute passed without a word from either.

"Mr. Shepard, we do understand your situation, but I am afraid it won't be quite that simple," she finally said. The nurse consulted the file she'd brought in—presumably Lachlan's. "Your son was arrested after being found wandering in the park shirtless, shoeless, and witless. The police brought him to us, and we take that responsibility very seriously. I am sure you can see why it would be impossible for Lachlan to leave today. Additionally, Dr. Marie has not yet made his final pronouncement on your son's neurological health."

"I have hardly begun my assessment," Marie interjected.

"While I do appreciate your efforts, my son is already being treated privately for his ailments," Cyrus firmly replied. "I believe it would be best for him if he continued that course, as he was showing great improvement. As for the police matters, I would be happy to pay the fines today that were imposed against Lachlan for his behavior." My boss withdrew a check torn from the syndicate's 1920s ledger book from his left inside jacket pocket, then a fountain pen from the opposite one. "I would like to make a sizable donation to your institution, as well. To whom shall I make out the check?"

Marie's expression turned amused, while Clara became flustered.

"M-Mr. Shepard, I...," she trailed off, her eyes darting to the doctor for help. He remained quiet, studying Cyrus with a curiosity that would've made me uncomfortable. "I am afraid that is simply not able to happen. I-I mean, not the money, well the donation...it is—"

"You cannot pay court imposed fines here," Marie finally broke in. "We are a hospital, not the préfecture, and certainly not a courthouse."

The beginnings of a scowl traced over Cyrus's features.

"Dr. Marie, I'd hoped to keep this civilized, but I cannot with good conscience allow Lachlan to remain in this facility. My son has grave physical injuries that no one seems to know the origin of, or even when they were inflicted. At best, he had them when he arrived, but your staff neglected to properly care for them. At worst?" Cyrus glared pointedly before continuing in a low voice that verged on menacing. "At worst, your staff has been abusing its patients. A fact I'm sure the authorities would appreciate me sharing with them."

Clara sucked in a deep breath, her hand flying to her heart.

"Mr. Shepard!" she cried. "We treat each patient with the utmost care and respect, we would *never* do such a thing. It is preposterous to even think that our nurses and aides are abusing these poor souls."

My eyes flew to Dr. Marie. I expected him to be equally outraged, but he was still intently studying Cyrus like a germ in a petri dish. Though my boss was definitely difficult to read, Marie was a world-renowned expert on matters of the brain. I wouldn't have wanted to be Cyrus in that moment; Marie's stare was making *me* feel awkward. Nonetheless, my fearless leader was returning the doctor's gaze, completely unfazed.

"I understand your concerns," Marie finally said, ending the awkward silence that had descended upon our group during their little stare-off. "However, I can assure you that no one working in this hospital injured your son."

"Though I can agree that it seems unlikely for such atrocities to happen under your tutelage," Cyrus replied, his eyes brimming over with faux worry. "I do hope you can appreciate my concerns over the state of his injuries. Lachlan has not been properly cared for while here."

"On behalf of Nurse Clara and her staff, I do apologize for the fact your son's injuries might have been overlooked. That mistake will not be repeated," the doctor assured us.

"Perhaps I may offer a solution?" Cyrus asked. "If it is amenable to both you and Nurse Clara, I would appreciate your allowing Lachlan's personal nurse to work here during his stay. It's a fellow named James, and I believe having a familiar face will be of comfort to my son."

"That is not necessary," Clara declared. "My employees are quite capable of providing excellent care. And besides, I do not have the funds in my budget to pay for another staff member."

"You misunderstand," Cyrus soothed. "I am just offering a bit of help for your staff, and I will of course pay for his time myself. I'd also like to make that donation we spoke of earlier. Perhaps it might alleviate any budgetary strains you are experiencing?"

Before Clara could voice the indignant words that were sure to come, the doctor interjected.

"That is exceedingly generous of you," Marie said. He gave the nurse a pointed look. "Nurse Clara would be delighted to have James on board. And, on behalf of our entire institution, we are deeply grateful for your contribution. Clara, won't it be a relief to have additional funding? We will be able to make some of those hires you presented."

"Yes," the nurse said quietly. She turned her gaze to my boss, the gift horse. "It is very kind of you to help, Mr. Shepard."

"Marvelous," Cyrus declared, taking up the fountain pen once more. "To whom shall I address the check?"

As the two men sorted out the donation, I glanced over at Clara. Though her disappointment in being undermined was obvious, her eyes lit up as she watched Cyrus writing zeroes on the check. Clara was smart enough to know how much the money would help, even if it meant putting up with an unwanted nurse for a few days.

Truthfully, I had no idea what the hell Cyrus was up to. Lachlan was a serial killer. Serial killers did not deserve private nursing care. Though I did feel bad for the rogue runner when we saw him, he'd left a wake of people in much worse conditions while essentially forcing people to watch. What he deserved was a lifetime of negligent care in a facility much worse than this one.

"Do you perhaps have another copy of that?" I asked Clara, pointing to Lachlan's patient file. "I don't mean to be any trouble."

"I'm sure I can rustle one up," the nurse replied, perking up. "Just give me a few minutes."

With that, she excused herself from the room. As I'd guessed, Clara was driven by being needed. She liked to feel helpful. True to her word, the nurse returned quickly. She held an identical folder in one hand, and a plastic bag in the other.

"Here you are," Clara said, handing me both items. "I also brought your cousin's possession inventory—it is everything he had when he was brought to us."

"Thank you so much," I said, holding up the bag and peering at the contents, which appeared to be only dirty blue fabric.

"Those are the trousers Lachlan was wearing when he arrived," Clara explained, wrinkling her nose. "That was all we had in the inventory for him. Perhaps you will bring him suitable attire when you come back?"

"Of course," I replied, placing my hand lightly on her forearm. I dropped my voice to a conspiratorial tone. "Also, Clara, I want to apologize for my uncle. He's been overly forceful today, and I am very sorry for that. Uncle Cyrus has just been so worried for Lachlan. We both appreciate your time and graciousness a great deal. Thank you for helping us to find my cousin."

Clara smiled brightly, as I'd hoped she would. In my experience, it was best to leave a trail of kindness behind when on a run. In our line of work, you never knew when people might become assets.

The nurse and I chatted easily while Cyrus and Dr. Marie finished their discussion. After handshakes and goodbyes all around, my boss and I headed outside. Waiting until we were in the car, safely out of range of prying eyes and ears, I turned to Cyrus and gave him a dubious look.

"Care to tell me what that was all about?"

"You haven't figured it out?" Cyrus asked with a chuckle. "We need to step-up your deductive reasoning training."

Being the mature professional I was, I stuck my tongue out at him. He snorted—very un-Cyrus-like—then started the car's engine.

"No, I'm afraid I don't understand the logic behind providing a private nurse for a murderer," I intoned. "Maybe too much time with

Gaige is dulling my mental capacities."

"I would not be surprised," answered my boss, the corner of his mouth quirking as he drove past the guard gate. "The alchemists will need some time to clear up the legal matters and convince the doctors that Lachlan should be released. They'll be working overtime to solve this problem."

My mind briefly filled with pleasant thoughts of Ines nursing scores of paper cuts after being forced to file the paperwork for it all.

"So…?" I asked, shaking my head to clear the mean notion. "Why put up such a fuss for a nurse?"

"James is not a nurse," he replied. "James is a bodyguard. Well, he will be. He's an alchemist, but his training included the skills we need right now. James is the perfect person to watch Lachlan for us, and pretending to be a nurse is the perfect cover."

"Are you sending him to protect Lachlan, or to protect people *from* Lachlan?" I asked, marveling at Cyrus's capacity for planning ahead.

"Both," my boss said simply. He gestured to the file still clutched in my hands. "Have you looked at that yet?"

"Nope, I was busy smoothing over things with Clara." I opened the folder and laid it across my lap. "Someone once told me that we shouldn't leave people on bad terms, if it can be helped."

"Thank you for being so helpful," Cyrus replied in a dry tone.

"You're welcome," I declared cheerily.

Turning my attention to Lachlan's records, I pulled the meager stack of pages from the folder and began flipping through them. Other than the police report, there were only result sheets from his psychological tests and the hospital's medical lab.

"Lachlan does not have polio," I announced.

"Good to know."

"He also appears to be suffering from several psychological disorders," I said, reading off the list of possibilities.

"Or time sickness," Cyrus corrected.

"Blah, blah, blah, Lachlan's only words are 'Not my name'," I continued.

"So I noticed."

"They inventoried his injuries when he arrived. Contusions… abrasions…lacerations," I recited, taking a closer look at the comments on his intake sheet. "The wound on his arm was indeed there then. According to this, 'the wound appears to be self-inflicted, most likely within the past forty-eight hours'." I looked up from the pages, incredulous. "How is it possible that they thought that? No one can cut a line that straight with their non-dominant hand, much less while enduring the pain."

"He was a crazy man they found wandering in the park—I doubt they thought about it too much," Cyrus replied.

Shaking my head, I flipped to the next page, which turned out to be the first one again. I straightened the stack and positioned it to fit the folder's clips through the holes on top of each piece of paper.

"That's it, there's—"

I fell silent as something caught my eye. Something that made me stare intently, then frantically flip back to his intake form.

"Find something?" Cyrus asked, his eyes darting back and forth between the road and me.

"I…," I began, turning back to each sheet to confirm what I'd found.

When I'd checked each page of Lachlan's records, I let my hands fall to my lap. Peering over at my boss, I wondered how he was going to take it.

"I have good news and bad news," I hedged. "Which would you like first?"

"Good," Cyrus replied without hesitation.

"Lachlan is definitely *not* the Night Gentleman."

He shot me a severe look.

"What's the bad news?"

"We have no idea who is."

FORTY THREE

"THURSDAY? ARE YOU sure?" Cyrus asked.

"Definitely. Thursday, March 26th," I assured him. "I noticed the date first on his police report, but the dates on all of the other pages match up with him being there from the 26th on."

"Well, shant," my boss swore.

We drove for several minutes in silence. I stayed quiet, allowing Cyrus's hyper-speed brain to work through all of the ramifications and possibilities of this new information. When we stopped at a traffic light, my boss turned to me.

"That was an excellent catch," he said. Cyrus's expression was a confusing mix of respect, worry, relief and…it looked like pride, but I couldn't be sure. "I'm sorry, I should've told you that right away. You did well, Stassi. I wasn't even going to ask for the file. I figured there wouldn't be anything helpful in it since we already know what's wrong with him."

"Just doing my job," I replied, hiding a wide grin. Cyrus wasn't promiscuous with compliments, which made it all the more rewarding when he gave one.

He pointed to the bag lying on the seat between us as the light turned green.

"Care to continue using those sleuthing skills?"

"Ugh, really?" I asked, my smile disappearing with the thought of touching the contents. "I was thinking that you might like to do it when we get back."

"Not a chance," Cyrus shot back.

With an exaggerated sigh, I picked up the bag, clutching it only between my thumb and forefinger. I took a deep breath and held it in, then pulled out the sole item—a pair of tattered navy pants caked with mud and other substances I preferred not to think about. When my lungs began burning, I gave up and took another breath. The eau de chamberpot wafting off of the filthy fabric was so strong that I immediately reached for the handle to roll my window down.

Glaring down at the offending pants, I wished we had sealant spray with us, or at least plastic gloves. Anything so that my skin didn't have to come in contact with the source of the noxious odor. I wasn't worried about germs or catching some old-time disease—the vaccines we received on the island made our immune systems practically impenetrable—it was really just the ick-factor that made me hesitate.

Cyrus glanced over when we were stopped at another light and chuckled.

"I don't think a visual examination will suffice in this case," he said with a grin. "I'm afraid you're going to have to get your hands a bit dirty…literally."

My glare was transferred from the pants to my boss. He was enjoying this entirely too much. Keeping my eyes on him, I grasped fistfuls of the filthy fabric with both hands.

"Does this make you happy, boss?" I asked.

"Delighted," he replied. "Now check the pockets."

When I complied with his request, I found only bits of pocket lint and two peppermint wrappers. As I grasped the waistband and turned to the other side of the garment to check the back pockets as well, my fingers encountered a small, square lump that made me pause. Bringing the garment uncomfortably close to my face, I peered down at the grimy fabric. Sure enough, on the inside of the waistband, a small opening was cut into the lining.

"No way…," I trailed off.

"Find something?" Cyrus asked, his brow wrinkled.

"Yeah," I replied, looking at him uncertainly. "A runner pocket."

By that, I was referring to the small, hidden pockets found in the clothing worn by runners when we were on missions. For the most part, we used them to keep our tech from the future with us on runs that required it, though they were also invaluable when absconding with small items. In instances when we were searched, runner pockets were rarely found, since waistbands, hems, and the linings of clothes weren't closely examined.

I slid my index finger into the opening I'd found and pulled out a slim, silver object.

"What's in it?" my boss asked, one eye on the road while the other peered at my find.

"His camera," I replied, furrowing my forehead in confusion. "But didn't we find his camera in the hotel room?"

"Yeah, we did," my boss answered, looking just as baffled as I felt.

"It doesn't make sense for him to have another one with him," I pointed out. "The memory on these things is huge—it's nearly impossible to fill up. Why would he bring two?"

Cyrus was quiet for a long minute as I tried to turn the device on.

"The battery is dead," I told him.

"We need to take a closer look at the photos on both of the cameras," he replied, pulling the car to a stop in front of our townhouse. "There's a reason for the second one, maybe pictures he didn't want anyone to see."

"Since he wasn't permitted to be here, wouldn't that be *all* of the pictures he took?" I reasoned.

My boss let out a deep sigh as he opened his car door.

"That would make sense," he said, sounding tired. "But nothing about this entire situation makes sense."

Movement from the sidewalk caught my eye, drawing my attention away from the nonsensical.

"Who's that?" I asked, pointing to a boy who was pacing in front of the townhouse. Cyrus's posture immediately tensed. He stepped out of the car, and I scurried to follow.

The kid looked to be in his early teens. He walked to the far window of the hat shop, his head sweeping from side to side as he kept alert to his surroundings. When he turned to begin the walk back to our doorstep again, he started when he saw Cyrus and me watching him. With a decidedly worried expression on his youthful features, he hurried over to us.

"May I help you with something?" my boss asked in French.

"Do you live here?" the boy replied, also in French.

"We do."

A relieved smile spread across the teen's smooth cheeks. He gestured to the steps in front of our door, where a vase sat with what looked to be several dozen roses. My blood ran cold at the sight. I didn't know how I'd possibly missed them, even with my attention on the kid.

"I have a delivery for Anastasia Prince," he said, still speaking to Cyrus.

"That's me," I said quietly, my gaze still locked on the offending buds. Would there ever again be a time when the sight of red roses didn't bring a feeling of unease?

Apparently the delivery boy's English wasn't great, or even good, because he simply tilted his head to the side and stared at me like a puzzled puppy when I spoke.

"C'est moi," I repeated, and then continued on in the boy's native language. "Who are they from?"

"This I do not know, miss," the boy said. He handed me an envelope from inside his jacket pocket. The contents were weighty, something more than a simple note. The pageboy retrieved the flowers, but Cyrus intercepted him before he could hand the arrangement to me.

Holding the vase away from him as though the flowers might bite, Cyrus fished some money from his pocket and sent the boy on his way with a handsome tip.

Once inside, Cyrus set the vase on the kitchen counter. "Do not touch any of it until I get sealant spray," he directed.

My boss returned a moment later with a can of hand sealant spray, tweezers, and Dr. Merriweather. Both men wore identical my-dog-just-died expressions that made my stomach plummet. After coating his hands, Cyrus reached for the envelope I'd set on the island countertop.

"Stassi, wash your hands," he instructed me, before turning to the doctor. "Tell her."

I turned to the sink behind me and complied, waiting expectantly for Merriweather's words.

"What do you know about Dragon Dust?" the doctor finally asked, his voice so low, it was hard to hear over the running water.

"Excuse me?" I sputtered.

"Oxydryaphane," Dr. Merriweather repeated. "The colloquial term used on the streets is Dragon Dust."

"Yeah, I know what it is," I said, rinsing the soap off my hands. Grabbing a cotton hand towel, I turned back to face the two men. "It's nasty stuff. There were some problems with it in the work camp...." I trailed off, not wanting to go back down that road.

"I figured you'd know what it is," Cyrus said in a low voice, not looking up from the envelope that came with my flowers. He'd already swabbed it for bio matter, and was now running chemical-testing swabs over the paper.

"Why?" I asked. "I thought it was a modern drug. That dryaphane element wasn't even discovered until the 2200s. That's like three hundred years from now—what does it have to do with this mission?"

"Gaige tested positive for it," Dr. Merriweather said quietly.

"No way!" I exclaimed. "You're wrong. Test again. It must be a false positive. That can happen, right?"

"Calm down, Stassi," Cyrus said, looking up from where he was watching the line of swabs turning different colors. "Unfortunately, we can't test another blood sample. Dragon Dust is fast-acting and only stays in the system for twenty-four hours. After that, it is nearly untraceable."

"Okay, well Gaige doesn't use that shite," I said stubbornly. "If you can't confirm that with a test, you'll just have to trust me. He didn't bring it with him. I would've known, and they would've found and confiscated it at customs."

"We don't think he brought it with him—" Cyrus started.

"So then you know it's a false positive!" I exclaimed.

"Actually…," Merriweather started, watching me with concern and apprehension. The latter wasn't surprising, since I'd bitten his head off about a million times since we'd met.

"We think he was dosed," Cyrus finished for him. He moved to the old-fashioned range to our right and turned on the teakettle.

"Wait, what?" I asked, confusion replacing the indignation. "When? By who?"

"Given the exceedingly short half-life of the drug, there's only a short window of time in which it could have happened," Merriweather explained. "Gaige must have ingested it within hours of passing out. The behavior you described—mania, hyperactivity, then wooziness—suggests we are looking at an hour or less."

"That means Gaige was drugged at the boxing gym. Or on his way home," Cyrus finished. "We need to account for every person he might have come in to contact with."

"Every person? Come on Cyrus, there are...," I trailed off as realization dawned on me. "Wait, you guys are saying that he was drugged in 1925 with a substance that won't exist for another three hundred years?"

"That seems to be the case," Cyrus replied.

"What about the alchemists? Could it have been one of them?" I asked. "Did you check the logbooks?"

"I took the liberty of looking over them while you were at Salpêtrière," Merriweather chimed in. "Of those who have travelled recently, only the transporters have travelled from here to a time when Dragon Dust was available. But they never left Branson Isle, since they were not vacation trips."

I began pacing the kitchen, verbalizing my stream of consciousness to work through the problem. "And we don't have Dragon Dust on the island. Another runner must have brought it here. But why? Are they selling it? Just dosing random victims for kicks?" I stopped pacing and faced Cyrus. "What are the odds that whoever had it just so happened to pick another runner to mess with? That doesn't make sense. Gaige was targeted. But by whom? And why Gaige? Why not me?"

My eyes were pleading as I met my boss's gaze. My faith in him was so absolute that I actually expected him to have the answers for me. He held up the envelope, as if they might be in there.

"There aren't any traces of hazardous materials, and definitely no Dragon Dust on this. Do you want to do the honors?" he asked.

"Why not?" I sprayed sealant on my hands and took the envelope from Cyrus. There were three sheets of formal writing paper inside. Somehow our villain had found the time to pick up custom stationary, judging by the monogram on the top—the initials MTB. I unfolded the pages and began reading the scrawling words aloud.

"My Dearest Stassi." I shuddered at the killer's familiarity. "Did you enjoy your visit to Salpêtrière? You are such a sweet girl to pay our Lachlan a visit. I do so worry about him; the mental health system here really is not up to the standards you and I are accustomed to. It was never my intention to harm our friend Lachlan. If not for him, I would never have become a famous figure in history. You see, I had no choice. He had something I needed, and his conscience was getting in the way of my work."

I looked up at Cyrus uncertainly. The Night Gentleman was apparently giving us the dramatic speech of all villains just before they committed a final heinous act. Not a good sign.

"Did your partner enjoy my present?" I continued, my eyes widening as I took in the words. "I had planned to gift you with the same. But you know what they say about the best-laid plans, do you not? They so often go awry. Please do convey to Ms. Richardson that it was my pleasure to share with her, and she is ever so welcome.

"Have no worries, dear Stassi. My next gift will surely find its mark and serve as a grand testament to my legacy. I sincerely request the pleasure of your attendance for my finale tomorrow night. You have made quite the impact on the Parisian social scene in your short time here, and it wouldn't do to perform without you there. Additionally, I am including tickets for Mr. DuPree, Ms. Richardson, and Mr. Hemingway himself. There must be a fitting audience, there simply must be.

"Finally, my Stassi, I humbly beseech you to not waste your time trying to find me. You have more important matters to attend to, do you not? I will disappear like the wind following my finale, and it would be a fruitless effort for you to attempt to follow me. The timewaves are a marvelous thing, are they not? Our mutual friend has provided me with all I need to travel throughout time. Tomorrow night will be my last performance in this era, and is sure to be my finest yet.

"When we meet again—and I solemnly swear we will, my dear Stassi—you must give me your thoughts on the show. A constructive critique is important for perfecting one's craft, don't you agree?

"With this, I leave you until tomorrow night. Please know that you have inspired me so, and I dedicate this final act to you."

Suddenly finding it hard to breathe, I reached for the counter to steady myself. My arms felt like lead as they fell to my sides, the letter still clutched in my right hand. My thoughts were dizzying as I tried to process all of this new information.

Cyrus reached for the letter and I readily handed it over. He read the final words in a measured voice that, despite its lack of emotion, left me cold all over.

"All my best, Mr. Mitchell T. Baylarian."

My boss held up four glossy rectangles that he'd pulled from the envelope. "He sent tickets to tomorrow's performance of the Flying Codonas."

"He's taunting us," I muttered. "He admits to drugging Gaige. And he knows we went to see Lachlan. Is he stalking us?"

"As disconcerting as that thought may be, I actually hope he is following us," Cyrus said. "If he's seen us, then we've seen him."

"Do you know how many people we've all come across? How many that I alone have encountered?" I demanded, frantic. Images zoomed through my mind like a slideshow on fast forward. "This is Paris, Cyrus. In a time when people are living voraciously. He could be anyone. A guest at the Fitzgerald party. A patron of Stein's. A cab driver. A bartender. A bellhop."

I gazed beseechingly at my boss, feeling overwhelmed and already defeated. We'd met dozens of people, and crossed paths with hundreds more. The thought alone was daunting.

"Gaige has seen him," Cyrus interjected calmly. "Somehow, this man," he tapped the creepy letter, "managed to get Dragon Dust into something Gaige ate or drank. He must have—"

"The man!" I exclaimed, cutting off my boss's deductions.

With the unfailing patience that never ceased to amaze me, my boss waited wordlessly while my thoughts came together.

"If Hadley's supposed hangover was actually the effects of Dragon Dust when he was trying to drug me, then I saw Mitchell. A man sitting at the bar sent over drinks while we were having lunch at the Ritz—it *had* to be him. It *was* him. That's why he sent tickets to the Flying Codonas. He must have overheard Hadley telling me that she wanted to see the show."

"Do you recall what he looked like?" Cyrus asked, a hint of excitement flashing in his eyes.

"Not particularly," I replied, deflating as I realized how little attention I'd paid to the man at the bar. "He was sitting in the shadows, and I only saw part of his profile."

"Would you recognize him if you saw him again?" Merriweather asked.

"I think so. I can look at the pictures on both cameras, maybe he's in one of the photos?" I suggested.

"Very good," Cyrus answered. "We know that Lachlan and this man—Mitchell—were together at some point, so it's likely that he'd be in at least one photo on the camera we found on Lachlan. In fact, I think it's a safe bet that the men traveled to this time together."

"Ah, time tourism," Dr. Merriweather said knowingly.

"Precisely." Cyrus nodded. "It is an easy, albeit risky, way for runners to make extra money. You might be surprised how much some are willing to pay for the chance to visit other times."

Actually, no, I wouldn't be surprised. Our clients were willing to pay obscene amounts to own a piece of the past. To experience the past was on a whole other level—entire fortunes had been spent on time tourism back when it was legal.

"Hopefully Gaige got a better look at him," Cyrus continued. "I'll take both of the cameras down to the police station and see if Gaige recognizes anyone. We should also see if the florist can tell us anything about who bought these flowers. Stassi, will you handle that angle?"

"I want to go see Gaige," I said hurriedly. "Please, Cyrus."

"I can visit the florist," Dr. Merriweather offered. "I know that it is not customary for alchemists to do fieldwork, but this is a simple task, and it sounds like you could use all the assistance you can get."

"Thank you, doctor. That would be a big help," Cyrus decided.

Even though I was pleased that he wasn't sending me off on the errand, my boss's approval was a worrying development. It was a sign of how desperate the situation had become that Cyrus was enlisting the alchemist's help. Their specialties were paperwork and diplomacy, not fieldwork.

"So, yes? I'm coming with you to see Gaige?" I asked, hoping my boss was too distracted to deny my request.

Cyrus's expression softened when he met my gaze.

"I understand wanting to see your partner, Stassi. But I need you to call Hadley Richardson and Charles DuPree and set up the date for tomorrow evening. Invite them to dinner and the show. While you are at dinner, I will search the Hemingways' apartment for the third piece of the manuscript. That will allow plenty of time for me to arrive at the theater before you do. I will hang back for the duration of the performance, and watch for anyone watching you. Several extra sets of eyes won't hurt either. I'm sure Bane and his people will be happy to help. And, of course, the alchemists."

"Of course," echoed Merriweather.

"Wait, we're actually going to follow the instructions of a madman?" I asked incredulously. "You must be kidding. We cannot invite Hadley and the others. We'd be purposely putting them in a dangerous situation. Can't we just have the show cancelled?"

"I know it seems risky," Cyrus said gently. "But if you and your friends aren't there tomorrow night—if *no one* is there tomorrow night—Mitchell will simply choose another time and place for his so-called performance. We have knowledge and forewarning on our side for tomorrow night. If the show is cancelled or he isn't satisfied with the audience, we will lose those advantages."

For several long moments, I weighed what he'd said. Though I hated the idea of endangering Charles and the Hemingways, Cyrus was right. If not tomorrow night, Mitchell would just attack some other time, when my boss and his team weren't there to stop him.

"Cyrus, those calls will only take a couple of minutes," I replied grudgingly. "Will you just wait until I'm done to head over to the station?"

"I don't like the idea of you being out and about with this guy on the loose and fixated on you," he answered. "I want you safe."

"The Night Gentleman knows where I live," I pointed out. "I'll be safer with you."

"Inspector Thoreau wants to speak to you about the murders," Cyrus hedged. "I'd like to avoid that, if at all possible."

"I can handle him, Cyrus," I replied with a wry smile. "Unless he is prepared to throw me into the cell beside Gaige's, we have nothing to discuss."

"That is precisely what I'm worried about." Cyrus sighed heavily. "I don't need both of you in jail."

I gave him my best puppy dog eyes. My boss took one look at my pleading expression and folded like an accordion.

"Go make your calls. We will leave when you are finished."

FORTY
FOUR

SURE ENOUGH, THE inspector spotted me at the préfecture's front desk as we inquired about visiting Gaige. He pounced on the opportunity, insisting that I join him in a windowless room for a "friendly chat".

Unfortunately, Thoreau was sorely disappointed in my conversational skills. Stubborn to the end, I refused to change my story, despite the glaring evidence that contradicted it.

"Miss Prince, you could not have arrived in England on March 24th. There were no commercial liner arrivals from America," Thoreau repeated, his face set in hard lines. "I presume that also means you did not take the ferry over from London on the 26th."

"My brother and I arrived in Paris last Thursday," I replied obstinately.

"By train?" he persisted.

Actually, by vortex.

"Yes," I said instead.

"From London? You previously said you left from Victoria's Station. Is that still what you say happened?"

"Yes."

"You have only been in France for one week?"

"Yes."

"Not three weeks? Maybe four?"

"No."

"And you and your brother arrived here together? Not on separate trains?"

"Yes. And no."

"He did not come earlier? Perhaps to settle your living arrangements?"

"My father's secretary arranged our accommodations before we left Baltimore," I answered, meeting his gaze directly.

"Miss Prince, we know that your brother's passage documents are not authentic. We know that he did not travel in the manner you have stated on the days that you have said."

I sighed. "Is my brother's mere presence in your city the only evidence you have against him? As I've said numerous times, he was not here when the murders began. Neither was I. But even if we were, we'd have been two among hundreds of thousands of other people." I leveled him with a cool gaze, inspired by Cyrus. "This is an absolute witch hunt. My brother's arrest is a travesty of justice, and it will not be tolerated."

"Those other people have not lied to us about their whereabouts, Ms. Prince," Thoreau replied warily.

"Have you questioned them all? I am impressed. Your station is far more efficient than the ones back home. Perhaps you should offer a seminar on interrogating every single person residing in or visiting a city at any given time. Truly, it is a remarkable feat, you mustn't keep these abilities to yourself."

Inspector Thoreau began tapping his pencil on the table. Lips pursed and jaw working back and forth, it appeared he desperately wanted to tell me exactly how much he appreciated my attitude. I smiled sweetly.

"Am I under arrest, Inspector? If not, I would like to visit with my brother now. I do believe you've wasted quite enough of my time for today."

"No, Miss Prince, you are not under arrest at this time," Thoreau replied, emphasizing the last bit. "But I do have more questions for you, if that is not too much trouble. Your brother will still be here when we are done."

Inspector Thoreau was showing his claws. I was getting under his skin.

"Actually, Inspector, I believe we *are* done here," I said, keeping my tone light and cordial. "My uncle has insisted that our lawyer be present for any further questions. You understand, of course. I came to speak with you today against his advisement, because I was of the mind that we could be civilized about this whole thing. But good manners only go so far."

Inspector Thoreau slid his chair back, the metal feet screeching against the tile floor. He stood, one hand on the table, and leaned down until our noses were indecently close. I didn't flinch. Evidently, we'd moved on to the bad cop portion of the program.

"We will find out the truth, Miss Prince," the inspector spat.

I eased my own chair backwards and stood. In my modest heels, I was a hair taller than the police officer. Taking full advantage, I stared down my nose at him.

"I hope you do, Inspector."

Cyrus was waiting in the station's front reception area when I exited the interrogation room.

"How did it go?" he murmured in my ear.

I tilted my hand to indicate so-so.

"Sir?" Cyrus called to the young man sitting behind the desk. The officer looked woefully bored; desk duty probably wasn't what he'd had in mind when joining the force. "We are ready to go back, when you have a moment."

"For Prince, yeah?" the officer replied in a thick cockney accent, eyeing me with interest.

"That's correct," I said with my most innocent smile.

"Just a tick, then." With that, he poked his head behind a door and bellowed something in French. The officer nodded to Cyrus and resumed his position behind the desk.

Another uniformed officer showed us to a meeting room several minutes later. He waited for us to sit, then gave us brief instructions about interacting—or, rather, *not* interacting—with the prisoner. Finally, two officers led in a shackled and cuffed Gaige. I stared at my hands as my partner's shackles were attached to the table legs, feeling almost embarrassed that I was witnessing his humiliation. The handcuffs were removed before the officers stepped outside the room, leaving the three of us alone.

For several long moments, none of us spoke. Dark circles hung beneath Gaige's eyes like black half-moons. His dark hair was sticking out on the sides but flat in the back, suggesting he'd spent a sleepless night staring at the ceiling.

"How are you?" I asked finally.

Gaige shrugged. "It's not the Ritz, but I've stayed in worse."

"We're working on bail," Cyrus assured him.

"I know. The lawyer stopped by earlier."

Cyrus glanced around the room, evidently gauging exactly how private our conversation would be. The lack of a two-way mirror was a good sign—it meant that the nosy inspector wasn't standing on the other side, eavesdropping on us. Since neither security cameras nor listening devices were standard yet, it seemed we were in the clear.

"Dr. Merriweather found Dragon Dust in your system," Cyrus said in a low voice, skipping the pleasantries. "I am going to ask you this once, because I have to—did you knowingly ingest it?"

A series of emotions quickly crossed Gaige's drawn face. I caught disbelief, horror, and then finally relief. If I had to guess, the latter was a result of knowing that there was a reason for his odd behavior and blackout.

"No," Gaige said emphatically. "Cyrus, of course not. You know I wouldn't do that."

Our boss leveled a gaze on him, measuring the truth of his response.

"I don't need that shant," my partner added, a faint glimmer of his unbroken spirit flickering through his eyes. "I get high on life."

I stifled an inappropriate giggle.

"That's what I thought," Cyrus replied, looking amused, too. "I just needed to be sure." My boss began pulling document sleeves from his pockets and setting them on the table. "Stassi and I found Lachlan."

Excitement flared in Gaige's dark gaze. "Was he arrested? Can I go home now?"

"He was in a mental hospital," I responded quietly. I watched as the flames of hope were doused as quickly as they were lit. "He's been there since last Thursday, so he's not the killer."

"Okay...so what does that mean? If Lachlan isn't the Night Gentleman...," Gaige trailed off, glancing between Cyrus and me for answers.

My boss didn't disappoint. He launched into an abbreviated version of our visit to the sanitarium, then told Gaige about the newest flower delivery and the accompanying note and show tickets. Cyrus finished by relaying the latest working theory—that Lachlan might've been moonlighting as a time guide. Gaige listened to it all with rapt attention, as if there would be a quiz later.

Once my partner was caught up, Cyrus slid the vacuum-sealed envelope containing the note across the table for Gaige to read.

"As of right now, it seems the Night Gentleman is the civilian who hired Lachlan to come to this time. It also seems he's taking credit for drugging you," our boss said, pointing to the line asking if my partner enjoyed the present. "We found another camera today, in the pants Lachlan was wearing when he was admitted to the sanitarium. Since the two men were most likely traveling together, there is a chance the Night Gentleman, this Mitchell T. Baylarian, is in at least one picture on one of these cameras." Cyrus tapped the devices, and then added a magnifying glass to the pile of gadgets on the table. "Did you drink or eat anything at the boxing gym?"

Gaige rubbed his eyes. "I don't know. The details of that day are a little hazy. I mean, I definitely didn't eat anything. I'm sure I had some water, though. It was hot and I was sweating. So, yeah, probably water."

"Where did the water come from?"

"I-I don't know," Gaige said, looking helpless. "It's almost like I was in a gray-out before I blacked out. I remember having breakfast with Stass, then walking over to the gym since it was nice out. Once I got there…." My partner shrugged as he trailed off.

"Close your eyes and focus, Gaige," Cyrus commanded.

My partner complied, his forehead scrunched up in a caricature of a thinking man.

"You've been in the gym for some time now. It's hot, and there's very little airflow in there," Cyrus said evenly. "You're thirsty. Where did you get the water from?"

My partner shook his head slowly.

"Where did your water come from the other times you were there?"

"Sometimes there are towel boys with water bottles who work for tips. There's also a water cooler with cups on a table off behind the back ring."

"Did you all have a towel boy that day?" Cyrus prompted. "Do you remember someone squirting the water into your mouth?"

Gaige shook his head more emphatically this time.

"No. I went and got water from the back."

"Okay. Do you remember—"

"Wait!" Gaige's eyes snapped open. "A kid handed me a glass before I could fill up my own."

"Is that normal?" I asked. "Was he filling up cups for other people, too? Or just you?"

Gaige thought for a moment, then shook his head in frustration.

"I really don't remember anything after I went to the water table. I'm sorry," he added. "I just can't remember."

I reached across the table and patted Gaige's arm. "It's okay. You're positive that it was a kid who handed you the glass, though?"

"Definitely. He couldn't have been more than like ten or so."

"Did you stop anywhere on the way back to the townhouse?" Cyrus asked.

Gaige looked helpless as he shrugged. "I don't know."

"Do you know what time you left the gym?" I chimed in.

"I know Ernest had to be somewhere at five o'clock, so I'm guessing it was a little before then?" my partner replied.

"And you were home already when I got back from lunch with Hadley. That was a little after four," I supplied. "If you did stop anywhere, it couldn't have been for more than a few minutes."

"I do remember being excited to tell you about Ernest having the third part of *Blue's Canyon*," Gaige recalled. "With such a big development, I doubt I would've gone anywhere on the way home."

Our boss closed his eyes and began rubbing his temple with one hand.

"I think it's safe to assume that the Dragon Dust was in the water at the gym," Cyrus decided. "And if Mitchell wasn't there…."

"It was probably him at the bar," I finished, pausing to process this new information.

Gaige shot me a questioning look, and I filled him in on the guy who sent Hadley and I drinks at the bar.

"I know it's a long shot," Cyrus said, once I'd finished. "But let's go

461

through the pictures and see if either of you recognizes anyone."

Gaige and I both nodded. Cyrus shot a glance at the door, then set the cameras on the heavy wooden table. It was a big risk, having our modern technology out in a public place, but there was no way around it.

"Just look for anyone who seems at all familiar," Cyrus instructed, pushing a camera towards the middle of the table. "We don't have much time, we need to make this as expedient as possible."

Much to my surprise, Cyrus slipped the small sleeve over his index finger that controlled our cameras in playback mode. Just having the cameras in the police station was risky enough, but utilizing the advanced hologram technology in public was downright dangerous. It was another worrying indicator of how desperate the situation had become. Nevertheless, we all knew from experience that it was impossible to make out faces on the tiny camera screens.

Even once Cyrus executed a series of swipes and gestures to project the pictures two feet wide in front of us, the process was slow and painful. Each camera held hundreds of images. Gaige became increasingly frustrated as we flipped through picture after picture of various landmarks and notable sights—the Eiffel Tower, Versailles, the Louvre, and the Arc de Triomphe. We inspected each and every shot for several long moments, stopping frequently to study all of the faces in the background with the magnifying glass. It might have gone faster if we'd extended the projection—the hologram could extend up to thirty feet wide—but it would be a lot more noticeable should someone walk in. Not that a two-foot hologram in the middle of an interrogation room in the 1920s was inconspicuous.

"I'm sorry," said Gaige, when we were about a hundred pictures in. He slammed a fist on the table. "This isn't working. All of these faces are blurring together. I couldn't tell you whether I've seen any of them before, not if my life depended on it. I'm usually so focused on—"

I snatched the magnifying glass from Gaige's hand and leaned in towards the middle of the table.

"So glad you're listening to me," Gaige grumbled. "And, why yes, I was done using that."

His words were lost on me as I held the old-fashioned brass glass in front of the current picture. It was a scenic shot from the gardens at Versailles. Standing off to the side, almost out of frame, was a man *I* recognized. His cheeks had a tinge more color and his eyes weren't quite so haunted, but it was the same man. I'd have bet money on it.

"Son of a…," I muttered. "I am so dense."

"What do you see?" Cyrus demanded.

"It's him," I replied, handing the magnifying glass to Cyrus and pointing to the figure in the hologram. "It's definitely the guy from The Ritz. I cannot believe I was sitting ten feet from him."

Tears threatened to come as guilt washed over me. More than anything, I felt like I'd let Cyrus down. And Gaige, too. If I'd just done something when he was there. If I'd just walked over and asked who he was, maybe we wouldn't have been sitting in a police station with my partner shackled to a table. I looked over at him, my eyes welling up against my will.

"I am so sorry," I began, furiously swiping at my eyes before the tears could fall. "This is all my fault. I—"

"You know it's not really your fault, right?" my boss asked gently. "You had absolutely no way of knowing who he was or what he was doing."

Cyrus wrapped an arm around my shoulders and pulled me to his side. Against the instructions of the guards, Gaige reached for my hand. The tears finally fell when he squeezed it reassuringly, small rivulets tracing a path down my cheeks. Their compassion was making me feel even worse. They were the only family I had, and I'd let them down.

As quickly as the thought came, I banished it to the darkest corners of my mind. I refused to become a sobbing mess in the middle of the shantstorm we were in.

"You're being ridiculous, Stassi," Gaige said. His tone was light and without a trace of pity. It was exactly what I needed; I hated pity. "You didn't murder anyone. And this guy didn't have 'Serial Killer' tattooed on his forehead." My partner leaned in closer to the hologram as if inspecting it. "I mean, he didn't, *right*? Because if he did, yeah…major screw up, missy."

His flippant tone instantly made me feel better.

"I thought it was supposed to be ironic," I retorted, brushing a stray tear from my cheek.

"Did you really?" Gaige shot back. "Or is this payback for your little swim in the Arno?" He held up one of the chains that attached his leg to the table. "If this is your idea of revenge, I officially concede. You win, Stass."

I rolled my eyes at him, squared my shoulders, and wiped the last of my guilt tears from my eyelashes. Cyrus smiled, the edges of his eyes crinkling as he watched me pull my shite together.

"Okay, that's enough time wasted on making me feel better," I declared. "Let's catch this son of a bitch."

FORTY FIVE

AFTER HUGGING GAIGE goodbye and promising that he would soon be a free man, Cyrus and I left the préfecture. Between visiting Salpêtrière, being interrogated, and then visiting Gaige, it had been one of the longest days of my life.

When we returned to the townhouse, I went straight upstairs and collapsed into my bed without changing out of my dress.

The sun had already begun its climb to the middle of the sky when I opened my eyes the next morning. Panicked, I bolted up in bed. There was an insane amount to do, and I couldn't believe that I'd overslept. After quickly washing my face and pulling on a clean cotton dress, I emerged from my bedroom.

The sounds of many voices and multiple conversations greeted my ears the moment I opened the door. Pausing at the landing, I looked down at the commotion below. There were at least a dozen people milling about downstairs with a frantic energy.

"There you are!" Ines's voice trilled above all of the others. She'd spotted me, beckoning me to join the party in the living room. "We need to get you over to the style team, they have lots of work ahead to get you ready for tonight."

Brushing off the offhanded insult, I descended the stairs and plopped down on the couch. Blueprints were stacked on the coffee table, and Cyrus was going over them with two men I'd never seen before. He paused to pour me a cup of coffee from the French press in front of him.

"Why didn't you wake me?" I asked grumpily, accepting the teacup and saucer.

"It's going to be a late night," my boss replied simply. "I need you well-rested, focused, and in top form."

My boss quickly went over the plans for the day—his to ready the strike team, mine to be accosted by the glam squad. It seemed odd that my sole responsibility was to look pretty, but Cyrus dismissed the notion as soon as I voiced it.

"We need you for a lot more than your pretty face," he said with a wink. "I'll be down to the styling stations in a bit to go over the plans with you."

"Is this all going to work?" I asked him quietly, gesturing to the chaos around us.

"Honestly? I really believe it will." Cyrus's quiet confidence was the most reassuring thing in the world. If he'd been frantic, like everyone else, I would've been even more worried.

"Stassi?" Ines called, standing by the door. She tapped her watch. "We really must let them get started."

I glanced over at my boss and rolled my eyes.

"I simply must be going," I drawled sarcastically, hoping Cyrus would appreciate the levity. "I only have all afternoon to get ready for dinner—an impossible task, I assure you."

"Hang in there," he replied with a wink. "I'll be down soon to give you a break."

FIVE HOURS LATER, Cyrus sat in the armchair in my room, shuffling through a stack of papers while I finished donning the jewelry that completed my look for the evening. After slipping thin gold hooks through my earlobes, I stood in front of the mirror in my bedroom and marveled at my makeover. Felipe and Naomi had truly outdone themselves. Of all the beautiful gowns and exquisite jewelry I'd worn while in Paris, the look Naomi picked for my double date with Charles and the Hemingways was by far the most amazing yet. The gown was a rich blue, so dark that it was nearly black, with embroidered gold swirls adding pops of color. The fabric hugged my frame in all the right places, somehow transforming my athletic figure into an hourglass. My neck appeared longer and more swan-like, encircled by thin gold chains of varying lengths.

The earrings I'd just put in were long and gold as well, anchored by teardrop diamonds that hung to my chin. Though I was certain I wouldn't have been able to afford any of my Parisian attire, the earrings would've been a stretch for even our wealthiest clientele. They were exquisite.

Felipe spent longer than normal styling my auburn locks into a sleek hairdo that would eventually become synonymous with "Old Hollywood Glamour". For the first time since arriving in Paris, the length wasn't pinned up, leaving my hair to brush my bare shoulder blades. Keeping with the style that would become popular with starlets in ten years, my eyes were winged with dramatic liner, and my lashes were long and dark with mascara. His final touch was a deep red lipstick that accentuated my cupid's bow. The overall look was bolder and more eye-catching than ever.

And that was the point. The Night Gentleman was expecting me tonight. He would be looking for me, and I didn't want to disappoint.

My job was to be the shiny object that distracted the killer, so he wouldn't notice Cyrus and his strike team.

"You just have to remember everything we've gone over," my boss was saying drawing me away from my reflection. "No one separates from the group. Don't drink anything unless you've seen the original container opened in front of you. Stay alert and in contact. Also, we managed to book the chef's table at the restaurant, to thwart attempts to drug your food. It is extremely unlikely that Mitchell will be at the restaurant, but we don't want to leave anything to chance.

"You won't recognize most of the alchemists," Cyrus continued. "We had to pull resources from all over France. Bane and his enforcement team will be there, too. Our people will be posing as ushers, ticket takers, stagehands, and other patrons. We'll be focusing a good bit of our resources on protecting the performers, though we have a whole team dedicated specifically to you and your guests."

"Do you think we're actually his targets, and not just his audience?" I asked softly. I would never forgive myself if something happened to the Hemingways or Charles. In addition to my personal guilt, history would never forgive me if something happened to Ernest.

Cyrus leveled me with an open gaze and slowly shrugged. There was evidently no sugarcoating on the menu for tonight.

"The fact that the flower deliveries were addressed to you *does* suggest he's developed a fixation of sorts. However, he seems oddly certain that he will see you again, so I would be surprised if his plan is to harm you. If any of you are the targets, I think it's more likely to be Mr. DuPree and the Hemingways."

My throat went dry and I nodded jerkily, unable to speak. This was not exactly news to me, but it was difficult to hear it admitted aloud. Since the roses and letter had arrived the day before, I'd been wondering if that was Mitchell's plan. Only my implicit faith in my boss was stopping me from cancelling the whole thing.

Cyrus placed his hands on my shoulders and pinned me with emerald eyes full of concern. "Nothing is going to happen to you or your friends. Okay? I will not let him touch you. *Any* of you."

A knock on the front door to the townhome interrupted the moment. In a truly shocking move, my boss placed a quick kiss on my forehead before going to answer it. I gathered my purse and shawl, and followed my boss down the stairs, expecting the driver was at the door.

"Cyrus, good to see you, mate," I heard a deep, booming male voice say. The accent was thick and Australian.

Bane and his team had arrived.

When I reached the living room, I saw four enormous men crowded in the foyer alongside my boss. With more tattoos than all of the Hell's Angels at the height of their popularity, and enough facial scars to make me wonder if they'd lost a fight with a propeller, these men looked every bit the enforcers that they were. The Atlic Syndicate had them, too—a crew who went in to deal with the unsavory side of our criminal enterprise—but our guys didn't look like extras from the Godfather.

Ten eyes turned in my direction when I was in view of the foyer. A guy with a diamond-shaped scar bisecting his right eyebrow and a neck covered in tattoos whistled appreciatively. I couldn't help but laugh—these guys were *so* not going to blend here.

"And who do we have here?" he asked, his smile bordering on a suggestive leer. He squeezed past the others, removed one fingerless leather glove, and offered me his hand. "I'm Wick. And it is a pleasure to meet you."

"Stassi," I said, returning the handshake.

Wick's smile widened, revealing twin dimples in his cheeks. The look would've been one of boyish charm, if not for the scars that told of violent fights and the snakes and skulls covering his skin clear up to his chin. The effect was oddly unsettling.

"Calm down, Wick. You're scaring the girl," Bane admonished, clapping the younger man on the back before turning to introduce himself to me. "I'm Bane."

"I know," I replied with a nervous smile. "I'm Stassi. It's really nice to meet you, thank you for coming."

Though we'd never actually met, I recognized him from pictures; he was one of Cyrus's original employees from back before the individual syndicates existed.

"These other goons are Raff and Tot," he said, pointing to each in turn. "We'll have your back tonight, Stassi. There's a car waiting out front, I assume it's for you?"

"Yes, it's probably Jacque," I confirmed. "I should be going, but I really do appreciate you coming here to help. Knowing you guys will be there makes me feel better."

And it really did. Bane and his goons were large, imposing, and slightly terrifying. Which meant they were perfect for taking down a serial killer.

The others chimed in with more promises to keep me safe, then I said goodbye to the muscle. Cyrus offered me his arm while the large men made a path to the door, then my boss escorted me on the short walk to the car.

"I know what you're thinking," he said as he pulled the door shut behind me. "They may not be the most sophisticated bunch, but they're extremely good at their jobs, trust me."

I smiled. "I do trust you. Good luck with the manuscript."

"Just keep the Hemingways with you and occupied, let me worry about the rest."

"That I can do," I promised. Surprising both of us, I gave my boss a hug before climbing into the car. Cyrus closed the door behind me, and stepped back to watch from the sidewalk as the car pulled away. He gave me a reassuring nod and smile, though his rigid posture belied his calm façade.

FORTY SIX

HADLEY TALKED NONSTOP through dinner—a blessing since I was too jittery to engage in anything more than polite conversation. By the time our main courses arrived, I'd managed to knock over my water glass, dribble champagne down my dress, and send a steak knife, blade down, into Charles's lap. The last incident had my heart beating out of my chest, as visions of nicked femoral arteries and gushing thigh wounds danced in my head.

Thankfully, no blood was actually shed, and Charles laughed it off.

Ernest asked after Gaige, inquiring about his treatment and wanting to know if there was anything he could do to help.

"I truly appreciate the offer," I told him, touched by the writer's compassion for a man he'd only known a short time. "My uncle already has an attorney working on bail. I am sure we'll have this mess cleared up soon."

"No one believes he did it," Hadley said, reaching across the table to pat my hand.

"Of course not," Charles added. He wrapped an arm around my shoulders. "We all know the police are under pressure. That inspector has latched on to your brother and is simply using him as a stooge."

The food was amazing, yet I ate very little of it. The Hemingways seemed to attribute my twitchy mood and lack of appetite to Gaige's arrest, which was for the best. Charles wasn't so easily fooled. He waited to broach the subject until just before we left the restaurant, while Hadley was in the restroom and Ernest was occupied at coat check.

"You are awfully quiet this evening, Stassi," Charles mused, leaning in close to speak directly into my ear.

"It only seems that way because Hadley is so talkative."

Charles laughed. "You are not wrong." He brushed hair back from my cheek, the light sweep of his fingers across my skin giving me shivers. "But there is something else bothering you. And not just your brother's arrest, I am assuming."

Staring into his earnest gaze, I wanted to tell him the truth. I wanted to tell him the Night Gentleman's real identity, and that it was my fault Hadley had been drugged. It was a miracle the combination of Dragon Dust and so much alcohol hadn't killed her. I wanted to tell him about the massive sting operation Cyrus and the alchemists were setting up. How Baylarian would likely be gone for good if we failed to trap him at the show. With Lachlan's name tattoo, Baylarian could jump on his own. Sure, he'd experience time sickness that might drive him as crazy as Lachlan, but how many more people would die before that happened?

"It's my cousin," I blurted out. "He is very sick. That's actually why my uncle came to Paris to begin with. My cousin, Lachlan, was supposed to meet Gaige and me here, but he never showed up. So, Uncle Cyrus came to look for him. Unfortunately, we found him yesterday. At Salpêtrière."

Charles's arms were around me, pulling me tight against his chest.

"I am so sorry, Stassi. You poor thing."

The sentiment was real and heartfelt, and tears pricked the backs of my eyes.

"Is everything okay?" Hemingway's voice interrupted the moment.

Charles and I broke apart. Turning away, I discreetly wiped the wetness from my eyes before facing the writer with a forced smile.

"Of course, Ernest. You have the coats? Shall we go?"

Cirque d'Hiver was already quite crowded when we arrived. Patrons milled around the lobby, conversing and sipping cocktails as they waited for the theater doors to open. Charles and I took the Hemingways' coats with us over to the coat check, while they went in search of drinks. Charles helped me out of the fur stole I was wearing, adding it to the pile on the counter. I glanced around anxiously, hoping to spot a face I recognized.

"Here is your claim ticket, Mr. DuPree," the attendant said to Charles. "Enjoy the show." Though the man's French was flawless, his slight accent gave him away.

I whirled back to face the counter just in time to see Wick give me a conspiratorial smile. A high-necked white dress shirt with long sleeves hid his tattoos. Paired with a standard black vest, the Australian enforcer was dressed identically to the theater's other staff members. A customs' makeup artist had done wonders on Wick's facial scars, even drawing in small hairs to complete his eyebrow.

While Charles was focused on pulling out bills to tip him, Wick gave me a wink, exposing his dimples. I let out a long bated breath that I wasn't aware I'd been holding. Seeing a familiar face—even one as unfamiliar as Wick's—made me feel immensely better. Cyrus and his team were here, even if I couldn't spot every one of them.

The enforcer thanked Charles for his generosity, then turned to the next couple in line. When my date began scanning the throng of theatergoers, I gestured to where I'd spotted the Hemingways waiting for us near the bar with glasses of champagne in hand. Charles placed his hand on the small of my back and guided me through the crowd, staying only a half-step behind me.

Even with my mind overwhelmingly occupied by thoughts of the Night Gentleman, Cyrus's strike team, and fears for the safety of us all, Charles's touch sent pleasant sparks up my spine. At one point, I paused to let a rowdy group pass in front of us, and took the opportunity to lean my head back against Charles. While we waited for them to file past, his other hand caressed my arm before his fingers intertwined with my own. His mere presence was both reassuring and fortifying, and I found myself feeling grateful that Baylarian had forced me to invite him.

I let out a long sigh as I realized this would probably be the last time I ever saw Charles DuPree.

When we'd finally made it across the lobby to the bar area, I saw that the Hemingways were chatting with another couple. As we approached, the woman talking with Hadley turned toward us. To my immense surprise, I saw that it was none other than Ines. Her sweeping black gown paired perfectly with her inky hair and snowy skin to create an overall look of monochromatic contrasts.

"Anastasia! Charles!" she trilled with faux surprise. My Parisian guide leaned in to brush a kiss on each of my cheeks, before repeating the gesture with my date. "How are you my dears? It is so wonderful to see you both."

At the sound of Ines's greeting, the man talking to Ernest turned to face us. It took several moments for my brain to swap out the immaculate tuxedo for a lab coat and realize who it was—Dr. Merriweather. For the second time in as many minutes, I was taken aback by the presence of an alchemist.

"I'm well," Charles was saying. "And you, Ines? You look wonderful, as usual."

"Right as rain," she cooed in response, then gestured to her escort. "Have you met Jonas Merriweather? Jonas, may I present Anastasia Prince and Charles DuPree."

The doctor shook hands with Charles, before leaning in to brush a kiss across the back of mine. For a man unaccustomed to fieldwork, he was doing an impressive job of pretending we'd never met.

Our group formed a small circle, with Dr. Merriweather positioning himself firmly on my right side.

"I had the pleasure of meeting your uncle earlier this evening," he told me conversationally.

"How lovely," I replied, unsure of what else to say.

Dr. Merriweather waited while Hadley handed me a crystal flute of bubbly and I thanked her.

"I am afraid he was not having the best night," he continued, giving me a meaningful look that I couldn't decipher. "Seems a business deal of his fell through. He had another meeting lined up for this evening. Here is hoping that venture goes more smoothly." The doctor raised his glass in toast.

"What line of business is your uncle in?" Hemingway asked.

"Acquisitions," I said smoothly, scanning the lobby for said "uncle". Cyrus was nowhere in sight.

"He's here, dear. No need to worry," Merriweather said under his breath, holding his glass up to his mouth to hide the movement of his lips.

Before I could ask him where, the doors to the theater opened. The crowd immediately began migrating in that direction. Instead of joining the stream, our little group stepped out of the way and continued chatting. I kept one ear on the conversation, as my eyes made regular rounds of the lobby. The Rosetta was firmly in place, and I reached up to discreetly adjust the receiver to its maximum range capabilities. Bits and pieces of conversations floated through my right ear, the device catching everything within fifty feet. The effect was overwhelming at first, though I gradually grew accustomed to it. Fortunately, I'd had a lot of practice using the Rosetta.

"—yes, he is—"

"—that is your third whiskey, please don't—"

"—where he—naturally found that—"

"—Stassi—glad you—so beautiful—"

The blood drained from my face as I froze, glass halfway to my parted lips. I didn't move a muscle, not wanting to lose the disembodied voice among the others in the crowd.

"—she never did find—"

"—sometimes I swear he just cannot help—"

"Yes, Stassi," the voice came through again. "I see you can hear me."

I whipped around, studying the faces around me in the desperate hope I would spot the man from the pictures.

"Oh, don't bother looking, you won't recognize me."

It was a distinct advantage. Not knowing that we'd identified him would hopefully make Baylarian careless.

A hand touched my forearm, and I jumped.

"Are you okay, Stassi?" Charles asked worriedly, sliding his fingers down to squeeze mine.

Ten very concerned eyeballs were locked on me. I forced a smile and laughed breezily.

"Of course," I replied, scrambling to find an explanation for my spastic behavior. "I'm just feeling a bit jumpy. I do believe I might've had a bit too much champagne with dinner." Forcing an embarrassed expression, I rolled my eyes.

As the others chuckled politely, Ines loudly asked Ernest and Hadley about their upcoming trip. Though she'd expertly deflected the attention of the rest of the group, Charles's focus remained on me. He peered at me with an unspoken question in his eyes, but the return of Baylarian's voice left it unanswered.

"Such the actress, Stassi," it taunted. "Playing so many roles must get confusing. How do you know who you truly are?"

My eyes darted desperately around the room. The crowd was dwindling, making it easier to see individual faces. I searched for a lone man who would appear to be talking to himself, but found none.

"Another drink, miss?" a server interrupted.

I looked down at the glass in my hand that was still filled halfway with sparkling amber liquid. Turning to the waiter to decline the offer, I stopped short when I met his dark eyes. Felipe was staring back at me. The stylist held a tray of cocktails in one hand, and a single champagne flute in the other. He subtly tilted the latter towards me.

"Yes, champagne, please," I replied, taking the hint. "Thank you so much."

I placed my drink on Felipe's tray and took the new glass. He handed me a cocktail napkin from the bottom of his stack, and then drifted away without another word. Ines witnessed my exchange with her fellow alchemist, and she immediately drew Charles into the conversation. Taking advantage of the opportunity, I quickly flipped the napkin open.

No sign of target yet. Has he made contact with you? Nod once for yes, twice for no, then head inside the theater. C.

P.S. Ines has something I forgot to give you—be sure to get it.

Nodding once, I crumpled the napkin in my hand. Felipe swept by again, and I placed it on his tray. Turning my full attention back to the group, I waited for an opening in the conversation. Ines was just finishing a story about the ridiculous woman she'd helped at the hat shop earlier in the day. When she paused to accommodate the obligatory laughter, I pounced.

"We should find our seats," I interjected, before someone else could speak.

Charles offered me his arm, and we joined the flow of patrons filing towards the entrance doors. Without warning, the Night Gentleman's voice found me once more. My pulse pounded, picking up tempo with each word.

"That dress really is exquisite. 'Tis a shame it might be ruined before the night is over." He clucked his tongue. "Now, you must be thinking to yourself, 'Why? Why will my dress be ruined? *How* will my dress be ruined?' Is it because you have a front row seat to my final performance? Or perhaps it is because you *are* my final performance? Careful what you drink, Stassi."

The champagne flute slipped from my fingers, his cackling in my ear drowned out the shattering of the crystal on the marble floor. I whipped my head frantically around, searching for the offending laugher. Locating the only man braying like a hyena should have been easy. But, everywhere I looked, all I saw were couples talking, waiters carrying trays, and concerned patrons eyeing the mess I'd made.

Thankfully, the rest of our group was lost in the crowd ahead and didn't witness my erratic behavior. Unfortunately, Charles had a front row seat. He stepped out of the tide sweeping us to the theater doors and pulled me along with him. Gently tugging my arm, Charles leaned in.

"What is going on?" he asked insistently.

It had been too much to hope that he hadn't noticed my behavior. I was acting like a schizophrenic, but that's because I had voices in my head.

"I-I...," I stuttered, desperately wanting to tell him everything. I met his warm honey gaze. "I'm sorry, Charles. I can't tell you."

He studied my face for several long moments, searching my eyes for the answers I couldn't give.

"Are you okay?" he finally said.

"I will be," I replied. "It's a long story, and...." I weighed the gravity of letting him in on what was happening.

"Stassi," Baylarian's voice trilled in my head. "Say goodbye to your

Prince Charming."

"You promised not to hurt them," I whispered, as if the killer could hear me. Unfortunately, the Rosetta wasn't designed for two-way transmission.

"You can tell me anything," Charles murmured, moving impossibly closer before continuing in a whisper. "I want to help you, whatever is it. I am here for you, let me help you."

The emotions that I felt at his words—gratitude, guilt, anxiety—tipped the scale. I tapped the Rosetta until it was muted.

"We don't have time for me to explain everything," I started. "But, the Night Gentleman has threatened to attack tonight. Here."

Charles's expression instantly hardened.

"We need to leave," he declared. "Go outside. Now. Wait for me out there. No, find a cab immediately and go home. I will get the others and meet you back at your place."

He turned, looking for an opening to reenter the crowd entering the theater. Before I had a chance to stop him, Charles whirled back around to face me.

"We need to have this entire place evacuated straightaway," Charles announced. His eyes were darting around, apparently searching for ways to do so. He suddenly stopped and locked my gaze again. "Wait, how do you know this? When did you find out? Why are we here?"

"Like I said, there's no time to explain," I replied, pulling him back to me so he could hear my whispered answer. It was my turn to take his hand and squeeze it reassuringly. "We know the Night Gentleman will be here, and my uncle hired a team to find and stop him. Cyrus's guys are here. They're all around us. They're going to keep us safe, I promise. But if we leave, if everyone leaves, so will the killer. And we don't know if we'll ever have another opportunity like this one. When we know where he will be. It might be the only chance we have to clear Gaige, to have my brother released."

As the words streamed out, I worried about the ramifications. Cyrus might not be thrilled with letting civilians in on the plan. Nonetheless, my bizarre behavior wasn't going unnoticed. I had to explain. Hopefully, my boss would understand.

"What about the police?" Charles asked, after several long moments of processing what I'd said. "Did you call them?"

"Of course," I said, immediately feeling guilty about the lie. "They said that they have the killer in custody. They thought…they thought this was an elaborate ruse to let him off the hook. But my brother didn't kill those people. I *swear* he didn't."

I implored Charles with my gaze, praying he would grasp the gravity of the situation.

"I know he didn't," he replied quietly. "I believe you. What can I do to help?"

"Just watch for anyone behaving oddly. Watch for anyone watching us. Keep in mind that my uncle's team of guards will have their eyes on us, but I know what they look like. Just point out anyone you notice."

Charles leaned in so his forehead was touching mine. We stayed like that for a full minute, our hands clasped. I wished I could pause time. That I could pause the frenzy around us and stay like that—in a secluded bubble with only Charles. He inexplicably made me feel safe, and that was something I craved.

Our brief interlude was interrupted when a janitor hurried over with a broom and mop to clean up the glass I'd dropped. I mumbled apologies to him, then Charles led me away from the mess. Ines appeared out of nowhere, whisking me from Charles's arms and ushering me off down a side hallway with a sign for the restrooms.

"If we hurry, we can get to the stain before it sets," Ines called to Charles. "We'll meet you in the theater in just a minute."

He looked uncertainly from the sticky liquid on my dress to my face.

"I promise," I reassured him. "We'll be right behind you."

Ines practically dragged me down the hallway and into the ladies' room. Only seconds after the door closed behind us, it swung open again and a waitress scurried in with towels.

"I am sure I can get it out. It is just champagne, after all," the newcomer announced. She patted my arm as I stared down at the mess I'd made. "This happens all of the time. Not to worry, Stassi."

My anxiety level was so high that my head snapped up suspiciously at the sound of my name.

"Naomi," I breathed, looking at the waitress for the first time. "I'm sorry, I didn't know it was you. I didn't know you'd be here tonight."

"Yes, well, when Ines said we were coming to the show, I did not realize I'd be posing as a service worker." The wardrober shrugged one slim shoulder. "Oh well."

With that, the two women set to work blotting at the champagne stains with hand towels. Naomi removed several fragments of glass that had latched onto the skirt of the dress. I stared in the mirror. My reflection, ghostly pale and wide-eyed, stared back at me.

Get it together, I thought. *Lock it up.*

But even that wasn't enough to combat the neon signs flashing "Danger, Will Robinson!" in my head.

Cyrus had warned me of this possibility. That *I* was somehow Baylarian's final act. The flowers, the taunting letters, the poems—all of it suggested a fixation on me. Still, this was the first time he'd threatened me directly. It made the reality all the more real.

"There, good as new," Naomi declared. She wrapped the glass fragments in a paper towel and went to throw the bundle in the wastebasket.

"Keep those," I said. "I want them tested."

Ines and Naomi exchanged uncertain glances. Okay, yes, maybe I was paranoid. Felipe brought me the drink himself, so it should have been safe. But Baylarian was crafty. For a week, he'd been toying with us, following us, and stalking us. Until spotting him in the picture on Lachlan's camera, we'd been blind cats chasing an invisible mouse. Even knowing what he looked like, we were playing the horror movie version of *Where's Waldo.*

Unfortunately, the cost of losing might be my life.

"Here, give them to me." I held open my purse for Naomi to drop the bundle inside, then looked at Ines. "Cyrus said you had something for me?"

"Oh, of course," Ines said, reaching into her own clutch. She pulled out something the size of a thumbtack and dropped it into my hand. It was one of the syndicate's smallest and most advanced communications devices. "He was quite distressed that he forgot to give it to you before you left."

"Thanks," I replied. After tapping the earpiece once to turn it on, I inserted it into my left ear. As if having the Rosetta and Baylarian in the right side wasn't enough, now I'd have Cyrus and the strike team speaking into the other ear. Perfect.

Nonetheless, I felt better knowing that I'd be in the loop as the evening progressed. If I turned the function on, the device would also allow them to hear me. Help would never be further away than a steady tap on my ear.

"If you guys want to go ahead, I just need a minute," I told them.

The alchemists exchanged loaded glances again.

"You really should not be alone, dear," Ines protested.

She had a point. But hearing Baylarian's voice had rattled me. I needed a moment alone to compose my thoughts.

"I'll be fine, Ines," I told her firmly. "And I'll be right behind you."

Reluctantly, the pair left the bathroom. I waited several beats past the door closing to ensure they were gone, then turned back to my reflection. Felipe had gone to great lengths to ensure my hair and makeup were perfect, so shoving my head under the faucet seemed like a slight. Instead, I wet a hand towel and dabbed at my neck to calm my nerves. When my breathing became less frantic, I cupped my hands under the faucet and greedily drank the cold water.

Feeling steadier on my feet, I squared off with the mirror for a rousing pep talk.

"You can do this. You are not alone. Cyrus is here. Bane is here. Wick is here. All of those other alchemists are here. And they're all here to protect you."

I scoured my reflection, looking for the girl who'd survived thirteen years in a work camp.

"You are *not* helpless. You took care of yourself for years, this is just one more night."

Sure, this one night happened to feature a serial killer who was borderline obsessed with me. But it wasn't the first time I'd dealt with taunts and bullies. I just needed to remember the golden rule: Don't ever let them see you sweat.

FORTY SEVEN

ENTERING THE THEATER, I felt marginally better. At the very least, I was outwardly more together, and projecting exponentially more confidence than before. Still, reaching up to unmute the Rosetta filled me with dread.

Showtime.

The house lights went down just as I walked in. A disgruntled usher, miffed by my late arrival, was instantly more helpful when he saw the front-row seat on my ticket. I followed behind him, my eyes sweeping the theater for signs of Cyrus and his team. Wick and Bane were leaned against the back wall of the theater, posing as disobliging ushers, but no one else was immediately evident. As though he'd been searching, Charles spotted me before I'd made it halfway up the aisle. Visibly relieved, he waved and stood as I approached.

"How is the dress? Were they able to salvage it?" he whispered as we took our seats.

"Good as new," I told Charles.

On the stage, a man and a woman had just finished ascending rope ladders to platforms high above. As the orchestra's music swelled, they launched themselves off in perfect synchronization. Another pair on adjacent platforms took off, followed quickly by two women who executed perfect flips before being caught by those already in the air.

The first act was a whimsical piece about a young peasant girl who made a wish upon a falling a star to meet a handsome prince. The peasant girl and her two sisters danced under the moonlight as flyers tumbled overhead in bright white costumes, playing the part of the shooting stars.

As engaging as the piece was, and as arresting as the performers were, I dragged my eyes away to scan the theater. With only the dim lighting from the stage, the audience was shrouded in shadows. Faces were indistinguishable from one to the next. I couldn't even make out the gender of those seated farther away—they all appeared as inky blobs.

"Do you see anything?" Charles murmured in my ear.

"Only the large, formidable men who are here to protect us," I replied in the same hushed tone, giving him a smile in the darkness.

Don't let them see you sweat.

Charles refocused his attention on the stage and reached for my hand. His fingers threaded with mine. I looked down and had one of the sappiest thoughts of my life: Our hands fit together so perfectly, it was as though the two were meant to join as one. Even through my embarrassment at the thought, I relaxed just slightly. Charles was here. It was going to be okay.

Naturally, the thought was about six seconds premature.

"Eenie…meenie…miney…mo…."

The Night Gentleman's voice was full of delight, which terrified me.

"Which star will no longer glow?" he finished.

My next breath caught. The tempo of the music increased along with my heart rate as a crescendo built. Just as it reached an impossibly intense apex, the song ended with a deafening crash of cymbals. Every light in the theater went dark, like candles being snuffed out all at once.

I closed my eyes, anticipating screams.

None came.

Instead, raucous applause and ear-splitting whistles invaded the silence. Shouts of enthusiasm rang out from the audience instead of terrified shrieks.

"Bravo!" "Magnifique!" "Incroyable!"

I exhaled.

He's screwing with you, I thought.

Settling back in my seat, I leaned against Charles. I allowed myself the brief, fleeting hope that perhaps the entire evening was simply an opportunity for Baylarian to make us dance like puppets. That perhaps no one would get hurt.

"Stassi?" Cyrus's voice asked tentatively in my left ear. "Can you hear me? Nod if you can hear me."

I complied, imagining Cyrus watching me through the binocular contacts the team was wearing.

"Good," he continued, evidently seeing me nod. "You don't need to respond, just listen. I tuned your earpiece to a different frequency, so you wouldn't hear all of the team's chatter and be distracted. Did you really hear from Baylarian?"

Subtly nodding again, I pointed to my right ear.

"He's using the Rosetta?" Cyrus asked, sounding almost impressed. "He must know our tech pretty well. Has he spoken to you through it since the show started?"

I nodded yet again, wondering if Ernest Hemingway was going to think I had a spastic twitch.

"Hang on," Cyrus said. "I'll be right back."

Just as my boss left my head—a weird thought, if there ever was one:

my boss and a serial killer sharing my head space—a pinprick of light appeared center stage. It grew bigger and brighter, until a young man's face was fully illuminated. The prince, a single candle clutched in his hands, crept across stage, constantly checking over his shoulder as if worried he was being followed. One after another, spotlights popped on to illuminate enormous gold picture frames on the prince's right side. Inside the frames, as many as three and four acrobats posed in gravity-defying positions, moving fluidly from one stance to the next. When the prince's eyes fell on one of the frames, the actors froze, comic expressions of shock and horror on their painted faces.

In my ear, Baylarian cackled. The audience laughed, too, unknowingly parroting the maniac.

"Or maybe it will be our prince who meets an early demise," Baylarian whispered. "What do you say, Stassi? The most famous people in history are always the ones who die tragically. Should we make Alfred Codona a legend?"

"No," I moaned.

I didn't realize I'd spoken aloud until I felt pressure on my hand, followed by Charles brushing a soft kiss on my cheek.

"Say the word and we will leave," he whispered.

I shook my head without turning to look at Charles, afraid his gaze would be enough to make me give in and flee.

"Stassi?" Cyrus asked. His voice wavered slightly, sounding as if he were trembling with adrenaline. "Bane said that it's impossible to hack the Rosetta signal. If you're hearing Baylarian, that means he's here. And he's close. Is he still talking to you?"

I nodded miserably.

"I'm going to join the others, we're going to fan out and find him. Will you be okay if I take eyes off of you? We have him outnumbered. But I think we need the manpower for scouring this place right now."

Again, I nodded. The passive act made me feel impossibly more helpless.

"Just sit tight," my boss continued. "I'll let you know as soon as we find him."

It felt wrong to sit and enjoy the show while my coworkers did the heavy lifting, but I kept telling myself that I was doing my part. If Baylarian wasn't already aware that he was being hunted by a strike team—which seemed unlikely—my joining the effort would instantly tip him off. Feeling completely useless, and longing for Gaige's presence, I curled up in my seat and watched the players on the stage.

The prince was just completing his walk down the hallway of living artwork. After only a moment, the houselights extinguished completely once more. My pulse kicked into overdrive, waiting for the inevitable screams. Instead, the lights came back up to illuminate the peasant girl and her sisters, now playing in a forest of human trees. Sitting on a tree limb three people high, the prince watched as the girl and her sisters joyously swung high above the stage like female Tarzans. Even with fear coursing through my veins, the sight transfixed me. The aerialists dressed as trees caught the small girls with ease, and then sent them somersaulting through the air to the next set of waiting arms. On and on they went, traversing the stage and back with unthinkable agility and precision.

"Do you like Shakespeare, Stassi?" Baylarian's voice startled me out of my admiration. "Perhaps our star-crossed lovers will die together, going out in a blaze of glory befitting any great tragedy."

I gritted my teeth and shook my head defiantly.

Why are you doing this? I wanted to shout.

"Stassi?" Cyrus's voice broke through in my other ear. "Wick spotted him. We're converging on his location. Do not leave your seat. I repeat, do *not* leave your seat. I'll let you know as soon as we have him in custody."

The receiver in my left ear went dead, as he switched back over to the other channel.

"Oh, I see you don't like that ending," Baylarian was saying. "Do you truly want to stop me, Stassi?"

The question made me bolt upright in my seat. Praying he could see me, I squared my shoulders, then nodded resolutely. My deliberate gesture drew Charles's attention, but I'd given up trying to pretend that there weren't voices in my head.

Surprisingly, Charles simply reached over and rubbed my back reassuringly. I couldn't imagine what Charles DuPree must think of me, but there wasn't time to dwell on it.

"If you truly want this to stop, Stassi," Baylarian taunted, "come and find me. I know that's what your boss thinks he's doing, but I've arranged a special distraction for him and the alchemists. This is about you and me, Stassi. Now come and find me."

I was halfway out of my seat the moment I heard his words. My instantaneous action must have amused the killer, because he chuckled.

Which just pissed me off more.

Anger and adrenaline were mixing with the fear to create a potent cocktail in my veins. I was ready to find him. I was ready to end this. I was ready to make him pay and get the hell out of this cursed time. Though his comment about Cyrus worried me, I knew that my boss and his team would take care of each other. If Baylarian wanted me to find him, I would. And I would make him regret it.

"Not so fast, my dear," the killer intoned. "Perhaps you should first whet your whistle. A little liquid courage, if you will. My gift to you."

On cue, a waiter appeared with a single champagne flute on his tray. He handed me the glass and disappeared in one fluid motion. Between the darkness and his stealth, I was unable to get a look at the waiter's face. I considered letting Cyrus know, to have someone chase the man, but I knew it wasn't Baylarian himself. I would've heard him speaking beside me. Instead, I focused on the dreaded "gift" I held.

"Drink up, Stassi," the killer prompted.

Hands trembling, I raised my glass. Though I pretended to take a sip,

I was careful to not allow a single drop to cross the threshold of my lips.

"Don't insult me, Stassi," Baylarian snapped, his tone no longer playful. "This is *my* game. Which means *my* rules. Drink the champagne, or someone dies. No help. Don't involve anyone else. This is between you and me. Drink. Now."

I swallowed over the lump in my throat. Drinking the laced alcohol was a definitively bad idea. But would he follow through on his threat if I didn't comply? He'd proven to be vicious in the past, and unapologetically so. What choice did I really have? Uncertainty tore my heart in two.

"Cyrus?" I whispered, using the flute to mask the movement of my lips. "Bane? Wick? Anyone?"

The only response was the dead line humming in my ear. I considered trying to scan through the other channels, but it would be obvious to the killer what I was doing. If he saw, he might murder someone, just to show me he was in control.

Indecision warred within me as the seconds ticked perilously past. If I was the ultimate target tonight, the champagne might very well kill me instantly. Images of the fire twins' horrific deaths invaded my mind.

No, no, no. I don't want to die like that.

"Cyrus?" I repeated piteously. My boss had chosen one hell of a time to disappear. What could Baylarian have done to distract them? What could make Cyrus disappear when a serial killer's crosshairs were set firmly on me?

"Do I need to raise the stakes?" Baylarian demanded. "Maybe the lives of strangers don't matter to you. What about *his* life, Stassi?"

He paused to let the idea sink in. Was he talking about Cyrus? Gaige? Hemingway?

"Who?" I breathed, even knowing that he couldn't hear me.

"Your own lover's life must be worth the gamble."

My lover? Oh, no....

Charles.

I turned in my seat, just in time to see a red dot appear on the back of Charles's head. Feeling my eyes on him, Charles looked over at me questioningly. Our eyes locked. His brimmed with concern and alarm.

I made my decision.

"Stay here," I demanded, imploring Charles to oblige. "Whatever happens, *stay here.*"

Without another thought, I downed the entire glass of champagne in one long swallow.

FORTY EIGHT

THE ALCOHOL SEARED my throat. Tears sprang to my eyes.

I'm dying.

Around me, the world went silent. In my peripheral vision, blurry shapes danced like shadow puppets. A dusky blob reached for me. Though a part of me knew that it was Charles, I instinctively pulled away, rocking unsteadily in my seat. My insides were on fire, as if acid was disintegrating my body from the inside out. My skin was set ablaze as the feeling intensified.

"Come and find me, Stassi," the killer taunted. His voice sounded a million miles away. "Now. Or he dies."

My arms and legs were leaden. Through some inhuman display of strength, I managed to get to my feet. Charles tried to pull me back down, but I yanked my hand free of his. Stumbling, I ran up the aisle towards the exit. A startled usher threw the doors open when he saw me coming, and I charged into the lobby.

Bright light assaulted my retinas. I blinked to gain my bearings. The world was spinning so fast. Why was it spinning so fast?

"I'm here!" Though I tried to shout, the words came out as a whisper. "Now what?"

"Hallway to the left. Go. Now," Baylarian instructed.

Barely able to see more than a foot in front of my face, I stumbled left and used the wall to support myself. Framed posters advertising the theater's productions crashed to the ground as I tried to grab ahold of anything to keep me upright.

Cyrus, where the hell are you?

Tears poured down my cheeks, brought on by the burning sensation in my throat and lungs.

Water. I need water.

Suddenly, there was no more wall. I fell to my knees, dropping something I'd been clutching in one of my hands.

"Halfway down the hall is a door to the balcony level. Join me, Stassi. But hurry, or your dear Charles won't live to see the second act."

Using every ounce of willpower in my being, I scrambled to my feet. My hand landed on something squishy. My purse. High, hysterical laughter escaped my lips. That was what I'd dropped. Somehow, through my forty-yard dash out of the theater and one-woman tornado through the lobby, I had managed to hang on to my purse. Snatching it up, I hugged the bag to my chest.

The hallway was dark, with only one thin line of illumination at the base of each wall. My vision was starting to clear, but the fire inside me was blazing hotter with each passing breath.

If I make it out of this alive, I'm going to kill Cyrus, I thought with a senseless giggle.

The first door I found was locked. Yanking on the handle with all of my strength yielded no results.

"Keep going!" Baylarian urged. "Hurry!"

I tried the next two doors, but neither opened. Groaning in frustration, I tugged on the fourth, nearly falling backwards when it swung open. I slipped through and began climbing a steep stairway in utter darkness. A silhouette stood at the very top, lit from behind. His hand extended towards me.

I hesitated.

"Don't be absurd, Stassi. You have come this far. Don't lose your nerve now." Baylarian's voice echoed in my ear as it reverberated off of the walls around me. He was surrounding me, inside and out. He was everywhere.

Panting heavily and in desperate need of something to douse the flames licking my throat, I began to climb the stairs. Whether it was the end of my adrenaline or a second round of effects from the drink, I stumbled. My feet felt preposterously heavy as I crawled up, one step at a time.

Without warning, the silhouette reached out and grabbed my arms, dragging me up the final steps. And suddenly, I was face-to-face with Mitchell T. Baylarian. The Night Gentleman. The mass murderer.

I'd seen his picture. I'd seen him that day in the Ritz with Hadley. But staring into his feverish dark eyes, I realized I'd also seen him numerous other times since arriving in Paris. Dancing at Fitzgerald's book party. Drinking at Closerie des Lilas. Walking down the sidewalk in front of Stein's house. Entering the milliner shop. He had always been there, right under our noses.

Baylarian dragged me to the front of the balcony. The entire box was deserted, as were the adjacent ones. There was no one there. No one to stop him from hurling me over the side.

"I went to a lot of trouble to get these seats," Baylarian said conversationally, as if we were on a date and he wanted me to know the lengths he'd gone to impress me. He had one arm wrapped around my waist, holding me uncomfortably close to his side. Though I wanted nothing more than to shove him away, to shove him over the ledge, my limbs refused to comply with my brain's screaming commands.

"Quite a few patrons were disappointed when they were told the private boxes were all unavailable. Do you even know how many tickets I had to purchase?" he continued. The killer gestured to the left and then the right. It wasn't just the surrounding boxes that sat vacant. The entire balcony level was empty. "It was worth it, though."

"You have me. Now tell me what you want," I wheezed, infusing as much bravado into my words as a scared-shiteless girl could muster.

Baylarian took a step away and stared down at me. His expression was puzzled, as if the situation should have been obvious.

"I want you to witness my final performance, of course," he said. "Someone needs to tell the world what happened here tonight."

Confusion swam through my mushy brain.

"Aren't you going to kill me?" I mumbled.

The Night Gentleman laughed. That same cackling laughter that had been taunting my mind through the Rosetta was even more terrifying in person.

"Of course not," he replied, nearly gleeful. "You are much too important to kill, Stassi."

A glint of red light drew my attention to Baylarian's left hand. The madman was twirling something between his long fingers. With my head tilting unsteadily, it took me a minute to realize what it was. Once I did, the molten lava swirling in my belly turned to stone. Even by the tiniest measure, the revelation returned some degree of my control over the champagne's effects. It wasn't enough to stop him, though.

The Night Gentleman was holding a small black box dominated by a round red button. A remote detonator of some type. He was going to blow us all up.

I let out a long, shuddering breath.

"Why?" I asked despondently. "What did these people do to you?"

"Nothing," Baylarian said simply. "They are merely necessary casualties. Pawns in the game, if you will. But important pawns. Do you know who is here tonight? This show brought out more notable people than I'd even hoped for. The Duke of Westminster and his mistress. Two princesses of Greece. A Russian Countess. Playwrights. Fashion designers. And of course, your friends. Ernest Hemingway, himself. Hadley Richardson. Your amour, Charles DuPree. Can you imagine? People who *matter*, Stassi."

He peered down at me in the darkness, imploring me to understand.

"Killing them ensures me eternal infamy. Each of these lives secures my place within history. Isn't that what we all want? To never be forgotten?"

Baylarian gently stroked the switch with his thumb. He bore down with just enough pressure to make my heart stop. But not enough to detonate his weapon. My horror shoved aside the densest of the fog in my brain. I needed to get control of myself. I needed to stop him.

I stilled the rocking of my body with sheer will alone. I clutched and unclutched the purse in my hand, demanding that my body follow the commands of my brain.

Squeeze. Release. Squeeze. Release. Miraculously, my fingers complied.

The killer closed his eyes. His hands raised. He began waving them in time to the music, like a conductor leading his orchestra down the final stretch of a piece. With utter horror, I realized that was exactly what was happening.

The building crescendo would climax with the final notes of so many lives.

I had to act. *Now.*

Eyes still closed, lost in his own world, Baylarian hummed quietly as he swung his arms to the beat. He thought I was too weak to put up a fight. He thought me too complacent to take action. Or maybe he truly believed that I was grateful to be the sole surviving witness to his act.

Whatever it was, the killer was wrong.

The music poured from him right up until the moment I smacked him across the face with my purse.

Sure, it wasn't the most elegant defense. But the clutch was the only weapon at my disposal. And I was resourceful.

Baylarian stumbled. The detonator slipped from between his fingers. We both dove for it, our heads colliding. Stars shot across my vision, flashing a blinding sheer white. Somehow, only explicable by pure luck, the switch and my outstretched fingers connected as I tumbled down. I fell to the ground at the front of the balcony, the detonator gripped tightly in my hand.

Don't squeeze. Don't squeeze.

Baylarian landed on top of me, his weight crushing my ribs. The little remaining air in my lungs rushed out through my parted lips in a strangled scream. Nails raked at the hand holding the switch, tearing desperately at my skin. I held on as though every life in that theater depended on it.

And it did.

I kicked and thrashed erratically, willing the killer away from me. But Baylarian was bigger than me. And stronger. And not suffering the effects of whatever poison he'd put in my champagne.

He had me pinned on my back in no time. His knees dug into my thighs, rendering my legs useless. A blur of movement flew towards my face. I turned my head, just in time to avoid taking the blow full-on. Baylarian's fist clipped my cheek, the brunt of the force landing on my ear. Then his forearm was on my throat, cutting off my air supply.

Guess he doesn't need a witness all that badly.

My vision was going dark. The hand holding the detonator was slick with sweat. I wasn't going to be able to hold on much longer. With my last ounce of fight, I arched my free hand into a claw. My nails dug mercilessly into the arm at my throat. But it had no effect on the madman.

Desperate to breathe, I thrashed my head from side to side. My cheek hit something smooth and soft. My purse, I realized through the ever-darkening shadows of death. That damned evening bag was still with me. A sharp prick of pain parted the dusk, bringing dim hope.

Baylarian's attention was focused on the switch in my right hand. The arm at my throat lifted a fraction, allowing one shallow breath before it resumed its torturous pressure. Millimeter by millimeter, he was pulling the device from my fingers. I gave up on the arm at my throat and went for the purse. In the fall, the clasp had come undone. Another stroke of luck.

My fingers inched into the bag, fumbling to find my salvation. My last dredges of hope ignited when I felt the sharp bite of jagged glass in my palm.

With a sound more animal than human, I plunged the broken glass into Baylarian's arm. The pressure on my windpipe ceased as he yanked back instinctively. I sucked in the precious air that burned my lungs with reprieve. My hand was sticky and slick with a mixture of my blood and his, but I maintained my excruciating grip on the glass. Even as it dug into my own palm, I pulled the shard from Baylarian's arm.

I swung with every ounce of energy in my being. I aimed the makeshift weapon at the killer's hand, which was milliseconds from freeing the detonator from my own weakening grasp.

Howling like a wounded wolf, Baylarian gave up the fight for the switch. He reared back, holding his injured hand. As he hurled obscenities at me, I braced for another fist flying at my face. Sure enough, Baylarian's came barreling at me. I flung the hand holding the glass towards his, praying his momentum would make the two connect.

I'd guessed wrong. It wasn't his hand that struck the blow. It was his head.

For a long, dazed moment, I thought he'd head-butted me on

purpose. But Baylarian wasn't moving. His body was deadweight on top of mine. Dizziness overwhelmed me, and bile rose up in my throat. I was an instant from blacking out.

Did he really knock himself out? I thought wondrously, hanging on to consciousness for dear life. My eyes closed, the weight of the lids too heavy to fight.

Just as I was drifting away, the weight lifted off of me all at once.

Shant. He's alive. He's going to blow this place up.

No adrenaline came. No fight. No will to live. I couldn't have moved if a hundred lives depended on it. My final thought was whether I would live to feel the fiery explosion.

A bright light was suddenly shining directly into my eyes. The white light of the afterlife. Unfortunately, I was too dizzy to handle it. Would I be forgiven for vomiting on the pearly gates?

"Too fast," I moaned. "Slower. Please..."

"Stassi? Stassi?" Saint Peter called. "Open your eyes. Bane, get Dr. Merriweather. *Now.*"

They died, too? I thought with immense sadness.

With a touch as light as butterfly wings, fingers eased my eyelids open. Two impossibly green dots consumed my vision.

"I'm sorry, Peter," I whispered. "I'm going to throw up on you."

"Stassi?"

"Who's Peter?" a voice asked from somewhere far away.

"I'm here, Stassi. I'm so sorry. Just lie still. Help is on the way."

"Cyrus?" I asked, wondering if I was only dreaming his voice.

"It's me. I'm right here, just stay with me."

I licked my lips and tasted salty, coppery liquid.

"Cyrus?" I repeated, my voice a soft whisper.

I felt someone lean in over me. "Yes?"

"If I ask later, lie and say that was my blood I just tasted."

And then, I passed out.

FORTY NINE

TIME PASSED IN a blur of fog, shadows, and disorientation.

Two days later, I was still in my bed at the townhome, recuperating from the fight with Baylarian and sleeping off the effects of the drugs. In a fleeting moment of clarity, Merriweather told me that the champagne had been laced with a large dose of a strong muscle relaxer and habanero pepper oil. Fortunately, the concoction hadn't caused any permanent damage. With rest and lots of ice cream, I was scheduled to make a full recovery.

The cut on my hand from the broken glass took twelve stitches to close. In time, I'd have a kickass battle scar to go along with the not-so-kickass story to tell my friends. The bruise on my cheek from Baylarian's fist was already fading. It didn't hurt too badly, and I was even eager to show Gaige that we now had matching black eyes.

But the purple and blue patches that encircled my throat like a tie-dyed scarf were not so easy to joke about. Every time I was shuffled to the bathroom and looked in the mirror, the tender, discolored skin reminded me of how close I'd come to dying. And every time Cyrus's gaze landed on my neck, his jaw began to work back and forth. The one positive result of my injuries was that my boss had been waiting on me hand and foot. He was clearly burdened with misplaced guilt about the last-minute rescue.

"Baylarian knew we were watching you," Cyrus told me, once I was finally able to stay awake. "The guy Wick spotted was a decoy. He led us right to a bomb as a distraction, so he could get you alone. I should have known better. I should've realized what was happening. I am so sorry, Stassi." Cyrus paused, his expression heartbreaking. "The worst part is, the bomb he led us to was only one of *ten* we found in our sweep of the theater afterwards. He played us, and I almost lost you."

I drank my milkshake through the pink twisty straw someone had procured upon my request. The cold, sweet deliciousness felt amazing on the blisters of my abused esophagus.

"I didn't know you cared so much," I joked, trying to lighten the mood.

Cyrus had been beating himself up since finding me on the balcony. Though his self-reproach did have some perks, I hated seeing him so sullen.

"Come on, Cyrus," I said, when he didn't so much as crack a smile. "You did the right thing. My life isn't worth the lives of all those people in the theater. You had to take the chance."

An unreadable emotion played across his expression. My boss took my uninjured hand in his.

"I am *so* sorry, Stassi," he repeated, his voice wavering. "I never should have put you in that position."

We fell silent. I slurped more of the milkshake, trying to think of something that would turn my boss's frown upside down. More than anything, I wanted to put the events on that balcony behind me. Until everyone stopped treating me like an injured bird, that wasn't going to happen. Ignoring it all might not have been the most emotionally healthy response, but that was how I'd coped my entire life.

My rescuers—Cyrus, Bane, and company—had not killed Baylarian. When they'd finally found us on the balcony, Cyrus had shot him with a tranquilizer dart. Dressed as medical staff, a team of alchemists had removed his unconscious body from the theater. They'd gone straight to customs, where Bane and his goon squad had jumped back to our time with the serial killer. When I asked what would happen next, Cyrus clammed up.

"The Founders will convene to decide how to handle the situation," was all he would say.

Vague yet ominous, the statement left me oddly uncurious as to the possible outcomes and subsequent fate of the villain known as the Night Gentleman. The glint of grim determination in Cyrus's piercing gaze told me all I needed to know: if Cyrus got his way—and he *always* did— Mitchell Baylarian would suffer greatly for his crimes.

Dealing with the situation within the syndicates, instead of handing him over to the Parisian authorities, left one very big problem. My partner was still in a jail cell.

"How's Gaige doing? Any word on bail?" I asked Cyrus.

My boss smiled. "He's fine. He's worried about you, though. Damn near broke his cuffs when I told him what happened. We're still working on bail. Hopefully, he'll only be in the jail for another day or two."

"Days?" I moaned. "Gaige is not a killer. We found the killer. It's not okay that he is stuck in an ancient prison."

"Once he's out, he'll need to jump back immediately," Cyrus continued, patting my hand. He didn't comment on the fairness of the situation.

I sat back, moping. Gaige and I had made a Herculean effort on this run. Ending it this way was woefully depressing. Cyrus had confirmed earlier that he didn't find the final piece of *Blue's Canyon* during his search of the Hemingway's home. Bane's men had managed to swap out the forgeries of the two sections Gaige and I found for the originals. Too bad "close" only counted in bocce and bison bombs.

"I'm sorry that you're going to have to deal with the unhappy client," I said. "I'm sorry we didn't complete the run. We had it locked up before the serial killer came along. We were *this* close."

"Don't be," Cyrus said, waving off my apology. "Besides, the Hemingways are still in Paris. Hadley was so worried about you, she insisted on delaying their trip. She's called numerous times to check on you." He paused and eyed me critically. "She isn't the only one."

A girly flutter went through my abdomen and I flushed.

Charles.

I had a small stack of phone messages from him, a large bouquet of flowers—Charles had no idea how much the sight of a flower delivery had terrified me—and I was told he'd dropped by several times. Officially, I'd "taken ill" during the performance, supposedly suffering from a wicked case of food poisoning. The numerous witnesses who'd seen me wheeled out of the theater into a waiting ambulance supported this version of events, though it was alchemists, not paramedics, who'd taken me.

I wanted to see Charles. Cyrus had forbidden it. My bruises, stitches, and overall just-got-the-shite-beat-out-of-me appearance were not in line with food poisoning. Too many red flags. As a peace offering, Cyrus had at least given me the messages and flowers, but was firm on my lack of contact with the outside world.

"I still think it's best if you return to the island as soon as possible," my boss said, drawing me from my thoughts of Charles. "You can finish recovering in your own bed."

This was an argument we'd had multiple times. Cyrus wanted to jump home with me immediately after the theater. Initially, Dr. Merriweather declared it wasn't a good idea for me to travel through a vortex in my condition. Once I was conscious, my tenacious refusal to leave Paris while Gaige was still in prison delayed my departure.

I shook my head. "When Gaige is free, I will go. You can't make me go before then."

Cyrus sighed.

"*Please* don't make me go before then?"

My boss eyed me for a long moment. I did my best to look as resolute as possible, hoping that my injuries would add to the tough façade.

"You're a stubborn one, you know that?" Cyrus asked, a hint of a gleam in his eye.

I nodded.

"Against my better judgment, someone will be coming to stay with you," he said. "I need to get back, and deal with the mess Baylarian has made. But I don't want you to be alone."

"No. No, no, no. *Please* don't stick me with Ines," I groaned.

The gleam grew into outright amusement on my boss's face.

"I know she means well," I continued my plea. "But, Cyrus…that woman drives me crazy."

"I know the feeling," Cyrus replied with a laugh. "I'm not sticking you with Ines. I think you'll be happy with my decision." My boss stood to leave. "For now, get some rest. Focus on getting better."

Cyrus started for the door.

"Wait," I called. "Aren't you going to tell me who it is?"

"You'll see," he called back, without turning around.

At least toying with me has cheered him up, I thought.

Curiosity battled my body's need for sleep. Eventually, the need grew into a painful exhaustion, and I drifted off.

The next time I woke, big blue eyes were peering at me over the top of a glossy magazine.

"Hey there, sleepyhead!" Molly exclaimed, her cheery tone a sharp contrast to the worry lines creasing her forehead.

I blinked and rubbed sleep from my eyes.

"Am I home? Did Cyrus knock me out and drag me back to the island?" I asked groggily.

"That does sound like something he'd do. But no. He asked me to come to you." She let the magazine fall to her lap and held her arms open wide. "So here I am."

I sat up, tears welling in my eyes, as realization dawned.

"You're my surprise!" I cried, the tears starting to fall. Having Molly with me was the absolute best-case scenario that I could imagine. I'd missed her so much over the past few weeks, and finally she was here with me. After everything that'd happened, the sight of her brought a rush of relief. Everything would be okay.

"Hey, hey, hey, none of that," Molly declared. She hurried from her chair to perch on the edge of my bed. I scooted over to make room for her. My roommate wrapped me in her arms, holding me while I cried into her shoulder.

"I'm sorry, I don't know what's wrong with me," I choked out between sobs. Molly rubbed my back and made strange comforting noises.

"You've been through a lot," she murmured. "You should cry, Stassi. Get it all out. You'll feel better."

And I did. Then I did some more.

I cried big, fat ugly tears. I rambled long, nonsensical sentences, while my best friend simply listened. Most of what I said verged on incoherent, and yet Molly seemed to understand perfectly. She never asked for specifics or interrupted me with questions. Instead, Molly just made soothing comments when warranted.

Of course, that was only for the topics of Baylarian and *Blue's Canyon*. Once the conversation veered towards Charles, my best friend had nothing but questions. I hadn't meant to bring him up. I mean, what did he matter any longer? I would never see him again. Still, once I started talking about him, I couldn't stop. I found myself telling Molly about our first dance, our first kiss, our trip to see Worchansky, and every other moment with him. When I recounted rolling down the street mid-make-out, she doubled over in laughter.

"I am so glad you're here," I told her.

The river of tears had long since run dry, but my overwhelming gratitude for her made the dam burst all over again.

"Are you kidding? Paris? 1925? Cyrus barely got the words out before I was in the vortex." She winked playfully, but her tone was no longer light and carefree when she continued. "Anytime you need me, I will always be there. That's how friendship works."

FIFTY

THREE DAYS AFTER Molly's arrival—three therapeutic days of French pastries, milkshakes, and laughing with my bestie—James sent word from Salpêtrière that Dr. Marie was willing to release Lachlan. Bane and Cyrus returned immediately to collect him.

Lachlan was jumped straight back to our time, where he would finally get proper treatment. Given the severity of his time sickness, it was unlikely that his mental faculties would ever be restored completely. But, in time, there was a chance he might be able to function again. At the very least, he wouldn't be subjected to the heinous conditions that twentieth century asylums were known for. Without his tattoo, Dr. Merriweather was concerned the jump might do Lachlan more harm than good, but Cyrus thought it was a risk worth taking.

Charles sent more flowers, called, and knocked on the front door with increasing frequency. On Cyrus's orders, Molly turned him away each time. Had I asked, she would have defied our boss and let him in.

As tempted as I was, and as badly as I ached to see him, I didn't protest the moratorium on face-to-face contact. While I knew that I couldn't explain away my visible injuries, it wasn't the only reason I went along with Cyrus's plan. When it came down to it, seeing Charles would only prolong the inevitable.

It was better for both of us if I cut the cord now.

Nonetheless, I looked forward to Molly's play-by-play each time Charles stopped by. Because, truthfully, I missed Charles. And I think my roommate knew it. She was heedlessly persistent that I grab life by the rhino and let him in for a little sexy time before I left.

"I see why you're so enamored," Molly told me, after a heated conversation with Charles that ended with her slamming the door in his face. "That guy is," she fanned herself dramatically, "*so* hot."

I refused to dignify her theatrics with a response, though it didn't slow her down one bit.

"You know," she continued. "If you want, I can step out the next time he comes by. Do a little shopping. Hit a nightclub or two. Maybe gamble at one of those clubs posh people love so much. I have a feeling that a little alone time with Charles is just what you need."

I glared at her. "Cyrus said no. And you know it's a bad idea, regardless."

Molly waved off my protests, rolling her big blue eyes skyward.

"Flings are okay, Stass. Everybody does it. Be bad for once. It will feel *oh* so good."

Yes, *flings* were okay. But I wasn't sure I would classify spending time with Charles as a fling. As unfortunate as it was for all parties involved, I had feelings for him. I wanted to know him better. I wanted to talk to him, laugh with him. And yes, eventually do *other* things with him.

Had my interests only been on those other things, I would have taken her up on her offer to skedaddle for an evening. But they weren't. So, I let his calls, flowers, and concerns go unanswered.

Though not nearly as persistent, Hadley's inquires after my health had increased, as well. Since my friendship with her wasn't as complicated, I accepted her calls. I promised Hadley I was on the mend, and even hinted that there was a chance I'd be feeling well enough to receive visitors before she left for Germany. Her enthusiasm over the prospect was surprisingly genuine. I felt awful and deceptive, since my interest in seeing her was more business than pleasure.

If I could get Hadley out of her house when Ernest was off writing or on a walk, Molly could search the apartment again. Cyrus had said to forget about the run, but I wanted something productive to come out of this disastrous trip. I wanted *Blue's Canyon*. Both because I am a finisher, and because Gaige wanted to read the rest of it.

One week after the theater night, Molly returned to the townhouse in a terrible mood after visiting Gaige. After a session with Felipe to rid her hair of the blue streaks, Molly had been to the jail every day to see him. Every other time, she'd returned in good spirits. But this day was different. She flopped angrily in the armchair by my bed, her expression a mixture of anger, fear, and immense sadness. The sight of her like that sent me into a panicked tailspin.

"The judge ruled today," Molly spat. "They're not letting Gaige out."

I stared at her for a long moment.

"Ever," she finished.

When she calmed down enough to explain, it was even worse than I'd thought. Between the pressure to solve the murders and the fact that the Night Gentleman had not struck since Gaige was taken into custody, the police were convinced my partner was their guy. According to the alchemist lawyer, the evidence against him was thinner than a heroin-chic runway model. Unfortunately, justice was both blind and senile in this case.

Regardless of what the Parisian police had decided, a trial was out of the question. There was absolutely, positively no way that Gaige could stand trial.

That left only one possible course of action.

"How do we break him out?" I asked.

In true roll-with-the-crazy form, Molly didn't bat an eyelash at my suggestion. Instead, she perked right up.

"Well, let's see," she began, looking almost excited. "We could bribe the guards?"

"Too chancy," I replied. "We could get him a hacksaw for the bars on his window?"

"It's halfway underground," Molly answered automatically. "Do you think we could get guard uniforms?"

"I don't think there are female guards in this time. Suffrage is just now rolling," I reasoned. "Do you think your mom could get us enough sleeping gas to knock out everyone in the station?"

"Too much airflow on the windows without glass. What about escaping through a ventilation system?"

"Do they even have ventilation systems yet?"

"A rat with a key tied to him?"

"How would we get the key?"

"Bribe a guard?"

Despite the seriousness of the situation, I cracked up. We stared at each other for several long moments.

"You'd think that we'd have some sort of advantage, being from the future and all," I intoned. "We're obviously not very good prison-breakers."

Suddenly, Molly bolted up. Had she been a cartoon, "Eureka!" would've appeared above her head.

"We might be able to jump him out!" she exclaimed. "You know, use our advantages. They've been taking me down to his cell when I visit Gaige. They lock it behind me, and a guard is stationed outside of it, but the cells are underground. The walls are *stone*. So we've got earth. We just need water. Or we could start a fire in his cell? That might be tricky, I don't know if they'd be cool with us taking matches in for a friendly visit with a supposed murderer."

"And water isn't problematic?" I said dryly.

She shrugged. "Maybe not. There are a lot of exposed pipes down there. We might be able to flood the cell."

Even though the jailbreak scenario had been my idea, I stared at her doubtfully.

"Flood the cell? Seriously? We'd have to flood the whole level."

"No. We just need enough running water to stand in. Then we could jump."

"Okay. What about the guard?" I asked.

"Hit him with a little memory modifier," she said, as if it were really that simple.

Memory modifier was a last-resort drug. It was typically only used by the cleanup crews, and only in rare, extreme cases when an individual saw something they shouldn't. Things that couldn't be explained away.

"All the guy will remember is Gaige being in his cell one minute, and gone the next," Molly continued. "It will look like a run-of-the-mill prison break. Except, no one will see Gaige leave." She grinned at me. "His disappearance will be one of the great mysteries of all time."

"What about time sickness? An unorthodox jump will make Gaige sick. And you, too. Although, you don't have to be there. I can go on my own, and you can go back through customs."

Molly gave me a look of exasperation.

"I'm not sitting out a prison break," she declared. "You commit a felony, I commit a felony. That's how we roll."

"Molly, do you really want to go through that again? Especially so soon?" I asked gently. "It was miserable. I don't want to see you like that ever again. Not to mention, the risks inherent with suffering time sickness repeatedly. Do you want to end up in a nuthouse?"

"Look around, Stass. We already live in one. Plus, I'm retired from running now anyway, so it isn't like I need to worry about time sickness in my future." Steely reserve shone in my best friend's eyes. "Besides, it's for a good cause."

"You really do care about him, don't you?" I asked gently.

Color infused her porcelain complexion.

"Of course I care about him," Molly replied, her tone matter-of-fact.

We stared at each for a long moment that seemed to stretch on forever.

"This plan is nuts," I said finally.

"Oh, totally," Molly agreed.

Another long pause.

"Should we get permission first?" I asked.

Molly scoffed at my rule-abiding ways.

"It's easier to beg forgiveness than ask permission."

FIFTY ONE

WE SPENT THE rest of the night working out the details of the most ridiculous, outlandish plan ever. Every time I mentioned how nuts it was, Molly just reminded me that it had been my idea.

Customs stations kept a stash of memory modification drugs, so they were actually easy to obtain. Almost scary easy.

"How many do you need?" Ines asked when we inquired about it. Nothing more, no questions about what we needed it for. Just how many.

In her defense, we'd just requested blueprints for the jail, so it was probably glaringly obvious what we had in mind. If the Frenchwoman found our plan crazy, she didn't let on. In fact, Ines was more than willing to help out with every one of our odd requests. She even went as far as to help us find the Department of Sanitation records, to ensure that the pipes down in the cells had water running through them, and not sewage. All that was left was figuring out how to break one of the pipes.

"Axe?" Molly suggested.

"Don't be absurd," Ines tisked. "How would you go about smuggling an axe into the prison? Where would you conceal such a large weapon? Let's be sensible about this."

"Fine." Molly threw her hands up in the air. "We need a blowtorch, then. We can burn a hole in the metal."

Ines's dark eyes flashed with interest.

"Now that is an idea. Not the blowtorch, of course. But blowing a hole in the pipe could work." She looked around the deserted customs station, as if suddenly worried about being overheard. As if we hadn't been there for hours, scouring random blueprints and discussing a prison escape. Fortunately, the likelihood of anyone bearing witness to our shenanigans was slim to none; it was the middle of the night, and Ines was the lone agent on duty.

"We do have small incendiary devices, no larger than a bandage," Ines continued. "The force is powerful enough to create quite a large hole. As an added bonus, the actual device is consumed in the explosion."

Molly and I exchanged glances. I couldn't decide if our plan suddenly seemed doable, or if involving explosives crossed the line from a little crazy to utterly batshite insane.

Choosing optimism, I grinned at my roommate. She mirrored my expression. Man, I loved the alchemists' toys.

"You can give us a couple?" I asked.

"Of course, dear. These desperate types of situations are precisely what incendiary devices are for. Now, fair warning, once the package is opened, you will only have so much time before it detonates."

"Exactly how much time are we talking?" Molly asked.

"That depends. How much time do you need? I have ones that will explode anywhere from thirty seconds to twenty minutes after being exposed to air," Ines responded, her tone all business.

Molly and I exchanged another glance. "What do you think?" she asked.

I shrugged. "Thirty seconds seems kind of short. Maybe a minute? Five, tops. I mean, we don't want to stand around twiddling our thumbs, waiting for it to go off."

"We'll split the difference and go with the two minute explosives," my roommate said decisively.

Ines nodded, as though approving of the choice. "Wait here and I will get them for you."

The alchemist disappeared inside of a storage closet, surfacing a moment later with five rectangular packages. She handed them to me.

"Do not open them until you are ready to use them," Ines reminded us. "Once they have been activated, you cannot deactivate them."

"Got it," I said, tucking the tiny explosives into my pocket.

"And try not to go overboard. We cannot have you blowing up the whole jail."

I laughed at her pragmatism. Somehow, she'd managed to make this situation seem utterly reasonable.

Ines glanced at a slim gold wristwatch on her arm.

"Thank you, Ines," I said, grabbing her hand and giving it a squeeze. "Thank you so much for all of your help."

She gave me a tight smile in return. "This is my job, Stassi. I am happy to help you." Ines gestured toward the stairway leading to the hat shop. "It's late. You should get some sleep."

Footsteps sounded from the other direction, down the hallway that led to the vortexes.

"Are you expecting a runner?" Molly asked. She wrinkled her nose and her eyes went wide. "Oh, shant. Is Cyrus coming through tonight? He *cannot* see us."

A brief moment of alarm made my chest tighten. It passed quickly. Now that we had a more solid plan, instead of the Hail Mary, half-court shot for the win that we'd started with, I wasn't overly concerned with

Cyrus's reaction. If anything, my boss might be upset I was out of bed and running headlong into danger.

He'll get over it, I decided.

"We should talk to him," I said to Molly, who was already sweeping the prison blueprints off the countertop. She glanced around wildly, looking for other evidence of our scheme.

"Are you crazy?" she asked, not pausing in her frenzy. "I think that's everything, let's get out of here."

"Molls, listen to me," I pleaded, knowing I'd feel better if Cyrus backed our plan. "We should talk to him."

"It's not Cyrus," Ines snapped, taking a deep breath before continuing in her typically apathetic tone. "I believe another member of Atlic is due to come through."

She glanced around the room, narrowing her eyes at the jumbled mess Molly had made of the building plans.

"Is there anything else I can help you with? No? Best of luck then."

Ines shooed us towards the exit.

"Don't worry, I won't let the door hit me on the ass," Molly muttered sarcastically, as we climbed the stairs to street level.

"I wonder who it is," I replied quietly. "Maybe we could enlist their help."

"Definitely not," Molly quickly decided. "Two of us are plenty. It's simple. Less opportunity for disaster along the way. Plus, we don't need to clog the infirmary with more sick runners than necessary. Cyrus *definitely* won't approve of that."

"Good point," I agreed.

It was late by the time I crawled back into my cushy Parisian bed. Molly had taken up residence across the hall in Gaige's room. We were both mentally exhausted. I was struggling physically, as well. Still, sleep didn't come easily.

Every time I came close to meeting Mr. Sandman, worry over one detail or another pulled me back to full consciousness. All of the tossing and turning was fruitless, and only exhausted me further. The first rays of dawn were streaming through my window when I finally gave up.

Donning a white silk robe over my pajamas, I plodded downstairs to make coffee and start my day. Thankfully, the door to Gaige's room was still closed.

At least one of us will be well-rested, I thought enviously.

After boiling water and figuring out the French press, I dug in the back of the cabinets for something bigger than the dollhouse-sized teacups the Europeans were so fond of. Being a modern, American girl, I needed my caffeine in large doses. Today, in particular, I needed it in an extra-large dose.

Victorious in my pursuit, I settled onto the couch with my twenty-ounce mug of strong black coffee in hand, feeling quite pleased with myself. The black writing on the ceramic read "Hogsbreath is Better Than No Breath"—evidently another runner with sticky fingers had left it behind. Instead of contemplating the meaning of the phrase, I spread out the copies of the prison and sanitation system blueprints that Ines had delivered overnight.

The main floor of the station consisted of an intake area with an adjacent waiting room, several interrogation rooms, and a large bullpen where all of the inspectors' desks sat. That was the area I was in with Thoreau, and while visiting Gaige. Administrative offices for city officials made up the three uppermost levels of the préfecture. Of the two underground levels, one was divided into a records room and an evidence storage area. The other was entirely devoted to prisoner housing.

According to Molly, only about half of the cells were in use on any given day, since the préfecture was meant for short-term incarceration. According to the map, there were twenty cells total. Though the presence of other arrestees was worrisome, we had a few extra doses of the memory modification drug if they became problematic. Given the sort of people down there, I didn't anticipate running into trouble with them. The jail was only used to house drunks needing to sleep off intoxication, individuals awaiting bail, and men and women currently on trial.

Visiting hours were from eleven until six. Molly and I intended to have our butts sitting in the uncomfortable plastic chairs of the waiting area by 10:45, ensuring we would be the first visitors taken down to the cells.

I grabbed a notepad to start a list of everything we needed to take with us. Yes, my inner control-freak was rearing its head. But being systematic was the only way we'd have a snowball's chance in hell of pulling off this harebrained scheme. I jotted down everything that came to me.

1. Explosive bandages
2. Memory modification injections

Okay, so my list wasn't a long one.

I tapped my pen and contemplated what item three could possibly be.

"For the love of chocolate!" Molly's voice called from the top of the stairs. Startled, I jumped in my seat, sloshing coffee over the rim of my Hogsbreath mug. "Why are you up so damned early?"

Molly's huge yawn turned into a throaty chuckle at my reaction as she descended the steps.

"Couldn't sleep," I muttered, setting the mug down next to my short checklist.

"Really? Because it sort of looked like you were just sleeping with your eyes open, Stass. You were completely zoned out. Everything okay?"

"Just tired," I replied with a sleepy smile. "And wracking my brain for things we might forget."

"You made a list, didn't you?" she intoned.

"I didn't not make a list." I stuck my tongue out at her, drawing another laugh.

"Is there more coffee?"

"Yeah, but it's probably cold by now," I said with an apologetic smile. "I can make more."

Molly waved me away. "I'll make it. You, my friend, definitely need more caffeine."

The telephone rang as Molly turned on the burner under the kettle. We exchanged glances. Though I'd been up for a while, it wasn't even eight o'clock yet. I couldn't imagine who'd be calling so early.

"Dishes for a week says it's lover boy," Molly called with a smirk, snatching up the handset. She was standing next to it, so my sleep-deprived self didn't stand a chance of beating her to the phone. Not that I wanted to talk to Charles. Definitely not....

I watched as the expectant grin faded from my best friend's face, her expression sinking as she learned the caller's identity. *Not Charles*, I thought, my own feelings of disappointment mirroring Molly's.

"Hi Hadley.... Yep, it's Molly.... So nice to speak to you, too.... No, no, I was already awake.... Of course, just give me a minute to see if she's up. I haven't seen her yet." Molly covered the phone receiver and raised a questioning eyebrow at me.

I shook my head in response.

"Take a message," I mouthed, tossing the notepad with my extensive list across the counter to Molly. The throw lacked oomph, and the notepad sailed only two feet before fluttering to the carpet.

Molly rolled her eyes at my pitiful attempt.

"It's not heavy enough," I whispered. "Not my fault—it's science."

"I'm sorry, Hadley," my roommate said into the receiver, sparing me an exasperated smirk. "It appears as though she is still asleep. Can I give her a message?"

There was a pause while she listened to Hadley's answer. The teakettle sang its shrill song, and she stretched to remove it from the burner. Cradling the awkward handset in the crook of her shoulder, Molly filled the French press as she listened.

"Of course.... Oh, today? The 10:15 from Gare de l'Est Station to

Frankfurt? Of course…. I'll let her know…. I'm sure she'll try…."

Molly glanced over at me.

"She's doing much better, but still a little weak…. Yep, of course…. Toodles."

"So she's leaving today?" I asked, as soon as Molly had replaced the receiver.

"Yeah, she said Ernest received a telegram last night from one of their friends in Germany. The guy is leaving for the U.S. in a couple of days, and Ernest really needs to meet with him beforehand. They can't delay the trip any longer. She said they're leaving for Gare de l'Est soon, and asked if you could possibly meet her for coffee at Le Petite Rose to say goodbye. It's apparently a café in the station."

"Well, damn," I swore.

"What's wrong?" Molly asked, bringing the coffee pot and another cup over to the sitting area. "I thought you liked Hadley?"

"I do," I said quickly. "That's not the problem. I mean, I know we don't have any spare time on our hands. In fact, it's quickly waning. It's just…well, the Hemingways leaving is decisively the end of any hope we might get the rest of *Blue's Canyon*."

Molly gave me a questioning look.

"Wanna try?" she asked mischievously.

"Right," I replied with a sigh. "Because we have time for that when we're planning a prisoner escape in three hours."

"We could do it," Molly declared. "You know how I love a good felony first thing in the morning. Always starts my day off right." She grinned broadly. "The question is, are you up for two heists before noon?"

I weighed our options.

"Even if we could get Hadley over here, and Ernest was somehow already on his way to the station, the manuscript won't be in their apartment. Hemingway will have it with him," I hedged.

"Exactly," my roommate said, excitement creeping into her voice. "They'll have it with them at the station. Call her back. We might be able to pull this off."

As always, Molly projected confidence into her words. I, however, was dubious.

Molly's big blue eyes narrowed to slits, a sure sign she was deep in thought. "You could swipe it from their luggage at your coffee date. Or I could. Either way."

"It's worth a shot," I decided. "We might as well try."

"Exactly!" she repeated. "And in a few short hours, you and I will be back on the island. With Gaige. And maybe even a complete manuscript of *Bluebells*—"

"*Blue's Canyon*," I corrected.

Molly sipped her coffee, her squinty thinking face still in place.

"Worst case, we'll be sitting in our own jails cells in a few hours," she decided. "You know, locked up with a suitcase full of Hemingway's tighty whities." Molly shrugged, as if that didn't sound so bad. "Either way, we have a very eventful day ahead of us."

"That sounds just peachy," I muttered, pushing the thought from my head.

Molly was definitely right about one thing: we couldn't have packed more scheming and heisting into our morning if we'd tried. It made me nervous, but I didn't voice the thought. Knowing my roommate as well as I did, it was a guarantee that she'd see it as a challenge to defy. Molly had never met a limitation she couldn't push. Two of her favorite words were "Challenge" and "Accepted".

FIFTY TWO

AN HOUR LATER, I fastened my locket around my neck and slid my camera inside the runner pocket of my dress. If everything went according to plan, we would not be returning to the townhouse. Anything I intended to take back to the island had to come with me. I wanted to say goodbye to the team at customs, but we couldn't risk telling the alchemists our plan. Instead, I wrote quick notes to Naomi and Felipe to thank them for everything, and to tell them I hoped we'd see each other again.

A brief feeling of sadness fluttered through me—a new reaction to leaving a run. I'd never before grown so attached to customs agents.

That's the beauty of time travel, I assured myself. *You'll see them again. Maybe you'll come back on a vacation trip.*

I crossed to the full-length mirror, to be sure I looked okay without the skills of the alchemist stylists. The girl staring back at me looked damned close to the one I'd been seeing after Felipe and Naomi worked their magic. Most importantly, the bruises and lacerations were gone, thanks to my boosted immune system.

"Mirror, mirror on the wall, is Stassi the fairest of them all?"

I spun to find Molly, arms folded over her chest, leaning against the doorframe with a smirk on her painted red lips.

"Ha, ha," I replied with an eye roll.

"You ready?" she asked.

"As I'll ever be. Do you have everything?"

"If you mean the exploding bandages and mind-erasing serum, then yes."

"It doesn't erase minds," I scolded, already feeling guilty about messing with someone's memory.

"Potato, potato," Molly replied with a grin, pronouncing both the same way. She held up a small black handbag. "Isn't it crazy that our prison break kit fits inside here? We might need to raid the alchemists' batcaves more often."

The distant ringing of the telephone came from downstairs.

"Just ignore it," I said. "There is nobody we need to talk to right now. We literally cannot detour at all, there's no time."

"You sure?" Molly asked. "It might be Charles. This is the last chance you have to say goodbye...."

Sadly, she was right. But I couldn't say goodbye to Charles. Not only because the mere thought of it made my heart hurt, but also because I couldn't explain where I was disappearing to.

"It's better this way," I told her, trying to convince myself it was true. I glanced at the clock on my nightstand. "Come on, we need to go if we're going to catch Hadley."

The phone was still ringing when I shut and locked the door for the last time.

We arrived at Gare de l'Est an hour before the Hemingways' train left. Through the plate-glass window of the café, I saw Hadley and Ernest sitting together at a table in the back corner. His head was bent over a folio, his hand flying across the pages. Hadley was staring off into space, looking impossibly bored, and more than a little irritated by her husband's lack of attention.

Such a lonely life, I thought sympathetically.

"They still have their luggage. That's a good sign," Molly muttered, pointing towards the stack piled up beside the Hemingways' table. There were two train cases sitting atop two old-fashioned suitcases—the kind without gliders. On the very top was a battered leather briefcase.

Molly and I exchanged glances.

"Think it's in that one?" I asked quietly.

"It probably is. Or it might be," she hesitated before squaring her shoulders. It was odd to see Molly in action on a run, though I should've expected her take-charge, take-no-prisoners approach. "Try to find out for sure which bag has the manuscript. I'm going to hang back. Once they hand the bags over to the porters, you distract them, while I make the grab on the platform. Unless you have any other ideas?"

We hadn't exactly planned out the details. I let out a long, slow breath and shook my head. "No, I can't think of anything. Wish me luck."

A bell tinkled as I pushed open the front door to the café. Hadley's eyes darted in my direction, and her expression lit up when her gazed landed on me. She jumped to her feet and waved me over.

"Stassi," she breathed, engulfing me in a tight hug. "I am so glad you came." Drawing back, Hadley held me arm's length and studied my appearance. "You look well! I am so glad, I heard how terribly ill you were." She hugged me again. "Ernest, dear, look who has come to say goodbye." Her tone was unabashedly annoyed when she addressed her husband.

Several beats of awkward silence passed, while Hemingway continued to scribble furiously in his notebook.

"Ernest," Hadley snapped.

This time he glanced up, clearly exasperated by his wife's interruption. Hemingway's expression softened when he saw me.

"Anastasia, how nice to see you." He closed the notebook, the pen still inside to mark his place. Ernest stood and offered me his seat.

"Oh, that's not necessary. I can pull over another chair," I began, looking around the café.

Molly entered through the front door, a black hat and dark glasses obscuring her features. I had no idea where the disguise came from, or why she was even wearing one when she hadn't met Hadley or Ernest in person. My roommate settled at a table near the entrance that provided an unobstructed view of the entire café.

"No need," Hemingway was saying. "I want to run to the newsstand before we board. How is your brother?"

"It seems that he will be let out very soon," I vaguely replied.

"Wonderful!" Ernest boomed. "Man wasn't meant to rot away in a cell. We all knew he had nothing to do with those killings, I'm pleased the damnable police finally came to their senses."

"I'll pass along your kind thoughts," I promised.

Ernest—*Ernest Hemingway*—set down his writing and clasped one of my shoulders.

"I'm so glad we were able to see you before we left, if only to say goodbye," he declared. "I apologize that I must dash so quickly, but I feel a headache coming on and need some powders for the journey. I do hope you will still be in France when we return from Germany, we can catch up then."

Hemingway placed a quick kiss on each of my cheeks, grabbed his notebook, and started for the door.

"Will you be back to help me with the luggage? Or do you expect me to schlep this all on my own?" Hadley called after her husband.

It was as though the brightest star of luck was shining down upon me. "I can help you, Hadley," I offered quickly.

Ernest paused and consulted his pocket watch. He glanced over his shoulder to us. "That is very kind of you, Anastasia. Much obliged," he told me. To his wife, he said, "I will meet you on the platform."

I settled into his vacant seat as Hemingway exited the café. I briefly wondered if I'd ever see him again.

"I apologize for his atrocious manners," Hadley said, drawing me back to the present moment. "We had a tiff this morning, and he has been in a foul mood ever since. But telling you about our squabbles is boring, and I do loathe boredom. How are you feeling? How is your dear brother faring in that terrible place? I read in yesterday's paper that his bail has been denied. Do you really think he'll be released?"

"I'm confident that he won't be there much longer," I replied. "And I am feeling much better. Thank you so much for all of your care and concern, I am quite appreciative."

Hadley waved off my gratitude. "Can I get you a coffee? Or tea, perhaps?"

"No, thank you. I've had my fill of caffeine already today," I said. "Depending on how things go with Gaige, I am not certain we'll still be here when you return. The lawyer is hopeful that we can have this mess cleared up shortly, despite what the papers say, and then our father is anxious for us to return home to the States."

"That is so good to hear about your brother. And I'm quite glad you came." She reached across the table and patted my hand.

For the next twenty minutes, Hadley and I exchanged small talk. I asked about her plans while in Germany, and she gave me a list of sights to see once Gaige was released. I tried unsuccessfully to bring the conversation around to the manuscript. Every time I mentioned Hemingway's writing, her expression turned sour, as if the topic left a bad taste in her mouth. Finally, she sighed heavily.

"I wish we had met earlier, Stassi. Goodness knows I could have used a close friend here this last year. I find you to be a breath of fresh air, and perhaps even a kindred spirit." Hadley paused, and it dawned on me that she was right; we'd both known great loneliness. When she continued, her voice was steadier than it had been. "Now, see here. Write down your address, both here and in Baltimore. That way I can write to you. I really would like to keep in touch."

The lump in my throat made it hard to swallow. For the umpteenth time, I had to quell the horrible feeling of betrayal making my insides squirm.

This is the job, I reminded myself.

I wrote the actual address of the townhouse and a fictitious one in Baltimore on a piece of paper, and handed it to Hadley.

"Please, do write," I said, with a bright smile to hide my regret that any letter she wrote would go unanswered. The thought occurred to me that a transporter could pass along letters between us, though I doubted the syndicate would find that to be an acceptable use of its resources.

Hadley stood and began to gather the luggage. I followed suit. When she moved the briefcase to the tabletop to collect the larger bags below, I took the opening.

"Be careful with that one," Hadley warned, when my fingers closed around the handle.

"Does it contain your family jewels?" I teased as I lifted it. The briefcase was startlingly heavy, as though containing bricks or gold bars. Momentary worry fluttered through me—a manuscript wouldn't weigh a fraction of the case's heft. I eyed the other pieces of luggage.

Hadley scoffed. "No, something much more valuable. Well, more valuable to Ernest, anyhow." She rolled her eyes. "He cares more about his precious pages making it safely to Germany than he does me."

I weighed her demeanor and opted against sympathy. She was like Molly, in that regard.

"I'll guard it with my life," I said solemnly.

Loaded down with all of the Hemingways' Germany-bound possessions, Hadley and I set off in search of the correct platform. Molly was still sitting by the café's entrance, sipping coffee from a small mug. She'd removed her sunglasses, but still wore the hat low, shadowing her face.

"Will you be checking all of the luggage with the porter? Or should this one stay with you, so Ernest can work on the train?" I asked, holding up the briefcase as we passed Molly's table. My roommate nodded subtly to indicate that she caught my not-so-subtle message.

"Oh, I am sure he wants it in the compartment. And so, we will check it. Then he will have to talk to me." Her laugh was brittle, and I once again thought about how terribly lonely Hadley's life must be. I might just inquire about the transporters.

Ernest was waiting for us on the platform. His relief upon seeing the briefcase was palpable.

"That one stays with me," he told the porter who hurried over with a cart.

No, no, no.

"Really, Ernest," Hadley implored. "Don't be silly. You have done nothing but work lately. Once we reach Germany, you will do nothing but work. I don't think it's too much to ask for a couple of hours without it."

"I have a deadline, Hadley," Hemingway protested. "Besides, luggage is always being lost in transit. I cannot afford to lose that briefcase."

"Sir, I can assure you—" the porter started to say, his frosty tone indicating just how offensive he found Hemingway's comment.

"It stays with me," Hemingway said flatly.

The porter loaded the rest of the luggage onto his cart and handed a claim ticket to Hemingway with a curt nod. I had the briefcase clutched tightly in my hands, wracking my brain for a way to prevent it from boarding the train along with Hadley and Ernest.

"Please give your brother my best," Hemingway said again to me. "If there is anything I can do to help, provide a character reference or the like, you will let us know?"

"Of course, thank you."

Hemingway gave me a one-armed hug and another kiss on the cheek. Then, to my dismay, he reached for the briefcase. Reluctantly, I let it go. My last hope of obtaining the third piece of *Blue's Canyon* evaporated like dew on a hot summer morning.

Swallowing my frustration, I turned to hug Hadley one last time.

The train's whistle blew a warning.

"I'll write soon," Hadley promised as we parted.

Off to the side, Hemingway withdrew a cigarette from his pocket and lit the end. He blew out a long plume of smoke.

"Dammit, this is my last one," he remarked, to no one in particular. "I am just going to run and buy more."

"We need to board, Ernest," Hadley said testily.

"I'll only be a minute. Here, do not let this out of your sight." He handed her the briefcase.

Hadley set it down next to her with barely a glance. "I swear, his writing is more intrusive than a mistress. At least I would stand a chance against a mistress."

I smiled sadly, at a loss for words. A crowd of people was moving in our direction on the platform, talking and laughing with one another. One figure, tall and slim, hung near the back of the group. Her hat was pulled low over her forehead, her sunglasses taking up nearly half of her face. In one hand, she carried a leather briefcase, roughly the size and shape of the one sitting near Hadley's feet. It wasn't beat up and scuffed like Ernest's, but hopefully no one would notice until it was too late.

The train whistle blew a second warning.

"I should go," Hadley remarked, reaching for the case.

"What about Ernest?" I asked, my voice coming out a little too loud and a little too frantic.

Hadley's head snapped in my direction at my shrill tone.

"For all I care, he can catch the next train," she said, attempting to sound blasé.

The crowd of people was nearly upon us. Molly was mere strides of her long legs away.

I grabbed Hadley's arm when she reached for the briefcase again. Squeezing her hand, I desperately tried to keep her attention focused on me.

"This trip will be good for you," I reassured her, pitching my voice to be heard over the chatter of the passing crowd. "Being in a foreign country, particularly where you don't speak the language, has a way of bonding people," I added, babbling now to hold her gaze.

A young Frenchman tripped, bumping into Hadley and causing her to stumble sideways. I caught Hadley before she could fall.

"Pardon me," the Frenchman said, flushing with embarrassment.

One of his friends made a joke about his large feet and lack of coordination. The group laughed. After making sure Hadley wasn't hurt, the young man and his friends moved on.

The train whistle blew a final time. Over Hadley's head, I saw Hemingway hurrying towards us. I hugged my friend one last time.

"There's Ernest," I announced as we drew apart.

Hadley checked over her shoulder. I gave her hand a parting squeeze. Then I melted into the stream of passengers on the platform, without so much as a backward glance.

Guilt sat leaden and solid in my gut. Deceit was nothing new, but the repetition of my moral crimes did not make them any easier to digest.

FIFTY THREE

AS I SLID a pair of dark sunglasses up the bridge of my nose, Molly fell in step beside me on the sidewalk. Ernest Hemingway's briefcase swung jauntily from her long fingers.

"Cha-ching," she said, steering me to the curb and extending her arm.

A taxi veered towards us, coming to a stop a couple feet away. Molly opened the back door and gestured me inside.

"Place Louis Lépine, s'il vous plait," Molly told the driver. She sat back and looked at me expectantly.

"Is it in there?" I asked, gesturing to the briefcase.

"There are definitely papers inside," she said as we pulled away. My roommate's eyes were teeming with excitement as she removed the oversized aviators. "I'm talking jackpot, Stass. I'm not sure yet what all is here, but there are hundreds—maybe even *thousands*—of handwritten pages. Regardless of whether or not *Blue's Canyon* is here, Cyrus is going to kiss your feet when he sees what all we got."

"Will the feet kissing come before or after the ass chewing for you, me, and Gaige jumping without a vortex?"

"Before. Definitely before," Molly declared. She fell into me as the cab driver swerved particularly hard to the left. He was driving through the streets as though playing Gaige's favorite video game—Grand Theft 387. Somehow, the driver seemed to be completely in control of the vehicle as he wove in and out of the sparse traffic.

"So it was worth the immense shame I'm feeling right now?" I asked Molly, helping her back to her side of the seat.

"More than worth it," Molly declared, opening up the briefcase in her lap. Sure enough, the suitcase-like compartment was stuffed with papers. Her estimate in the thousands suddenly didn't seem so outlandish.

"Holy shant," I breathed.

Molly took a handful of pages from the top, and I did the same. We spent several minutes flipping through them, cataloguing our loot.

A page at the bottom of the section I'd pulled grabbed my attention. The handwriting was different from the others, and completely familiar to me. Filled with hope, I scooped up the next stack from the briefcase. Sure enough, it was also in Andre's scrawling script.

"The entire thing," I whispered.

"Did you say something?" Molly asked, looking up from the pages she was reading.

"It's the whole thing," I repeated, staring wondrously at my roommate. "*Blue's Canyon*—the whole book is here. Including Hemingway's notes on it."

Her eyes grew into saucers. "You mean…."

"Yeah," I replied, sitting back in the seat and staring out the window as the streets of Paris flew by.

Emotions were sailing through me with a speed that rivaled the racing cab. Though I felt relief at completing the run, I couldn't help but think about how much easier the entire thing would've been if we'd just gone to Hemingway initially. I found it difficult to regret a single night spent chatting people up, our trips to Closerie des Lilas, or the visit to Shakespeare and company. Not only did Gaige and I have fun, but they'd all been incredible experiences. And I'd met Charles. And befriended Hadley. And Gertrude Stein. And Ernest *freaking* Hemingway.

"There was no way of knowing that he'd have the whole thing," Molly said, patting my hand.

"I know," I replied piteously.

"Don't worry, I have just the thing to cheer you up," Molly promised, holding up the pages in her hand. "There's also what looks like a full draft of another of Hemingway's novels, one I'd never heard of. *Juvenalia*?"

"Never heard of it," I said, eyeing the title page.

With a heavy sigh, I grabbed another stack of papers from the briefcase.

We spent the next ten minutes trying to make sense of it all. In total, there seemed to be bits and pieces of at least three of Hemingway's other unpublished works, plus carbons of several more. When I came across a carbon copy of another title page, my heart stopped. It was *The Sun Also Rises*. Written in Hemingway's hand.

The briefcase was a veritable gold mine. Grabbing Molly's arm, I shoved the page in front of her face. Our excited screeching drew the attention of the driver. I couldn't even imagine what he was thinking of us as we filled his backseat with loose papers and squealed like schoolgirls.

"You know," Molly started, once she'd completed her seated version of our happy dance. "If we weren't honest, upstanding members of a crime syndicate, we could sell these ourselves on the black market. Think about the dough we'd get. Yachts, mansions, deluxe electric transpo vehicles. Ooh, or an island of your very own! Stassi Island. It has a nice ring, right? Or Stolly Island? Mossi Island?"

I rolled my eyes. "We wouldn't live long enough to spend all that money. Cyrus would hunt us down and pull the trigger before you could say, 'Three of everything in each color, please'."

Molly let out a breathy laugh. "True. But he's going to make *bank* on this loot. Which means you will, too. You'd better...."

"Um, not just me," I pointed out. We were only a minute or so from the préfecture, so I began gathering up the papers and putting them carefully back in the treasure chest. "You and Gaige get equal shares, obvs."

I finished packing up the pages, only half-listening to her protests about the division of wealth. It wasn't like any of us were hurting financially, or that we couldn't afford to buy pretty much anything we desired—okay, maybe not an island, but almost anything else—so my exhilaration wasn't actually about the money. I was far more excited to tell Gaige that we'd successfully completed the run. And Cyrus, too.

As the driver pulled to a stop in front of the préfecture, I checked the briefcase clasps for the third time while Molly paid our cab fare. Stepping onto the sidewalk, I paused to take a long look at the building. It had been the bane of my existence for weeks. And now It was to be our salvation.

All the elation drained out of me in an instant. It was replaced with fear, dread, and a modicum of hope. We were about to commit the most insane heist of my career. Quite possible the most insane heist *ever*.

"You ready to do this?" Molly asked, looking just as worried as I felt.

"No," I replied simply.

We stood there for several minutes, just staring at the building. The reality of our plan was staring us in the face and weighing heavily in my mind.

"Lock it up?" Molly finally asked, her voice wavering.

"Lock it up," I repeated quietly.

The phrase lacked even a trace of conviction.

FIFTY FOUR

WAITING IN THE near-empty reception area of the préfecture was agonizing. We'd given our names and signed the visitors' log, and then there was nothing to do but sit and stew until eleven o'clock. The seconds ticked by at an impossibly slow pace. Uniformed officers passed in both directions, some dragging cuffed perps and others consoling distraught victims.

"A watched pot never boils," mumbled Molly, when she noticed me checking the clock on the wall for the umpteenth time. It appeared to be stuck at 10:51.

"Yeah, yeah. I know," I grumbled. "It's a compulsion."

I glanced around. Only the desk sergeant was there, engrossed in the morning newspaper.

"Besides," I continued in a low voice, "it gives me something to do. Otherwise, I'll just keep thinking of all the things that could go wrong.

I mean what if those bandage thingies don't work? It's not like we tested them. Or what if there are more guards down there than normal? Or what if it's packed with prisoners? We only have so much memory modification serum. We can't dose a crowd. Or what if the pipe doesn't actually have water? What if—"

"Stassi, stop," Molly cut me off. She rested a comforting hand on my arm. "Yes, all of those things could happen. Or they could *not* happen. We did our due diligence and devised a plan that allows for as many complications as possible. All we can do now is hope for the best."

"I don't like leaving things up to fate," I replied. "I like to be in control."

"I know, I know," she soothed. "But I'd say fate's been on our side today."

Molly gestured to the briefcase in her lap.

"Ms. Prince? Ms. Ringwald?" The intake officer's voice made us both jump.

As he stared at us expectantly, I wondered if he was about to declare that Hemingway had reported the theft, slap cuffs on us, and then take us down to join Gaige in the jail. Perhaps taking our stolen treasure trove to the police headquarters wasn't the best idea. My roommate was probably considering the same possibility, because her snowy complexion had turned ashen.

"I can take you down now," the officer prompted, speaking slowly as if we were lacking mental faculties. Not surprising, since Molly and I were staring at him with identical shocked expressions, as though we'd suddenly woke to find ourselves in the police station without any knowledge of how or why we'd come.

"Yes, of course, thank you," Molly said, regaining her composure before I did.

My roommate nudged me hard in the ribs, and we both stood. My palms were suddenly slick with sweat. My head spun from the influx of adrenaline that instantly began coursing through my veins. It was go-time.

"This way, please," the man continued, still speaking in that drawn-out and deliberate tone. He pointed to the door only two feet away marked "Les Visiteurs", as if it weren't glaringly obvious where we were going.

"Ringwald? Really?" I whispered, rolling my eyes at Molly as we followed the officer down a dimly lit hallway. We turned several times, heading into the depths of the station.

She shrugged, covering a terse smile. "Why not?"

"Excellent logic," I quietly declared.

Once we reached the basement level, the uniform led us through three sets of locked doors. He used a different metal key from his massive key ring on each, relocking the doors behind us. Watching the station's careful security precautions in action, I couldn't help but think how futile his efforts would prove to be.

When the guard opened the third and final door, the smell of body odor and human waste assaulted my senses. I took a deep breath through my mouth and passed through the doorway, getting my first look at the Parisian jail.

An uneven stone walkway that was coated in a thick layer of slime and grime divided the two sides of the holding area, flanked by metal bars down the entire length in either direction. The same metal bars divided the long space into cubes that were ten feet square, according to the plans we'd studied. Each cell contained two cots, a metal toilet, and a sink.

Still breathing through my mouth, I trailed the guard and Molly down the dim corridor. My eyes darted back and forth as we passed cells, inventorying the space and its occupants. Without warning, a face appeared a foot to my right, pressed against the bars. I scrambled away. The mug belonged to an older man, with a scraggly salt and pepper beard and wild mane of frizzy hair. A broad toothless grin spread across his features, the expression bordering on maniacal. He wore an undershirt that had probably once been white, but was now a disturbing shade of dirty dishwater, and black trousers meant for a man three times his size.

"Hey, Billy," Molly said as we passed.

The man's grin became impossibly wider.

"Back again, is you?" he shouted in a thick cockney accent. I winced at the volume of his voice, which was entirely unnecessary given our proximity. "Bring me a present this time?"

A scuffle of feet drew my attention to the last cell closest to the wall—Gaige's cell. My partner's strong fingers wrapped around the bars, and I caught a glimpse of his nose and unkempt hair.

"You flirting with my girl, Billy?" Gaige called to the other inmate.

The sound of his voice gave me the strength to cast aside the worst of my doubts.

Molly winked at the other prisoner, who looked like he'd fit right in at Salpêtrière.

"Don't pay him no mind. He's just jealous, he is," she replied in a painful imitation of Billy's accent. "Had a right busy morn, I have, luv. Next time, I'll have something for yous."

"Yous a proper touff, you is. That boy don't treat yous right, yous come and tell ole Billy. I'll set 'em straight."

Stifling the nervous laughter in my throat, I marveled at Molly's ability to make friends in the most unlikely of places.

"Sweet talker," Gaige called out.

The uniformed guard stopped in front of Gaige's cell.

"Step away from the bars," he ordered my partner.

Gaige moved out of sight.

I glanced back at Billy's cell, estimating his sightline. With even greater luck than I could've hoped for, the only other prisoner was across the aisle and six cells from the end of the row.

"You have thirty minutes," the guard told us in a stern tone. "I will remain right out here. No touching. No passing items to the prisoner."

"I know the drill," Molly replied pleasantly.

The officer furrowed his brow, confused by her not-yet-used colloquialism.

"We understand the rules," I explained.

"Thirty minutes," he snapped.

The guard turned his back, reaching for the lock with his key ring— his mistake, our good fortune. In one fluid motion, Molly slid a syringe loaded with the memory modifier from beneath the sleeve of her dress. Without hesitation, she plunged the thin needle into the exposed skin at the nape of the uniform's neck.

The officer was a big man, with a substantial amount of bulk hanging over the waistband of his pants, and yet the serum dropped him like a bad habit. The key ring clattered to the floor when the officer slumped forward against the bars. Molly and I both moved to catch him, trying to minimize the bruises he'd wake up with. It took both of us to ease him to the ground and drag him down the hallway. We propped the unconscious man against the bars of a cell, his head lulling to one side and tongue protruding from between parted lips.

"How long before he wakes?" I asked anxiously.

"No clue, I didn't look at the strength of the serum. But he isn't likely to remember the last week with that much in his system, let alone the last hour. He could be out for days, for all I know. Get the keys."

"Hells yes! Is this a prison break?" Gaige exclaimed. Molly and I ran back to his cell, keys in hand. "That's so hot."

That was when I got my first good look at my partner.

Unkempt hair stuck out in every direction. A week's worth of stubble covered his jaw, the facial hair noticeably lighter than that on his head. His short nails were caked with black grime. Dark circles under his eyes brought to mind images of a raccoon. And yet, despite it all, my partner was grinning like a kid on Christmas morning.

"'Ey! Whatcha doing down 'ere?" Billy called.

"Mind your horses, old chap!" Molly yelled back, grinning. "You'll wait your turn, you will."

"Can we save the excess shenanigans until we're back on the island?" I asked, holding the key ring up to the bars in front of Gaige. "Any clue which key it is?"

At the other end of the hallway, Billy continued to yell.

"I'll deal with him. Just get the door open," Molly said. "Oye Billy! I have yer present right here, I do," she called in a sing-song voice as she headed for his cell.

Ignoring the chaos around me, I picked a key at random. When I fit it in the lock and turned, nothing happened. Next key. Same thing.

"What's the plan?" Gaige asked anxiously. "How are we going to bust out of the station?"

"We're not." I tried a third, and then a fourth key with no luck. "Why didn't we dose the guard *after* he unlocked the cell?" I muttered, frustrated.

"What do you mean 'we're not'?" Gaige asked.

The sixth—or was it the seventh?—key finally did the trick. The locking mechanism turned with an angry scrape of metal on metal. The instant the door opened, Gaige flung his arms around me. He pulled me hard against his chest in a bone-crushing bear hug. My partner smelled horrific—a mixture of boy's locker room, mothballs, and mold. And yet, I didn't care. Gaige kissed my cheek, the stubble from his beard rough against my skin.

"I've been so worried about you. Molly told me what happened at the theater and I.... Shant, Stass. I should have been there to protect you. If you'd di—"

"I didn't," I cut him off in a fierce tone. "I'm fine."

Gaige hugged me tighter. When we broke apart, my partner's eyes were wet. So were mine.

"We've got to move, guys," Molly said, coming up behind us. Her face was paler than usual, her blue eyes wide and nervous. "I took care of Billy, but someone probably heard him shouting. We could have company at any moment, we have to go." She glanced up towards the thick exposed pipes running across the ceiling of the cell. "Help me with the cot."

The metal frame was flimsy, and we easily moved it into position in the middle of the cell, directly beneath the center of the pipe. Molly kicked off her shoes—igniting explosives while breaking out of prison was *so* not the time for stacked heels—and stepped up onto the metal slab. It bowed slightly under her weight, just enough to make her sway unsteadily as the metal wobbled. Gaige wrapped his hands around her waist to help her balance, then glanced over at me with a companionable smile.

"Any chance you want to let me in on the plan now?" he asked pleasantly. "For instance, why are we redecorating my cell instead of getting the hell out of here?"

"Not the time," I replied simply, watching my roommate trying to gain her balance. When she appeared to be somewhat steady, I handed her several of the bandages from her purse.

"Oh, right," continued Gaige conversationally. "Old-fashioned bandages. Thank goodness you brought those, I have a paper cut."

Shooting him a withering look, Molly removed one of the explosives from its wrapper and slapped it on a pipe.

"Two minutes!" she yelled.

"Of course," my partner groaned. "You're here to fix the pipes. We might need something more for these old things, but why not, might—"

The sounds of the metal bed creaking beneath Molly's weight cut him off. All three of us froze in place.

Gaige swore. Molly and I exchanged alarmed glances. Frantically, Molly tore two more explosives from their packages and stuck them to the adjacent pipes.

"Yep, we'll just do some routine maintenance with first aid supplies with a guard unconscious two feet away," Gaige grumbled. "Good thinking."

"Get out of here!" Molly snapped at him. She took two tentative steps to the edge of the bed, the metal wobbling like a saw that had been plucked. "And stop complaining while you're being rescued—it's just ridiculous."

In reply, Gaige swept his arm behind her knees and scooped her off the bed.

"Thank you for being my gallant knight," he intoned, waggling his eyebrows.

"Not the time!" I yelled, pulling on his arm. "Ninety seconds!"

We scurried out of the cell and into the walkway. Molly scrambled out of Gaige's arms.

"Plan?" he demanded.

"We're jumping," I replied simply. My partner's eyes swept from me to Molly to the explosives on the pipe as he filled in the details.

Without warning, two men entered the cellblock. The first was another uniformed officer, this one with a baby face and bewildered expression. The second man made my heart stop. His golden-brown eyes smiled when they landed on me.

"Charles?" I breathed.

For a pulse-pounding second, Molly, Gaige, and I just stared at each other. I shot a frantic gaze at Charles and the guard.

"What are you doing here?" I demanded, my voice frenzied and high-pitched. My eyes darted to the officer, who was staring dumbly at the chaos around him. Between the unconscious guard, the unconscious prisoner, the open cell door, and our crowd in the hallway, the poor rookie was clearly overwhelmed. Thank heavens.

"You are not answering my calls or my letters," Charles was saying.

"I thought your brother might know what…" He trailed off as his eyes landed on my partner. Realization dawned as Charles noticed that Gaige was on the wrong side of the bars.

"Do you have any more memory mod?" Gaige hissed to Molly.

She wasted no time answering, her stocking-clad feet slapping against the stone as Molly headed towards the men.

"Guard first!" I yelled at her.

"Stassi, what is going on here?" Charles asked. His tone was eerily even and calm, given the situation. Our eyes locked.

"Take cover," I demanded. "Now!"

The sight of my rabid-looking supermodel roommate barreling at him with a needle in hand finally jolted the officer out of his daze. He began shouting shrilly in French. Syringe in one fist, Molly collided with the man at full speed. Surprised, he caught her in his arms and they began to struggle. Charles wore an almost comical expression of disbelief as he watched the two fight for the syringe. Wordlessly, Gaige and I hurried to help Molly.

The first explosive detonated.

One hundred and eighty pounds of stinky man flesh knocked into me with the force of a moving truck. We hit the ground together, Gaige's body shielding me from the flying bits of metal. The force of my skull hitting the stone floor left a ringing in my ears and spots in my vision. I lifted my head to see Charles grab the officer from behind, wrenching his arms behind his back and providing Molly with a clear shot at the guy's jugular. The rookie stopped struggling the instant the needle pierced his skin.

Gaige rolled off me, groaning and moaning while shaking shrapnel out of his hair. Water gushed from the pipe, leaking out into the hallway and soaking through my dress.

Charles held the unconscious officer in his arms, looking utterly stunned. As the reality of the situation came crashing down, Charles dropped him and stepped back.

"What have I done? What the hell have I done?" he groaned, repeating the phrase as he ran his hands through his hair.

Unable to help myself, I moved towards Charles.

"He's fine," I promised. "Just asleep. And you saved us. You saved *me.*"

The second two explosives detonated in fast succession, the force knocking me flat on my stomach in the pool of water. Charles scrambled over to where I lay. When he met my gaze, Charles looked like a bewildered child.

"It's okay," I continued. "I swear, it's going to be okay."

"Dose him, Molls!" Gaige shouted.

My roommate turned terrified blue eyes on us. "I can't. I'm out," she said weakly.

Gaige darted to where I lay in the hallway. In one fluid movement, he grabbed both of my arms and hauled me to my feet, dragging me over to the stone wall just outside his cell.

"We have to go, Stass," my partner said, compassion brimming in his eyes. "I'm sorry."

My neck snapped as I whipped my gaze between the two men.

"What are we going to do about him?" asked Molly, her voice tinged with panic.

"We're going to leave him," Gaige called back. "It's fine. He won't say anything."

Stunned, Charles's looked from Molly to Gaige to me, unable to comprehend the situation.

"Stassi?" he asked, his voice barely audible over the water pouring from the pipes.

"I'm sorry. I'm so sorry," I whispered, unsure if Charles could even hear me.

Gaige held his hand out to Molly. She sprinted in our direction, not breaking stride as she bent to retrieve the briefcase with the manuscripts.

Her fingers slid between Gaige's.

My partner was still clutching my arm as I reached for the stone wall with my other hand. The *prima* within my wrist warmed instantly. I focused on what was about to come, welcoming the golden glow that began to swirl in front of me.

"Stassi, wait!" Charles yelled, his voice already sounding as if it were a million miles away. Or perhaps a million years.

My tattoo was singing powerfully when I felt his fingers brush the bare skin of my arm.

And then I was gone.

FIFTY FIVE

MY BODY HUMMED with the beat of the siren's song within as I greedily gulped the cool air enveloping me. I felt cold, smooth stone beneath my hand. No longer was the stone slimy, nor the air fetid. Comfort washed over me. I was in the familiar vortex, deep within the island I called home.

Gaige's hands ran up and down my goosebump-covered arms, his touch as reassuring and familiar as the vortex. Several feet away, someone coughed, then gagged. I heard the sound of liquid hitting stone as she— it had to be Molly—spewed the contents of her stomach. My own gut flip-flopped out of sympathy.

Gaige pulled me closer. With my eyes squeezed tightly shut to stop the spinning sensation in my head, I leaned my forehead against my partner's chest. He stroked my hair and murmured soothing words in my ear, as though I was a child who'd just awoken from a nightmare.

"Go help Molly," I told my partner. "I'm fine. We're home. I'm fine now."

"Molly has all the help she needs," he replied.

More coughing. More sickness.

"I feel like death," a hoarse voice proclaimed.

Gaige's hoarse voice. Coming from several feet away. Not inches.

I shoved back, struggling free of the arms that held me. Golden-brown eyes, wide and bright with shock, stared back at me in the darkness.

"No. No. No!" I cried. "No, no, no *no*. No! You can't be here! You *can't*. Oh shant. This is not happening. It *cannot* be happening!"

"Calm down, Stassi," Charles DuPree said calmly. He reached for me.

Shooting backwards, I batted him away. Charles let his hands fall to his sides, but moved towards me. For every step I took back, he took one forward. I continued to backpedal until the comforting stone wall was pressed against my spine.

"Stassi?" Molly's voice called. "You good?"

"Not exactly," I replied, my voice wavering with hysteria.

"I know," she replied. "My stomach did *not* appreciate our exit strategy. Though, oddly enough, I don't feel nearly as bad as last time I did this." Her silhouette emerged from the darkness as she moved towards me, but quickly came to a dead halt. "Oh *shite*."

For a long, quiet moment, she took in the scene—me pressed against the cave wall as if it might somehow save me, Charles only a foot away. In our time.

"Shant!" Molly exclaimed. "Is that Charles? Oh, frack. Frack, frack, *frack*. Cyrus is going to—" My roommate broke off mid-sentence, collapsing against the side of the cave as she dry-heaved. Though he wasn't doing well either, Gaige stumbled over to stand beside her. He rubbed her back and held her hair as Molly's entire body convulsed.

"Stassi? Is that you?" a voice called from the entrance to the vortex.

"We need medics!" I called, not bothering to look at the newcomer.

It was Rupert. His sleepy voice was music to my ears.

"Um, who's your friend?" Rupert asked uncertainly. "Should I call security?"

An unauthorized jumper coming through the vortex was usually cause for alarm. Protocol demanded that both security and Cyrus be notified immediately.

"No, don't call them," I replied, fighting to keep my voice steady. "Just get the medics down here. Both Molly and Gaige need attention. Tell them that two runners are down here with time sickness."

"Okay." Rupert's voice sounded small and uncertain.

"Please, Rupert?" I pleaded. "I have this under control."

The attendant scurried back to his post.

Send Charles back, I thought, my brain switching into survival mode. *Get him out of here before anyone else sees him.*

Looking over at my roommate and my partner, I hesitated. I didn't want to choose between helping them and saving my own ass from exile.

"Go!" Molly prodded. "I'm telling you, I don't feel *that* bad. You need to handle this, now."

I grabbed Charles's arm and dragged him from the vortex into the main gate. He didn't resist.

"Medics are on their way," Rupert told me from behind his console of knobs and buttons.

"Move," I demanded. "No, wait. I need you to program a jump to Paris. 1925. Same date we left. Um, I guess that would be April 4th? 5th?"

Rupert stared at me as though I'd lost my mind.

"You can't jump again so soon," he protested weakly. "Especially since you didn't use the—"

"Just do it," I snapped. Softening my tone, I implored Rupert to play accomplice to my crime. "*Please*, Rupert. Please just do it?"

Boots pounded stone—the medics running down the steps. They'd be inside the gate any second.

"We need to hurry," I pleaded.

The teenager chewed his bottom lip and ran a hand through his hair. What I was asking him to do went against a number of syndicate rules and regulations. But Cyrus was going to kill me if he found Charles on the island. Exile would be the best-case scenario.

Just as he looked like he was going to relent, Rupert's eyes widened so much that white was visible all around the iris. The color drained from his face in an instant. He stepped back from the controls.

"Stassi, what is going on?" The voice came from behind me.

Cyrus's voice.

Too late, I thought.

My boss's tone was utterly calm, which made it all the more terrifying.

"Cyrus, I can explain," I began, whirling to face him.

"So do it."

Medics came crashing down the stairs.

"Vortex five!" Rupert told them.

The four men hurried inside the tunnel.

I met Cyrus's expressionless green gaze and swallowed thickly.

"I didn't mean to bring him here, Cyrus, I swear. I don't know how or why, but I *swear*, I didn't bring him here on purpose," I began, my voice quickly picking up pace. "It all happened so fast. We were in the middle of a prison break when he showed up. Molly had used all the memory mod. We were just going to leave him. I mean, who would believe him anyway? Three people vanishing into thin air? Not exactly something that happens every day, you know? But, I don't know what happened. I guess...I guess he grabbed me right as I was jumping."

Aware that my explanation was devolving into incoherent rambling, I clamped my lips shut and took a deep breath through my nose. Cyrus's blank mask never wavered. Charles shifted uneasily from foot to foot beside me. I didn't dare look at him.

"Two patients. One female, one male," a medic barked into his walkie-talkie as he reentered the gate. "Both made a jump without customs. Prepare beds." The other three were close on his heels, half-carrying, half-dragging Molly and Gaige from the vortex.

Arms crossed over his chest, Cyrus never took his eyes off of me.

"Both of you report to medical," he finally said.

I opened my mouth to protest, to say that I was fine and didn't need medical attention.

"That is an order, Stassi," Cyrus warned. "I want you both checked out. Then I will determine the best course of action. For now, do not let him out of your sight. At all. Stick to him like white on rice, do you understand?" Not waiting for an answer from me, my boss turned to Charles. "Welcome to Branson Isle, Mr. DuPree. Your stay here will be brief."

Cyrus spun on his heel and left the gate without another word.

"Come on, let's go get poked and prodded," I muttered to Charles.

Pale but determined, Charles nodded. Together, we trailed my boss up the stairs.

As we emerged, I saw the bright stars twinkling above, like diamonds strewn across blue velvet.

Charles sucked in a breath of air. "Where are we?"

"Branson Isle, like Cyrus said," I replied stiffly.

"Which is where, exactly?"

I stopped walking and stared at Charles, appreciating for the first time how bizarre this had to be for him. And it was only going to get more bizarre when we reached the infirmary, and he saw all of the syndicate's medical gadgets.

Charles stopped, too. I reached out and gave his hand a brief squeeze.

"It'll all make sense soon," I promised, not sure that it would. How was Cyrus going to explain everything to him? Would Cyrus explain anything to him? Or would my boss simply hit Charles with memory mod and call it a day?

"I trust you, Stassi."

You shouldn't, I thought.

Aloud, I said, "Come on. Cyrus will be pissed if we don't get our butts up to the infirmary."

"We would not want that," Charles replied in a light tone. He reached for my hand, but I pretended not to notice and started walking again.

Along the path to the infirmary, we passed a group of off-duty runners who were enjoying a dip in the hot springs. Loud music and raucous laughter rang out from the pools down below. Out of the corner of my eye, I caught Charles staring with interest at the spectacle.

"Hey, Stassi!" a silky voice called out. I glanced in the direction it came from—one of the bungalows not far from the path. Squinting into the darkness, I found the source with relative ease, thanks to a neon pink bikini. Arin, whose swimsuit was secured by little more than dental floss, was standing on the back porch of her bungalow. Her hair was wet and her eyes slightly unfocused.

"Totes bummer about Paris and the whole serial killer thing," she continued, sipping from a red plastic cup in her hand. "Cyrus was majorly P.O.'ed about that rogue runner. Wouldn't want to be him right now, you know?"

"Yeah, me neither," I called back.

I really don't want to be me right now, either, I thought.

Charles simply gaped at the exchange, his expression a mix of embarrassment and fascination.

"You're drooling," I said. Tugging him forward, I hurried on before Arin sobered up enough to realize there was a new hot guy on the island.

"What is she wearing?" Charles asked. "And why was she walking around outside in it?"

"She was swimming," I replied.

"Is that a bathing costume?"

"Yeah, something like that."

"But it is so…small."

I didn't bother telling him that the neon two-piece was probably one of her more modest suits.

Unfortunately, he'd opened the can of questions and couldn't seem to get the lid back on. From there, Charles peppered me with every query I would've expected, and then even more: Are we near Baltimore? Who lives here? Do you live here? Is Cyrus really your uncle? Is Gaige really your adoptive brother? Why are we going to an infirmary? Are we sick?

The last one gave me pause. We'd reached the medical center, but had yet to enter.

"You aren't sick," I said definitively, realizing for the first time that Charles, unlike Molly and Gaige, was not puking his guts out. I studied him. No pale or waxy complexion. No feverish eyes. Sweat was beading on his forehead and he did wear a look of confusion, but both were explainable under the circumstances. "Do you feel sick?"

"I am well," Charles replied.

"It's the adrenaline," I said. "Jumping gives you lots of adrenaline. Just let me know when it wears off and you start to feel sick."

But the more I looked at him, the less certain I felt that it would prove true. Myself excluded, I couldn't think of a runner immune to time sickness. And Charles didn't even have a tattoo. No *prima* embedded in his skin to help ease the journey through the space-time continuum. I shook my head. He was going to be hurting very soon.

"Jumping?" Charles was asking. "Is that what you call what we just did? We 'jumped' from Paris to here? Branson Isle, was it? I have never heard of it."

I sighed heavily and stepped within range of the door sensor. Frosted glass doors slid smoothly apart. Charles sucked in air as he was struck speechless by our not-so-modern marvel.

I felt the corners of my mouth turn up at his expression. Adapting to new surroundings was part of my job as a runner. Even when something shocked or surprised me, I fought to keep it from showing on my face. Then again, I had the added benefit of jumping back to times that I could prepare for. There was no preparing for the future.

Which was precisely why runners didn't travel forward beyond their own time; it was a fundamental rule agreed upon by all of the syndicates. One glance at Charles's ghost-white face confirmed that it was a sound decision. He swayed unsteadily on his feet as we approached the reception desk, gaping in an undignified, very un-Charles-like manner.

A wave of sympathy washed over me. The poor guy had to feel like a lost puppy separated from his family. Which he sort was.

The night nurse on duty was a year or two older than me. Her waist-length silver hair was twisted into three separate buns at the nape of her neck and shimmered under the bright infirmary lights. Silver mascara had been liberally applied to her long lashes, and her eyebrows were dyed to match the exact shade of the hair on her head. As she typed on the keyboard in front of her, the text displayed on a clear screen behind her desk.

"Stassi, nice to see you have returned in one piece," Roxi, the nurse, said with a smile. "Are you here to see Molly and Gaige? I'm afraid the medics are still tending to them, but you can wait if you want." She gestured to a row of sleek chrome chairs off to one side of the room. "Or, if you'd prefer, you can wait at your bungalow. I'm sure you'd be more comfortable there, and I will comm you as soon as they are able to receive visitors."

As amazing as heading back to my bungalow sounded, it wasn't in the cards. I might never be allowed back there. Would Molly pitch my stuff and revel in the luxury of having the bungalow to herself?

"Actually, Roxi, I'm here for an eval," I said shakily. I nodded towards Charles. "Cyrus wanted both of us to be checked out."

"This must be our visitor." A man with the tall, lean body of a swimmer appeared in the entranceway to the treatment wing. Dr. Wain Carver was head of the infirmary, and a man I only knew from a distance. The fact that Cyrus felt the need to call him made me queasy. He rarely treated runners for anything as routine as time sickness. Return from a run with the plague, Spanish flu, typhoid—whatever that was—and Dr. Carver was your guy. Time sickness was left to the underlings, particularly in the middle of the night.

"Dr. Wain Carver," the doctor said, offering Charles his hand.

"Charles DuPree," Charles replied, the picture of manners and etiquette.

He must have a high tolerance for weird, I thought, marveling at Charles's ability to speak in the face of technology that had to seem like something from an H.P. Lovecraft novel.

"Mr. Atlic has asked you be given a physical." The doctor spoke in low, soothing tones meant to be reassuring. Naturally, they had the opposite effect on me. "No need to worry, we just want to make sure you are healthy."

Two large medics loitered in the hallway behind the doctor. Their nonchalant attitudes weren't fooling me. Probably not Charles, either. The medics were hanging back far enough as to not be threating, but close enough to tackle Charles should he flip his shant.

Charles ignored the men and smiled serenely at the doctor, nodding politely.

"Of course, doctor."

Dr. Carver gestured Charles towards the hallway. "This way." He turned to me. "Someone will be with you shortly, Stassi. Have a seat for now."

The first sign of true distress appeared in the form of a deep frown line between Charles's eyes. "You are not coming with me?" he asked, voice cracking on the last word. "I thought you would be staying with me. Your uncle said you were to stay with me."

The medics moved closer to Dr. Carver. I shot them a look that said,

"Back the hell up", and reached for Charles's hand.

"This is very routine, no big deal," I told him with a large fake grin. "Dr. Carver will take good care of you. I promise. And as soon as he's finished running some tests, I'll come see you."

"Precisely. All very routine," Dr. Carver agreed.

"You said I wasn't sick," Charles said to me, lowering his tone as though there was a chance the others might not hear him in the quiet reception area.

The medics took another step forward. Too much more protesting or procrastinating, and they were going to dose him. I hated to admit that it might be for the best. Thus far, Charles was handling all of this amazingly well. But he was beginning to crack. One look at the medi pods, and he was likely to freak out.

"You probably aren't," I replied slowly, feeling terrible for him. "The island is very isolated, though. Cyrus just wants to make sure you don't have any communicable diseases."

The lie slipped out easily enough, partly because it was rooted in truth. Someone from a different time period could very well be carrying a disease long since eradicated. I didn't want to think about the other reasons Cyrus might want him to undergo a medical evaluation. Or, possibly, a psychological one.

"Stassi, when are—"

I cut him off abruptly, planting my mouth firmly over his. Charles stiffened at first, but relaxed quickly. The kiss didn't last long, just long enough to shut him up. Then, I brushed my lips softly over his cheek and murmured quietly in his ear.

"Cooperate, please. They won't hurt you. You'll be safe. And you'll be back with me soon." I straightened and gave him my fake smile. "I'll see you soon."

Heart heavy, stomach a bundle of nerves, I watched Charles disappear through the doors.

FIFTY SIX

THOSE SLEEK CHAIRS in the waiting room were torturous. My butt had more knots than a sailing rig by the time someone came for me. To my surprise, and dread, that someone wasn't a medic.

Cyrus entered the infirmary waiting area and took a seat next to me. Without a glance in my direction, my boss leaned forward, elbows propped on his knees, and stared at the floor in front of him. I rubbed my eyes, stifling a yawn as I steeled myself for my beheading.

"I'm so sorry, Cyrus," I whispered.

He didn't answer. For several extremely long minutes, I stewed in the silence. When I finally couldn't take it anymore, I broke down and asked the question weighing heaviest on my mind.

"How much trouble am I in?" I asked quietly, bracing myself for his judgment.

"Depends. Which transgression are you referring to?"

I hesitated, and then opted to wait him out.

"Afraid you'll hang yourself with the rope I'm giving you?" he prompted after another lull.

"A little," I admitted.

Finally, my boss turned to look at me. Those emerald eyes studied me with the intensity of a high-powered microscope. It wasn't long before I began to squirm under the scrutiny.

"Answer me one question, Stassi. And answer it honestly. Did you intend to bring Charles DuPree back with you?"

"What?" I exclaimed. "No. Of course not, no. Cyrus, I swear. It happened just like I said. He must have grabbed me right before I jumped. I didn't even realize he'd been brought along, until we landed here and I gained my bearings. I swear."

Cyrus nodded. "I believe you. I just wanted to hear you say it."

"You do?"

"Of course."

Though I was grateful that he believed me, I wasn't sure it was enough. Bottom line, Charles was here because of me. Did my intentions matter?

"What is the punishment for stowaways?" I asked, my voice low and wavering. "Exile?"

Cyrus looked alarmed as he met my eyes. The kindness I saw set my hopes aflutter.

"Accidents happen, Stassi," he said gently. "You're not going to be punished for it."

My sigh of relief could be heard on Mars as the crushing threat of exile was lifted from my shoulders. Without thinking, I wrapped my arms around Cyrus and squeezed.

"Thank you, Cyrus," I said, my voice cracking.

"We'll still have to hold a council meeting for you to tell the other Founders exactly what happened. They need to hear it in your own words."

"I understand," I replied quickly. "No problem."

A genuine smile played across Cyrus's lips. "Nice job with the prison break. You and Molly make quite the team."

Blushing, I looked down and waited for a reprimand. When none came, I ventured a question of my own.

"Have you seen her?" I asked. "Molly? How is she?"

"Not too bad. If I am being honest, surprisingly well, in fact. I expect she'll make a speedy recovery."

"Thank goodness," I said, relieved. "Gaige, too?"

"He's a little worse for the wear. Being locked in a damp cell for a week was already taking a toll on him. And, in general, jail food isn't the most nutritious. No need to worry, though. He'll be good as new in a couple of days."

"And Charles?"

"Now that is interesting." Cyrus furrowed his brow, perplexed. "He demonstrates no signs of time sicknesses. For his sake, let's hope he's just as lucky on the return trip."

My heart sank. Until that moment, I hadn't realized how much I'd been hoping that somehow, someway, Charles would be able to stay on the island with me. The notion was ridiculous, of course.

He didn't belong here.

He didn't belong with me.

Our lives were so very different. Our worlds couldn't have been further apart, our times less compatible. He could stay in 2446 no more than I could stay in 1925. At least, not indefinitely.

"When will he go back?" I asked quietly.

"Soon," Cyrus answered, leaning back in his seat. "Dr. Carver wants to run some tests. I need to speak with him. When we're finished, I'll take him back to 1925, give him a heavy dose of memory mod, and send him on his way. Then the alchemists will monitor him for a while to ensure his mental and physical health are unaffected."

Make sure he doesn't go blabbing about futuristic islands and time vortexes, I thought.

"Can I take him back?" The question slipped out, spoken so softly I thought for a second I'd simply thought it.

"That might not be best," Cyrus said, not unkindly. He squeezed my shoulder affectionately. "His feelings for you are very strong, Stassi. I'm not even sure the memory mod will erase them at this point. The less contact he has with you, the better it will be for him."

Averting my eyes, so Cyrus wouldn't see the ridiculous tears gathering in the corners, I nodded.

"Can I at least see him before he goes?"

Cyrus's hand tightened on my shoulder. He took a painfully long time to answer.

"I suppose one last visit won't hurt. Not too long, though."

My head shot up, the tears forgotten. "Really?"

"Think of it as a reward," Cyrus replied, nudging my shoulder with his own.

"For bringing back a guy instead of a book?" The sarcastic response slipped out without thinking. I clasped my mouth shut, not wanting to test the limits of my boss's benevolence.

To my surprise, Cyrus chuckled at my comment. "Definitely not. Rupert found the briefcase in the vortex. It seems you not only completed your assignment, but also went for extra credit. Those Hemingway novels will fetch quite a bit." He shrugged. "Who knows? I may keep them for myself. I have always loved ancient literature."

"How crazy is it that we got those?" I asked, faint guilt still tugging at me. "I feel terrible for stealing from Hadley, we were only after *Blue's Canyon*. I cannot believe everything else we acquired, too."

"C'est la vie," my boss replied with a wink. He checked his watch. "Voulez-vous voir votre ami maintenant?"

Even without the Rosetta, I knew what he was asking.

"Yes, please," I replied.

Cyrus personally escorted me back to Charles's treatment room. Despite the late hour—or early, depending on how you looked at it— Charles was awake and alert. He wore pale blue scrubs and the wide-eyed expression of a man sure he'd blink and find the last twelve hours had been a dream.

"Hey there," I called from the doorway. "Can I come in?"

Charles sat up straighter and ran a hand through his mussed hair.

"Stassi." He said my name on a long sigh, visibly relieved to see me. "Yes. Please, come in."

This was truly the last time we'd see each other, our final goodbye. I'd done this once already, but hadn't appreciated exactly what it meant during the chaos with Baylarian. Realization dawning, the cold fist of fate grabbed hold of my heart and squeezed. I hid my pain behind a smile. He didn't need to know the truth. No need for both of us to be upset.

"I apologize for my attire. Dr. Carver took my clothes and gave me these." He plucked at the scrub top, giving the shirt a look of disdain.

His expression made me take stock of my own appearance. I was still wearing the day dress I'd put on that morning in Paris, the fabric now rumpled and stained. I could only imagine what he must think, coming from a world of people who never looked less than perfect.

"How are you feeling?" I asked, inexplicably nervous in his presence.

It was odd. On my home turf, I should have been more relaxed, more at ease with him. But I wasn't. I couldn't think of anything to say, couldn't find a place to put my hands, and couldn't stop fidgeting.

"Well, thank you," Charles answered. "You?"

So formal. He's nervous, too.

"Good. It's always nice to be home, you know?"

Silence erupted between us like an invisible barrier that we were both afraid to cross. Finally, Charles pointed to an armchair in the corner of his room and invited me to sit with the arch of an eyebrow. I started towards the chair, changed my mind, and altered course.

Charles's face relaxed into a genuine smile. He held out a hand as I approached, and I threaded my fingers with his. Leaning down, I kissed his forehead, then rested my cheek against his silky golden hair.

"This is goodbye," he whispered, voice thick with emotion. It wasn't a question.

Lying no longer seemed necessary. Not trusting my voice, I only nodded in response. I wasn't sure how much Cyrus would tell him, maybe nothing at all. Either way, Charles would soon have no memory of the island, the jump, or our conversation. If they gave him enough memory mod, I might be little more than a whisper in his mind. An itch he couldn't quite seem to locate, let alone scratch. The thought sickened me.

"Forever goodbye?"

I nodded again.

"Is that what you want?" he asked.

"What I want doesn't enter the equation," I replied.

Gently, Charles pushed me back so we were facing each other.

"Is that what you want?" he repeated.

"You don't understand. You can't understand. And I can't explain it to you," I said, my frustration seeping out.

"I understand more than you might think," Charles said quietly.

I shook my head. "No. You don't."

"Technology beyond comprehension? Women prancing around in less than a cabaret dancer? People who speak English, and yet I cannot understand half the words? I am in the future."

There wasn't a trace of uncertainty in his voice.

"Wha—"

Before I could form the words swirling through my mind, Charles grabbed my hand and tugged the sleeve of my dress back to expose the tattoo on my wrist. I tried to pull free, but his grip was firm. Delicately, as if I were made of spun glass instead of flesh and bone, he traced the loops and scrawls of *prima* as he spoke my name. The act was oddly sensual, and gave me a thrill that started deep in the pit of my stomach. When he brought my wrist to his soft, full lips, my knees went weak. Closing my eyes, I sank onto the bed beside Charles.

His breath tickled my skin as he whispered in my ear, "Is that what you want? Do you want this to be goodbye forever?"

"No."

His lips found mine, and I lost myself in that kiss. Like puzzle pieces falling into place, we seemed to just fit together.

A knock on the door interrupted our goodbye before it became as involved as I'd have liked. The unfocused look on Charles's face told me that he felt the same way. A second knock sounded, louder and more insistent.

I reluctantly crawled off of the bed and attempted to smooth my dress.

"Stassi, I'm afraid your time is up," Cyrus said, poking his head through the door.

Embarrassed, I refused to face my boss.

"One minute, I'll be right out," I called.

"Sir, could I speak with you?" Charles asked, tone formal.

"Of course. I have some questions for you, as well."

Cyrus stepped inside the room.

"Alone," Charles added.

"Excuse me?" I stammered.

"I think it is best if we speak in private," Charles told me, his neutral expression rivaling one of Cyrus's.

"Um, no." It wasn't the most eloquent response, but perhaps the truest.

"You need to get some rest, Stassi. You've had a long day," Cyrus chimed in.

"I'm not tired," I snapped.

"Stassi, please," Charles pleaded. "Just trust me?"

Trust or not, I was unceremoniously ushered from the room by Cyrus, feeling dumbfounded by the dismissal. I paced the hallway outside of Charles's room, pausing every so often to listen at the door for snippets of conversation. The damned thing was virtually soundproof. All I could make out was the dull hum of conversation, but no actual words.

I considered visiting with Molly or Gaige to pass the time, but curiosity kept me pacing the same four square feet like an invisible fence held me captive.

What were they talking about? Why wasn't I allowed inside? How could that have possibly been the last time I'd see Charles? I wasn't going to be able to say goodbye in private?

I touched my fingertips to my lips, still warm from Charles. My cheeks flushed at the thought of our kiss. I had to see him again. Screw Cyrus and his orders. I just needed a little more time to say a proper goodbye. Both Charles and I deserved that much.

An hour after closing behind me, the door to Charles's room finally swung open again. A pale, drawn, and, if I didn't know better, troubled Cyrus emerged. His hands shook slightly as he ran them over his face. Shoulders hunched, the confidence my boss always emanated had vanished. He seemed to have aged ten years in that one hour.

Forgetting my irritation, I hurried over to my boss.

"Cyrus? Cyrus, what's wrong?"

"Oh, Stassi. You're still here. Good. Very good." He cleared his throat, attempting to compose himself. "We need to talk tomorrow. For now, you should go back to your bungalow. It's very late."

"But, Charles.... Please, Cyrus, just give me—"

"Charles will be here in the morning, Stassi. You can see him then," my boss quietly interjected.

"Really?" I asked hopefully.

"In fact," Cyrus continued, talking over me. "You can show him around the island. He'll be your responsibility until he starts his training."

"Training?"

"Yes, Charles DuPree is our newest runner."

Want more Stassi, Gaige,
Molly, Charles and Cyrus?
Visit: www.TimewavesSeries.com

Enter **STARLES** on the password-protected
pages to unlock special content!

NOTE TO THE READER

Dear Reader,

Thank you for reading The Syndicate! We genuinely hope you enjoyed the book.

As an indie author, reviews are incredibly important. As we all know, reviews can make or break most anything now; I rarely buy anything without checking out what others have to say, especially when it comes to books. And the more reviews something has, the more likely it is that others will take a chance on it.

Because of this, I hope you'll consider reviewing The Syndicate. Posting an honest— good or bad!—review on your blog, the retail site for your E-reader, and Goodreads allows authors like us to gain new readers and keep doing what we're doing.

Read on!

XOXO, the Sophies

ACKNOWLEDGEMENTS

First and foremost, I want to thank my partner in crime, hetero-lifemate, and the best friend a girl could ask for. You've never given up on me, and I will never be able to thank you enough for that. I know it's been really hard since I became sick, but you never stopped pushing me to make our collective dreams come true. And even though this one, silly idea of mine ended up taking us a full year to research and write, you never gave up on it. Thank you for being the kindest, most thoughtful, and most compassionate person who's ever lived. Here's to another ten years of laughing hysterically, painful singing, dance parties, traveling the world, finding adventures, and dominating life. I love you!

Thank you to our whole BEA crew! We honestly could not have done it without all of you, and are so grateful that you guys came from all over the country to help us. It was great getting to hang out with all of you, and we hope we'll be able to do it again soon, sans stress. SD retreat in the Caribbean??

As always, thank you to Barbara Gordon, who holds a very special place in our hearts. You've been with us since the beginning, and we will never be able to convey how grateful we are for your help, time, dedication, and support. Thank you for always being there for us, we appreciate you more than you'll ever know. No matter where this journey takes us, we hope you're up for the ride! And even if we never write another word or post another promo pic, I know our friendship will endure.

Thank you to Jaclyn Mara, who came up with the tagline for the cover of this book! But more than that, thank you for being so incredibly supportive of us. From making quote edits to acting as our blog liason, you dove into this craziness with both feet and an infectious enthusiasm. We are so glad we met you, and so grateful for your friendship.

Thank you to Victoria Schmitz, for the years of support you've given us. You were *such* a trooper in New York, and such a huge help to us. Thank you for being an invaluable member of our team! We adore you, and hope we'll be able to get together again soon.

Thank you to Patrick Gordon—for BEA, for all of your time, and for insisting that we keep the metal stand that now holds our dog leashes and keys. It was great to meet you, and we are really grateful for all the time you've spent helping us. I know your sister roped you in to all of this, but you've been so supportive and we really appreciate it!

To Justess- my kindred sleuthing spirit! Thank you for being so supportive of our writing, taking a chance on our books, and for telling others about them, too! I'm so glad I've gotten to know you, and hope you enjoy your surprise.

To Kelly Hillman, thank you for showing such a keen interest in this crazy journey we're on, and for being so proud of us. Your enthusiasm spurs us on, and you remind us to stop every once in a while and appreciate how far we've come. I'm so happy that Bunny has officially made you my sister. We love you!

Thank you to our families and all of our parents, for teaching us to dream big and work hard. You guys taught us both that anything is possible, and we never would've been able to do all of this without you. Thank you for your unfailing support.

And finally, but mostly importantly, thank you to our readers. It never ceases to amaze us how you guys have embraced the wild stories in our heads. We wouldn't be where we are without each and every one of you. Every time you read and review one of our books, tell a friend about them, or post on social media, you're supporting our dreams. For that, we are eternally grateful.

ABOUT THE AUTHORS

"Sophie Davis" is the pseudonym for two best friends, roommates, and now writing partners. The pair met at Penn State's Dickinson School of Law in 2005 and instantly bonded over their love of great books and bad horror movies. After they graduated, when one longed for the ability to read minds so she wouldn't have to study for the bar exam, a Saga was born. When the Talented Saga went on to be an internationally bestselling series, the girls decided to throw caution to the wind and follow their shared life-long dream of being writers.

The duo currently lives in Washington, D.C. with a poodle and a rescued mutt. The pups are their faithful companions—with frequent social media appearances—as the girls navigate the world of Indie Publishing.

For more information on Sophie Davis, visit:
www.sophiedavisbooks.com
To contact the girls directly, email them at:
sophie@sophiedavisbooks.com.

FOLLOW SOPHIE ON SOCIAL MEDIA:
Instagram: @officialsophiedavis
Twitter: @sophiedavisbook
Tumblr: officialsophiedavis
Facebook: www.Facebook.com/SophieDavisBooks
Pinterest: https://www.pinterest.com/sophiedavisbook

Made in the USA
Middletown, DE
11 August 2017